Volcrian's Hunt

The Cat's Eye Chronicles

Book 3

T. L. Shreffler

www.catseyechronicles.com

The Cat's Eye Chronicles

Sora's Quest (Book #1)

Viper's Creed (Book #2)

Volcrian's Hunt (Book #3)

Caprion's Wings (Novella #3.5)

Ferran's Map (Book #4)

PROLOGUE

Born into the colony, they lived without names and without parents. They became in all ways invisible. Brothers and Sisters. Servants of the Shadow. The Hive.

And the highest members of the Hive, those who fought and lived by the teachings of the Dark God—only they were given Names. Titles earned through combat at fragile ages, when children were the most eager to spill blood.

There was no word for *child* in their tongue. Only the word for the unnamed—*savant.* The same word for silence and sand and stagnant pools of water.

By the age of fourteen, he had waited long enough. He was ready to take a Name.

It was early, early morning. The shrine stood in a clearing of tall grass covered in dew. It was the day before the Naming ceremony. The grass had a grayish hue, as did the dawn. Clouds covered the sky, drifting inland from the nearby ocean, which he could hear if he listened carefully. The air was heavy and brisk with moisture. Trees surrounded him—long, narrow things with smooth trunks, branching into wide canopies above. He had grown up with the smell of salt water, the rush and hiss of the waves.

His teacher Cerastes, one of the Grandmasters that had held the dagger of the Viper long ago, always trained him next to the sea.

"Look at it," Cerastes had said the night before, speaking in his low, rough voice like the curl of waves against rock. *"At how it moves, coming and going. Look at all of the life that spills out of it.*

The ocean regurgitates life like a drunken sailor."

The nameless savant had studied the ocean with his teacher.

"If it weren't for us," Cerastes had said, *"for our kind, life would overtake the world. It would cram itself into every corner. Multiply out of control. Do you understand the danger in that? Just like the ocean waves, all things have a balance. The wave rushes in, then rushes out. It cannot just come in and in and in— then the whole world would be an ocean."*

The savant had watched the sea, alert.

"It is not beautiful or glorious, what we do," the Grandmaster had continued, *"but it is necessary. We are the outgoing wave. The harvesters. Hands of the Dark God. Soon you will enter into our tradition. Are you ready to take a Name?"*

Savant had nodded slowly. In that moment, it felt as though he had waited a lifetime, counting each passing minute. *A Name,* he had thought. *A presence. A history.* He would become more than just a shadow—more than an unknown child of the Hive.

Then they had meditated, looking out across the iron-gray sea. He didn't let himself consider failure. Those who failed at the Naming were scorned and shunned, often forced to leave the Hive. He didn't have to compete. He could refuse. At least then he wouldn't risk losing his home. *But that's the way of a coward, not an assassin.*

And now it was morning and he was ready.

He walked across the meadow to where the ground caved downward abruptly. Grass turned to gray, rough stone. The shrine of the Dark God was underground, hidden inside a massive cavern that was formed by a centuries-old stream of perfectly green water. The dancing water could be heard throughout the cavern, resonating off the granite rock.

He stood at the edge of the pit for a long moment, looking through the ancient crags. Between the rocks, only darkness gazed back.

After a final glance around the clearing, he started down the rocky crevice. He gripped the loose shale with his feet. His fingers found crooks and handholds in the rough stone. He was quick and nimble, and slid easily downward.

Shadows enclosed him. It was a familiar darkness, soft and cool. A brief walk through the cavern brought him to the stream of green water, illuminated by shafts of sunlight, which filtered through the layers of the ceiling. He leapt the stream easily.

On the opposite side stood a brass door embedded in the wall, wedged into a natural fissure in the rock. It, too, was centuries old, dating back to the founding of the Hive. The door had no key, and it took only the slightest shove of his shoulder to crack it open.

He entered the shrine of the Dark God—a long, stone cavern perhaps a quarter-mile long. The walls were almost five times his height. Dim lanterns hung from the rocky ceiling, rusted by age and moisture. The stone was colored green by its high copper content and crumbled under his fingers, but the room itself was well-swept and maintained. The ceremonial offering of a dead shark had been laid on an altar the night before, toward the opposite end of the hall. This morning, the corpse had no stench. A sign that the Dark God had accepted.

Along the greenish stone wall hung an expansive collection of ancient weapons: dirks, maces, claymores, battle axes, pikes, staves, crossbows, chakrams and whips. Almost every kind of weapon that the world had to offer. The Grandmasters maintained them regularly.

But these weapons were not of average make. Forged from superior metals, blessed by the Dark God's fire, they were each imbued with a Name. When a warrior displayed the right skills, he earned the weapon and its title—and status within the Hive.

There, hanging from the ancient wall, he saw the one he wanted. The weapon he would use in the fight.

It was a recurved dagger with a trailing point, serrated toward the hilt, about twenty inches long. It hung from the end of the bottom row where all the unclaimed blades were stored. He couldn't touch it, not yet. But it was the same one his Master had used, the one he had been trained for. The Viper. *He who hides in the grass.*

"Aye!" a voice suddenly reached him. It echoed around the stone walls with startling volume. "I know you're in there!"

The voice was immediately familiar. He glanced out of the shrine, into the shadows of the underground cavern.

She stood ankle-deep in the dewy green water, a piece of oatbread in one hand, her shoes in the other. His eyes flickered over the girl's plain black uniform. Although most in the colony were without names, he always thought of this girl as "Bug," both because she was small for her age and because she often trapped moths, putting them in small boxes or jars around her hut.

"Preparing for the Naming?" she asked, a slow smile spreading across her face. A dimple stood out on one cheek. He was surprised by it. The Hive did not encourage smiling—or any show of emotion, for that matter. He felt something swell within him: a certain strength.

"I am already prepared," he said. "Will you be watching me?"

"I will be competing too."

"What?" He stared. She was only twelve, far too young to fight for a Name. Most of the boys competing would be older than even he was, sixteen or seventeen.

She nodded. "My Master says I must. She says that she has no other students to compete in her Name."

He watched her with careful eyes. There was uncertainty on her face. Adults knew how to mask their emotions, but she was still young.

To fail at the Naming was to be shunned from the Hive. Everyone knew that. He wondered why Grandmaster Natrix would force her to fight....Maybe she wanted to get rid of her. It was not unheard of, and Bug had always had it rough. She was small for her age and showed too much kindness toward animals. He couldn't count how many times he had caught her leaving food out for wood-cats and squirrels.

"Come on," he said, and held out his hand. "Let's look at the weapons. Show me which one your Master used."

She nodded. As they entered the long, cool stretch of limestone, she turned to glance at him, her green eyes still uncertain. All members of the Hive had the same make and coloring: black hair and green eyes. It was a trait of their people.

"I knew I would find you here early," she said, perhaps shyly; he couldn't tell. "I watch you practice sometimes. You are very good. They say Cerastes sired you himself; that is why he wanted you as his student."

Savant only shook his head. "That's rude," he said. "We're all brothers and sisters in the Hive."

She shrugged, still grinning. "Perhaps. But not by blood. The humans say that you can only be related by blood."

"We are different."

"You think so?"

Savant didn't answer. The only ones who knew the true bloodlines of the Hive were the women, and they kept that knowledge well guarded. Biological siblings were usually traded with other Hives to keep them from intermixing blood. Every now and then, a mother would be reprimanded for favoring her own child over others. All children of the Hive were supposed to be raised communally. All elders were to be treated with equal respect except for the Grandmasters, who were revered.

"Which weapon?" he asked, turning to the wall, hoping to change the subject.

She pointed at a short, curved sword. "The Adder," she said. Then she wrinkled her nose. "To be honest, I don't want that one. I want the Krait or the Asp. I'm much better at them."

He glanced over her in thought. She referred to the whip or the shortbow. To be honest, he couldn't imagine her with either one. She was too small. Too skinny. He felt his heart sink at the thought, though he quickly quelled the feeling. It was not the assassin's way to show pity.

And yet, here they were. "Do you want to practice?" he asked slowly.

She blinked. "Practice? With the Named weapons?"

He nodded.

"But...it is forbidden!"

He shook his head. "Only if they catch us. I've been training for the Viper for seven years. Let's try them out."

She watched him warily for a moment, her assassin's mask

slipping back in place, then she grinned again. "Alright," she said. "But only for a half hour, and in the forest where they won't find us!"

He nodded, looking up at the dagger of the Viper. *What's come over me?* he wondered, suddenly uncertain. He wasn't one to break rules. It was especially forbidden to touch the weapons in the shrine...but something about Bug made things different. Something about her large, wide, slanting eyes. Their particular shade of green, like moss grown over a lake.

And the fact that he truly felt sorry for her. He doubted that she would win a Name. She might even be killed.

He grabbed the dagger before he could change his mind.

At first she went to take the short sword, but then she hesitated. She took the whip instead.

They dashed into the forest, the dawn light ever brightening, leaving the gray meadow behind.

* * *

Toward the back of the cavern, the rocks narrowed into a series of tunnels, leading to a secret exit shrouded in ferns and bushes. The green water of the stream led to a dense woodland. They walked into the forest and found a place about a half-mile away from the sacred ground. Large, mossy elm trees swayed on each side. Ivy coiled across the ground.

They waited to regain their breath, then Bug loosened the whip from its coil, dangling it in front of her. "Prepare yourself," she said, eyes glinting.

He leveled the Viper before him. It was a long, thick dagger, the blade jagged and sharp enough to pierce metal. He gripped it backwards from the handle and went into a crouch.

It was difficult to tell who lunged first, but suddenly they were fighting. Her whip lashed out, faster than the eye could see. But he heard it snapping through the air. He leapt to one side, the whip striking the tree behind him, tearing off a strip of bark and moss.

Then he lunged at her. She tried to engage him in combat, but he quickly slipped under her defense and grabbed her by the arms. Within seconds he had her pinned against a tree, the knife against her throat. He was skilled enough not to cut her.

Her eyes widened. Then she glared. "Again!"

She ducked under his arms as soon as he released her, then spun, kicking him behind the knee. She was fast—faster than he. She caught his foot and he fell to the ground, but was up again within seconds. They circled slowly, each studying the other opponent, looking for a weakness.

Then she flicked the whip, catching him on the cheek. A shallow cut. He could tell that she had avoided his eyes on purpose.

He touched the thin streak of blood.

She lunged at him while he was distracted, drawing a knife from her belt. He turned slightly out of reflex and the knife barely missed his neck. Then he ducked under her short arms and grabbed her by the shoulders. Rammed her up against the tree again. Pushed the Viper to her throat.

She dropped the small blade. "I give!"

He released her, barely even panting. It was somewhat disappointing. He had hoped she would be better than this.

"You'll never win a Name with these skills," he said.

She avoided his eyes. She knew the truth. "I know," she said quietly. "What should I do?"

Savant couldn't answer. He could only look at her, that peculiar feeling swelling in his chest again—pity.

There was a sudden crackling in the underbrush.

They both snapped to attention, then Savant grabbed Bug and shoved her back behind the tree. They crouched low among the roots, breathing lightly, painfully alert. They shared a wide-eyed glance. If someone caught them with the Named weapons....

The crackling in the underbrush continued. Savant turned slightly, angling his head to see between the leaves. At first he couldn't make out much...but then he caught a shuffle of movement. A peculiar glow seeped through the ferns, like a highly concentrated patch of sunlight. It shifted across the forest floor.

The light moved closer.

Savant felt his mouth turn dry. He had heard tales of such a light, but he could scarcely believe his eyes. He could *feel* the light, too. It vibrated against his skin in an annoying, buzzing way. The hair on his arms stood on end.

Only one of the races glowed in such a way....

There was the low mumble of speech. He turned his head again, straining his ears.

"We only need one," he overheard. "Don't put yourself at risk." The voice was small and distant, as though held in a cup.

He shared another glance with Bug. She had overheard it, too.

"I know. I'm waiting for a young one. An adult will cause too much trouble." This voice was far stronger than the last, only a few yards away.

Savant gripped the handle of the dagger. The Viper was still new in his hands, yet it felt comfortable, familiar. It gave him courage. With a slight nod to Bug, he crept around the tree and darted forward, staying low to the ground, using the underbrush as cover. His footsteps were absolutely silent, not even a crunched leaf. Stealth was the first lesson of an assassin.

Bug scampered after him, mimicking his every move.

The light was fully visible through the trees. It hurt to look at it. Savant found himself averting his eyes, even as he crept closer. He wanted to hear more of the conversation....

He paused again behind a thick copse of trees. The light was brightest on its opposite side, perhaps only a few feet away. In this position, he could hear the conversation clearly.

"Make sure you're not followed," the thin, hollow voice said.

"Don't worry," the person replied, soft and melodious, his words dripping with nectar.

Suddenly, the light vanished.

Bug let out a small breath, barely audible. Her hand clutched at Savant's sleeve.

Then a shadow fell over them.

Both savants turned, their expressions guarded. The man who stood behind them was strange indeed, not of the Hive. His coloring was far too exotic. Pale, pale hair, like the white sands of the beach. A white tunic and fawn-colored breeches. His skin held a strange glow, barely visible. In his hand was a small white stone.

"Who are you?" Savant asked. He raised the Viper before him, brandishing it viciously.

"Just passing through," the man replied. He stood only three paces away. A strange smile was on his face, cruel and sharp. Then he turned to Bug. "Here, little one. Catch this." He tossed the stone.

Savant's hand shot into the air, trying to intercept the throw, but Bug was too fast. She easily snatched the stone, perhaps out of reflex.

"No!" Savant yelled.

Bug screamed.

White light flashed, exploding outward like a miniature star. The force of it actually pushed Savant back, almost toppling him to the ground. The whiteness pierced his eyes and he clamped them shut, ears ringing, pain splitting his head like an ax.

"Don't look at it!" Savant yelled. His eyes were tightly shut, his head buzzing from the intensity. "It's a sunstone! It will blind you!"

"How considerate," that melodious voice spoke again.

Savant didn't hesitate. He lunged toward the voice, the Viper singing in his hand. He plunged the blade into thin air, missing his target, but he didn't stop—no, he kept lunging, kept listening. The handle felt hot, as though warmed over a fire.

Savant now recalled lessons about the sunstones, about bright lights and white-haired strangers. He had heard all of it while studying the War of the Races. He should have thought of it sooner, but he had never heard of a Harpy traveling so close to the Hive. This stranger was a child of Wind and Light, one of the First Race and a sworn enemy of the Dark God.

And a sunstone was not just a pretty pebble. It was a dangerous magical weapon used for hunting and killing the Dark God's children.

"Where are you?" Savant roared, anger rushing through him like hot fire. He could hear scuffling in the underbrush and a dull moan. Bug's voice. He followed it. His vision was beginning to clear and he blinked his eyes repeatedly. He could now make out vague shadows and outlines, imprints of leaves and branches.

There, to his left. The Harpy!

He lunged again, knife plunging, and this time hit flesh. He sank the dagger deep into the leg of the Harpy. The man let out a cry of pain and outrage, then whirled, backhanding Savant across the face. The blow was fierce and Savant stumbled backwards again, still sensitive to the light, hardly able to focus his eyes.

The sunstone flashed again. It felt like having his face thrust in a fire. He cried out, throwing up an arm to shield himself, dropping his dagger. The ground tipped—his head swam.

He tried desperately to recover, to open and focus his eyes. He could see Bug—or at least he thought it was Bug—scrambling through the bushes, biting and scratching at her captor. She was screaming in pain, smoke rising from her hand. The sunstone was burning through her skin and into her flesh, where Savant knew it would fester. The light would bind her limbs and steal her senses. Eventually, it would burn out her eyes.

He was overwhelmed. His blood felt like it was boiling in his veins; his head pounded. He pulled himself to his feet and tried to follow them through the forest, tried to listen, but his ears were consumed by an intense ringing. The ground kept tilting beneath him.

He fell to his knees, curling up in pain.

The light grew and grew...and then faded....

* * *

An hour later, he came to. He hadn't expected to be still alive.

The forest was empty. After a brief, desperate search, he uncovered the Named weapons, the whip and the dagger. That eased some of his tension, but he was still worried about Bug. *Assassins do not worry.* But he could not quell the sense of guilt and panic.

A few scuffs marred the dirt, but besides that, there was no sign of Bug or the white-haired stranger. He searched for a trail and found a few white feathers littered in the underbrush, but they led to nowhere. No path, no evidence. Upon examining the feathers, Savant wasn't surprised. Harpies could fly. How did one follow the air?

There was nothing more he could do. He took the Named weapons back to the shrine, mounting them carefully on the wall. His ears were still ringing, his eyes sensitive. In the dark, cool recesses of the cavern, he knelt by the green water and plunged his head into its cold depths, allowing the current to run through his hair. The peaceful shadows slowly permeated his mind, calming his heart, soothing his skin.

Finally he sat back, taking deep, moist breaths. He felt numb and uncertain. Should he address the counsel of the Grandmasters? If he told them about the Harpy in the woods, they might gather a team of huntsmen and track down Bug, rescue her....

Or perhaps not. The Grandmasters were not warm or understanding. They would ask what he had been doing in the forest. Ask about the Named weapons. About the nature of his friendship with Bug.

And he would be severely punished for using the weapons. They might disqualify him from the Naming—perhaps permanently.

It chilled him. The thought of waiting another year for the Viper left him sick and uneasy, if they even allowed him to compete. Perhaps his actions would render him unworthy of the title. Another Savant could take his place. Cerastes had other students to compete for his Name.

Cerastes. He let out a slow breath. He couldn't go to all of the Grandmasters about this, but perhaps he could speak to his own. The bond between student and teacher was built on loyalty and unquestionable trust. Cerastes would know what to do.

It took a half-hour to return to the beach, a stretch of sand on the outskirts of the colony. He found his Grandmaster easily. Cerastes sat above an alcove of rock that sank down into the ocean, like the mouth of a gaping giant. Ten foot swells crashed against the rocks—the giant's breath. His teacher was deep in meditation, perfectly still, almost invisible against the dark rock.

Cerastes opened his eyes, aware of his student's presence. "You are late," he said. "In four years, you have never been late for our training. What happened?"

Savant fell upon his knees before the Grandmaster, propping his hands against his legs, bowing his head. "Master," he began. He had rehearsed the words, but they failed him now. His mouth grew dry. "There has been...an accident...."

"Assassins do not have accidents," his Master replied automatically. Then his brow furrowed. Cerastes was far older than his student, well past his prime, and yet his forehead was still smooth, his black hair long and sleek down to his waist. "What happened?"

Savant hesitated only for a moment, then he rushed through the story, explaining the morning's events. He kept his voice soft, his tone quiet. Those of the Hive had ears everywhere.

When he finished, Cerastes lowered his head in thought. He

remained silent for a long stretch of time. Savant almost relaxed, lulled by the rush of the ocean and the caw of gulls.

"I know the female you speak of," he finally said. "She was Grandmaster Natrix' student. She was weak."

"We must save her."

"*She was weak.*"

Savant looked up sharply, unable to hide the surprise on his face. He stared at the Grandmaster for a long moment, countless words on his lips, tangling his thoughts. He shook his head to clear it. "But, she is of the Hive."

"You are not listening, Savant." Cerastes spoke slowly and clearly. "You are my best student. The best I have seen in twenty years. Your logic is as keen as your blade."

Savant waited, forcing himself to listen, barely contained.

The Grandmaster carried on at a leisurely pace. "Harpies are not weak. Their very nature, in fact, is designed to destroy us. Their Light burns our eyes, their Voice binds our limbs. Does it make sense for the Hive to send full-fledged assassins—some of whom will be killed, I assure you—to rescue a weak child?"

Savant felt anger spark to life. It rushed up from his stomach, burning his throat like molten rock. "But...."

"You were friends with this girl?" Cerastes' stare pierced him. Savant lowered his eyes. Friends were not encouraged in the Hive. They were tolerated, perhaps, but only as a thing of childhood. He was too old for such sentiment, now—a friend was a weakness, a crack in one's armor. "No, Grandmaster."

"Then give me one reason why we should save her." Cerastes' words were unexpectedly direct.

Savant looked up and opened his mouth. Paused. He had no

reason.

The Grandmaster nodded. A slow, knowing smile spread across his lips. His green eyes glinted coldly in the afternoon light. "This is the way of the Hive, savant," he murmured. "Now let me ask you a far more important question. Are you sure that you are ready to take a Name?"

Savant gazed at his Master, still reeling from the day's events. "Yes," he finally said.

"Because your weakness is most apparent right now."

The words shut him down. Savant realized what he was risking; what his Grandmaster was threatening. He locked his jaw, wiped his expression and cleared his thoughts. He let out a short, tense breath. "It was an unexpected morning," he said abruptly.

The Grandmaster nodded again. "Understandably. Take a run on the beach. Clear your mind for the Naming."

Savant bowed, his head touching the rock, then stood up. He reminded himself that he was lucky. Cerastes was far more understanding than some, and he was true to the ways of the Hive.

He climbed to his feet and turned, leaping nimbly across the slippery rocks.

Cerastes called from the peak of the giant's mouth. "You did not fail her, savant," he said, and his student turned briefly, catching his eye. "Remember. *She was weak.*"

CHAPTER 1

Volcrian stood outside the shop and gazed at the faded blue sign. A mixture of fish oil and salt water mingled in his nose; it was a scent that brought back painfully clear memories.

It seemed like only yesterday when he and his brother had stood before the very same shop. They had been mere children then, sixteen years of age, with the world at their feet. The year before, their father had died of a chronic illness, leaving them orphaned. The two brothers had grown inseparably close, relying on each other to survive. They had lived like that through their youth, far into adulthood.

But his brother had been dead now for three years. That haunted him like a sickness, plagued his thoughts, stole his sleep. He couldn't forget his brother's face, nor that of the killer.

Volcrian flexed his left hand, a crippled knot of twisted fingers and curling tendons, maimed the day Etienne had died.

That's why I'm here, is it not? he thought with a small smile. Yes, so many years ago, he and his brother had run across a struggling merchant who was trying to sell fish. The fishmonger had begged them for money, for any sort of help. Etienne had worked a simple spell, a mixture of blood and fish eggs. He had anointed each barrel of fish, then the threshold of the door, the frames of the windows. The customers would crave the man's stock, feeling rejuvenated after eating it.

They had done the job in return for a favor. A favor that

Volcrian had not yet collected.

The population of the docks passed by him quickly, hunched against the low clouds and stiff wind. The air was heavy with moisture, though it had yet to rain. Behind him, miles upon miles of moored ships stretched across the shoreline, from passenger vessels to fishing boats to giant freighters. Delbar was a bustling city, full of eager merchants and cunning thieves. Yet no one approached the door.

Volcrian had to wonder at that. Blood magic had a price. There was a balance to it—one couldn't just take and take. Eventually, one would have to give back. Usually the mage suffered the consequences, falling ill for days, drawing too much blood to recover, his life force drained.

But Etienne had been young, his magic fierce and unfettered. It took years for a Wolfy mage to build up discipline and control over his spells. Volcrian eyed the sign dubiously. Who knew what waited beyond the storefront?

"Are we going to stand out here all day?" came a woman's voice to his left, slightly slurred, as though her lips were numb. "I may be dead, but I'm still freezing."

Volcrian grinned at the irony. "A cold corpse," he murmured. "Quaint."

The priestess rolled her eyes. They slid too far back into her head, almost full white. It took her a moment to refocus them, the eyeballs spinning lazily about, clouded by death.

Volcrian watched in fascination. She had taken on a kind of beauty these past weeks since he had killed her on the steps of the Temple of the West Wind. Her skin had turned gray and ashen; her lips were swollen and bloated, a dark purple. Her hair had turned white and was beginning to thin. Between the patches of missing hair, he could glimpse the curve of a perfectly smooth head.

She was bundled in a thick brown cloak several sizes too big, the hood shoved down over her head. His own silver hair and pointed ears drew enough looks. He didn't need people noticing a walking corpse in tow.

With a shrug, Volcrian reached for the old, weathered door. It creaked as he opened it, protesting the movement.

Inside, the store was small, cramped, and full of the overpowering stench of rotten fish. Something else lingered in the air, tainting the walls, sickly sweet. The old, old spice of magic. Volcrian's nose recognized it immediately, although he knew no human could detect the smell. He instinctively grimaced. The scent shouldn't be this strong, this sour. Something had gone wrong with the spell. Not entirely surprising.

"Lovely," the dead priestess muttered, her eyes wandering haphazardly around the room.

"Almost as lovely as you, my dear," Volcrian murmured back.

Something shifted in the gloom of the shop, hidden amongst the crates and barrels of fish. His eyes adjusted to the light, then landed on a stooped figure in the corner.

"Malcolm?" he said into the darkness, and the figure flinched as though struck. Volcrian took a step forward, peering into the shadows, ears twitching. He detected the faintest creak of floorboards as the creature within shifted. "Come out," he ordered.

There was a croaky laugh from the depths of the room. The figure scuttled between two boxes, attempting to hide. Then a voice muttered, "A Wolfy, is it? Your kind are not common."

Volcrian's eyes narrowed. Yes, finding a Wolfy was rare

indeed. It was sad to think that humans, the weakest of the races, were now in control. The other races had all but perished—including his own.

"It's been years since I was last here." Volcrian addressed the shadows. He sniffed the stagnant air again, wrinkling his nose. "I take it you remember."

That odd croak answered him from the fish crates. "Oh, how could I forget?" he grumbled.

The mage shuddered despite himself. The voice that spoke was not natural. The vocal cords were warped, twisted, struggling to pronounce.

"At least twenty years I've been waiting," the voice snarled. "Etienne, isn't it?"

Volcrian straightened up. Etienne's name was far too pure to be tainted by that voice. Sliding through those dirty lips, the name sounded more like a curse, like sodden wood dropping on the floor.

He glared into the shadows, his temper piqued. He strode deeper into the room, shrugging through the tendrils of magic as though they were cobwebs.

"Etienne is dead," he said calmly, despite the anger in his gaze. "I am Volcrian."

"Ah, yes. The elder brother. But no different. Still a Wolfy. Still a mage." The shadowy figure spit on the floor before Volcrian's feet, a gob of yellow phlegm that looked toxic. For a moment, the mage turned livid. The atmosphere of the room, so drenched with magic, began to shift.

The figure moved away from him, scuttling between boxes, remaining half-hidden.

"Show yourself," Volcrian called. The magic squirmed,

contracting. Although it had been years, the spell still responded to his presence. Its power was still alive.

The storekeeper had no choice. Abruptly, Malcolm stepped from between the boxes, pausing in the hazy light from a window.

Volcrian's lips twisted in disgust.

Before him stood something that might have once been a man. Now it seemed more of a toad. Hunched double, his skin was wrinkly and loose, clinging to the bone like a wet curtain. His ears were large and dangling, his hair all but gone, and his eyes...large, blind disks in a ruined face.

The man was aging almost three times as fast as normal, his life drained by the bloodspell.

Volcrian recognized the side effects of amateur magic. He and Etienne had caused much damage when they were younger, before they discovered their great-grandfather's journal. Volcrian shared a sideways glance with the priestess. She, too, had been changed by magic. Yet for all of her swollen, blue-tinted skin, she still held a semblance of beauty, something ethereal, vaguely human.

This man, on the other hand, was like a slimy animal dragged from the ocean.

"What do you want, Wolfy?" the creature bit out. "I take it you have not come to lift my curse. Name your purpose and leave so I'll never have to look at you again."

"Gladly," Volcrian replied. He wanted to leave the shop as quickly as possible. "I am looking for a group of travelers: an assassin, a Wolfy mercenary, and a girl. Have you heard any news on the docks? Anything out of the ordinary?"

The man muttered to himself in thought, croaking and warbling. "A gang of Dracians stole a large seafaring vessel about two weeks ago," he said. "Word had it that a Wolfy was with them. Big he was, almost seven feet tall."

Volcrian nodded. He had noted a large population of Dracians in the city, another one of the magical races living side-by-side with the oblivious humans. But a giant Wolfy was exactly what he was looking for.

The Wolfy race was split into two factions—the mages and the mercenaries. All of the mages were short, effeminate, and silver-haired. The mercenaries were robust warriors, broad as an oak and tall as a bear. The only commonalities between them were their pointed ears and sharp teeth. The mercenaries could not use magic. In that respect, they were as useless as humans.

"Do you know their destination?" he asked smoothly.

The creature rolled its caving shoulders. "No," he said bluntly. "But there's a mapmaker on Port Street. He might know. I'll warn ye, though," he held up a finger. Volcrian noted the webbed skin. "He's a bit batty."

A batty mapmaker? This, from a frog-man? It almost made Volcrian smile.

"Is that all?" Malcolm asked, a hint of relief in his voice.

"I have need of a ship," Volcrian said, his voice ponderous, distracted by this new information. What was the assassin up to now? Fleeing overseas? "And a crew."

The fish-seller grunted, almost a laugh. "You want my ship? Can't fish without a ship...."

"That is none of my concern," Volcrian snapped. He refocused on Malcolm and took a threatening step forward. "I am hunting a deadly assassin and time is of the essence. If you will not give me your ship then I will take it."

The man recoiled from the mage, muttering a stream of garbled croaks. Then he limped back into the shadows, attempting to hide behind another box. Volcrian followed after him, walking steadily through the cluttered room.

"And if I refuse?" Malcolm finally grunted.

"You can't refuse me," Volcrian said in a low voice. "The price of your spell was one favor. It is in the magic that taints this store. In your blood."

"I *will* refuse," Malcolm replied bitterly, turning to face the mage, a small spark of defiance in his eyes. "You'll have to kill me if you want my ship."

Volcrian knew that the frog-man was goading him. Malcolm wanted free of the spell, even if it meant death. The mage smiled grimly. "I could make your situation a lot worse," he threatened. "How about another spell? One that takes your voice away? Or...one that takes your soul?" He raised an eyebrow.

The man's eyes widened, becoming perfectly round moons. "Y-you can do that?" he cringed.

"Of course," Volcrian smiled thinly.

"Just...j-just a moment," Malcolm said, his voice quivering. He limped into the depths of the store, vanishing in the maze of fish barrels. Volcrian's pointed ears twitched. He heard the sound of rummaging, the slide of a desk drawer, the man muttering to himself all the while.

When Malcolm returned, he held an oily scrap of paper in hand. "The title to the boat," he said. "'Tis old, but sturdy. The crew will sail if you can promise them coin."

"Oh," Volcrian murmured, "I'll promise them something...."

Malcolm didn't seem to hear. He thrust the paper into

Volcrian's hand. The mage took it, grimacing at the creature's wet grip. "Now leave," Malcolm spat. "Leave, and never return here."

"Oh, I don't plan to," Volcrian smiled. It was a cold look. Then he turned and walked toward the door. As he passed the priestess, he put a casual hand on her shoulder. "Do your work," he said darkly.

The corpse-woman groaned.

Volcrian winced. "Now."

"Wait," Malcolm said from the back of the room. "What do you mean? Who is this woman?"

Volcrian ignored the fishmonger and passed through the door. He closed it tightly behind him. He strode onto the docks, pausing next to the ocean, listening to the gentle lap of the waves against the wooden posts.

After a minute, he heard muffled screams from inside the store —only audible to his sensitive ears.

He didn't like the reminder of Etienne's untrained magic. It felt like a blight on his memory, some backhanded insult. There was no way to reverse a bloodspell, but he could kill the victim. Make the man's suffering shorter—perhaps end it completely. Only death would undo the curse and erase what his brother had done.

And he also wanted to test the priestess. See what she was capable of—if she would obey him completely, despite her rebellious spirit.

He lingered on that thought. He had killed the priestess only a few weeks ago, then raised the corpse. According to the spell he had used, she shouldn't be able to remember her old identity. And yet she maintained some semblance of will...part of one, at least. It wasn't supposed to be that way.

It was troubling. Perhaps his magic wasn't as perfect as he had thought. Maybe he had made a mistake, a flaw in the timing, in the amount of blood he had used.

No, he thought. He had read the spell in his great-grandfather's journal, over and over again, careful to follow each step.

He listened to the scuffles from inside the store. Eventually, the store grew silent. He felt a surge of satisfaction. The priestess had fulfilled her duty.

He thought back to when she had first greeted him on the doorsteps of the Temple, with her proud nature and hard brown eyes. She had spent her previous serving the Wind Goddess. Perhaps those Winds still protected her, retaining in her some sense of the woman she had been. Perhaps that's why his spell wasn't as perfect as he had hoped.

He didn't care to dwell on it. As long as she carried out his orders, he could handle a bit of complaining.

CHAPTER 2

Sora leaned over a bucket and tried to puke. She heaved several times, but her stomach was empty.

A week on the ocean and she still hadn't adjusted to the constant roll of the waves. It was constantly with her—a vague, lingering nausea that dogged her heels. She had tried everything to cure the sickness, from mint leaves to a bottle of wine. Nothing helped.

Sora sat back on her bed, closing her eyes, trying to distract herself from the nausea. Thinking of her quest only made it worse. A plague was sweeping over the mainland, brought on by the bloodmage, Volcrian. Crops were rotting, people dying in the streets. As it turned out, she was the only one who could stop it. *Ironic, that.*

It was a little strange considering that a year ago she had been no more than a noble Lady, dreading her birthday party and her marriage to come.

Volcrian hadn't intended for his spells to grow out of control. He had summoned three wraiths from the underworld, but they had brought a dark power with them. The residue of the Dark God, released back into the land. The only way to stop the plague was to kill Volcrian and return the Dark God's weapons to their rightful place, wherever that may be. The first half was easy enough. Kill the mage, stop the plague.

I wouldn't be in this situation if it weren't for Crash, she thought bitterly. The assassin had kidnapped her after discovering her Cat's-Eye necklace, an ancient device from the War of the Races.

Sora grimaced and forced herself to stand up. *I need some fresh air,* she told herself firmly. She walked out of her cabin, a small room barely large enough for her bed, and into the ship's hold. A long, salt-worn hallway stretched in either direction. She chose the stern.

Halfway down the hall, a group of Dracians lingered in the doorway of another cabin. They were short men, only a few inches taller than herself, with bright coppery hair and eyes like the ocean waves, a mix of green and blue. They snickered when she passed. Sora tried to ignore them. They had all sorts of names for her now: Upchuck, Oatmeal and her personal favorite, Spew.

Good-for-nothing clowns, Sora thought. The Dracians were the most obnoxious race she had met so far. If they weren't teasing her in the hallways, they were cat-calling to her on deck or dumping seaweed on her head.

One day, when this was all over, she would get back at them. Somehow.

Sora climbed up the short stairs to the deck. The topsail flapped above her in a strong breeze. It was still overcast, the clouds roiling about like a frothing stew. They hadn't seen a day of sun since leaving Delbar. The Dracians had warned that queer storms hovered over the Lost Isles, magic that lingered from the War of the Races. It astounded her that the storms had lasted so long. The War of the Races was a legend to most on the mainland, an ancient history all but forgotten, having taken place countless centuries ago.

She shivered against the cold wind. A few drops of rain struck her nose. Another storm was brewing, a few minutes away from breaking loose. Perhaps this hadn't been such a good idea, but there were only so many places one could go on a ship, even a three-masted seafaring vessel.

"Sora," she heard a voice call.

She looked up, surprised to see Burn approaching her. The Wolfy towered over her by almost two feet. He usually wore a giant greatsword strapped to his back, but today he was dressed in a linen shirt and snug breeches. His gold eyes met hers and he grinned, two fangs pushing against his lower lip.

"How are you?" he asked, pausing next to her.

"Oh, same old," she muttered, and grimaced as another wave swelled beneath the ship.

"You look pale," he observed. "Still haven't found your sea legs?"

"I'm beginning to think I don't have any," Sora replied. Then she glanced around. "Where is everyone?" Usually the Dracians were all over the ship, clearing off the decks or manning the rigging.

"Jacques called us all to the captain's quarters. I believe he wants to discuss our course," Burn said.

Sora frowned. "I haven't heard anything about this...."

"That's why I came looking for you." Burn offered his arm, a surprisingly chivalrous gesture. "Let's go below deck."

Sora sighed. The waves were worse downstairs, where she could hear the creaking of the timbers, the various rocks and debris that struck the thick wood. It made her shudder. She wasn't sure how reliable this vessel was. She felt terribly concerned about the storms, as though a thin sheet of paper stood between her and drowning.

Another thought occurred to her. A bit of anxiety cramped her stomach. "Will Crash be there?" she asked slowly.

"Of course," Burn replied, a small frown on his face.

She took his arm anyway. "Right," she said. She didn't treasure the thought of seeing the assassin. She had avoided him since the first day of the voyage, which was truly saying something, given the size of the ship. "Let's go."

* * *

Burn and Sora entered the room just as Jacques opened his mouth to speak.

Jacques, the self-proclaimed captain of the ship, wore a slightly oversized, flamboyant blue coat. He had found it in the original captain's cabin, tossed over a chair. Although they had commandeered the ship, he had taken to wearing it. Sora thought of telling him how silly it looked, but she got the impression that he already knew—and he liked it that much better.

A large black crow sat on the chair behind him, shuffling its wings. The eccentric pet followed Jacques everywhere. It had the tendency to collect shiny objects. Sora had found a stash of small coins, buttons and thimbles on top of Jacques' bookshelf in his cabin. It was now eyeing the round compass on his desk, turning its head in interest.

"Ah, and we are joined by the last two members of our merry crew," Jacques said. "Sora, I saved a seat just for you. Next to that bucket."

Sora glared at him as a round of laughter moved through the room. Then she saw the chair he had offered and glared even harder. It was right next to Crash.

The brooding assassin stared stoically at the wall. She was glad that he didn't meet her eyes. A week ago, he had fought off a Kraken on the docks, saving her life once again. The sea dragon's bite had carried strong venom, and from what she had heard, the assassin was still recovering. Not that she cared. She had spent an entire night by his side, using her limited healing knowledge to pull him back from the brink of death. Then he had awakened in a thankless mood and she had stormed off, tired of his sarcasm.

Now that she thought back, she couldn't quite remember why she had been so angry, but she held onto the grudge anyway. *It's about principle,* she told herself. He should apologize, and perhaps even thank her for saving his life.

She sat down with a stubbornness to her mouth, then glanced sideways at him, taking in the assassin's black hair. It clung to his forehead, dampened by sweat. His face was slightly pale, his lips tight. His green eyes stayed focused on the same spot on the wall. It occurred to her, suddenly, that he might be seasick, too.

Burn stood next to her, bracing his legs against another roll of the ship. He nodded for Jacques to continue.

The bright-eyed Dracian turned back to the room. "As I was saying," he continued, "our ship has sailed a little off-course. These storms are growing difficult to navigate."

There was a murmur of concern from the crew.

"I propose we set a new course, try to find a way around the storms." Jacques began pacing, walking up and down the front of the room. It was a broad cabin, doubling as a game room when it wasn't used for meetings. The tables were nailed to the floor, as were the chairs, to resist the motion of the ship. Just watching him made Sora dizzy. How could he maintain such perfect balance as the deck rocked and swayed? "This is why we have called all of you together, so we can take a vote on the best way to go. Tristan, will you do the honors of explaining our first choice?"

Jacques stepped aside and a younger Dracian took his place. Tristan winked at Sora, though the gesture was lost on her. He was a handsome specimen—two bright blue eyes, dimpled cheeks, and a strong chin. She looked down, swallowing hard, trying not to retch. The younger Dracian had been vying for her attention since they had first met. *A bottle of hormones, that one,* she thought blearily. He had brought her soup for a while until she vomited on his shoes.

Tristan turned to face the crew. Sora tried to listen to what he was saying, but she was too distracted by the storm outside. The clouds had amassed thicker and thicker; it looked like night beyond the porthole window, with the ocean turned a murky gray. The noise of the waves was deafening.

A flash of lightning split the sky. She heard a distant rumble. A shudder passed through her body, a hint of foreboding. This was a new development. It had rained constantly since the ship left the docks, but this storm looked far worse than the others, titanic clouds roiling above an iron-gray sea.

A few more flashes of lightning passed. Sora tried to listen to what Tristan was staying. Something about a coral reef. No one seemed worried about the storm.

No one except Crash, perhaps, who was trying to hide his seasickness. Sora stole a couple of quick glances at him, hoping he would puke all over the cabin floor. A smirk touched her lips. *Looks like he's finally getting what he deserves,* she thought smugly.

Then the ship gave a mighty roll, tossing them all back in their seats. Sora keeled over, dry-heaving.

Tristan glanced at her, grinning. Then he waved to the back of the room. "You owe me ten coppers," he called to a friend.

Sora sat up, recovering from her episode. "You made a wager?" she demanded.

A round of giggles erupted behind her. She shot a glare over her shoulder. The Dracians ignored her look, muttering amongst themselves and passing coins back and forth.

Crash turned to her, unexpectedly. She looked at him in surprise. "It helps if you stay focused on one point," he said quietly.

She rolled her eyes.

"Childish," he muttered.

Her face flushed. She bit her lip. She was not going to be forced into a conversation.

Tristan collected his payment and continued speaking. He was describing a coral reef to the north, which he had spotted from the crow's nest earlier. "We either need to backtrack and go around it or head to the south to avoid the storms."

"The clouds are thicker in that direction," Joan interjected. The female Dracian sat next to the window and pointed outside. "Looks pretty bad right now."

"Do we have lifeboats on this ship?" another voice piped up: Laina, the street child who had accompanied them from the lower plains. Her pale blond hair was slightly mussed, as though she had forgotten to brush it that morning. She looked small and thin, even next to the Dracians.

Sora glanced over at her. Just yesterday, she and Laina had

met for an hour to sew. It was a womanly task that she didn't relish, but someone had to mend the sailors' torn clothes. The thirteen-year-old had taken a liking to Tristan and had insisted on darning his socks. Sora couldn't imagine why—perhaps because of the Dracian's dimpled chin and straight teeth.

"There might be a few lifeboats," Tristan said.

"You mean...you don't know?" Laina pressed, her voice turning petulant. "You've stolen a ship without lifeboats?"

"We assumed you all knew how to swim," Jacques said defensively, standing up in Tristan's place. "Raise your hand if you need swimming lessons!"

No one budged.

Sora sighed. The meeting was wandering off-topic fast. Typical.

There was another loud boom and the ship tossed more violently, tilting to one side. The crew members turned to the window, watching the massive, turbulent swells. Everyone listened to the storm, the thrum of heavy raindrops on the deck above. It was difficult to see outside; the sky was darkening quickly, obscuring the vicious ocean.

The timbers creaked, groaning like a wounded animal. Sora's hands grew clammy. There was a sudden commotion on deck, drifting down through the ceiling—the dim shouts of voices and thrumming feet.

Suddenly, the door flew open.

A Dracian crew member rushed into the room, a wild look in his eyes. "Get down!" he yelled, and threw himself to the floor.

No one moved, but looked amongst each other in confusion. The ship began to dip downward. Sora turned to look out the window. The blood drained from her face.

A solid wall of water met her eyes, blocking out the clouds. The wave was huge, far higher than any she had seen before. It peaked above their masts....

The ship dipped down, then tossed sideways as the massive wave crashed over them. One moment Sora was sitting in her chair, the next moment the room was backwards. The floor became the wall, the walls became the ceiling. She crashed to the ground, rolling to the side as the entire ship tipped and kept tipping. A loud, terrible *crack!* split the air.

"The masts!" someone yelled. "We've lost the masts!"

The lanterns flickered out. Darkness. The room was filled with scattered cries and screams. Sora scrambled to her feet and then slammed into a table. A body crashed into her from behind, knocking the wind from her lungs. Her thoughts spun in panic.

Then the windows shattered inward.

The table blocked her from the glass, but not from the flood of water. It gushed into the room like a spewing mouth. She was struck by an icy wave. The ocean greedily forced itself in, sweeping over the floor, consuming every inch of space. Before she knew it, she was up to her waist in freezing black salt water.

There was no time to think. The Dracian on top of her was panicking, trying to claw his way over her, away from the water. Sora shoved him off and struggled toward the door. It took her a moment to realize that the room was sideways and the door was, technically, beneath her boots. Submerged. More people bumped into her, panicked members of the crew. *Burn*, she thought. *Laina, Crash*....Where were her companions?

She was pushed back by the force of the next wave. The ship

rose again, then plummeted downward, rolling and spinning. She sucked in a desperate breath, then the water slammed her up against the wall. Or was it the ceiling? The ship listed drunkenly on the waves, tossed back and forth by the violent ocean. The meeting room was on the lower deck of the ship, flooding by the second. They were sinking.

The water was now over her head. She swam upward, searching for air, and caught a quick gasp. The entire room was almost submerged.

Sora forced her eyes open and almost gasped—the bloated form of a Dracian was in front of her, pale white again the dark water. She pushed the drowned man away, trying not to panic.

It was less violent underwater. The waves tugged and pulled, but nowhere near as forceful as at the surface. She noted the other crew members fleeing the room. Some went downward, prying open the door and swimming into the lower hallway—mainly the Dracians, who moved powerfully through the water. The ship was on its side; there could be oxygen in the hallway, or not. She didn't think she could last that long. It was horribly, paralyzingly cold.

Suddenly, she saw Joan. The woman swam smoothly through the water, as elegant as a seal. Sora watched her friend take on her Dracian form, the true appearance of her race. Her skin rippled and gleamed. A layer of scales emerged, silvery-blue in color. Her feet and hands elongated, webs spreading between her digits. Joan's eyes flattened and darkened until they were two ovular black disks. The only thing remaining of her old self was her thick mane of red hair.

Each of the Dracians was born with a different elemental power. It defined their magic. Some took to fire, some to air. Joan, it seemed, had taken to water.

The female Dracian then slipped agilely through the broken window. Grasping the idea, Sora swam to the surface one last time to take a breath, then dove downward again. She moved with painfully slow strokes toward the shattered opening.

She had always thought of herself as a strong swimmer, but the tug and pull of the ocean made her movements awkward and clumsy. It was her first time swimming in salt water. Her eyes were burning.

I'm going to drown, she thought, her lungs aching. No, she had to get out! On inspiration, Sora swam toward the wall and used it to launch herself at the window. Thankfully, it worked. She hooked her fingers on the sharp glass and pulled herself through. The cuts stung, but she could hardly feel them. She was too focused on escaping.

She propelled herself into the dark, open water beyond the ship and fought her way to the surface. It seemed an impossible distance, but she kept swimming. She grabbed onto floating debris from the deck, barrels and shards of the masts, using the wood to launch herself upward.

Finally, right when she thought she would pass out, her head exploded above water. She had only enough time for one short, desperate breath before a wave crashed over her. She was sent spiraling down, but was caught in the force of a second wave and shot to the surface again. The ocean tossed her into the air before dropping her back down. She felt like a small ant trapped in a river, spinning in useless circles.

Half-conscious, all she concentrated on was keeping her head above water. Now she was too numb to feel the rain, or even the freezing ocean that surrounded her. Basic instincts took over. Her world became very small—dark, swirling water and moments of blessed air. It was a battle against the sea and she only hoped that the Goddess would show her mercy.

The waves suddenly seemed to calm. She drifted upon the top of the ocean, barely keeping her head up. Although the rain and waves still lashed around her, no sound met her ears.

She turned and saw a large, dark object plummeting toward her on a fifteen-foot swell. It looked like a door broken off its hinges....

It crashed down on her head, forcing her under the water.

CHAPTER 3

Volcrian paused before the door of the mapmaker's shop. The dead priestess wandered along behind him, scuffing her feet against the cobblestone road. He ignored her.

It was a circular building with a domed roof, thatched windows and a large brown door. The shop was located on the corner of Port Street and Sanction Way, far from the cheap inn where he had stayed the night.

It had taken him all day to find it. At first he had gone uptown, away from the fishmonger's shop, only to discover that he was on the wrong side of the city. Delbar was massive, sprawling at least twenty miles down the coast. It was slightly slanted, the roads wending downward or upward. The poorer districts were at the "sunken end" while the expensive mansions and hotels were opposite. The mapmaker's shop was right in the middle at the fringe of the merchant's district.

A small rose garden decorated the building. Thorny vines thrust into the streets like beckoning fingers. The windows flickered with lantern light.

Good, he had arrived in time. The mapmaker would still be inside. He walked up to the front door and knocked.

No one answered. After a few seconds of waiting, he let himself in.

The shop was a chaotic mess. Tables upon tables stacked with papers. Bookshelves lined the walls, stuffed full of leather-bound tomes. Most didn't carry titles. Oil lamps rested on several of the tables, burning quietly.

"Hello?" he called out. His voice echoed from the domed ceiling.

"A minute!" replied a voice from the back of the room. Volcrian squinted, scanning the tables. He didn't see anyone.

Then, abruptly, a figure stepped out from behind one of the bookshelves. It was an old man, stooped and weathered, a brown hat shoved over his head. Stiff gray hair jutted out from under the rim. The old man looked him over with small, shrewd eyes. Volcrian thought of Malcolm's words—the mapmaker didn't appear batty. Only eccentric, his gaze keen with intelligence.

The mapmaker observed him for a moment, then raised one thick, bushy eyebrow. "Eh?" he said. "Well? What do you want?"

Volcrian didn't like his tone. It was sharp, unwelcoming. "I am looking for an old friend," he said. "He might have stopped by here a few weeks ago. Black hair, a young man, in his prime. He might have been here with a girl, or perhaps...a Wolfy."

The old man let out a short bark of a laugh. "A Wolfy? Now that's a first. If such things exist, I've never seen one. You'd best search the docks. All sorts of rumors down there. I'm sure you'd find someone claiming to have seen a Wolfy." He continued, one thought after the next. "I have many customers—sailors, treasure hunters, even nobility. Perhaps a hundred people cross my doorstep in a week. I certainly can't remember a black-haired man and a girl."

Volcrian took a step forward, running a hand over the table nearby. He touched the cover of a large leather book. "You'd remember this one," he murmured. "She wears a Cat's Eye."

The mapmaker's expression shifted momentarily, a glimmer of thought. Then he turned away, shuffling across the room, putting a book back on the shelf. "As I said, I have many customers. I don't remember anything of the sort."

"Ah," Volcrian said thoughtfully. He glanced at the priestess behind him, her body shrouded in the heavy brown cloak. She stood quietly by the wall, taking no interest in the conversation. She had been admittedly quiet since their run-in with Malcolm. He wondered, for a moment, if she could be of any assistance to him. Then thought better of it.

Volcrian turned and crossed the room toward the old man. The mapmaker glanced up and saw him, then circled around another table, keeping it between himself and the mage. "What do you want?" he asked again, his mustache bristling.

"The truth," Volcrian growled. "Don't test me. I can smell a lie at twenty paces. Tell me the truth...or I will force it out of you."

The man's eyes flickered to Volcrian's silver hair, his pointed ears. The mage waited, practically hearing the man's thoughts. He might not have seen a Wolfy before, but he was staring at one now.

"You have a queer energy about you," the mapmaker finally said. "From where do you hail?"

Volcrian was taken aback by the question. "The north," he said briefly. It was somewhat true. Wolfies had originated from the northern mountains, adapted to cold weather and icy climates. Yet he had been born in the fields, far from his native homeland. The mapmaker didn't need to know that.

"Hmph," the man grunted. Then he pulled a sheet of parchment from the stack in front of him. "I have a map here that may interest you," he said directly. "I think I remember the girl you speak of. As I recall, they were going to the Lost Isles."

That was easier than he had expected. Volcrian glanced out the window. He might have time for supper after all. "The Lost Isles?" he echoed. But why? The islands were all but a myth to humans. Long ago, back in the time of the Races, they had floated in the sky as the majestic island of Aerobourne, home to the Harpies. But that had been centuries ago. What could possibly be on the Lost Isles now?

The only way to find out would be to go there himself.

"Give me the map," Volcrian grunted, and reached for it. The mapmaker pulled back, holding the parchment in the air.

"For a few silvers," he grinned. "If it's so important...."

Volcrian felt a slow heat move through him. It built up in his chest—rage. He was on a hunt for vengeance—time was of the essence—and this man was toying with him?

"I have not the coin, nor the patience."

"You're a customer in my shop," the mapmaker cut him off. "Buy the map, and perhaps I shall give you a few parting words of wisdom."

Volcrian felt the rage grow. A year ago, he might have been able to control it, but not now. Not when his prey was so close to slipping his grasp.

He launched himself across the table, hands grasping, his fingers eager for blood. The mapmaker let out a yelp and fell to the floor, scrambling away. Then the old man got back on his feet with surprising agility and dashed toward the door, abandoning the map on the table.

"Stop him!" Volcrian roared.

The priestess moved, but slowly, as though underwater.

The mapmaker dodged past her and grabbed the door handle, yanking it open, plunging into the street. A moment later, he turned the corner and was gone.

Volcrian stared after him, heaving. He had half the mind to give chase—but that would be an even bigger waste of time. Instead, he stood and brushed himself off, then turned back to the map. Glanced over it. It was new parchment, a copy of the original, by the freshness of the ink. He folded the scrap of paper and tucked it in his cloak, then ran a hand through his long hair, regaining some sense of composure.

"We have what we came for," he said, turning back to the priestess. He crossed the floor to his minion and gave her a withering stare. "Next time, act quicker."

"If you haven't noticed," the woman said, "this body is not what it used to be. How am I supposed to waylay a man?" Her voice was like dust.

The anger bloomed again, rising quickly to the surface. Volcrian shook his head slowly. "I don't care if he takes your arm off," he growled. "Do as I say."

The priestess remained silent, staring at him with cloudy eyes. He couldn't read her expression. It was beyond the point of coherency.

He whirled toward the door, walking with swift steps. "Come," he said. "We have a boat to catch."

The two made their way out to the street and into the late afternoon light.

* * *

The sea breeze ruffled Burn's hair. His light-brown locks flashed in the sunlight and brushed against his long, pointed ears.

He gazed at the ocean, watching the constant roll of the waves, the breaking of the surf. He stood on a rocky beach, the white sand speckled with a myriad of smooth stones: deep reds, pale greens, slate blues. For now it was sunny, though he could see a long stretch of storm clouds in the distance, spinning turbulently as though conspiring amongst each other.

He could see little else from the shoreline. Still, his eyes searched and his ears listened. He was desperately hoping for any sign of her. Of Sora.

The ship had beached itself on a small island perhaps thirty miles wide, Burn judged by the curve of the shoreline. The hold of the ship was ripped open, gutted like an old shoe on a river bank. Shards of masts, crates, and other debris scattered the shoreline for miles. The Dracians were searching up and down the sandy beach, tending to the survivors and trying to scavenge what they could.

The frame of the ruined ship was about a half-mile away, lodged firmly on an underwater reef. The majority of the crew was still intact, only three fatalities...and one missing girl. Burn supposed they were lucky. Most had clung to the upper deck, the only part of the ship that hadn't been submerged. It had been their protection against the merciless storm.

He shuddered just thinking about it. He still couldn't quite believe that he was alive.

Burn glanced down at the compass in his hand. He wasn't sure if it was broken or not; it was partly waterlogged. He had no idea where this island was located, if they were anywhere near the Lost Isles, or if this was just another rock in the ocean, a resting point for migrating birds.

He squinted, still searching the water. Sometimes, far off in the distance, he thought he saw a large, gray shape against the horizon. Another island? It didn't appear to move. Then the clouds would shift and it would vanish again.

"We found the weapons," a voice said from behind him. He glanced to the side, noting Jacques' presence. The Dracian Captain still wore his blue coat, though it was frayed and tattered, long rents on his arms and back. The black crow sat on his shoulder, its feathers slightly ruffled. It held a twisted piece of metal in its beak, perhaps a door hinge or a bolt.

"Good," Burn said. It was an empty sound. At this point, recovering the chest of weapons seemed trivial.

Jacques cleared his throat and spoke again. "Your greatsword is intact, the assassin's equipment, the sacred weapons...and Sora's things," he murmured.

Sora. Burn shook his head slowly. At least they still had the weapons of the Dark God, the key to undoing the plague. But first they had to destroy the mage who had caused all of this. And for that, they needed a Cat's Eye. "Without Sora, this quest is as good as finished," he murmured.

Jacques' hand landed on his shoulder. It was an awkward position since Burn was almost two feet taller than the Dracian. "She'll show up," the Dracian said. "A few of my men are flying over the island and won't return until it's fully covered. It might take a couple of days. Most of the wreckage turned up here, but she could be farther up the coast."

"Right," Burn muttered. *Or at the bottom of the ocean.*

He turned and looked at the ravaged crew. They moved across

the stone-studded beach, stiff and subdued. They were attempting to build a shelter out of ruined shards of the ship. By the looks of it, they weren't having much luck. They would do better to move into the forest, take shelter amongst the trees.

His eyes traveled to Laina, the young girl they had rescued on the mainland. She was throwing stones into the ocean, her pale hair matted with saltwater, her clothes ripped and salt-stained. Sora had found the girl in a jailhouse, slated for hanging, and had saved Laina's life. Thirteen was too young to be executed—too young to be in a shipwreck, to be stranded on an island. They shouldn't have brought her, but there hadn't been much choice. They couldn't have abandoned her on the streets of Delbar, with nothing and no one to turn to.

A bit of guilt lodged in his throat. He had once had a daughter her age. Two daughters—an older and a younger. Four years ago... only four years ago had Volcrian taken them. He had found his older daughter Alanna next to his wife's body, curled and blackened in the fire of their house. His younger girl, Avian...he had only found her bloodied cloak, wrapped around the tips of her pointed ears, cut from her head. He had searched for her...for weeks he had looked, but he had not found her body. He had nightmares about it, imagining what Volcrian had used her for. A sacrifice? Black-blooded magic? His heart twisted in his chest, stealing his breath.

"Laina," he called to the girl.

She glanced up at him. Her eyes were a light lavender-brown in the sunset. Her gaze traveled from Burn to Jacques, then narrowed. "If you're wondering why I'm not fishing," she said defensively, "it's cuz I don't know how!"

Burn glanced down at the Dracian. Jacques shrugged in

response. "I was just trying to give her something to do," he muttered.

Burn sighed. Laina was a street child, skilled at nothing but picking pockets. "Gather driftwood and help make camp," he called to her. He pointed to the ridge of trees behind him. "Somewhere over there. Jacques will bring our weapons over."

Laina dropped the rock in her hand. "I want to look for Sora," she said.

"Stay close to us for now," Burn replied. "We don't know the dangers of this island."

Laina rolled her eyes and then turned, walking up the beach, picking up driftwood as she went. Burn took that as her agreement.

"Wolfy," the Dracian said at his side, drawing his attention again. "You should tell Crash about the weapons."

Burn raised a brow. "Why? Can you not do it yourself?"

Jacques shrugged. "He took off into the forest a little while ago. Honestly, he's your companion, not mine."

Burn nodded, a quiet breath passing through his lips. The assassin did not make friends, did not suffer fools. And the Dracians were a friendly, foolish lot. He turned from the ocean and started across the beach.

"We'll start a bonfire," Jacques called after him. "Catch some food and eat well tonight. You'll see. Everything will be better in the morning!"

"Just find Sora," Burn said over his shoulder.

"Right."

He started into the forest, picking his way through scrub grass, then into the shade of the trees. The dirt was grainy in texture, mixed with sand. The trees of this island were similar to those he had seen in the far south—long, naked trunks with bursts of giant leaves toward the top. Tropical. Others grew low and winding, spreading outward more than upward, wide and waxy.

He sniffed the air, taking in the new scents of the forest: saltwater, dense pollen and a fruity, sweet haze. Listening intently, he picked up the assassin's sounds. Crash was not trying to hide—otherwise he would be inaudible, invisible, as notable as mist. He continued in the direction of the noise.

* * *

Crash paced restlessly through a small patch of jungle, back and forth, flattening the grass. He didn't need to go deeper into the brush, but was content to cover the same clearing once, twice, thrice...countless times. The air was surprisingly humid beneath the trees, given the close proximity of the ocean. If he listened, he could still hear the distant rush of waves, the call of gulls. It brought back memories—visions of a past that he lingered on, perhaps too much over the years.

A cloud of gnats had grown quite attached to him. They followed in his wake, back and forth across the small clearing. He flicked his hand in the air, focused on his thoughts. Or rather, on his lack of a solution.

His mood darkened with the fading light. He kept listening for a sound from the Dracians, a whoop of excitement or the shout of a name, but there was none. Which only meant one thing. They were still searching for Sora.

And it was growing dark.

Damn. He glanced at the sky, cursing the sun. Usually he had plenty of patience, a requirement in his line of work. Calm and collected, his thoughts clear and precise. But now his mind buzzed uncontrollably, terribly loud, conjuring pictures of Sora's body, crumpled and lifeless on the beach. Or even worse—a league under the ocean, eaten away by fish.

Waiting is necessary, he told himself. He was a man of action, but pacing would have to do for now. He felt like he should be walking the beach, scouring endless miles until he found her—but a larger part of him knew that it was in vain. *Don't fancy yourself a hero.* The Dracians could fly over the island much faster and return with any news. A whole body of news, perhaps, wrapped in a damp cloak, one lifeless hand drifting toward the ground.

Don't think of it, he told himself. What had happened to his training? He was out of control. No, he was doing all that he could —it just wasn't enough.

There was a thrashing in the underbrush. He recognized Burn's steps, heavy with exhaustion. Crash felt that same weariness tug down at shoulders. Defeating the ocean was no small feat. He was surprised that any of them had survived. Part of him had almost wished for death. It would have been an unexpected—if welcome—end to this ridiculous quest.

Burn emerged between two waxy leaves, his clothes smeared with bright orange pollen. He gazed at the assassin, his eyes a deep amber in the evening sun. Crash wished he would look away. He saw far too much sympathy in that gaze.

"They found our weapons," the Wolfy said, indicating over his shoulder. "They're a little stained by salt water, but salvageable."

Crash nodded curtly and resumed pacing.

Burn hesitated for a moment, watching him. His eyes traveled to the bent grass. "Do that much longer and you'll flatten the forest," he remarked, humor in his tone.

Crash didn't respond. He waved another hand at the gnats around his face. He grimaced in annoyance.

Burn cleared his throat slowly. "I'm sure she's alive."

"I don't care," Crash growled.

Burn paused, watching him closely. Then the Wolfy crossed the clearing, stopping before the assassin, cutting off his steps. "You don't need to lie to me," he said solemnly.

Crash sighed. At this point, Burn was his oldest companion. He used the term loosely. In the wide scheme of things, the two barely knew each other. He had approached the Wolfy long ago, seeking help to defeat Volcrian, or at least more knowledge of the mage's power. But Volcrian had found them first.

Burn's family had suffered the consequences. One night, they had returned to find his daughters and wife dead, the house razed to the ground.

Crash hadn't asked the Wolfy mercenary to join him and hadn't expected him to. But Burn had lingered with him on the road, perhaps on his own hunt for vengeance, perhaps because he had nothing left. Both options were ultimately empty. Crash didn't pretend to know the man's motives, and they made no difference. Volcrian was a menace, and now his magic tainted the entire mainland, a spreading plague.

They hadn't spoken of Burn's family since that night. They had shared very little of their pasts, spent too much time and energy on survival.

"Volcrian will find us," Crash muttered. "The plague will continue. Without the Cat's Eye, we will have to face him as we are.

And you know how that will end."

Burn's frown deepened. "That's all you care about?" he growled. "Volcrian's wrath?" He took a step forward. "Sora risked her life for us countless times. The least you can do is show concern. You should be out searching, just like the Dracians, not wasting time on your own selfish motives."

Anger surged. Fire burned in his arms, his chest. Crash felt his skull throb. Before he could stop it, a dark shadow rose up from the grass, gathering in the air. The Wolfy's face flickered, a hint of fear.

The assassin shoved Burn away and glared, seething. "Search the beach?" he snapped. "And not be here when she returns?"

A sudden, inexplicable smile cracked Burn's lips. "Ah," he murmured. "So you do care."

Crash paused, still breathing hard. The blackness glinted in his eyes again, and he passed a hand over his face, trying to clear it. No. He had to regain control. He could feel the fire spreading down his legs, up his back, dancing around his skull. Assassins were not meant to show emotion. He had been warned from a young age of its danger, the peril of losing oneself to wrath, to fear, to love—to anything.

He turned away, pacing again, this time in a new direction. "We covered five miles today on foot," he said bluntly. "The Dracians have searched farther. She's gone."

"Sora is resilient," Burn murmured. "Don't give up hope."

"Hope?" Crash said bitterly. "Open your eyes."

His words hung in the air between them, an impenetrable wall. He gazed at the Wolfy, unflinching. Then he turned and stalked into the forest, back toward the beach. He rubbed his other hand over his face, swatting at the gnats. Burn was right about one thing

—he needed to make himself useful, and now that his weapons had been found, he had plenty to do.

CHAPTER 4

Sora felt a strange tingling sensation. A dull roar filled her ears, rushing in and out, over and over again. At first she thought it was a dream or some trick of her mind. Then she felt the gritty texture of sand beneath her, the light brush of wind.

A sudden thought jolted her awake. *The ocean.*

Then a hot, terrible pain struck her. The tingling in the back of her skull moved forward, throbbing down her forehead, her nose, her teeth. She groaned, feeling as though her head had been split in two.

But her shoulder...her shoulder hurt worse. Every beat of her heart brought a terrible, swooning ache. She clamped her jaw shut, seething, trying to breathe. *By the North Wind,* she thought. *What happened?*

A shallow wave rushed up, licking her foot. The water was ice-cold. She groaned again, opening her eyes and blinking against the harsh light. The sun was blinding, as though her face was an inch away from fire. *No more storm clouds,* she thought vaguely. *Where am I?*

After a moment, she attempted to sit up and almost screamed. Her arm was useless at her side, her shoulder stiff with a deep pain. She glanced sideways, almost afraid to look, and saw her shoulder jutting out at an awkward angle. Dislocated.

A wave of nausea rolled through Sora and she gritted her teeth. This would not do. If she waited too long, the shoulder would swell up and she would be crippled, which left only one option. She had to push her shoulder back in.

She wished, for a very long moment, that she were back at her manor, before she had ever met Crash and Burn or her mother. It seemed so long ago now. The world of wealth and riches was like another life, the story of another girl, one she had known in a distant past. She could still remember that girl's room, the gauzy white curtains blowing inward, the smell of bath salts and jasmine.

In that life, a half-dozen Healers knelt by the girl's bedside, applying ointments and soothing lotions. They would have gently relocated her arm, strapping it tightly to her chest. There might have even been a minstrel in the corner, playing sweet acoustic music on a guitar.

But she hadn't lived there in a very long time. No, for the past year she had been with her mother, in a log cabin in the wilderness, learning the tricks of the healing trade. Lorianne had taught her well. She could do this herself. She would have to.

Sora took a deep breath, trying to remember the technique that her mother had used. Countless children had been brought to their house with this kind of injury. Eventually, some had been able to right their dislocated arm by themselves. *If a child can do it, I can do it,* she thought. She kept breathing, trying to think through the pain.

Finally, she laid back down on the sand, easing her arm outward. She winced several times, slowing the movement. *It doesn't have to be painful,* she heard her mother's voice, gentle and warm in the sickroom. *Reach over your head like you're scratching your back.*

Sora did so, trembling with the effort. It hurt no matter how slowly she moved. Finally, she thought she had her arm in the right position, with her elbow over her head and her hand down. She turned her hand outward, stretching the arm up and back.

There was a slight pop from the bone, the sense of something smooth and curved sliding into place. The pain flared for a moment and then subsided. Her body still ached, but her shoulder dislocation was much less pronounced.

Sora sat back up carefully. She straightened out her arm, flexing her fingers. Winced. It was still sore—but workable.

Finally, she was able to take stock of her surroundings. She glanced around the abandoned beach. The shoreline was long and curved, stretching into the distance with nary a flaw. Pebbles speckled the sand, glints of color against the fading sunset. Shards of driftwood interrupted the landscape, twisting up from the beach like tortured skeletons. Color drenched the sky, deep orange and vibrant pink, sinking into a glorious royal purple. She had less than an hour to find shelter for the night.

*Crash, Burn, Laina...*she thought, still searching the horizon. She scanned the ocean, looking for a sign of the shipwreck. She saw shards of wood and tangled ropes that might have been from the ship. Then her eyes landed on a large broken door, listing in the shallow water. She vaguely remembered it slamming into her during the storm. She had managed to cling to the wood, possibly the only reason why she was still alive.

Besides that, there was nothing. No footprints. *I'm alone.*

The sole survivor?

At the thought, her body shuddered uncontrollably. Alone. On an unknown island. Stranded.

Don't panic, she told herself firmly. Goddess, were they all dead? The thought crushed her, suffocating, her heart rising to her throat. It couldn't be true. But as she searched the beach, she saw no sign of civilization—of life.

She couldn't accept it. Her head spun. Perhaps this beach didn't even exist. Perhaps she had woken up in the unknown limbo between life and death, in the twilight realm where ghosts lingered, trapped by memories. But no, her body was too sore. Her dislocated shoulder was evidence enough that she was still alive.

They're dead, she thought again. It kept repeating in her mind, over and over, making her sick.

She took another deep breath, pressing her good hand to her chest. To her Cat's Eye. The stone was smooth, perfectly round, glinting with a secretive green light. Strength flooded through her, warming her muscles.

You don't know that for sure, her inner voice murmured. *Calm down. Focus.* She needed to contain herself, to fight off the urge to scream. No, now was the time for survival. She forcefully quelled her emotions, shoving them into an old box somewhere deep in her mind. She would look at them later. She needed to find shelter and safety, some place where she could piece together what had happened.

Sora dragged herself to her feet. Her muscles quivered, then grew solid and firm. Her entire body felt as though it had been chewed up in a giant's mouth, then spit out on the ground. She glanced down at her torn clothing, bruised skin visible through the holes. Seaweed clung to her pants and shirt, tangled up in the cloth. She tried to rip the strands off, but the effort was too much.

She stumbled over to a pile of driftwood and pulled a large, long branch from the mess. It was fairly straight, made smooth by the ocean. She felt a sudden pang of loss, reminded of her witchwood staff, her favorite weapon. She would never see it again.

Then she turned toward the forest, staggering up the beach. She could see a mountain covered in bright green foliage jutting over the tops of the trees. It was small compared to the mountains of the mainland. The sun touched the horizon behind it, sinking fast in the sky.

She turned her gaze back to the beach. Her eyes combed the trees, looking for a likely place to set up camp. She didn't know what kind of animals lived in this forest. It would be wiser to sleep in the trees.

She spotted a perfect climbing tree further up the beach. A large, thick trunk sprawled outward, split into many branches. The bark looked flat and shiny, different from the tall pines of her homeland. The leaves were longer than her hand, waxy in texture, bright green.

She walked to the tree, quite a distance across the sand. Strange, spiky gourds hung from its branches, dark brown in color, bigger than her fist. *At least I'll have something to throw if I'm attacked*, she thought wryly. Then she set about climbing the tree. She was barely able to pull herself up to the lower branches, her left arm still weak and useless.

She settled into the nook at its center, curling up against the shadows. The smells of the forest were strange—minty and sweet, tangy, like the lemon tree in her mother's garden. Harsh sounds pierced her ears—loud, shrieking birds and croaking frogs. The click of insects. Distant roars of unseen animals.

She curled tighter into a ball, squeezing her eyes shut, wishing she were invisible. The faces of her friends swam before her. Burn's easy smile. Laina's awkward grin. Crash's enigmatic gaze. *They're dead,* she thought, tears slipping from between her closed eyelids. Grief struck her, an abyss opening in her chest, large enough to swallow her whole. She fell into it, pain coursing through her, overtaking her body. She felt minuscule, as though still trapped in another ocean, tossed by the waves, helpless.

She began to sob, a choking sound. The pain was so great; it forced her throat to close, made her tears weak and pitiful. She couldn't even begin to fathom what she had lost. *They're all dead... and I'm alone.*

* * *

Lori frowned. She thought she recognized the horse in the distance. It didn't seem possible, but she would know that dark coat anywhere, the white socks and blazed nose. She even recognized the saddle.

The sun was setting at the small port of Cape Shorn. It was a narrow hook of land that jutted out into the ocean, the last port town for the next sixty miles.

Ferran had brought her here in search of a book. A rare, priceless book that he had given to a whore some months ago. She winced thinking about it. The book had then been sold to some kind of a pirate that was supposedly anchored off of Sylla Cove. According to Ferran, the book held the secrets of the Dark God's weapons—and the method of returning them to the underworld. It was exactly what Sora would need once she killed Volcrian.

Without returning the sacred weapons, the plague would continue to spread, taking one victim at a time. She had kept a careful eye on the population of Cape Shorn, noting a few coughing sailors and merchants with pale, sallow skin. The plague had yet to take root on the coast, but it was only a matter of time. It was already sweeping across the farmlands.

She sat on the docks, coiling up various lengths of rope, repairing the weaker strands as fast as possible. The sun was setting fast and soon there would be no light to work by. Ferran was on board, stocking the cabin with dried meats and jarred vegetables, preparing his small houseboat for the voyage north. It was quiet this evening, unusually so. In a port city like Cape Shorn, countless merchants and fishermen stocked their ships before heading out to deeper waters. Tonight, however, the docks were unusually subdued, the sky gray with dusk, the sun at the brink of the horizon.

The horse approached them, coming to a stop. It whuffed in greeting, flicking its ears. Yes, she would know that steed anywhere. It was her stallion Mingo, the sire of two little foals back on her ranch.

A low, hunched shape struggled from the saddle. Her frown deepened. It could be none other than Cameron, her stablehand. But how had he found them? She couldn't guess. Her horses were well-trained, related to a distant bloodline that stretched back to the War. They were far more intelligent than most, in high demand amongst soldiers and the nobility. She had managed to secure a pair as payment from an especially thankful breeder. Since Cameron was mute, she could only assume that the horse's instincts had led him to her.

"What's happened?" she demanded, dropping the rope in her hands. Ferran glanced up, leaning out from beneath the roof of the houseboat. He looked at her questioningly, but she ignored him. She leapt to the wooden dock and ran inland toward Cameron, who looked ashen in the fading light.

The man didn't say anything—he couldn't speak, he was shivering so hard. He must have ridden all day. His face was bitten by the wind, bright red across his cheeks and nose. *Why is he here?* She could only think of one reason: trouble.

He held out a shivering hand, with a piece of paper clamped in it. She took the paper from his grip, prying his fingers open, and quickly read over the note.

It was from Sora. Lori gnawed her lip as she read. Her daughter had sent it from the Port City of Delbar, perhaps a week or two ago. But why the urgency? She kept reading, her heart in her throat, waiting for some indication that her daughter was wounded or trapped. But the message was much more surprising than that.

"The Lost Isles?" she muttered in surprise. Sora's letter detailed her journey to the city of Barcella, where she had met with the Priestess of the West Wind. Now she was taking a ship out to sea to the Lost Isles. Lori balked at the thought. It was a place of notorious shipwrecks. Sailors avoided those waters, at times making hundred-mile detours around the weather. The Lost Isles were said to be cursed by mysterious storms, residue left from the ancient War.

She was speechless.

"What is it?" Ferran called, stepping off the boat. He was a tall man, lean and muscular and in his late thirties, a few years older than her.

"Nothing," Lori said quickly, and shoved the letter in her pocket. She was worried for her daughter, but it only made her own journey more urgent. Sora would need Ferran's book to deal with the sacred weapons. Killing Volcrian was only half of the problem. They would have to undo the curse, bind the Dark God back into the earth, and seal shut whatever terrible gate had been opened. *Stay focused,* she told herself firmly. *You need to help Sora, not chase after her.*

She looked to Cameron, searching his face. Ten years ago, the man was kicked in the head by a spooked horse. He had been brought to her cabin for healing, but the injury had been too traumatic to heal even for her formidable skills. Eventually the wound mended, but not his mind. Lori agreed to take him on as a stablehand, providing room and board in exchange for labor. He had lost his ability to read and write and almost the ability to speak. They used a simplistic series of hand signals to communicate.

She glanced at the note again, then at her stablehand's face, assessing the situation. Cameron had probably received the letter and panicked, uncertain of what it meant. Still, she was grateful for the news from her daughter. It was better than knowing nothing and imagining the worst.

"You did a good job," she said, laying her hand against the man's cheek, which was icy-cold. "Thank you, Cameron."

Her stablehand nodded, still wheezing with exhaustion. She reached into the pouch at her belt and withdrew several silver coins. "For your trouble," she said. "Thank you for giving this note to me. Ferran and I are taking a quick journey up the coast. If Sora returns to the cabin during my absence, try to keep her there, all right? We will return soon."

He nodded again, then made a few signs with his hand. Cameron spoke at times, but sign language seemed easier for him.

It was difficult for him to pronounce certain words, especially with his jaw locked up by the cold.

"Aye," she said, answering his silent question. "Two or three weeks, I suspect. I will write you if it takes longer. Have a farmer in town read the note to you. Will you watch over the land for me?"

Cameron nodded.

"Good. Now wait here for a moment. I'll take you to a nice inn."

Cameron nodded again and grinned. He had a blunt, dopey countenance with large ears and a fragile chin. Lori watched as he climbed onto his horse. Then she turned and walked back down the narrow dock, raveling up the rest of the rope. She preferred that Cameron stay at an expensive place; it ensured his security. There were all sorts of hoodlums who would attack a simpleton on the docks. Best to avoid the poorer districts.

"What's that about?" Ferran asked as Lori returned to the boat. His expression turned wry. "Is that your husband? A lover?"

Lori smiled sweetly at him. "Yes, he came to say goodbye. We are very happy together."

Ferran's face went momentarily slack. Lori laughed at his expression. "Oh please, I'm joking."

"Of course," he replied, glancing away. "I knew that."

Lori watched him, the smile slowly fading from her face. "A letter from my daughter," she said briefly. She needed to process the information, the instinctive fear that rose within her at the thought of Sora's journey. There was so much danger in the world; she couldn't protect her daughter from all of it. *But that's what I'm trying to do,* she thought, considering her journey to Sylla Cove. If she could just get her hands on that book, she would have answers.

Answers that Sora could use.

"I'll be right back," she said, dropping the bundle of rope into the boat. "I won't be long, just to get Cameron settled. We need to leave tonight. We don't have much time."

CHAPTER 5

The next day, Sora felt numb and empty, as though the life had been drained out of her. The grief stayed with her like a heavy cloak, weighing on her shoulders, dragging at her steps. She forced herself to scavenge for food, using that as a distraction, something simple and primal on which to focus.

She didn't recognize any of the plants on the island, which made things difficult. She stayed away from the red berry bushes, which she suspected were poisonous. Most of the trees had prickly fruit of different sizes and shapes. She tried a bright orange specimen; the shell was sharply spiked and had a green interior, similar to a cucumber. It was bitter to the taste and she tossed it away.

Then she ran across a tall tree surrounded by large, brown pods. She cracked open the husk of one pod, finding a white, fleshy substance inside. The juice of the fruit was sweet and creamy, like watery milk. The white flesh was chalky and crunchy. She wasn't sure if she liked the flavor, but she ate it anyway. It was not as satisfying as she had hoped. The moment the sweet juice touched her lips, her stomach let out a loud growl, and she was consumed by hunger.

After an hour of wandering down the coast, she found an orange tree. Her eyes grew wide. When she had lived at the manor, oranges had been an exotic affair, served on special occasions and highly coveted. She hadn't eaten one in at least four years.

She gathered up the fruits and made a feast of it, peeling off the skin and biting into the pulpy, juicy interior. The oranges were warm and overwhelmingly sweet. Nectar dribbled down her chin and stained her clothes. Their smell attracted bees so she moved closer to the ocean to finish her meal, washing the juice from her hands in the shallows.

When she was done, she looked around the island, gazing at the slope of the mountain. She entertained the thought of searching for her companions, but the grief returned, splitting her heart, and she shuddered. She couldn't give herself hope—that would be a cruel joke to indulge in and she knew better. If there was one thing Crash had taught her, it was to be honest about her situation. One could deal with reality. Fantasy was much more difficult.

She grasped for another distraction. *I wonder if anyone else lives here.* The beach was obviously isolated and she hadn't seen any ships pass by on the horizon, but perhaps a town or village existed on the opposite side of the island. She pondered the thought, then wrapped as many oranges as she could into her shirt and tied the garment tightly around her waist, exposing her midriff. It might look a little strange, but she had no other way of carrying the fruit.

Sora walked along the beach for almost a mile, but it was hard-going in the sand. Eventually she returned to the shade of the treeline where the ground was firmer, entertaining herself by counting the plants she didn't recognize. There were vines of bright magenta flowers, far more saturated than a rose. Wide yellow blooms that smelled of exotic perfume, dense enough to make her sneeze, their stamens as long as her forearm. Countless species of trees, some of which sat low to the ground, trunks as fat as barrels, leaves sprouting in wide fronds. Others stretched high into the air, their branches jutting out like parasols. There was a large mix of ferns and bushes. Some resembled lizards' tails, twisting up from the sandy ground, thick and spiked. Some were green, some purple, others a vibrant red.

She saw several animals. Black snakes that curled through the rocks, small spotted frogs and large scabby insects. A flock of bright green birds passed overhead, screeching horribly. A family of small pigs trotted past, covered in dark brown fur. And, to her astonishment, monkeys. They sat high in the trees, chattering amongst each other, with their sleek black fur and white-masked faces. She had only seen one monkey before, in a cage on the docks of Delbar.

Toward mid-day, she saw a strange sliver of gray smoke against the sky. She blinked twice, staring at it, uncertain if she were dreaming. The thin trail drifted across the beach. She was hardly able to believe her eyes. A flurry of emotions passed through her—hope, fear, uncertainty. She had seen no sign of a shipwreck, but maybe...maybe she wasn't the only survivor. Maybe a few Dracians had made it out alive. She couldn't wish for more. *What's if it's Crash?* Guilt rose up inside of her. She hadn't made amends; no, they had still been arguing when the ship had gone down. No apologies. Only anger.

The guilt stifled her, a hard lump solidifying in her chest. The thought that her companions might be sitting in the forest, perhaps dining on pork or fish...was too much to bear.

Sora changed course and plunged into the jungle. She kept one eye to the sky, following the thin trail of smoke. Its origin couldn't be too far away.

The forest was thick and overgrown, untouched by human hands, almost impossible to walk through. The air was humid and heavy with pollen. She ducked under several spider webs—giant, glinting strands that wove up into the trees. She couldn't imagine the size of their makers, and she prayed that none of them dropped on her head. She kept a careful eye on her feet, hesitant to step on a snake in the brush.

It took her almost an hour to reach the source of the smoke. Finally, she stumbled out of the forest into a cleared space of land. She stood there for a moment, staring in awe.

The clearing was roughly an acre in width. The brush had been tamed back, hacked by a blunt blade. Wooden posts outlined the border of the trees. The grass was thin on the ground, torn up until nothing but dirt and rocks remained.

A building resided in the center of the clearing. Solid wooden beams were roped together with vines; the roof was covered in dry yellow grass. Smoke poured out from ventilation holes in the top of the roof. On one side, a rough door had been fashioned out of driftwood. Sora stared at it, surprised. A house? Was it on fire? She couldn't imagine why so much smoke would be coming out.

She paused, wondering what to do. There was no immediate way to put out the fire, and she wasn't sure she wanted to. The hut looked like it had been standing there for a while, not something the Dracians could have constructed overnight. A cold chill moved through her belly. That only left one other explanation.

She wanted to hide herself in the trees, but curiosity won out. With tentative steps, she crossed the clearing and paused next to the building, reaching out to touch the door. Dare she go inside? This close, she caught the scent of roasting meat. It made her mouth water. It smelled...*good.*

But where were the owners?

As though answering her thoughts, she heard distant voices to her left, the hubbub of conversation. She whirled, wide-eyed, and stared at the treeline.

Two men emerged from the jungle.

She didn't recognize them. Their hair was long and tangled, full beards down to their chests. One had brown hair, the other blond. They were dressed in animal skins, their feet wrapped in fur and leaves, deerskin cloaks over their shoulders. One carried a walking stick and limped heavily on his right leg. The other had a stone ax in hand.

They froze in their tracks and stared at her, eyes widening beneath their bushy brows. The blond's jaw dropped. Their expressions could only be described as awestruck. It was as though they looked upon the Goddess Herself.

Sora reached up and touched her hair subconsciously. She hadn't even thought about her appearance in the last day.

"Um...hello?" she called, unsure if they would understand her.

The brown-haired man reached out a hand, clapping his friend on the shoulder. "Now we've truly lost our minds," he said.

"Aye," the other replied, his expression hardening.

"Oh, good," Sora muttered in relief. She started across the clearing toward them, walking easily through the dirt. "I'm so glad I found you. I thought this island was deserted."

"Halt right there! State your name!" the blond man with the ax yelled. He waved the ax at her. After an uncertain moment, he called, "Are you a ghost?"

Sora paused a dozen feet away, put off by the ax. Were these men dangerous? *Startled, perhaps.*

She held up her hands cautiously. "No, not a ghost," she said. Ironic, since she felt like one. She pointed over her shoulder, back toward the beach. "My ship was caught in a storm. I washed up on shore. Is there a town nearby?"

The man's ax dropped back to his side. They stared at her for another long moment, then his brown-haired companion let out a deep laugh. "The Goddess has finally shined upon us!" he yelled to no one in particular. "How long I have prayed for a woman!"

"I saw her first!" the blond man growled, and shoved his friend away. "She's mine!"

Sora shifted uncomfortably, her eyes combing the jungle. *Maybe it would be better to leave.* She had fought off Catlins, wraiths and bandits before. She could probably handle these two— but she had no weapons and no easy route of escape. The forest was thick on all sides, tangled with vines and plant life.

The two men continued to argue. The blond man swung his ax haphazardly at the cripple, who dodged with startling ease. The cripple lashed back with his walking stick.

Sora turned and started back across the clearing, searching for a place to enter the trees. She would have run, but she didn't want to draw more attention to herself. The two men were suitably distracted for now.

Then, abruptly, a third man dashed out of the trees. It took her a moment to recognize him as human—he was covered in animal furs and vines. He ran directly in front of her and threw out his arms, blocking her way forward. He held an old, rusty saber in one hand. His face carried less facial hair, though he was still grimy and dirty. His chestnut-colored hair was tied back in a leather thong.

Sora stared at him, taken aback. Now she didn't know what to do.

"Sorry," he said, panting. "But you can't leave."

Sora frowned at the stranger, keeping a close eye on his sword. He was just as shaggy as his fellows, only his face was easier to see. His beard was thin and stringy, not bushy. He tried to smile at her, but that was an alarming sight. His teeth were yellow and crooked, his lips split, his skin creased by sun and dirt. He looked absolutely wicked.

She took a slight step back. "Don't come any closer," she said, shifting into a fighting stance, hands up, knees slightly bent. She glanced behind her. The two men had stopped arguing and were watching the confrontation. The blond one looked infuriated.

"My name is John Witherman," the third man drew her attention. "Perhaps you've heard of me? Captain Witherman of the Strongarm Pirates. I am quite a well known treasure hunter on the mainland."

Sora shook her head wordlessly. *Pirates?* That didn't bode well.

The man's grin widened, twisting his face into a wrinkled map. "Then I will educate you, my dear. Join our fire tonight and I will share my story."

Sora gave him a tight smile. "I'll have to decline," she said bluntly.

"She's mine!" the blond man yelled behind them. "I saw her first!"

"Idiot!" the cripple said. "She's the Captain's now!"

Sora balked at that. It was time to run. She turned on her heel and dashed for the trees without a second glance. The forest was several dozen yards away—a towering wall of impenetrable leaves. She emptied the oranges from her shirt as she ran, leaping over the round fruit, moving as fast as she could. The men shouted behind her and gave chase.

A second later, something hit the back of her head. *Thwak!*

It was hard enough to cause her to stumble. Then a body slammed into her from behind. Sora was tackled to the ground just before the fringe of trees.

John Witherman rolled her over, a second orange in his hand. He tried to smash it into her face, but she twisted to one side, trying to break his grip. They scrabbled for a moment, wrestling, Sora gaining the upper hand—but he was too strong, and her left arm was starting to throb. She didn't want to dislocate it again.

Then, suddenly, a second man landed near Sora's head. It was the blond one with the ax. He pinned her with one hand and pressed the dull blade to her throat, effectively stopping the fight. Sora spat at him and glared. He licked the fleck of spit from his mouth.

John Witherman pulled a length of rope from his belt while holding her down. The rope appeared to be woven of plant fiber and vines.

"Tie her, Benny!" he ordered, and passed it to the blond man.

Benny flipped her onto her back, dragging her arms behind her. Sora grunted in pain. She wanted to fight back, but she was outnumbered and weaponless. He tied her wrists firmly, then stood up, rolling her over.

Sora's heart hammered. Her vision narrowed with panic. Would they kill her now?

"Pick her up and take her back to camp," John said. Then he

nodded to the crippled man who stood behind them. "Help me gather the catfish from the shed, then douse the fires. We don't need any of her crew finding us." John Witherman gave her a wide smile. "Not until we're done with her."

Sora's body went cold.

Benny happily obliged, throwing her over his shoulder, putting a firm hand on her buttocks. Sora tried to squirm away, struggling as hard as she could. "Help!" she screamed, on the chance that someone else might hear her. "Help me!"

"Gag her," John said with another disturbing grin. "Your crew won't find you. We're the only people on this island. Been that way for the past seven years." Then he turned to his companions. "Let's go."

Sora kicked and writhed, trying to break free, but Benny's grip was like iron. Of course he wouldn't let her go. He probably hadn't seen a woman since leaving the mainland.

Goddess. The thought made her sick. She had to get away somehow. If only she had her staff and daggers, she could have made short work of these three. *There's still time,* she tried to calm herself. As long as they thought she was helpless, they might get clumsy, overconfident. In fact, she was certain of it.

Sora went limp and laid against the man's shoulder, awaiting a chance to escape.

* * *

Crash looked up. The sound of wings met his ears—giant, leathery wings of emerald hues that glowed in the late afternoon light. The sun shimmered against their outstretched skin, dancing across their scales. A group of five Dracians emerged from beyond the treeline, headed slowly toward their camp on the beach.

They were not so strange in their natural forms. Still humanoid in shape, their limbs were longer, more powerful than humans. Their jaws and foreheads had become pronounced, their mouths extended into short muzzles, long tails stretching from their backs. They were clumsy fliers, not like the Harpies, who could glide gracefully through the air like eagles on an updraft. No, the Dracians were heavy, bulky, and flailed against the wind with exhaustive efforts, dragged down by their own weight.

Only Jacques flew easily. He kept to the front, his scales a bright gold in the sunlight, leading the pod of Dracians. His elemental magic was the Wind, and he used it to help him fly, creating a strong draft beneath his wings.

Crash could remember when Jacques had demonstrated his magic, back on the docks of Delbar. A giant dragon, made completely of nimbus clouds, had been summoned from the sky. Lightning flashed from its mouth. Its jaws could have swallowed a bell tower whole. Still, the magic had been all show and no force. It had taken a Cat's Eye to defeat Volcrian's wraith. Sora's Cat's Eye— and almost her life.

He stood as the Dracians landed. Their wings kicked up a cloud of sand. Laina leapt to her feet and dove into that cloud, one arm thrown across her eyes. She ran up to Jacques. "Did you see her?" she demanded. "Did you find her?"

The sand slowly settled, blown away by the ocean's breeze. Crash watched the Dracians, wondering the same question, though he wouldn't voice it aloud.

Laina danced about from foot to foot, repeating her question eagerly. Crash eyed the girl in annoyance. Her shrill voice pierced the air—"Where is Sora? Did you find her?!"

Jacques turned his eyes to Crash. There was no warmth there. "No," the Dracian said finally.

"But we did find a town," Tristan piped up. The younger Dracian stood at Jacques' side. His scales were bright red in color, the shade of fresh blood. His element was Fire.

"A town?" Crash asked quietly, tilting his head in question. Tristan wilted under his gaze.

"Aye," Jacques agreed. "Old abandoned buildings made of stone. Looks like they've stood for a long time. We would be smart to go there, see if we can recover anything."

Crash nodded sharply. "How far?"

"Roughly ten miles to the north," Tristan offered, and pointed aimlessly over his shoulder.

Crash absorbed this news. A town. Could it be that they were on the Lost Isles after all? When the great island of Aerobourne crashed into the ocean, it had splintered into several smaller islands, lodging itself into the side of a massive underwater coral reef. It made sense, suddenly. Perhaps they were on one of the smaller outlying islands. His eyes shifted to the horizon where the storm clouds roiled and thrashed. The storm kept its place in the sky, several leagues out, not moving with any natural weather patterns. Perhaps they had made it through the magical boundary of the Isles.

"Ho!" a new voice interjected. Burn strode into camp, two boars hung over his shoulder. An arrow to the heart had killed both beasts. He twitched his long ears at the crew. "I overheard you in the forest. You Dracians are so loud, you scared off all the game in a half-mile!"

Jacques winced. "Sorry 'bout that, old boy."

"No matter," Burn replied. "As you can see, the hunt was successful." He shrugged his massive shoulders, jostling the two dead boars.

Their camp was nestled between a sand bank and the border of the dark, tropical forest, enough shelter to keep them out of the wind. Last night, they had attempted to camp on the beach proper, but the winds off the ocean had scattered the fire, stealing their warmth. They would have camped closer to the trees to begin with, but Laina had protested, claiming that Sora might drift in with the midnight tide. A morbid, if likely, notion.

Burn slung the boars onto a large log that bordered their new camp, then turned back to the crew. "We will head to the town in the morning. Perhaps we can find a map in one of the buildings, some indication of where we are."

"And you saw no settlers? No people?" Crash asked, looking back to Jacques.

The Dracians all shook their heads, murmuring the same answer. *No. Nothing. No one.*

Crash took his seat again on the sandworn log, next to the dead boars. The Dracians continued to talk amongst themselves. The rest of the crew drew close as Tristan described the old town, the weathered buildings and overgrown foliage.

Crash went back to cleaning his blades. They were damaged by the ocean, but not beyond recovery. He was attempting to redirect his thoughts, but no matter how hard he tried, Sora's face kept swimming into view, lifeless and cold under the waves. He closed his eyes briefly, trying to clear his mind. He had left her for a reason, long ago, at her mother's house. She should have stayed put. He hadn't wanted to see her again—right? No, of course not. And he had forced himself not to think of her while they were apart. Not until he had stumbled across her in the forest, Laina in tow, fleeing from bandits in the field.

He had accompanied her, fully knowing the risks. She needed someone...someone better than he, perhaps. But who else could protect her? Who else could shield her from Volcrian? *Don't think of it that way.*

She had been trying to rectify the problem, put right what was wrong, even though it wasn't truly her responsibility. He had kidnapped her, intending to use her necklace against Volcrian's magic. Then the bloodmage had summoned the wraiths from the underworld, releasing the Dark God's presence back into the land of Wind and Light. Sora had taken it upon herself to stop the pending disaster, but really, none of that was her burden. No, it was his.

He needed to set things right. *It's why I left the Hive.* Why he had turned away from his Grandmaster, his past, everything he had ever known. He had wanted to change. *But you can't outgrow the past, can you?* No, not when it was still so much in the present.

Guilt was a strange feeling, as alien and unwelcome as fear or doubt. And yet he couldn't push it away. Sora had relied on him, helped him, fought alongside him...and for what? An icy death, smothered in salt water.

Then the guilt bit at him again. They had argued the last time they saw each other. He hadn't tried to bridge that gap. Instead, he had pushed her away. *I had to.* She couldn't grow close to him, couldn't see what he really was. He couldn't let her. *If she had known the truth*...the darkness that lived inside of him, churning his gut, aching to escape....All he had done to contain that shadow, only to have it burst out at odd moments, a writhing, destructive force....If she had known his true nature, she never would have trusted him, never would have accepted his help.

But now she was dead. She would never look to him again. *Was it worth it?* No, of course not. He should have told her his secrets, made his confessions while he still had the chance.

Darkness passed over his eyes, strange and flitting. His shadow shifted on the ground, coiling up to his feet. Crash stared at it, wondering if he was losing control, if he would do so right now, in front of the Dracians, the Wolfy, the bastard street child who sat across the fire, twiddling her thumbs and asking a thousand questions....He knew he couldn't contain it. Not in the face of all this.

He stood up wordlessly. Burn cast him a questioning look. The Wolfy knelt by the edge of the fire, preparing the pigs, his eyes soft from the dimming sun.

Crash turned away from him. From the entire camp. He picked up his weapons, strapping them to his belt. "I'll make my own way to the town," he said bluntly.

The small company stared at him. Then Tristan spoke up. "This late? It'll be dark in a few hours. You won't get far in that kind of wilderness."

Jacques held up his hand, silencing his younger companion. "If the man wants to get lost, let him."

"'Tis a matter of space," Burn said loudly. He was back to skinning the boars, running a sharp knife under the skin, stripping it from the flesh. He glanced at Crash, briefly meeting his eyes. "Be safe, friend."

Crash nodded briefly, then stalked into the forest, unfazed by the Dracians. He was focused on something deep within himself, a terrible emptiness, a blackness that he had tried to escape, to control. It moved inside him, begging to be released. He wrestled with it, hoping he could leave the camp far behind before the demon came out.

He was a monster. They all knew it—he could see it written on their faces, in the subtle glances of the Dracians, in the way their voices faded in their throats. Volcrian's hunt was justified. His kind wasn't meant to save lives. Only to destroy them.

CHAPTER 6

Volcrian paused by the docks. The evening sun glinted across the bright water of Delbar. He held two pouches of sand he had scooped from the beach. He viewed the ship from the distance. It was smaller than he had hoped, perhaps only fifty feet long, two masts and a small cabin with a single lower deck. The entire ship could be manned by twenty people. He watched the sailors that lingered on the docks, wondering which were his crewmen. A series of large, burly men sat close to the vessel, eating a plate of crabs. He decided to start there.

But before he could negotiate, he needed some leverage.

"Here," he said, handing the bags of sand to the priestess. "Turn these to gold."

"What?" the woman asked. She raised an eyebrow, which was a strange expression, since her brows had almost completely fallen out. He glanced over her blue-tinted face. It was half-obscured by a wide hood.

"Turn. Them. To. Gold," he repeated.

The priestess took the bags and stared at them with her milky, blue-filmed eyes. "And how am I supposed to do that?"

Volcrian sighed. Who would have thought that the dead needed to be trained? "You're a ghost," he said.

"A corpse," she corrected.

"Either way, you are one of the dead, and the dead have a certain...power of illusion. I have placed a drop of my blood in each of these bags. You're not physically changing the sand. You're just making it look different."

The priestess let out the mimicry of a sigh, parting her lips, shrugging her shoulders. But no air passed through her lungs. "I don't know how," she said.

"You don't need to know how," Volcrian replied, his voice strained. "It is in your nature. Just do as I say." The bloodmage turned back to the sailors. More men had joined the crew, all sitting in front of the ship. Today was their scheduled departure date. If Malcolm had been in charge, they would be setting sail into the gray waters, on the hunt for tuna or mackerel. But Malcolm had yet to join them at the boat—he never would, Volcrian had ensured that—and so the crew waited, propped up on barrels, throwing dice and stuffing their faces.

"Are you finished?" he asked.

The priestess hesitated. "I think so."

Volcrian opened one of the pouches and glanced inside. Satisfied, he started across the docks, weaving through a group of women haggling over clams. He passed by large coils of rope, some thicker than his forearm. Past a stray dog, an old man and two young children, dressed in rags.

The sailors glanced up as he approached them. He reached into his pocket and withdrew the title of the ship, then paused a few feet away from the group; sailors were notoriously superstitious. At times, they showed surprisingly keen intuition. He could tell that they were unnerved. They paused from their games, turning to look at him.

"Hello," he said, a forced smile at his lips. "I am the new owner of this boat—and, I would hope, your new captain."

The sailors stared for a long moment, taking in his blue cloak, his expensive—if weathered—boots. A few glanced at his long silver hair, suspicion in their eyes.

"Where's Malcolm?" one asked, a large man in a red tunic, a bandana wrapped around his shaggy brown hair.

"He's left town," Volcrian said coldly. "I bought his store and his boat. And I would like to hire his crew."

"You got coin?" a second man asked, a blond man with a cob pipe in his mouth.

"Better than coin," Volcrian replied. He lifted up the two heavy purses He opened one of them, letting the men catch a glimpse of the gold dust inside. "Each is worth five-hundred gold, to be split evenly amongst you."

The sailors' eyes widened. They glanced back and forth, raising eyebrows, curling lips. "Hell," the blond man said. "That's quite a bit of coin."

"To be paid upon our return," Volcrian replied, and tucked the bags of sand back into his belt. The wind blew, pushing his cloak around him, brushing his hair across his face. He swept it back with a fine-boned hand. " We will travel into deep waters for the fish I seek—further than you're used to, I expect. But you will be rich men upon your return."

"What kind o' fish?" one of the sailors spat. "Marlin?"

"Yes. Among others," Volcrian murmured.

A few of the sailors frowned. One of them stood up, an older man, perhaps in his forties. He shook his head. "Doesn't sit right with me," he said. "I'll try my luck elsewhere."

Volcrian watched him depart, his eyes narrow, calculating. Two other sailors stood up to leave. The rest stayed in place.

The one with the bandana called out to him. "How do we know you're going to pay us?"

Volcrian grinned slowly. "I'll pay you once we begin our return voyage. If I don't, you can throw me off the ship."

The blond one grinned, showing blackened teeth around the corncob pipe. He leaned over to his mate, speaking softly. "Aye," he whispered, "why not slit his throat now and be done with it?"

The sailors chuckled together. Volcrian's keen ears picked up every word, but he didn't flinch. If he had to, he could kill every single one of these men and raise them back from the dead, as obedient as his dear priestess. He didn't want to waste the energy or the time, but the thought made his blood pound, his fingers twitch eagerly. A deep, unknown hunger burned inside him, fueled by rage. Nothing would stand between him and his prey.

"I'll take the deal," the sailor in the bandana said. He turned to glance at his fellows. "With any luck, the rest of this crew will quit. More gold for me."

At his words, there were murmurs of agreement. A few more men rose to join him. Volcrian watched them count amongst each other, calculating their payment on their fingers. Four more stood. The remaining few took to the docks, walking quickly away.

Volcrian hooked the pouches of sand back to his belt. He nodded to the man in the red tunic and bandana. "I shall return at midnight with supplies. Be ready to cast off." Then he turned away from the ship toward the docks. He casually linked arms with the priestess, nestling her hand in the nook of his elbow, almost chivalrous.

"Right, lads!" the man in the bandana called. He stood up, tucking a deck of cards into his belt. "Ready the boat! Pretty her up!

We set sail tonight!"

Volcrian waited until they were out of earshot, then glanced to the priestess at his side. "Well done, my dear."

"What are you going to do with them?" she asked, her voice a quiet rasp.

His eyes glinted. "Nothing...for now."

* * *

Sora was tied to a tree. Her shoulder ached from the abuse. She flexed her fingers, checking the bonds. Plant fibers didn't make the strongest ropes. She thought that maybe, if she wiggled enough, she could slip one hand through. But she couldn't make her move yet. The men were still in plain sight.

They stood around a small fire nestled deep in the jungle. Full night had fallen. They were preparing their beds and chewing on the last strips of catfish from the smoke hut.

"I saw her first and I carried her all the way here. She's mine," Benny was saying, waving his ax around. He had been muttering much the same for the past hour. She didn't like the fanatical gleam in his eye. He stood protectively in front of her, glaring at his fellows.

John Witherman looked displeased. He tucked his thumbs into his pants, his saber swinging at his side. "As the captain of our crew, I get the first pick of our bounty. I'll have her first, then you can take her."

"I don't like going second," Benny growled. "Besides, we ain't your crew anymore, not for the last seven years. Time for a new leader."

John Witherman's eyes narrowed. "Are you challenging me?"

"Aye," Benny replied seriously.

"Hold on," the older cripple said. He stood slightly to the side of the campsite, out of the way. "You can't fight each other. We've already lost so many! Stand down, Benny. Mayhap we can toss a coin."

"What coin?" Witherman snapped. He looked Benny solidly in the eye and drew his saber. "If he wants his neck slit over a woman, so be it."

They discussed her rape casually, as though she were just a bit of stolen treasure. Sora glared at the three men, disgusted and infuriated. Benny had carried her the entire way through the jungle, groping and fondling at every opportunity. She felt violated and enraged. Too much rage, more anger than she had ever known. *Patience.* With any luck, the two would be at each other's throats. Soon she would make her move.

And do what? her inner voice asked again. Her gut churned at the thought. But she couldn't leave these men alive to hunt her down. She had to survive no matter what. Everything had changed since the shipwreck. No one would come to rescue her. Burn was dead. Laina was dead. Crash....

She cringed at the thought of her lost companions. She was alone now, stranded on this island. She had to help herself.

"If you want her first, then try to stop me," Benny said stubbornly. Then he whirled to face her.

Sora met his eyes and curled her lip in disgust.

Benny leered and started untying his pants. His hands shook with anticipation, and Sora could see a large bulge growing beneath his belt. She curled her legs up to her chest instinctively.

"Cut her bonds, will you, Fonsworth?" Benny said gruffly to the cripple. "Y'might have to hold her down at first. I'm a bit out of practice." He winked at his companion.

Sora wanted to think better of the cripple, but Fonsworth's eyes grew bright with excitement. He hurried to her tree, limping across the campsite. "Don't hate me, little miss," he said as he crouched behind the trunk. "It's been years since any of us have seen a woman...I'm sure you understand."

The situation was quickly slipping out of control. A few more minutes and she might find herself underneath this scum. Sora made eye contact with Captain Witherman, who was fingering the hilt of his blade. She looked at him desperately, widening her eyes, simpering her lips. *At least, I hope this is how one simpers.* "Please," she said, looking directly at him. "Please, I prefer you!"

Witherman frowned at her, then at Benny's back. In the blink of an eye, he drew his blade. "Never double-cross a pirate," he growled, and lunged at Benny without further warning.

Benny dropped the strings of his pants. He turned on Witherman and swiped his ax to one side, deflecting the saber's blow. The two faced each other, faces red with rising passion. "I've had enough, Witherman!" Benny roared. "She's mine!"

Benny threw himself on Witherman. The two men stumbled backward, into the fire. They started yelling and screaming at each other, scattering the flames. Small embers caught light and the fire spread around their camp. The two men wrestled back and forth in a shoulder-lock, each trying to throw the other to the ground.

Perfect. Sora took full advantage of the situation. Her ropes were loosened by Fonsworth and she slipped her hands free easily. She quickly jumped to her feet before the crippled man could respond. His walking stick rested at the base of the tree. She grabbed it and swung it firmly down on his head. *Crack!*

The man crumpled to the ground, blood oozing down the back of his neck.

"Aye!" Benny called. "The wench is untied!"

Sora responded immediately. She leapt into the camp and gripped the walking stick with both hands. With a strangled battle cry, she brought it swinging down on Benny's head.

Benny twisted away from Witherman and threw up his arm. *Snap!* He caught the blow on his forearm. The wood shattered, splintering around the campsite. Benny roared in pain. Sora was certain that she had cracked his bone.

Benny fell to his knees, gripping his arm. He dropped his ax to the ground. Sora threw herself at the ax and scooped it out of the leaves, rolling back to her feet. Then she swung it at Benny's face.

Thunk.

The dull blade wedged into his cheek. Blood spattered. Chips of teeth flew through the air. Benny's scream increased in volume, reaching bloodcurdling intensity, but the man did not fall down. He reached out and grabbed Sora's legs, trying to drag her to the ground with him.

Sora felt cold and distant, removed from the fight; she was lost to her adrenaline, desperate to survive. She fell with Benny to the ground, coming out on top of him, and wrenched the ax from his face. Then, with a two-handed swing, she brought it down again—hacking at his hands, his chest, his neck, any piece of flesh that was exposed. Blood sprayed the air. Benny's screams saturated the night.

Then, finally, he fell silent.

Sora paused, sitting astride the body. She wiped the droplets of blood from her face. Her hands were shaking, her breath heaving. She stared down at the man beneath her and shuddered. Her heart raced. She couldn't look away from his ruined, tattered face. With a twinge of horror, she noted that Benny was still breathing—barely. Considering the amount of blood-loss, he would die soon.

She was shocked at herself. She had fought before...but never like this.

Suddenly, someone grabbed the back of her head.

John Witherman dragged her head up. He briefly looked into her face, snarled, then slammed her forward, shoving her off Benny's body and into the dirt. He landed on her back. Sora struggled to throw him off, but the captain was unexpectedly strong, fueled by rage. He pressed her face into the ground, suffocating her.

"You bitch," he seethed. "You killed my best mate!" He tightened his grip, uprooting a lock of hair. Sora cried out in pain, dirt filling her mouth. "Seven years on this island—these men were my family! You nasty wench! Now I'm going to make you suffer!"

He grabbed her left arm and dragged it behind her, back and up. Pain shot threw her from the unnatural position. She tried to turn, to break free—but he was too strong. With an audible *pop*, the bone slid out of place.

Sora's back arched and she screamed into the night, pain coursing through her. Tears pressed her eyes. It was unbearable— far worse than she could have anticipated. John Witherman rolled her over, his face contorted into a terrifying grin. His eyes glinted with blood lust. He licked his lips. "We're not done yet," he growled.

The flames from the fire were spreading, crawling across the dry leaves toward a nearby tree. Sora's free hand searched the dirt and came in contact with a burning stick. She gripped it and swung it at Witherman's head, catching him on the side of the face. He shouted in surprise and released her.

Sora climbed to her feet again, gritting her teeth in pain. She ran a few steps only to have Witherman tackle her, once more carrying her to the ground. She tried to throw her arms out to catch herself, but wrenched her bad shoulder—pure agony. She screamed again. Lost her footing. Her body felt clumsy and useless, broken and disorganized.

She and Witherman fell to the ground, kicking and scuffling. The fire slowly crept toward the trees.

* * *

Crash was poised on a large branch, silently watching the night. He had walked three miles to the north, then had knelt in the brush, his knives ready. He wanted to hunt. It was the only way to settle the beast inside of him, to calm the rage that boiled beneath his skin.

He watched his shadow move and play in the trees, wrapping around branches, sliding down trunks. *Remember your master,* he thought to the shadow, trying to calm himself, to rein it in, but it did not obey. It seemed to be laughing at him. He closed his eyes. *Remember....*

Abruptly, a scream pierced the night. A human scream. His eyes shot open and he turned toward the sound. It was a man's voice. A shiver went down his spine and his adrenaline surged. His shadow leapt to attention; it snapped back to his feet, sensing prey. The voice continued yelling, carrying across the forest. The birds and insects fell quiet.

Who else is on this island? The shouts carried from a direction opposite the Dracians' camp, perhaps a mile out. He listened keenly, sorting through the echoes, finally deciding on a direction. A second scream answered the first—a woman's voice. A voice he thought he recognized. His heart began to pound, piercing his chest. *No, she's dead.* She was supposed to be dead.

He started through the brush, swift and powerful, like a panther on the hunt.

CHAPTER 7

After a short and useless fight, Sora found herself with Witherman on the ground again. Twice she regained her feet, trying to flee from the spreading fire, but he tackled her, unwilling to let her go. This time she rolled with him, trapping his arms, kneeing him in the stomach. The man let out a soundless *oof.* Old breath struck her face.

They grappled on the ground for a long minute. Sora fought one-handed, using her legs to keep him at bay. She searched for his saber, but the weapon lay amidst the spreading fire, unreachable.

"You killed them," Witherman sobbed, anger clogging his throat. His hands flew to her neck, trying to strangle her. "You killed them!"

"Get off me!" she yelled back, trying to stab his eyes with her fingers. Nothing seemed to work. He slammed her into the ground again and a branch lodged beneath her back, jarring her dislocated arm.

Sora screamed. Pain rushed through her, tears stung her eyes, her arm fell limp and useless next to her body. John Witherman laughed, his hands finally at her throat, choking her with blind rage. "You bitch," he repeated, over and over again. "Die, die, die!"

She couldn't breathe. Her strength drained out of her; her head spun in panic. *This is it,* she thought, mentally opening her arms, embracing the idea of death. Her friends were gone, their quest useless, failed. This was the only answer. Strangely, she felt a bit of relief. She wondered, distantly, if their ghosts would meet her in the afterlife. She could imagine them now, all lined up in the darkness, waiting for her to cross over to the other side.

Shing! The sound of steel whistled through the air. Sora braced herself for the blow of a saber—but none came.

John Witherman inhaled suddenly, his mouth gaping wide. She caught a glimpse of rotted teeth. Then he crumpled on top of her, his hands still clamped to her throat, his body pinning her to the earth.

She closed her eyes. She couldn't move. *Damn.* Still alive—she was in too much pain to be dead. Her body trembled with adrenaline. She thought she might pass out.

She was afraid to look at her arm, to try to move it. She couldn't register what had happened, couldn't question it. She was too shocked.

Then the body was rolled off her. Another figure replaced it.

For some reason, she imagined a giant animal crouching above her, an ape or a bear, some hulking beast in the darkness. She closed her eyes, wondering if she was next, expecting a giant claw to take off her head. But when she looked again, she saw a smaller shape, something more like a man. Fear pierced her. Were there more stranded settlers on this island? Had John Witherman's friends come to help him?

If so, then why was he dead?

Was he dead?

The figure knelt next to her, completely silent. His footsteps made no sound. Sora stared up at him, helpless, in pain, struggling to breathe.

"Please..." she whimpered through clenched teeth. "Don't

touch me."

The shadow hesitated. And then he whispered, "Sora."

Her eyes widened. She felt struck in the stomach. She knew that voice—knew it as well as her own. Was it a dream? A nightmare? Some horrific joke of her subconscious....

"C-Crash?" she stuttered. *No!*

"Sora...."

No, no, no!

She could only stare at him.

He knelt gently and pulled her into a sitting position, his hands traveling to her injured shoulder. She gritted her teeth, tears stinging her eyes. He grabbed her arm and pulled it swiftly up and out, before she could flinch, and she felt the bone slide back into place. She screamed again, the pain intensifying. Then she collapsed against him, the wind taken out of her. He held her firmly in place. She wanted to speak, but she couldn't even breathe through the pain.

He said nothing but picked her up, gently resting her body against him, carefully adjusting her injured shoulder. He stood up, lifting her effortlessly into the air. His silence steadied her, gave her a moment to regain herself. He briefly gazed at the ruined campsite, the spreading fire and mutilated bodies. Then he carried her quietly through the trees, swiftly guiding them up a deer trail, over roots and shrubs.

The fire faded behind them until they could only smell its smoke. Finally the pain in her arm subsided and Sora was able to gather her thoughts. "You're alive," she finally said. Tears pressed her eyes. *I will not cry in front of this man!* But she couldn't keep the emotions contained. She let out a choked sob, then leaned further into him, pressing her face against his shirt, his smell, the mixture of sand, salt and sweat. So familiar. "This is impossible."

He glanced down at her. His expression was fierce, his jaw tight. But she wasn't afraid. She gazed at the familiar silver scar that ran down his neck and into the collar of his shirt. He was alive. She couldn't seem to adjust to the thought. She wondered again if she had imagined the body of John Witherman lying above her. Perhaps she had died after all and this was a phantom, come from the dark forest to escort her beyond the grave.

But her arm hurt too much and she could feel the weight of her bruised body. She wanted nothing more than to sleep. Her limbs dragged downward, burdened by weariness. *By the Goddess....*

* * *

They made camp about a mile away, next to a shallow stream that cut across the deer path. Crash set her carefully on the ground and she jolted awake, returning to consciousness, gazing with blind eyes until a fire was struck. She almost wished he wouldn't. She looked a mess—barely decent, her shirt ripped down the front, tied far above her torso to conceal her breasts. Her pants were in shreds, her feet bare. She didn't even want to think about what her hair looked like. *Why should I care?* she admonished. They had spent countless nights in the woods before. A woman's pride, it must be. Some remnant of her forsaken nobility.

The fire was lit. They stared at each other across the flames. She drank in the sight of him, tall and broad, his clothes as ripped and stained as her own. She kept blinking, expecting him to disappear, but he stayed solid and firm.

Finally, she said, "I thought you were dead."

He seemed tense. His face was drawn into a strange expression, unreadable. He wouldn't look away from her. "Burn and the Dracians are about three hours from here, near the beach," Crash explained. "We searched for you."

She nodded numbly. It took her a moment to absorb the information. The lump in her stomach eased. "Laina? Jacques? Tristan?"

He nodded.

She let out a slow breath. "The ship?"

"Gone."

She nodded—she had suspected as much. She waited for more news, but none was forthcoming. He remained as quiet and enigmatic as ever.

Abruptly, Crash stood up, as though shaking himself from a trance. He began to remove his shirt. It took her a moment to realize what he was doing.

"What...?" she started, then the shirt came off. Her voice died in her throat. *Oh, my.* She had seen him shirtless before, had denied to herself that he was an attractive man, tight with muscle, his skin nicked and bitten with scars. She watched as he crossed the fire to her side, the light licking his skin, playing across his defined chest. He knelt next to her, only a few inches away. She could feel the heat radiating off him like a furnace. Or was it the fire that warmed her? She tried to shake herself out of it. *Most definitely alive.*

He took the shirt and ripped it into long strips, then began tying the cloth around her, binding her arm in place. She sat stiffly, trying not to touch him, to lean against his muscled chest. *Look away,* she told herself. *Don't stare.* But she couldn't stop.

Finally, her bindings were knotted tightly. He sat next to her, a certain familiarity falling between them. He was a quiet man, but his silence was no longer uncomfortable. She expected it.

"I'm sorry." It burst from her lips.

He glanced at her, waiting for an explanation.

"For the fight on the ship. It's all I could think about..." she said in an attempt to explain herself, though maybe she didn't have to.

He nodded, accepting her words. "That's all you could think about?" he asked quietly. She heard a smile in his voice. She wondered, suddenly, if he was laughing at her.

She shook her head, pushing her tears back. "I still can't believe it," she said. "Perhaps the Goddess has favored us."

Crash shrugged. She could tell he was growing uncomfortable. But she couldn't let the silence choke them. She made a vow to herself in that moment—she would speak her mind, her true thoughts.

"I was so scared, Crash," she said quietly. She cast her eyes away, searching the darkened tree trunks, the small rocks on the ground, anywhere but his face. "Please...don't die again."

She sensed that he was smiling, though she still couldn't meet his eyes. It was difficult to say these things to a man like him. He let nothing show.

Gently, he took her hand. The motion shocked her. It was a small touch, unexpected. "I won't," he said.

She glanced sideways at him. He was staring into the fire, his gaze distant, solemn. "Did you really think I was dead?" she asked.

He nodded slowly. "It was...unpleasant."

She couldn't help the smile that tugged at her lips. It must have been pretty terrible, for him to admit that much. He sat so close to her, their legs almost touching, his hand over hers. She looked down at his strong fingers, his wide knuckles and hard, calloused palm. It was several shades darker than hers, tanned by the sun.

Then her thoughts turned inward. If her companions were alive, there was a chance that they might still defeat Volcrian. Their quest could succeed. They couldn't give up yet.

"We have to keep moving," she said, the thought spilling from her mouth. "I know we don't have a ship anymore, but perhaps we can build one. Perhaps the Isles aren't so far. Or there could be old wrecks around the island."

Crash shook his head. "Don't worry about it."

His words were surprisingly confident. Sora sat back for a moment, surprised, wondering if she should argue with him—then she felt the tension leave her shoulders. His words held more power than she wanted to admit. Just like that, her worry was gone.

She let out a long sigh. "We're going to survive this, right?" she asked, perhaps more to herself. It had been almost welcome, the thought that she could give up, that nothing mattered anymore.

She thought of the Wolfy bloodmage who followed them, of the plague spreading across the mainland. The sick people she had seen on the streets of Barcella, begging for help. It would be selfish of her to give up so easily. Selfish, but natural. *You can still give up,* some smaller voice murmured. *This isn't your responsibility. Let someone else fix the world.*

It was an alluring lie, but a lie all the same. She had played a hand in this situation. Without her, the wraiths never would have been summoned. Volcrian's wrath had been brought on by her actions. And if she didn't shoulder the burden, who would?

Crash watched her warily. "Sora," he finally sighed. "I can't give you false hope. Your Cat's Eye is the key to everything."

"I know."

"And at the end of this journey...the necklace might be destroyed. It could shatter."

She nodded. She had tried not to think of that part of their quest. The Cat's Eye shared a psychic bond with her mind, like a vine grown into a tree, entangling the same roots, drinking the same water. Uproot one and undo the other. She had worn her Cat's Eye for over a year now. If she removed it, she could go into shock, a coma, or even death...and in order to defeat Volcrian, she may have to.

He continued to watch her face.

She knew he was concerned. She hadn't seen him like this before, so attentive, so close. She tried to smile. "There has to be a way to survive a broken bond," she said. "We just have to find it."

He nodded. But for a moment, she saw a hollowness inside of him that was too great to bear. She looked away, unnerved. He obviously thought the worst. Expected it.

"And if I don't survive?" she asked quietly.

His grip tightened on her hand. "Then I will go with you."

She raised her eyes to his, looking him fully in the face, shocked. "What?"

"You won't die alone, Sora," he said quietly.

Her mouth went dry. She couldn't accept his words, their meaning, the heaviness that weighed between them. She had never expected this, not from a man like him, one who killed for a living, who had ended far too many lives.

She remembered their confrontation on the streets of Delbar, in a back alley next to a crumbled statue of the Wanderer. It had been a cold night, windy and moist. He had held her then, whispering in her ear: *"I came to protect you."* Protection, from a man who had once kidnapped her? Who had killed her supposed father? Who had introduced her to the world of magic and peril?

Yet here he was, still by her side. He must have meant his words. *More than you know,* her inner voice murmured.

Finally, she leaned against his shoulder, pressing into his warmth. "We'll find a way," she repeated.

He settled his head against hers, his jaw against her cheek, sharing the light of the fire, their fingers entwined. The night stretched on, spreading out around them in a dark blanket. They stayed like that for a long, long time.

* * *

Krait stood in an old cabin on the outskirts of Delbar.

It was a small shack, once a guardhouse, now abandoned. The walls sagged inward, like the ends of melted candles. The roof was damaged by rain and wind, smothered in cobwebs. Several of the floorboards were rotted to the point of breaking, yet she rested her weight easily on top of them, sure of her feet.

She watched out the window, staring at the waterfront, black waves lapping against the docks. People scurried by, quick to head home before the hour grew too late. This was the sunken end of town, where good folk avoided the streets at night.

To the left of the lonely cabin was a freight yard. It stretched along the very tail end of Delbar. Rows of giant crates lined the dock, bordered by a tall pulley system to lift them onto merchant vessels. For now, all was quiet. It was close to midnight. She watched a few of the King's soldiers wander the empty yard, casually patrolling up and down the long lines of cargo.

A small moth landed on the windowsill. Krait knelt slightly, looking at its tawny wings. The moth fluttered again, balancing on a shard of broken glass. It looked soft and delicate, graceful and orderly, belying the chaotic pattern of its wings. She reached out a slow finger, tempting the little bug into her hand. It waved its long antennae, exploring her fingernail, timidly brushing her skin.

Abruptly, the moth flew away.

"You are early," a voice said from behind her. It was quiet, silty, like sand slipping through an hourglass.

Krait turned, fear jarring her body. She immediately knelt on one knee, her forehead bowed, her eyes focused on the floor. The shadows of the room shifted, gently reaching and grasping one another, until they solidified into a tall figure. The man seemed to be made of darkness—like the night itself.

"Grandmaster," she murmured, and bowed lower.

"I take it all did not go well." The voice slid across her skin.

She paused for a moment, her thoughts spinning. In the past two weeks, she had sent countless men abroad in search of the Viper. None had returned. A few had sent letters, notes by pigeon, detailing their fruitless attempts. No one knew where the assassin had gone. It was damned eerie, as though they hunted a ghost.

Since their brief fight in the bell tower, she felt odd, out of sorts. She couldn't forget the gleam of his green eyes, cold and deadly in the darkness. His swift hands, how he wielded the dagger as an extension of his body. A worthy opponent—far worthier than she.

"They have the Dark God's weapon, Master," she murmured.

"And?"

"And...we've lost the trail. We don't know where they've gone."

Grandmaster Cerastes remained silent. She glanced up through her eyelashes. He stood in the middle of the room, perfectly still. He was long and rail-thin, his skin a pale, ashen color. His dark hair was perfectly straight and fell to his navel, blending with his robes. A black cloak cascaded down to his feet. He appeared to be an extension of the floorboards, a living wax figure.

"Rise," he hissed, and raised one long, white hand.

She did so, looking into the face of the Grandmaster. Gaunt cheeks, a sharp chin and large, ovular, entrancing eyes, sickly green in color, a toxic hue. They were slitted like a serpent, a sign of his mastery of the dark arts. His aura filled the room around him, causing her skin to tingle, the tiny hairs on her arms to stand at attention.

She waited for the blow to come. Braced herself for it. She had failed her duty. As a hand of the Dark God, she deserved punishment. Yearned for it.

"Something is on your mind, child," the Grandmaster said quietly, deceptively calm.

"Yes," she whispered and dropped her gaze again, avoiding his serpentine eyes. She focused on the bottom of his black robes. "The one who came to us with the weapon...he was of our kind."

"One of our own?" Cerastes echoed. She could hear the surprise in his voice. It startled her almost as much as his arrival had. It reminded her that he had been a man, once. More human than demon.

"Yes," she confirmed.

"A savant?"

"No...a Named assassin, Master. I saw his tattoo and the dagger he wielded."

"A dagger?" Cerastes hissed.

"Yes...the Viper."

Her Master turned, surveying the room, his eyes focused on something far more distant. A slow, thin smile spread across his face. She had come to recognize that look—it held a memory, something she was not privy to.

"How very interesting," he murmured. "You're certain?"

"Yes, Master."

"And where has the Viper gone?"

Here it was. The moment of truth, of confession, of eager atonement. "We lost him, Master. He killed Jackal and Widow, and then disappeared."

Surprisingly, Cerastes' smile stayed on his face. He looked harder into the invisible distance. "Did he, now?" he said softly. His eyes flicked down, pinning her in place. "And he did not kill you?"

Krait flinched slightly. Cerastes' voice was tinged with disappointment, out of place, as though he hoped for her death. "I escaped in a moment of distraction, sir," she admitted. "He recognized your Name."

Cerastes' silence grew dangerous. "And why," he murmured, "would you tell him my Name?"

"I...." Krait's voice died in her throat. *Because he would have killed me.* The words of a coward, of a traitor. She couldn't speak them aloud.

But Cerastes seemed to lose interest. He moved around the room—glided, really—hovering above the floor. His robes trailed on the wooden boards, his steps silent, eerily smooth. "I have a new assignment for you," he finally said.

"Yes, Master."

"We have need of a book," he said. "*The Book of the Named.* It has been missing since the War, but at last I have located it in the pirate city of Sonora. Retrieve it for me."

Krait dropped to one knee again, bowing her head. Cerastes watched her dispassionately. Then he turned back to the wall. "Time is of the essence," he said. "Travel by shadow. I have opened a pathway. This corner," he pointed with one long, thin finger, "shall take you directly to the city. Be quick about it."

Krait nodded. "And once I have the book, Master?"

"Bring it to me in the City of Crowns. Contact me once you have it and I will arrange for another portal."

Krait bowed lower, her nose almost to the floorboards.

Cerastes turned once more, walking toward the center of the room, then paused again. "Fifty lashes," he murmured. "For saying my Name." Then the shadows twisted off the walls, the floors, and stretched down from the ceiling. They grasped his body, seeming to pull it in all directions. He lifted slowly into the air, the darkness becoming his robes, his hair, his face. The pressure inside the cabin increased, the air turned dense, charged with magic, unbreathable.

Krait blinked.

He was gone.

Still kneeling, she uncoiled the short crop from her waist. She had several different kinds attached to her belt—leather, cord, gut.

She was the Krait, after all, and the whip was her namesake. Her Naming weapon was coiled in the niche of her back, pressed against her skin, a long and powerful bullwhip of over twenty feet. Its handle was made of sturdy metal, covered in dark braided leather. It pushed against her now, as though begging to be released, but the weapon was not appropriate for her own punishment. She needed something shorter. More personal. The cat would do.

Her heart pounded as she undid her black shirt, pulling it up from her belt and over her head. The cold air tickled her, drawing goosebumps to the surface. She shivered in anticipation, her senses heightened. Her eyes and ears became keen and clear. She turned her face away from the moonlight, deeper into the room, toward the shadowy, rotted wood.

She licked her lips. She yearned for the fire, for the sharp crack of the whip. It taught her obedience. Discipline.

Some might see the ritual as barbaric, gruesome, needlessly cruel. But they didn't understand. From suffering arose truth. It was the only way to know oneself, stripped down to the raw bone, naked and alone, in a place where mind met body. The hands and feet of the Dark God were bound together by suffering, the shared burden of punishment and intrinsic pleasure.

When Cerastes had first found her, she had been a shell of a woman, a ghost of her former self. Only sixteen, practically a child, washed up from the ocean and left for dead.

She had belonged to a Hive once, long ago, before the Harpies had taken her. Before the years of burning Light, which still seared her memory, creeping through dreams, awakening her in a cold sweat. The Harpies had used her as a slave, blinding her with sunstones, controlling her on a leash. They had burned her eyes out. She had been sightless for those years, practiced upon by young Harpy warriors, knowing nothing but pain and horror.

Then somehow, she had escaped. Despite her attempts, she couldn't remember how—it had been blocked from her memory, forgotten in a haze of anguish and desperation. She had awakened on the beach, alone, somewhere far out in the countryside. She had crawled away, slithering through sand and wet grass, keeping her head low, her blind face pressed to the earth. She had eaten bugs and leaves to survive, taking shelter beneath low blackberry bushes, wrapping her legs to her chest every night, eager to die. She had waited for some sign from the North Wind, the herald of the Goddess, to escort her into the beyond.

Then Cerastes had found her. In his dark and majestic power, he had healed her eyes—and given her new life. A new world. A Name.

Kneeling on the floor, she bent her head to the ground again. *Master, I am indebted to you.* With a strong flick of her wrist, she brought the crop down on her back. She grimaced, grunting in pain. *One.*

She struck again. Blood flicked into the air, spattering the window behind her. *Two.*

By the tenth strike, her body was singing, her skin tight with a mixture of fire and pleasure. She grew lightheaded, adrenaline pounding through her system, stealing her breath. She felt alive. Truly alive. Elated.

And deep in her belly, something stretched and unfurled, rippling with strength, turning its head toward her with eager attention. She felt its eyes upon her, red and burning in her stomach. She had never met her demon. Had never summoned it from beneath her skin. Cerastes had told her that she was damaged, that it would be impossible for her to summon her darker self. The Harpies had broken it out of her, stealing it with her sight, leaving her a useless shell.

But in these moments she felt it. Some shard of darkness, of unimaginable strength. A body more powerful than her own, an aura greater than her shadow, begging for release. *Yes. Yes. Yes.*

She cried out, overwhelmed by sensation. Her voice carried through the night, across the shipping yard and over the ocean waves. She lost herself to the sound, to the crack of the whip, to the stinging blood that trailed down her back.

CHAPTER 8

Sora blinked, foggy from sleep. Her left side was warm and she had a vague memory of curling up next to a body—someone strong and familiar. She looked up blearily, confused for a moment, wondering if she was still caught in a dream. Her eyes landed on Crash's back.

By the North Wind....

She sat up, startled, then winced at the pain from her arm. Her shoulder ached dully, throbbing in its socket. She was relieved that it was strapped to her chest. The extra support made the pain bearable.

The sight of Crash, however, took much longer to adjust to. She stared at his naked, muscular back, the tanned skin flecked with scars. *We slept next to each other.* It wasn't the first time, and yet she felt different now, too close, somehow exposed.

The assassin stirred next to her. He sat up and turned toward her, pausing when he met her eyes.

"How is your arm?" he asked. Practical, as always.

Sora shifted her bandaged limb and winced. "I'll be fine," she mumbled, though at that moment, she wished she had some of her mother's valerian root extract—an excellent salve for pain.

Crash stood and gathered his weapons, scattering the fire, throwing dirt on the remaining embers. She studied him, lost in thought. He was smooth and graceful, powerful, his actions precise and controlled. His black hair swept down around his ears, longer than she had last seen it, obscuring his eyes. His jaw was sharp and clean, his nose straight, his eyes the color of moss, deep-set beneath two elegant black brows. *Handsome,* she thought now, though she had forced herself to ignore it before. He always reminded her of a wolf, a cunning beast of the wilderness, sleek and dangerous.

When she had first met him, she had feared him more than anything else. He had killed Lord Fallcrest at her own Blooming, her coming-of-age ceremony. He had stolen her away into the night. Threatened her life, held a dagger to her throat. She had hated him.

Yet somehow, over so much time, things had changed. They had grown close. Become...friends? Could one be a friend to an assassin? They relied on each other. He had saved her life on countless occasions and she had returned the favor. After his actions of last night, she could only assume that he was fond of her. That he cared. Perhaps more than just cared. But she couldn't guess his thoughts....

He caught her eye. The hint of a smile touched his lips, secretive. She blinked, then looked away quickly, embarrassed. Her gaze traveled to the sky, a pale blue, quickly brightening in the east. It could be no more than an hour past dawn.

"Are we going to the Dracians' camp?" she asked, her voice husky and dry. She licked her lips, suddenly desperate for water.

"No," Crash said briefly. He straightened and pointed to the northwest, opposite the dawn. "They found a town out that way. Abandoned. We're meeting them there."

Sora nodded. She was relieved that he wasn't looking at her— his presence still made her nervous, like a child. She focused on his words instead. Soon, she would see her friends—Burn, Laina, everyone....*They're alive.* It was enough to make her forget her thirst, her hunger, even the ache of her arm. She couldn't wait.

They packed up camp quickly. There was little to take with them, only Crash's weapons. Then they started down a deer path in the opposite direction of Witherman's remains. She tried not to think of the dead men that lay in the forest, rotting under the sun, perhaps charred by flames. Witherman had been stranded here for seven years and no one had come. This island was far away from the mainland, completely isolated. She tried not to worry about that, too. With her friends by her side, they would find a way forward. Their quest would continue. It had to.

Crash and Sora walked all morning through the thick forest, following the natural deer paths that led through the woods. It was a hot day, the air dense and muggy under the trees, thick with pollen, laden with a vaguely citrus scent. The shade protected them from the intense sun, but still, Sora's shirt was soaked with sweat after an hour. She swatted at gnats and mosquitoes with her good hand, gritting her teeth in annoyance. The bugs seemed endless, clouding the air, following in their wake.

At times, they had to cut their way through the brush, hacking back thick vines and wide, waxy leaves. Snakes were common in this part of the jungle and she saw several different species of vibrant colors: green, yellow, black and red. Crash held up a hand when they crossed paths with a snake, remaining motionless until the beast slithered away; or he would pick up a stick and guide the reptile off the path. They forded several streams of clear, sweet water. He stopped at one stream and took a long drink, splashing his face, wetting his hair so it stuck to his forehead. Sora did the same and tried to wipe off some of the grime. She winced, avoiding her reflection. *What I don't know can't hurt me.*

Crash filled his water flask and they continued after a short break. The assassin was unusually conscientious: stopping to help her up a steep ledge of rocks, waiting patiently as she pushed her way through the thick brush. She was surprised by this—usually he was the one to push them forward, intolerant of any complaints. Her injured arm slowed her pace, and she was weary, her feet sore after only a few hours. They stopped to bind her feet with cloth, but it hardly seemed to help. Perhaps the past two days had affected her more than she thought. She didn't feel like her usual energetic self.

"What's that tattoo on your wrist?" Sora asked after a long span of grueling silence. She didn't have much breath left to talk with, but she tried anyway. Crash wasn't the type to begin a conversation.

He glanced down at his wrist as though annoyed with it. "My namesake," he said, then looked back to the path ahead.

"Namesake?" Sora echoed, curious. Usually Crash avoided answering any sort of personal question.

He nodded. "The Viper."

The Viper. She hadn't heard him called by that name—not by Burn or anyone else she knew.

"That's your name?" she dug.

"Yes. It was," he said briefly.

"Was?"

Crash shrugged, resigning himself to the conversation. "Dorian started calling me Crash after we met you. A joke, I suppose." He glanced at her, as though self-conscious about the story.

Sora grinned. "That's cute."

"Dorian thought so."

She snickered at this. Leave it to Dorian to nickname an assassin. The thief was long dead, but he had a way of living on. She wondered, briefly, what he would say in their situation. *"Bad luck, sweetness,"* she heard in her head. *"Just the way we like it."*

"Why Viper?" she asked. "That's a strange name."

Crash sighed. She knew he was uncomfortable with all of these questions, but she wasn't going to back down. His faux death had given her a new perspective on things, at least for the time being. She wanted to know as much about him as possible. As much as he would let her know.

"Where I grew up, we had to earn our names," he explained. He paused briefly to jump over a fallen log, then turned, reaching out a hand. She took it and he helped her over the obstruction. On the other side, they resumed walking. "I earned the name Viper because I was the best."

Abruptly he reached to his belt, pulling out a long, viciously curved dagger. She had seen him use it before, but had never looked at it closely. She gazed at the sharp blade, noting the worn handle, the intricately carved snake around its pummel. Her eyes widened. It was beautifully made and very well-maintained for its age. "I won the name and the blade with it," he added.

She gave him a sour look. "Humble, aren't you?" she grunted.

A thin smile came to his lips. "It's the truth."

"The best at what, then? Blade work?" she asked brusquely. He certainly knew how to use a dagger and a sword.

"All of it," he repeated softly, and looked to the ground. A sudden, cold shiver went down her spine. His meaning was clear.

Not just blades, but the spear, the bow, the fist—the best at killing.

She looked away, suddenly unnerved. *You know who he is,* her inner voice said. *Don't act so innocent.* It was true, she knew he was a trained killer, a master of the deadly arts. But she tricked herself into forgetting sometimes, lost in his enigmatic presence. They had grown so close over the past year. *Have we really?* She hardly knew anything about his past. Still, she couldn't look at him as just a murderer—a man who took money in exchange for lives.

She forced herself to push through it. She was afraid of his answers—but she needed to hear them, and she was suddenly full of burning curiosity. "What...." She paused to clear her throat. "What made you leave? Did they force you out? Did Volcrian have something to do with it?"

He shook his head slowly. His eyes clouded for a minute, focused on something that she couldn't see. She wondered where his mind was. She had seen that expression before, a glimpse of his inner thoughts.

Finally he said, "No, not Volcrian. I wanted something else. A different life."

Sora let out a long sigh of relief. *There, you see?* she scolded herself. *He's not evil after all.* And yet when she looked at him, he didn't seem happy. There was no peace on his face. Only a small grimace, as though focusing on some unsavory detail of a larger painting.

"I take it you haven't found it yet," she said wryly.

He glanced at her. A glimmer of surprise registered on his face. He gazed at her until she turned away, unable to stand the intensity.

"Perhaps," he agreed slowly. "I don't know." And he turned

back to the trail.

They continued walking, entering a lush grove of strange fruit trees. Their leaves were bright green and spade-shaped, hanging close to the ground, supported by fat, short trunks. As they walked, he pulled two exotic fruits from the lower branches, large pinkish orbs with soft skin that reminded her of peaches, only larger and heavier. He handed her two and took two for himself. They ate as they walked, peeling the skin from the rich fruit. The meat of the fruit was a deep yellow color, soft and juicy, warmed by the sun. Sora thought it was the best thing she had ever eaten. She took two more before leaving the grove.

* * *

"Why are we just waiting here?" Lori muttered, rolling up the sail and tying it to the yardarm. Ferran assisted her on the opposite side of the mast, securing the closed sail in place.

Despite its large size, Sylla Cove had been difficult to find, tucked between high cliffs almost forty miles past Cape Shorn. The trip up the coast had been fraught with short, choppy waves and bursts of wind. Now staring across the cove, Lori saw no evidence of a pirate ship, just a broad half-circle of land scooped from the cliffs and a friendly batch of seals that clambered on shore, honking and yelping at one another. The evening sun lowered softly behind her, casting its net across the sky.

"Patience, my dear," her companion replied, his hands tugging deftly on the ropes. "Isn't *patience* required of Healers?"

She shot him a disgruntled look.

Ferran grinned flippantly. His "loft," as he called it, was a small and shabby affair, a sailboat that had been constructed into a dwelling, not meant for the high seas. It sat low in the water with a roof built over it, housing a single cot, small table and kitchen area. At least it was clean. The mast was thin and pointed, attached to the front of the boathouse where he could fly a sail. But they wouldn't need one beyond this point. Once the tide came in, the current would carry them forward and Ferran would rely mostly on the long rudder that jutted from the aft of the boat.

To one side of the cove, a narrow inlet cut through the shelves of rock, flowing inland from the ocean, leading to some unknown destination. Its mouth was about fifty feet wide and blocked by a series of jagged stone teeth. For the past hour, she had watched the water inch upward incrementally. Soon the teeth would be submerged and the inlet free to travel. She assumed, given the direction of Ferran's gaze, that they were going through it.

"It looks too narrow for a schooner to sail," she said, noting the cliffs on either side of the inlet. "Certainly too narrow for a squarerigger." Luckily, their boat was about a third of that size.

"The channel is broader than it looks," Ferran replied. "And deeper." He was chewing on a cinnamon stick, rolling it about in his mouth. He pointed over the low railing to the broad cliffs. "On the other side of that inlet lies Rascal Bay and Sonora, the Pirate City."

"Pirate City?" Lori balked. He hadn't mentioned a city when they had left Cape Shorn a week ago. She had never even heard of one before. Then again, she didn't consort with any pirates.

Ferran nodded, biting down on the cinnamon stick. She remembered the days he would smoke thin rolls of tobacco leaves, back in their youth when they had adventured together. She was relieved he had put them aside; they smelled horrible. Or perhaps he just didn't have the money to buy them.

She lingered on that history for a moment, remembering the younger Ferran, far less weathered and much skinnier, without the tightly-roped muscle of the man next to her. He had spent his time gambling and brawling on the streets of Delbar, twenty years old and already a successful treasure hunter, building a strong reputation. Rumors had circulated about him back then. She remembered vaguely that the prince had hired him—though for what, she wasn't sure. She had heard the story fifty different times over the years, all from different mouths, but none were ever the same. He had never mentioned it to her directly during their time together and she hadn't bothered to ask.

She wondered at his current occupation—or lack thereof. She didn't understand how one of the most renowned treasure hunters in the Kingdom could end up like this. Perhaps it was becoming an antiquated business. All of the important relics from the War had already been found.

"You didn't mention a pirate city," she repeated.

"You don't just *mention* pirate cities," Ferran muttered distractedly. "Sonora is one of the worst kept secrets on the coast—but secret, it remains. If you go about telling the world, you're likely to get your throat cut." He secured the ropes in a tight knot and abruptly turned, striding toward the rear of the ship. "The tide is almost in," he said. "Secure yourself."

Lori took her seat at the center of the boat. She sighed briefly in irritation. Ferran insisted that she sit with a rope tied about her waist in case she went overboard. She had reassured him that she knew how to swim, but he wouldn't hear of it. She didn't remember him being so cautious in the past.

Ferran hunched next to the rudder, too large for the very back of the boat, his legs stretched out before him. He was a tall man, a few years older than she, in his late thirties, yet time had been kind. With the exception of a few sun lines, he was fit and strong, his hair thick and full, deep brown, tussled by the wind. A few distinguished strands of gray showed at his temples, hardly noticeable. He held a tousled sort of charm—an easy, thoughtless smile and quick gray eyes. A handsome man, Lori admitted, if a bit weathered. He carried himself with a reckless sort of confidence that she had always thought of as foolhardy. Back in their youth, women had flocked around him, drawn to his mischievous aura and deft hands —the promise of mystery and excitement, like drinking from a forbidden cup.

Now, at thirty-five, Lori knew better. Men like him were dangerous to fall for; they drifted into one's life and then out again, as errant as the wind.

Abruptly, the water of the cove swelled beneath the boat, the tide rushing in like a final sigh before sleep. Ferran gripped the handle of the rudder.

"Hang on," he called.

Lori barely had time to grab the ropes. Suddenly the boat shot forward, sucked toward the inlet by an unexpected current. Her eyes widened. The teeth at the front of the inlet were now fully submerged. The water swelled through the rocky crevice in a small tidal wave.

Ferran manned the boat expertly, maneuvering them toward the rocks. For a terrifying moment, she thought they would run up against the teeth, but their narrow boat skimmed through. The teeth dragged against the hull of the boat; she felt the long scrape in her bones. She held her breath, wondering if the rocks would bite through the wood. Given the long nose of the sailboat, it was a wonder that the boards didn't split and shatter.

"Witch wood," Ferran called to her above the roar of the water, as though reading her thoughts. He held the rudder firmly under his arm, using his weight for leverage and forcing it to the side, steering them into the deep canyon.

"Witch wood?" she asked, shocked. She glanced back at Ferran, catching his eye.

"Aye," he winked at her. "I was a treasure hunter once, you know. I held onto a few of my possessions."

A witch wood ship. Lori looked down at the shabby little boat, her opinion changed. Very impressive. Witch wood was only found in the Bracken, an ancient forest far to the East, where the trees were so old that they grew together as one giant organism. The wood couldn't be dented, even with a sword. Any relic made of witch wood had to be from the time of the Races, back when magic had been used to cut the wood and meld it into weapons. Humans had no tools that could mar its surface.

Lori looked at the wood beneath her, noting its smooth, bluish-gray hue. Then she let out a shriek as the boat tossed to one side, pushed by an upsurge of water. It tilted sickeningly, but didn't overturn.

After the initial rush of white water, the waves calmed and the current propelled them forward at a steady pace. She was surprised by how fast they moved. Hesitantly, she leaned over the side of the railing, watching the deep blue water rush past them, skimming the bow. She could see shards of wood against the sides of the cliff where larger boats had smashed into the rocks. Not a comforting sight. If they were to sink, there would be no land to swim to. The cliffs were steep and perfectly parallel to the water. She wondered how many sailors had drowned in the strait.

She looked back at Ferran. "Why did you give it up?" she called above the rush of the water. "You know...treasure hunting?"

Ferran managed to shrug, even as he manned the rudder. At this angle, his shoulders looked wide and taut with muscle, his back rippling with strength. "Too many death threats," he replied. "Thieves and cutthroats trailing me through every city...." Then his voice softened. "After Dane died, I continued for many years, but it lost its novelty."

Lori frowned. Ferran and Dane had been close friends when she had met them. She had fallen in love with Dane almost from first sight—his roguish smile, his carefree spirit.

Dane's face had grown dim over the years, clouded by memory, more than a decade since his death. But she saw his features in their daughter. Sora had his proud chin, his wide palms, his lower lip. His laugh. Every time she thought of her daughter, a mixture of fierce love and deep, roiling pain wrought her heart, stealing her breath. And guilt. Far too much guilt.

"Dane was a good man," she said. Far too young to die. When she thought very hard, she could almost picture his face, piece it all back together, the exact curve of his jaw and the fall of his dark hair.

"He gave his life for a useless trinket," Ferran said stiffly. "A couple of urns and an old statue. No artifact is worth a man's life."

"Aye," Lori agreed softly.

The water grew rough and fast, splashing over the edges of the boat. Before she knew it, Lori was soaked from head to toe. The wind was brisk and cold in the canyon, the sky darkening, making it difficult to see.

Finally, they burst from the opposite side of the inlet, skipping across the water as though spit through the air. The boat shot forward into a large bay, and immediately the current changed, slowing, broadening. In the last rays of the sun, she could see the color of the water, deep navy tinted with aqua green.

"Rascal Bay," Ferran's voice drifted to her above the rush. "The secret entrance to Sonora, the Pirate City. Look there." He pointed into the distance where Lori could see the glint of lights bobbing in the darkness. The city, or perhaps just the docks. "This is a freshwater bay. The salt water sinks to the bottom. There are tributaries that feed it from the Crown's Rush, about fifty miles to the East."

She nodded. As her eyes adjusted, she could make out the drifting outline of ships against the dusk. Graceful. Mysterious. Finally they were close enough to see this alleged pirate city, bright with window lights and street lamps. She was surprised.

Sonora was built on the foundation of beached ships. Massive holds were hammered together, crossed by rope bridges and wooden decks, three or four stories high. Buildings had been resurrected between them, filling in the gaps, backed by a series of cliffs that enclosed the bay. She could see the figureheads of mermaids, horses and other statues that adorned the old bows. Many of the windows were portholes recovered from old wrecks. The roads were paved with sandstone, the docks made of mismatched wood, pieced together over the years.

Several boats were in the bay now—large, seagoing vessels

with unmarked flags. Pirates, of course. And a few merchants, she suspected. She noticed them only because of the crates they held on board, a familiar sight from the port city of Delbar. A merchant wouldn't be fool enough to fly his colors in these waters. There was no evidence of the King's guard. In this alcove of a city, she doubted the King's law held much sway.

Ferran rowed them to a smaller area of the docks, occupied by houseboats like his, all tethered together. He left the rudder and perched on the keel as they neared, then leapt to the floating planks, a length of rope in hand. He guided the boat into the dock, his hands firm on the railing. Then he tied the keel in place, parallel with the houseboat next to him.

Finally, he held out a hand to assist her onto the dock. Lori picked up her satchel—she didn't like the idea of leaving her belongings on board, especially in a pirate city. She glanced at his hand, gave him a wry smile, and jumped off the boat by herself.

"Aren't you worried that your boat will be stolen?" she asked. There was a watch tower in the distance, but no guards on patrol. Paper lanterns bobbed along the waterfront, strung across the docks, casting pink, blue, and yellow light across the dark water. She could already hear the roar of voices, the distant strain of music, the general hubbub of the city.

"Pirate's honor," Ferran said, returning her ironic smile. "A pirate city wouldn't last long if they were all stealing from each other. No one steals from Sonora's port."

Lori frowned. "But what if...?"

"Otherwise, they'll be captured and killed. Trust me." He gave her a knowing look. "You don't want to be chased down by a fleet of pirates."

Ah. Lori nodded, imagining the long and narrow strait they had just passed through. The man had a point. A sailor would be hard-pressed to make it out of the bay.

"What now?" she asked.

Ferran looped an easy arm around her shoulder. He was more than a foot taller than she. She felt as though a lanky coyote stood at her side, loping easily down the boardwalk. "Now, we have a drink."

"I thought you were broke."

"I know the crew of the *Aurora*," he said, "a tavern in town. Trust me, a few drinks and some idle chit-chat, and we'll find the man who has our book."

"And what then?" she asked. She didn't like the thought of drinking with Ferran. The last time she had seen him drunk, he had been splayed out on the floor in the aftermath of a bar fight.

"You plan too much," Ferran said. "You should live more in the moment. What happened to you, Lori? You used to be so much fun."

She frowned. She hated the way he said that, as though she had become her worst fear—an overbearing worrywart of a woman. Maybe it was true. She had seen a lot of sickness and injury during her years as a Healer—a lot of death. For a while she had become reclusive, clinging to her cabin in the woods, hiding from the dangers of the world. Irrational fear, she had finally realized. One couldn't control death, just as one couldn't control a harsh winter, a fever, or a runaway horse. To live was to live dangerously. Precaution couldn't stop fate.

He was waiting for an explanation. "I'm an angry drunk," she said brusquely, hiding her thoughts.

Ferran laughed at that. "Then you'll be in good company."

* * *

They first spotted the town about two hours before sundown. Sora was shocked by how long they had walked. Five miles, perhaps seven, she couldn't be sure—only that her feet were bruised and scratched from the long trek.

They paused atop a small ridge, a precipice of rocks jutting above the forest. Crash pointed into the distance. She could see a bright, gleaming line of quicksilver across the sky—the ocean dancing with sunlight. There was an indentation along the coast where the trees tapered off, unable to take root in the silty soil. Then she saw the shapes of buildings, blunt stone mounds that leaned inward, rounded toward the top. At one point, their roofs might have been made of wooden boards or grass, but they had long since rotted away, leaving only the stone blocks.

Then she saw a large pillar of smoke wafting into the air. Their companions had already arrived.

A thrill of excitement moved through her. Sora felt her heart begin to race. Another hour of walking, and she would see her friends again. *Safe and alive.* It was more than she could have asked for.

Crash helped her walk back down the rocks and maneuvered them to the deer trail that led toward the coast. They cut through a few acres of wilderness, wherever the underbrush grew thin, taking the most direct path possible. Finally, *finally* they reached the rim of the trees. The ground became grainy and dry beneath her feet. The soil gave way to sand. Large rocks speckled the coast, swept in by the tide, the same brownish-gray stones that the buildings were made of.

She could hear voices bickering back and forth.

"The fire is too large," Joan's voice reached her, husky for a woman, immediately recognizable. "It's too visible from the water!"

"How else are we going to cook two deer and a boar?" Jacques argued back. His words were stout and rolling, in a strange accent that Sora had never been able to place. "From what we've seen, this island is deserted. There's no danger in a large fire."

"What if we are seen by a passing ship?" Joan pressed. "What if pirates travel these waters?"

"I hear a lot of 'ifs'," Jacques grunted.

Sora stepped from between the buildings. At first no one noticed her. Burn had his back turned and was stacking firewood next to a large pyre. The flames were still low compared to the amount of wood they had gathered. A pile of fruit lay adjacent to him in the overhang of one of the old buildings.

Jacques and Joan stood on the other side of the fire, facing each other. Jacques had a deer carcass slung over one shoulder, already skinned. His pet crow sat on top of the carcass, hopping back and forth across it, inspecting it with an eager black eye.

"Look at this town," Joan said emphatically. "People lived here once. We are not as isolated as we think."

"These buildings have to be over a hundred years old," Jacques replied. "If people used to live here, they are long gone."

Joan rolled her eyes in exasperation, then paused, peering over Jacques' shoulder. Sora met her gaze; she couldn't keep a broad smile from spreading across her face.

"What?" Jacques asked, then turned. His eyes landed on Sora.

His face went slack and white, as though staring at a ghost. "Oh, my."

They all stared at each other for a long, shocked moment. Then Crash stepped up next to her, his arm gently brushing hers. To anyone else it would have seemed like a meaningless touch, but Sora knew him better than that. She glanced sideways, still grinning. He met her eyes. A small smile played about his lips.

"Sora!" Burn's voice reached her. She turned around. The giant Wolfy charged toward her, sand flying beneath his feet. He crossed the beach in a matter of seconds and grabbed her in a fierce hug. Sora felt all of her breath leave her at once. The mercenary lifted her far off the ground, held in his powerful arms, then spun her in a circle. Her bandaged arm throbbed at the contact, but the pain was lost in happiness. She started laughing, her face buried in his soiled shirt. He smelled good—salt and citrus mixed with the metallic tang of sweat. She would have hugged him back, but her arms were pinned to her body, trapped in his tight hold.

Finally he set her back down. The world spun around her, slightly off-kilter. She turned to find the entire crew of Dracians at her back. One by one, they came up to touch her good shoulder, or her hair, or take her hand in welcome. They were all in their human forms, their hair bright coppery-red, their eyes like gleaming jewels. She didn't know most of their names, and for a moment, she felt guilty about that. She had been so worried about Crash and Burn, she had hardly thought of the entire Dracian crew.

Laina squeezed through the crowd, ducking under arms and stepping on toes. The small, thin girl stared at her for a moment, a dark frown on her face, then suddenly lunged, her arms wide open. Sora wrapped her good arm around the street child, gripping her tightly.

"I knew you weren't dead," the young thief said into her shoulder. "I knew it! I told everyone, but they wouldn't believe me!"

Sora stroked her head. "Well, I'm here now," she said in amusement.

"I was worried," the girl sniffed. Her tone bordered on accusatory. Sora couldn't tell if she was angry or just emotional.

"Oh, hush," she said. "See? I'm just fine."

"I knew you were fine!" Laina said defensively, then pushed back, rubbing her eyes, blinking back tears. "I take it back, I wasn't worried at all!" She turned to glare at Tristan, who stood close by, part of the ring of Dracians. "See? I told you she was alive!"

Tristan gave the girl a tight smile, then took Sora's good hand in his, raising her fingers to his lips. "We're relieved to see you," he murmured. His deep-blue eyes glinted in the sunlight. Then he glanced over her shoulder at Crash, his expression darkening. "Thankfully all in one piece."

Sora frowned, wondering what the Dracian meant by that. For a moment, the tension between him and the assassin was palpable, like the static before a lightning storm.

She shook her head, pulling her hand back from Tristan and rubbing her fingers, a slow blush creeping onto her cheeks. "Crash saved my life," she said quietly.

The Dracian turned to look at her, surprise registering on his broad, handsome face. Then he nodded. "That's good to hear. He was in quite a mood when he left our camp. I'm surprised he didn't slaughter the first thing he saw."

A mood? Crash? She glanced at the assassin, who still stared coldly at the Dracian. Crash was a few inches taller and a few years older than Tristan. His look was pure intimidation.

"This is a cause for celebration," Burn said abruptly, interjecting. His arm landed around Sora's shoulders, and he guided her to the shade of one of the buildings. "Let's cook that meat," he called to Jacques. "I think we could all use a hot meal and a quiet night."

Sora let out a small sigh of relief. She crossed the short stretch of beach with Burn. Crash followed them at a distance, observing the series of buildings. She sat down next to the sandstone wall, pressing her back against the cool rock. Closing her eyes briefly, she finally asked, "What is this place?"

Burn handed her a flask of water and sat by her side, putting his back against the wall, mirroring her position. "A town, I suppose," the Wolfy said. His voice was low and deep, like a small avalanche, soothing and familiar. "We arrived a few hours ago. The Dracians have been exploring. It looks like this might have been a mining town at one time."

"Mining?" Sora asked, her curiosity piqued. "Mining for what?"

"We don't know yet," he said. "But we found large metal carts in one of the buildings, and there's a series of mining tracks that begin at the rear of the village. It's a bit late to go into the jungle. We'll take a closer look in the morning, see if we can't find a way off this island."

"A mining cart is a far throw from a ship," Crash said wryly. He stood a few feet away, still gazing at the buildings. He looked thoughtful. Something must have caught his interest because he turned abruptly and walked into the cluster of buildings, his steps fast and silent.

Sora watched him go. "It wouldn't hurt to look," she muttered. *And I don't have any better ideas.* Her eyes slid back to the ocean. The sun was descending in the sky, creeping toward the silvery water. It was too bright, too difficult to look at. She guessed they had another hour before nightfall.

Burn searched her face, her entire appearance. "We were able to recover your weapons from the ship," he mentioned.

She turned to look at him. She was reminded of all the little details she had forgotten over the past two days while focused on survival. "My staff and daggers?" she asked.

"Aye," he murmured. "And the sacred weapons, too. They were all stored in a large chest. Thankfully the ocean didn't take them."

The sacred weapons? She was shocked by the news. She had assumed they were at the bottom of the sea by now. She shook her head slowly, absorbing his words. They had recovered the Dark God's weapons from the wraiths they had killed: the hilt of a rapier and a blackened spearhead. With the weapons intact, they could still move forward.

"We won't get far without a ship," she sighed.

"We might not be as far off-course as it seems," Burn said gently. He pointed to the horizon, out over the water. "I've seen other land masses out that way. Jacques sighted them too when he and the Dracians were flying. We might already be on the Lost Isles —just not the main island."

Sora's eyes widened fractionally. "Are you sure?"

Burn shook his head slowly. "As sure as we can be. But you're right. Without a ship, we still won't get far."

Sora started looking around, taking in all the trees, the wreckage of the buildings. "Perhaps we can build one," she said, her mind suddenly racing with possibilities. "Tie a few logs together, just enough to float. If we're already close to the main island, it can't take long—"

"Slow down," Burn laughed, and put his hand on her head. "We've thought of that and a few other possibilities. We'll decide on something tomorrow. For now, we all just need to rest."

Sora knew he was right. She was physically and mentally drained, but his words had sparked her determination. There was still a chance left that they could succeed—and she would take it.

Burn gazed at her face, his hand tugging at a knot in her hair. Then he frowned. "We found a well, too," he offered. "You can take a bath."

Sora's eyebrows lifted. "Really?" she said, then got to her feet, holding out one hand for balance. Her legs were sore and stiff, but she couldn't pass up this opportunity. "Show me."

Burn laughed deep in his throat. He took her arm and led her into the village. They entered what must have been the main street. Mounds of sand were pressed up against the buildings, carelessly arranged by the wind.

It was a short walk from one end of the town to the other, perhaps fifteen buildings in all. The houses were short and stout, nothing like the towering structures on the mainland. In the center of the town was a deep hole with a small brick wall around it, chipped down and worn away through the years. Sora saw a rope hanging over its edge that looked new, probably scavenged from the ship. She assumed there was a bucket tied to the side of the well.

"You'll have to bathe here," Burn said, indicating the rope.

Sora's eyes widened. "In the middle of the town?"

"Aye," he grinned. "Don't worry. I'll let the others know what you're doing. You can kneel behind that hill of sand over there."

Sora glanced over her shoulder, noting a small dune perhaps ten feet away. Hopefully the rope would stretch that far. She nodded, trying to focus on the positive. At least she would be clean. She trusted Crash and Burn to stay out of her business, but the Dracians were a mischievous lot. She would have to keep an eye on the rooftops.

The Wolfy turned and lumbered away, calling out to the Dracians, forbidding them to run about until she was finished bathing. They laughed distantly, joking with each other, though Sora couldn't make out the words. She shrugged and turned back to the well, then gripped the rope with both hands and began to pull. She heard a splash of water somewhere far below her. A small grin lit up her face. Finally, a bath!

CHAPTER 9

Lori wasn't fond of ale. She was more of a wine drinker, when she drank at all. The bubbly, amber liquid made her stomach burn unpleasantly, but she kept sipping away, watching Ferran from the bar. Her friend had attracted a lot of attention since entering the *Aurora*, and for good reason—he was a head taller and more handsome than most of the tenants. Women flocked around him, waitresses and other pirate riffraff, and Lori looked away as one tried to sit in his lap.

The *Aurora* had once been a grand ship, made of brass filigree and dark redwood. The inside had since been gutted and turned into a massive tavern or a gambling hall, depending on how one looked at it. Tables stretched in all directions, fifty rows down and twenty across, three decks high. The noise of the patrons was contained to a dull roar, drowning out the musicians that sat on the opposite side of the room. A wide range of card and dice games were set up, everything from poker and spades to roulette. Gold coins flashed in abundance. Chandeliers hung from the ceiling, lit with hundreds of candles. Wax spilled down the sides of the candles to the floor planks; the experienced patrons avoided walking underneath them.

As she watched, a dollop of hot wax fell from the ceiling and struck a drunk sailor on the shoulder. He yelped loudly, dropping a stack of cards on the floor.

A massive kitchen was located on the bottom deck. The

tantalizing aroma of roasted meat and herbs wafted up through the upper floors of the establishment. The top floor was roped off, reserved for special guests. Lori peeked up the large, wide staircase, catching sight of a bright red stage curtain. Perhaps they held performances there, too. It was far grander than anything she had expected to see in a pirate city. She couldn't imagine how the sailors had moved this giant ship from sea to land. They must have rolled it on more than a hundred logs, up the shallow bay to the base of the rocky cliffs.

The patrons of the tavern were a wide and various lot, a broad mix of grimy sea dogs, young thugs and wealthy merchants. Lori watched them with removed interest, far from intimidated—she had seen similar crowds in the City of Crowns. A few fat, bald merchants sat at a nearby table, throwing down cards and laughing into their drinks, their faces bright red. She identified them by their thick, heavy robes of a more expensive make than the average population. The sailors were just as easily spotted, hunched over tables, flexing their muscular, tattooed arms. She even saw a few men who reeked of the King's guard—perhaps soldiers on holiday? They wore clean linen tunics, their hair cut close to their ears.

Sultry waitresses prowled the room, refilling drinks and cheering the men on, coaxing them to bet more coin. In Lori's opinion, the women looked haggard and malnourished, with deep circles under their eyes and bones jutting from their wrists. As she surveyed the room, she couldn't help but note other physical conditions. *Rotted teeth—bad for the heart. Yellow eyes, liver condition—too much drinking. A lingering cough—too much pipe. Blackened nails—poor blood flow. Flaking skin—cured by fish oil. Runny nose—common cold. Sores around the mouth—could be allergies or a kissing disease.*

Any of these symptoms could be connected to the plague. Especially the blackened nails, the flaking skin. She had treated the illness first in livestock, receiving numerous complaints that chickens' beaks were turning black, their feathers falling out. Then the chickens would start attacking each other, eating one another, turning cannibalistic. The plague moved from the flesh to the mind. The hosts became crazed, erratic, violent.

When the disease spread to the farmers, she knew something was amiss. An illness rarely afflicted more than one species, especially where livestock was concerned.

"You look troubled," a voice reached her. It was unexpected. Lori gave a start, surprised out of her reverie.

She turned, her eyes landing on a redheaded man of medium height and build. Around her own age, handsome, with a square jaw and quizzical blue eyes. His hair was tied back at the base of his neck. He wore a silky blue shirt that shimmered in the light of the chandeliers, smooth as water. A wide belt cinched his pants at the waist, which were soft brown in color, snug, perhaps leather or deer hide. A single gold ring adorned his lower lip, pierced through the center.

Lori was only five feet tall, so even if the man was of medium build, he was still a hand or two taller than she. And, by the look of him, he was a Dracian.

She frowned, staring a bit too long. "Perhaps I need another drink," she said, lifting the corners of her mouth.

The Dracian sat at the bar next to her and nodded to the waitress. "Maria, two shots of rum."

"I don't drink rum," Lori said. "I'll do with a glass of wine."

The Dracian nodded to the barmaid, who winked at him in turn. "On the house, Lucas." Then she turned to get their drinks.

Lori looked at the man. *On the house, huh?* Was he a pirate? Probably. He seemed like a regular. Perhaps he was a resident of the city—and maybe he knew something about their book. She wondered if Ferran was having any luck at the craps tables. Her old friend had taken up a few games, claiming that men's tongues loosened after a few drinks. He planned to snoop around, but he had been gone a long time. He was probably doing more playing than snooping. She had lost sight of him in the crowded room.

"So what brings you to Sonora?" the man said casually.

Lori had her guard up—as much as she could, after a half-tankard of ale. "Sightseeing," she said bluntly.

"Ah...and have you seen much yet?" he grinned at her disarmingly.

"Just got in tonight."

"Hmm. New then? First time to the city?"

Lori watched him carefully. It probably showed on her. Despite being a peasant, she was better dressed than most of the women in the bar. Her white shirt was buttoned up to her neck, her green skirts long and flowing, reaching just above the ankle. All of her clothes were newly stitched and clean. "Aye," she said softly. "First time."

Lucas nodded. "I pegged you for a newcomer," he said. Then he leaned in close. "You look mighty uncomfortable, sitting at this bar by yourself. A pretty lady like you shouldn't be here unescorted."

Lori was surprised at this. Admittedly, she hadn't been trying to blend in. She had figured that in a tavern this size, no one would notice. But apparently this man had. What else did he know?

"Actually," she said, deciding to lay her cards on the table, "I'm a rare book collector. I hear there are a few books in this city that might be hard to find elsewhere."

Lucas sat back. In one smooth motion, he turned to the bar and picked up his shot. Lori was surprised. She hadn't noticed the drinks arrive. *Maybe I'm further gone than I thought.* He took the shot of rum in one quick toss to the back of his throat, then slammed the glass down and signaled for another one.

"Rare books?" he said, glancing at her. "Can't say I've seen many around here. Mayhap you haven't noticed, but pirates aren't the type to read."

Lori quirked the corners of her mouth up, a teasing smile. "Yes, but they are the type to steal. I figured I'd try my luck."

"Sonora is certainly a city of luck," the man muttered.

Lori turned and picked up her glass of wine. She wondered what this man was doing here. He didn't look like a lowly sea-scarred pirate. No, if he was a sailor, he was mighty well-off. Or knew how to loot. That shirt couldn't be cheap.

"Do you know this city well?" she asked casually.

Lucas searched her face curiously. "Aye," he murmured. "A permanent resident, you could say."

"Then would you know anyone who has an interest in old artifacts?" she asked. Lucas appeared to hesitate. *I have to make him talk somehow.* She pulled her hair back off her neck, fanning herself as though hot while allowing him to see the smooth curve of her neck and shoulder.

When she turned back to him, he was assessing her with his eyes, a pleased expression on his face. She saw his gaze flicker down, then up, making his intentions obviously clear.

"Old artifacts, you say?" He leaned in closer, a flirtatious smile perched on his lips. "The owner of this establishment is a collector, in fact. 'Tis an expensive hobby, you know."

The owner? Lori suddenly wondered if Ferran knew this. Perhaps it wasn't such a coincidence that they had come to the *Aurora*. Not only was it the biggest tavern in the city, but it was owned by a collector of rare and ancient artifacts. She felt slightly irritated. Of course Ferran must have known. His luck wasn't that good. *He should have told me.*

"And how does one go about meeting the owner?" she asked.

Lucas frowned. The question made him uncomfortable; she could tell by how his eyes shifted. "You don't," he said.

"Oh?"

"Aye...Captain Silas is not a kind man. And he likes blond women, perhaps a bit too much. You wouldn't want to catch his eye. You've come to a dangerous place, Miss...?"

"Lori," she said.

"Lori," he echoed. "Nice to make your acquaintance."

"You are rather well-mannered for a pirate," she smiled.

"Wasn't always a pirate." He raised his shot to her. "A toast?" he asked.

"To what?"

"To good luck." He tipped his shot back, and Lori took a sip of her red wine, allowing the bold flavor to linger on her tongue. It burned on the way down, leaving a warm knot in her belly.

There was a sudden crash from the side of the room. Lori jumped, surprised. She turned to look over her shoulder and spotted a card table tipped on its side, with several men standing around it, arguing. She let out a long breath. One of the men was a head taller than the rest, long and lanky, athletic—Ferran.

"Goddess," she muttered, staring at him. The crowd of women had somewhat dispersed, but several still hung around the table, their voices rising in Ferran's defense. The other sailors looked furious. She heard the words "cheating" and "check his sleeves."

She sighed to herself. Couldn't he play fair at least once? She wondered if she would have to step in and rescue her friend from his own reckless stupidity, but she was on to something with Lucas, and she couldn't let him go, not yet.

Lucas watched her face. "So you know Ferran?" he asked quietly.

Lori turned back to him, taken off-guard. Of course Ferran would be recognized in a pirate city. She should have expected that. *Goddess! Does his depravity know no bounds?*

She gave him a small smile. "An acquaintance," she said. "We just met."

"Ah," he murmured. He nodded to the barmaid, who immediately put another drink in front of him—a tankard of ale, the high-end stuff.

Three drinks and no charge. He had to be someone important. Lori looked at him curiously. "I want to meet your captain," she said bluntly. She might have slurred a bit. She hoped not.

Lucas turned back to her, his eyes wide. "Pardon?"

"Captain Silas, right?" she said. Her eyes glinted. He looked shocked. "Your drinks are on the house, you're wearing that ridiculous shirt—your captain owns this place, I'm guessing."

Lucas blanched.

Her grin widened.

Then he shook his head, a strained smile alighting his face. "You're an observant woman, Miss Lori."

"And I take it you're an observant man," she said back.

He shrugged nonchalantly. "I like to know who is visiting the *Aurora*. Particularly any new and attractive faces." He held her eyes, and she was surprised to feel a blush creeping into her cheeks.

She shook her head, unwilling to flirt. "Take me to see your captain," she repeated.

"Impossible," Lucas replied, but his grin became magnetic, secretive.

There was another crash from the side of the room—an overturned chair. The argument was escalating. Lori saw one of the sailors take a threatening step forward, pointing at Ferran's face. Her friend had his hands up, showing his sleeves. By his sly grin, she assumed he was trying to talk them down.

Lori turned back to the Dracian. "What would it take to meet him?" she continued.

"Nothing. I won't do it." Lucas shook his head solidly. "Captain Silas is a smarmy, disingenuous sea dog. Everyone in Sonora fears his name. He's captured over a hundred merchant vessels, sold all of his captives into slavery. Once, he beheaded a man just for mispronouncing his name. Trust me, you wouldn't like him, and..." Lucas gave her a playful look. "He might not let you leave this city after laying eyes on you."

"I can pay you," Lori said, reaching for her bag of coins.

The man pursed his lips. "No, no, that won't do."

Lori frowned. *Captain Silas has our book, I know it.* She knew it as surely as the symptoms of smallpox. But how else could she meet this pirate captain? Asking was getting her nowhere.

A thought occurred. It was spontaneous, a little risky. But hell, she was on her third drink, and perhaps Ferran was right. Maybe she needed to trust her gut and live in the moment.

She met Lucas' eyes sweetly. She smiled.

Then she pulled back her fist and punched him in the face.

Lucas fell backward out of his chair. Lori leapt after him, pulling him up by his silky blue collar. She punched him again, squarely in the nose.

Then, automatically, thirty men stood from their seats. A strange hush fell over the front of the tavern. Lori looked up, surprised to see so many pirates standing, staring at her, drawing their weapons. They were a gruesome lot, weathered faces and bright gold piercings. They were all marked with identical tattoos on their necks—a small anchor with a star beneath it.

Lucas stumbled to his feet, one hand clutching his nose, blood staining his pretty blue shirt. He held up his other hand to the men, palm open. "Stop," he said. "Dammit, everyone stop!" He paused a bit longer, his eyes closed. "You broke my nose!" he finally said, then glared at Lori.

She raised an eyebrow. "It's not broken," she said knowingly. "But I will break it if you don't take me to Captain Silas right now."

"You infuriating woman," he breathed, still holding his nose. His face was turning red. "*I'm* Captain Silas and this is *my* establishment!"

Lori gawked, horrified. She looked around. Everyone was staring at her—all of the men at the bar, the barmaids, the serving girls. They were pale as ghosts.

Silas glared at her harder, then turned on his heel. "Bring her," he said, flicking his wrist, then he stalked across the floor toward the roped-off staircase.

Immediately three brutes left the table closest to her. The patrons at the bar scuttled away, giving the men a large berth. Lori looked at the sailors disdainfully. She could have laid them flat out —considered it for a moment—but she needed to talk to the captain. Perhaps this situation could work in her favor.

"No need," she said stiffly. "I'm coming." She stood from her seat and followed the captain up the stairs.

Silas paused on the landing, turning to address his men. "And bring me Ferran Ebonaire!" he snarled.

Lori's eyes widened. She looked back at Ferran across the crowded room. He gave her a quick smile and then bowed out of his game, nodded farewell to his female entourage, and turned to greet the approaching sailors.

"Now, now," he said amiably. "No need to use force."

Lori turned back to the staircase and closed her eyes. Ferran Ebonaire. He had never mentioned his surname before. They had known each other for eighteen years, and never once had she heard him speak it. *Ebonaire.* Why hadn't he told her?

* * *

The third deck of the *Aurora* was something like a concert hall. A large stage stood at the far end, hidden by long red velvet curtains, perhaps forty feet high. Intricate chandeliers hung from the ceiling, far larger and grander than the chandeliers on the floors below. The majority of the light in the room, however, came from wall sconces lit by torches. Countless wooden tables covered the floor, each circular in shape with four or five red-velvet armchairs positioned around them. This was definitely a room for entertaining high-end guests, but for now it was empty.

Two large sailors were positioned on either side of her. Ferran stood a few feet away, his hands shoved into his pockets, leaning on one leg, as though he did this kind of thing every day. She half-expected him to ask for a drink. Before them, Captain Silas had pulled out a chair and was sitting with his head back, a cloth pressed to his nose.

After a long pause, he said, "Tell me why I shouldn't have you both killed."

Lori's eyebrow raised at this. She shot a glance at Ferran and saw him open his mouth to reply. *No!* she thought. Whatever the treasure hunter was about to say, she doubted it would help their cause. She rushed to cut him off. "If you had just told me who you were, this would have gone a lot smoother."

Silas sat up and glared at her. His bright blue eyes gleamed in the torchlight. His hair was slightly mussed; a few silky strands had slipped loose from their tie and brushed against his face. "I don't need to tell you anything," he said menacingly. It was quite different from the way he had spoken before, at the bar, playful and intimate. "Now state your business or I'll gut you with my knife. Believe me, the thought is very appealing."

"You wouldn't dare," Lori said angrily, raising her chin a notch. "I'm a Healer."

"A Healer?" Silas echoed. She could see the thoughts pass behind his eyes. Healers took an oath to serve all people—all races and creeds, good or bad, even criminals. They were surrounded by a sense of mysticism, and were thought to have the protection of the Goddess.

It was commonly said that to kill a Healer was the worst luck of all; to be cursed with a lifetime of misfortune. A human might ignore that superstition, but not a Dracian. The Races knew better.

"I'm listening," Captain Silas said icily.

"We are looking for a book," Ferran's voice cut into the conversation. He spoke lazily, unconcerned with the tension in the room. "I gave it to a whore in Cape Shorn. She said she sold it to a pirate from Sylla Cove. You're the only collector in this town. I figured it was you."

Captain Silas cocked his head to one side, thoughtful. Lori stared at Ferran, resisting the urge to clock him over the head. *All this time—he didn't tell me!* She didn't know whether to be furious or laugh at the irony.

Any minute now, she expected him to start threatening their captor, provoking Silas into a fight. That's what the young Ferran would have done—anything to prove he was tough. But this new Ferran did no such thing. She looked him over for a second time. He seemed bored.

"Aye, I remember buying that book," Silas finally said. "Couldn't make head nor tail of it. Half the pages were blank."

"Do you still have it?" Ferran asked.

Silas paused. "Yes."

Lori felt a knot of tension loosen in her stomach.

"I take it you want the book back?" Silas asked mockingly.

Ferran shrugged. "We have need of it."

"What kind of need?" he demanded.

Ferran glanced at Lori. She shifted on her feet. Now what? The only thing left to do was to explain the situation.

Silas spoke before either of them could. "*The Book of the*

Named is a rare artifact," he said. Lori was surprised again. Ferran hadn't known the title of the book—he couldn't remember it. Obviously Silas had done his research. A collector, indeed.

But there was more to it than that. She remembered *The Book of the Named* mentioned in old stories about the War of the Races. It had been lost shortly after the final battle, when the world had been torn by chaos and disarray. It was an evil book dedicated to the teachings of the Dark God, the ways of the assassins.

"I won't just give it away," Silas continued. "I paid a large sum for it."

Ferran turned to look at Lori fully. "Tell him about the plague."

Lori noted the frown on Silas' face. She licked her dry lips. The alcohol was beginning to make her feel sick and sleepy, and she wanted to sit down. "All right," she said. "As I told you, I am a Healer. Six months ago, I began to see a strange sickness infecting the farm animals around our town." She dove into the story, describing the symptoms, how she had attempted to treat the illness, to no avail. Then the disease had spread to the farmers.

When she mentioned her daughter's Cat's Eye and the magical quality of the illness, Captain Silas sat forward. She sensed that she had his full attention now. Lori quickly explained the events that had led them to this place—why they had come, and what they hoped to do.

Captain Silas tapped his fingers against the arm of the chair, his bloody nose forgotten. After a moment he said, "Some of my crew have fallen ill."

Lori's eyes widened. Had the plague already spread so far?

The captain was thoughtful once more. He glanced at his men, then at Ferran with a look of distaste rather uncharacteristic of a

Dracian. Lori wondered if his supposed reputation was true—perhaps he really was feared in all of Sonora.

"Fine," he finally said. "I will give you the book. In exchange, I want you to save my men's lives."

Lori balked at that. "Of course," she said automatically. "But if it's caused by the plague, there's not much that medicine can do."

"We'll do it," Ferran said, almost at the same time.

She turned to stare at him, horrified. She wanted to wring his neck. What were they supposed to do when she failed? When the sailors died? And what if she and Ferran contracted the plague? There was nothing to protect them from the Dark God's curse. She hoped against hope that he had a plan—but she suspected that he was flying by the seat of his pants.

"First, the book," Silas said, oblivious to Lori's thoughts. "And then, my men." He gave Ferran a menacing glare. "And if you can't heal them, I will kill you." His eyes turned to Lori. "His life is in your hands."

Lori gave him a tight smile. "Right," she said, still secretly furious. *If we fail, I'll kill Ferran myself!* She tried to catch her friend's eye, but Ferran was gazing at Silas placidly, as though hardly concerned by his threat.

The captain jumped to his feet and signaled to the sailors. The men grabbed Lori's arms and hauled her forward, following the Dracian's quick pace. Surprisingly, Captain Silas led them to the side of the room, where he pressed his hands against a panel of ornately carved wood. After a small shove, the wood gave inward and slid sideways—a hidden door. *Of course pirates would have hidden doors,* Lori thought, almost amused.

Silas led them onto a dusty staircase, lit by oil lamps that hung from the walls. The group started downward. One of the sailors kept a firm hold on her arm, though it was impossible to walk side by side. The staircase wrapped around in a narrow spiral; Lori felt dizzy from the alcohol and swallowed hard, hoping she wouldn't throw up. Eventually Silas paused and opened another panel. She had no idea where they were, possibly underground or in a separate building adjacent to the ship.

The room beyond was shrouded in darkness. Silas took one of the oil lamps from the wall and stepped through the doorway, casting the light around until he found and lit a nearby candelabra.

The candlelight spread in a broad circle, but even with the illumination, Lori couldn't make out where the corners of the room were. The chamber was massive, like a fourth deck, though now she could tell that it wasn't part of the Aurora. The walls were made of old stone, the floor was dented wood caked with dust. The room was filled with all kinds of things: boxes, chests, crates and barrels. As they started to walk through, she saw stranger things in the lantern light. Old statues worn by time and, perhaps, saltwater. Suits of armor, pieces of wagons, ox yokes, old furniture and a broad assortment of weapons. Most of the weaponry was rusted beyond use: axes, swords, spears, halberds, countless arrows, some of them mounted on plaques on the walls. A few appeared to be labeled. She was hit with a sudden, burning curiosity. Were these relics from the War? Pieces of ancient kingdoms? Some of the swords didn't look human-made. Their steel had a yellow sheen and their blades were ornately curved.

Silas didn't offer an explanation. She wondered how many of these things he had bought and how many he had salvaged from abandoned shipyards.

Finally they reached the end of the room. The entire back wall was lined with bookcases carefully spaced apart, with each book given ample room. Most were delicately encased in wax paper for preservation. Lori felt her fingers itch. She longed to touch the spines of the books, run her fingers over the ancient pages. How much knowledge was stored in this warehouse? She was in awe. She had a humble library back home, an assortment of old books that may or may not have been from the War—but nothing like this.

Abruptly, a small movement caught the corner of her eye. Lori turned her head, staring into the shadows. She listened carefully. She had seen something shift in the dark corners of the room. Or was it the flicker of lantern light? The back of her neck tingled. She glanced at the tall, burly sailors on either side of her, trying to reassure herself. They didn't seem concerned. *It's just your imagination,* she thought firmly. Nothing more.

But the sense of unease remained. She couldn't shake the feeling of being watched. She glanced around the giant room one last time. The walls and ceiling were curtained by darkness. They could have been surrounded by people; there would be no way to tell. It was an unnerving thought. *And illogical. We're the only people here.* She hadn't noticed any footprints in the thick dust. Even the air currents seemed undisturbed.

She tried to focus her attention on Captain Silas as he browsed a bookshelf, occasionally pulling out a title, then putting it back. Now that he was in front of his collection, his entire expression had changed, turning from a solemn frown to a wondrous smile, his eyes bright with passion. She knew how he must feel. She felt the same way when brewing a tonic or salve—she would lose herself in the scent of herbs, the feel of the mortar in her hands.

"Here it is," Silas finally said, and pulled the book from the shelf. It was surprisingly small, not a grand tome as she had imagined. In fact, it resembled a diary, easily held in one hand, bound by thick leather. The Dracian winced as he held it. "It's a bit cold to the touch."

Just like the Dark God's weapons, Lori remembered. She took it as a sign that this was the right book.

Suddenly, something launched itself from the side of the room. Lori gasped, turning. A shadow detached from the wall. It darted over the carpet so fast that she could barely make out its shape. It tackled Silas, who cried out, stumbling backward. The book was snatched from his hands, then the shadow dashed into the depths of the room, following the opposite wall.

Ferran responded first. He charged after the shadow, reaching for it. He grabbed its ankle, stumbling to the floor. The shape twisted skillfully, turning in the air like an acrobat, breaking his hold. For a moment, the darkness seemed to slip and fade and she caught sight of a face—long black hair, a feminine figure, the glint of green eyes. Lori's mouth fell open. She recognized those features. An assassin. One of the Sixth Race.

Lori shook herself into action. She turned and charged down the length of the room, running parallel to the wall, hoping to cut the figure off. It was difficult to follow with her eyes. The woman used the shadows as a cloak, flickering through the air like a ghost, moving faster than humanly possible. How had she gotten into the building?

Silas roared to his men, pointing after the apparition. The sailors had been standing slack-jawed, but they leapt to action and chased after her, drawing their cutlasses.

Lori's eyes followed the woman's path. She was heading to the far corner of the room, trying to escape. They said that the Sixth Race could transport through shadows, using them as doorways to separate lands.

She dodged between chests and boxes, sprinting as fast as she could. Suddenly, a second shape leapt in front of her. She saw the gleam of a sword, the flash of green eyes in the lantern light. It was too late to stop her momentum, so Lori threw herself forward, down to the ground, rolling beneath the blade. She came up on the other side of the man, whirling, holding up her arms in defense.

The man turned on her and raised his hand purposefully. His shadow lifted from the ground and shot toward her, creating a billow of darkness. Some sort of magic. Lori flinched backward.

Wham! Someone slammed her to the ground. Ferran wrapped himself around her, shielding her small body with his own. He raised his left hand, his fingers clenched into a fist. There was a flash of brilliant crimson light, a sense of energy flooding the air, electrifying, powerful. *Shhiing!*

The darkness struck the light and split apart, like a wave against rocks. Then it was sucked into the red shield, quickly nullified and absorbed.

Lori stared up at Ferran. She couldn't believe her eyes. A Cat's Eye?

Then Ferran was off her. He launched himself onto the darkened figure, wrestling the man to the ground. Lori was surprised that he could hold his own. Assassins were highly trained —fierce warriors, even those without a Name.

She scrambled to her feet, leaving Ferran to deal with the man, and sprinted toward the far corner of the room. The shadow-woman had been briefly waylaid by the pirates, but Silas' men were now groaning on the floor, and the woman continuing to run. If Lori hurried, she could still cut her off.

Lori took a sharp right and ran toward the wall, cutting toward the fleeing woman. Her figure darted past, quick as a whip. Lori reached out her hands. The dark cloak was merely an inch from her grasp. She leapt, her fingers splayed out desperately.

Wham!

Lori slammed into the wall.

Her face hit the granite. She stumbled backwards, dazed, then threw herself at the wall again, pounding the stone, scrabbling her nails against it. *No! Not now! Sora needs that book!* But it was too late—the shadow-woman had disappeared, vanishing completely.

Lori kept pounding at the rock in frustration, trying to find the portal. "Dammit!" she screamed. "Damn damn damn!"

Suddenly Ferran was behind her, dragging her away. "Get back," he said, throwing her behind him. He placed one of his hands on the stone. It immediately glowed with a red light. She could see the source of the light now—a leather cuff that he wore around his wrist. She hadn't noticed it before—she wondered how she could have been so blind. Embedded in the cuff was a circular stone, gleaming with scarlet energy. A yellow swirl moved in its depths, turning in slow, lazy circles. Yes, she had guessed correctly, a Cat's Eye. *But how? When? How long has he worn one?*

Ferran paused for a moment, his eyes closed, listening to some unheard voice. It was unnatural, like watching someone commune with a ghost. A chill passed through her. Then he turned to look at her. "The portal led to the City of Crowns," he said.

"But...but who?" she demanded. "Why take the book?"

"My guess," Ferran said, "is that the Sixth Race wants it as badly as we do."

Lori let out a slow breath. *Well, of course.* It made perfect sense. The Dark God was stirring, the sacred weapons had manifested—there were others who would want that power. Especially the Sixth Race. But for what purpose?

Tears of frustration stung her eyes. She had been so close, inches away from stopping the shadow. "Now what?" she groaned, running a tired hand over her face. The one thing she could have done for her daughter—and of course, she had failed.

"We'll get it back," Ferran said, watching her. His confidence was reassuring. When she looked up at him, he had a cunning gleam in his gray eyes. "Don't worry, we know where they went," he said. "They can't do anything without the sacred weapons. We'll find the book."

Lori nodded, still shaken. She hoped that was true. She took a deep, steadying breath and turned back to the room. Surprisingly, the large warehouse wasn't nearly as dark as before. The lantern light seemed stronger, bigger, more brilliant. She realized now that the shadows had been overly exaggerated, tainted by the assassins' magic. The air felt clearer, too, as though an invisible cloud had lifted.

Silas approached them. His nose had started to bleed again, and he pressed a stained handkerchief to it. "Well," he said. "That was unexpected." Despite his tone, there was a slight grin around his lips, a glimpse of excitement. Lori recognized the mischievous look of a Dracian.

"Big help you were," she muttered.

He raised an eyebrow. "That's what lackeys are for." He

glanced at the two pirates, who were standing by uncomfortably. One had a black eye. "Though I'll admit, they're better sailors than fighters," he concluded.

"We caught one," Ferran said. "All is not lost. We can question him."

Lori turned, surprised, to find an unconscious form slumped in the middle of the room. It was the second shadow who had attacked her—the male.

"How did you manage that?" she asked wryly. She crossed her arms, impressed.

"They might move like smoke," Ferran said, "but they bleed just like any man."

Lori nodded. She liked his show of humility, but she knew he was downplaying his skill. Those of the Sixth Race were notorious for their phantom-like abilities, their swiftness and prowess in combat. It wasn't every day that one was caught. It was like trying to trap vapor—they always slipped away.

"Tie him up," she said. "Before he can escape."

Captain Silas signaled his men, who stalked off across the room. One pulled a length of rope from his belt. *Trust a pirate to carry rope at all times,* Lori thought ironically. They lifted the prone figure by his arms and bound his hands and feet. The man appeared very young, now that Lori got a close look at his face. Practically a teenager, scraggly and unkempt.

Once the sailors were done tying the knots, Ferran approached. She watched her friend carefully. He touched the Cat's Eye at his wrist and murmured, "Bind him."

The prisoner's ropes glowed faintly red, then faded. Lori's arms prickled again—she rubbed herself, staving off a chill. She had never seen a Cat's Eye used in such a way. She assumed that the necklace would counteract any magic that the boy could use to escape. At least, she hoped so.

She stepped up to Ferran's side, leaning toward him so he could hear her soft words. "You never told me you had a Cat's Eye," she breathed.

He didn't meet her eyes. "I didn't want to worry you."

"How long?"

He glanced at her briefly, then away. "Since I was eighteen."

Lori counted back the years. He must have acquired the necklace before his career as a treasure hunter. But how had he come by it? Dane had found a Cat's Eye in the same caverns where he had died; it was now worn by Sora. But she didn't remember Ferran ever mentioning such a stone—or using one.

That meant that he had been wearing the Cat's Eye for twenty years. Just how much had he learned about it?

"What now?" Ferran asked, turning to look at Silas and his men.

The pirate Captain shook his head, appearing deep in thought. "The City of Crowns is more than two hundred miles away," he said. "No sense chasing after them tonight."

"What of your sick men?" Lori asked, remembering their deal. She felt a new sense of confidence, knowing that Ferran had a Cat's Eye. From what she could tell, it was the only way to counteract the curse—though last time, the experience had been less than pleasant.

"Aye," Silas nodded, meeting her eyes. "I'll take you to them."

"And the assassin?" Ferran asked.

Silas glanced at their silent captive. "Take him to the brig," he ordered.

Lori would have laughed if he hadn't sounded so serious. *A brig!* The *Aurora* wasn't a true ship anymore, though Silas was keen on treating it like one. The sailors leapt to attention and picked up their prisoner, heaving him easily off the ground, then started toward the exit. She watched them go, shaking her head, a small smile on her lips.

Captain Silas turned back to her. He either ignored her bemusement or didn't notice it. "Follow me," he said. "I'll show you to the sickroom."

Lori nodded. She and Ferran fell into step behind the Dracian. They left the room, following the same path as the sailors. Silas raised his lantern when they entered the stairwell, closing the door tightly behind them, sliding several locks into place. They climbed back up the staircase toward the upper halls.

CHAPTER 10

That night, Sora and Laina camped inside one of the abandoned houses, a single-story building with no roof. It was damned eerie. The wind seeped through the rocks, keening wildly like the cries of a mourning woman, dipping and rising with startling intensity.

Sora kept waking, staring out of the gaping, empty doorway. Sand gusted through the air, obscuring her vision. She could almost imagine the settlers who had once lived here, as though their ghosts still wandered the streets, peeking out of windows and from behind walls. She shuddered, shutting her eyes, trying to block out the noise. She focused on the roar of the ocean instead, letting it lull her to sleep.

Laina slept by her side, curled close. The two girls huddled together for warmth against the brisk ocean air. At one point, a dense fog rolled through the town, dampening their clothes and streaking the walls with moisture.

The next morning, Sora awoke to the sound of exotic birds. She blinked, staring up at the open ceiling, her eyes on a bright blue sky. The sun was warm, the air crisp, the breeze light and playful. It had to be close to noon.

She heard distant shouting from outside. It sounded like the Dracians. They were already packing up camp. She ran a hand through her disheveled blond locks, wishing fervently for a comb.

"I'll help you with that," Laina offered briefly. The girl was sitting by the side of the door, eating an orange.

"Thank you," Sora muttered. Her injured arm was fast becoming a nuisance. *I can't even tie back my own hair!*

Laina finished the last piece and wiped her hands on her shirt, then sat down behind Sora and pulled her hair back off her face. She wove her hair into a quick braid. Sora could tell that it was crooked, but at least it would stay out of the way. She stood up and adjusted the sling on her arm, then smiled at Laina, clasping her hand. "Let's see what all the commotion is about," she said.

Outside, a small party of Dracians had formed, carrying knapsacks and makeshift walking sticks. Burn waved her over. He was packing a large rucksack; she caught a glimpse of a black hilt and a dark spearhead inside. Beneath the sacred weapons were a series of tightly packed supplies, meat wrapped in large waxy leaves, nuts and roots. She glanced around for Crash but didn't see him.

"We're heading into the forest," he told her. "Are you coming? A small band will remain here to look after the wounded."

"I'll come," Sora replied. Her eyes swept over the buildings, low and hunched to the ground. A mining town. She wondered what minerals could be found on such an isolated island.

As she approached, Burn reached into a large chest that she recognized from the ship. The Dracians must have carried it with them down the beach. Burn unlatched it and opened the heavy lid; Sora sucked in a quick breath. Her staff was lodged crosswise against the length of the chest, her daggers wedged beneath it.

It was a welcome sight. Sora eagerly removed her weapons and slung her staff across her back, fitting it into the sling. The daggers fit in her belt. She felt stronger now. More confident.

"We're ready," Burn said.

Jacques, Tristan and the rest of their group all turned toward the opposite end of town where the mining tracks disappeared into the jungle. They walked through the settlement in under ten minutes. The Dracians spread out in search of useful items or weapons, though most everything appeared to be decayed.

Sora observed the buildings closely. Over here was evidence of a fire; some of the rocks were scarred and blackened. Over there was an especially large structure that may have once been a tavern or a meeting hall. A patch of berry bushes existed behind the rear wall of the settlement, separating the town from the thick leaves of the jungle. She paused, taking a handful of the dark, juicy morsels.

The steel tracks began at the far side of town, winding inland through the forest. They were so thickly covered in vegetation, the Dracians had to use their knives to cut back the brush. Countless birds squawked in offense, taking off from their nests, watching the travelers from nearby branches.

In one place, a tree had sprouted between the rails, its roots entwining around them. Part of the trunk had grown into the metal itself, binding and lifting it into the air, forcing the tracks off the ground. The group walked around the large tree, gazing at the entangled roots, a testament to how long it had been since the settlers had perished. Sora was unnerved by the thought. *What happened here? Where did they go?*

After close to an hour, the party came to a halt before the mouth of a cave, perhaps twenty feet wide and fifteen feet tall. The tracks led downward, swallowed by blackness. A few mining carts lay to one side, rusted metal boxes half-buried by dirt and plants. Sora stared at the carts, then back at the tracks, then at the cave's mouth.

"Now what?" Tristan asked, leaning against the rocks. "These people were probably mining for coal or gemstones. Hardly any use to us here."

Jacques bowed his head in thought, the crow settling on his shoulder, mimicking his position. The rest of the group hovered around the cave, uncertain of what to do next. No one moved to enter. It seemed almost too dark, as though the sun shied away from its depths. Sora took a tentative step inside and immediately shivered. It was icy-cold in the shadows.

Suddenly, Laina's voice reached them from the other side of the tracks. "Look over here!" she called. She was several yards from the rails beneath a fringe of eucalyptus trees, half-obscured by foliage. Sora followed the sound of her voice.

The young girl pulled back a curtain of vines, revealing a large metal slab that was rusted and worn, fastened to the side of a large rock.

Sora knelt before it curiously, brushing some of the dirt from its face.

"What is it?" Laina asked, staring at the tarnished surface.

"It looks like a sign..." Sora murmured, tilting her head to one side. It reminded her of the plaque outside the courthouse near her mother's town. A large brass piece, fitted into the rock with thick bolts.

Laina nodded. "There's writing on it. I don't know the language."

Sora squinted. Despite the years of age and wear, she could make out vague letters embedded in the metal, carved by a chisel. She brushed at the dirt again, chipping away the stubborn flakes with her nails. It certainly looked like writing, but the letters were strange, oddly shaped, almost like backward numbers or occult symbols.

A shadow fell over her. She instinctively knew it was Crash. She glanced up at the assassin. "What do you think?" she asked. A few of the Dracians appeared behind him, gazing curiously at the rock. Burn approached and stood at the rear. He could see easily over the group from his great height.

Crash gazed at the metal plate for a long moment, frowning. "It's written in the Old Tongue," he finally said, "the original language of the world."

"Can you read it?" she asked.

He nodded slowly. "Part of it has been rubbed out."

The Dracians huddled in closer. They all looked at the lettering and a few nodded. "That's the Old Tongue all right," Joan said. "I can only recognize a few of the symbols. There's a 'C' and a 'D.'"

"No," Burn said from above them. "It's a 'V.' The sign reads *Cavnea Sheen Len.* 'The Crystal Caves,' or, more literally, 'The Shining Caverns.'"

Sora wasn't surprised that her friend could read the language. Burn had admitted to being a scholar before he had taken to the mercenary life. "The Crystal Caves?" she echoed. It sounded familiar. Where had she heard that name before?

"Yeah, it does seem to say that," Jacques agreed. "That's strange. Were they mining for diamonds?"

"No, not diamonds," Crash interjected.

The group paused, turning to look at the assassin. He raised an eyebrow. "The Crystal Caves were mined during the War of the Races. The Harpies gathered sunstones from their depths."

"Oh!" Laina said loudly, interrupting the dark man. Crash gave her a frown, but she ignored him, turning to the rest of the group. She clapped her hands, excited. "I know this! My grandmother told me about it. The caves are legendary! The sunstones were used to bind the sixth race and imprison them with Light." She laughed. "And to think, we're actually here at the mouth of the cave!"

Sora rolled her eyes. Laina had mentioned her grandmother's stories before, but they weren't accurate. There was no sixth race of darkness. When the Elements had combined to create the races, the Dark had been shunned, feared for its unknowable depths. There had been no offspring.

"That's not all they mined," Burn rumbled.

Sora met his eyes, curious. *The Crystal Caves.* She had heard that name before. It tickled the recesses of her memory, something she had read in a book long ago, perhaps one of the stories of Kaelyn the Wanderer.

"Well?" Jacques prompted. "Out with it, man!"

"The Cat's Eye," Burn said. "This is where the Cat's-Eye stones were discovered. When humans were enslaved by the Harpies during the War, many were used as miners. They uncovered the Cat's Eye deep beneath the ocean. That's when they rebelled and the tide of the War changed."

Sora inhaled sharply. Yes, she remembered now. Not the story of Kaelyn, but another woman, a rebel during the time of the Saddened, the darkest period of human history. The woman had discovered the Cat's Eye, gathered an army and spread the secret weapon across the coast.

"Here?" she asked, bewildered. Perhaps this was the very site where the rebellion had started. It would certainly explain the burned buildings. Her imagination ran wild, issuing visions of the past, of soot-faced humans and magical, glowing Harpies—and of course, the Cat's Eye stones.

She shook her head, trying to clear her thoughts. She felt as though she had stepped into an old legend, straight out of a history book. "*Here* is where they mined the first Cat's Eye?" she repeated.

Burn nodded. "It must be," he said. "I don't know of any other cave by this name."

"My grandmother told me that the mines were destroyed when Aerobourne crashed into the sea," Laina said softly, interrupting the stunned silence. "Once Aerobourne started to fall, the Harpies maneuvered it on top of the Crystal Caves. They wanted to cut off all access to the stones, but it didn't quite work out that way."

Burn nodded. "As I recall, after Aerobourne fell, the humans used the mining caves to dig under the Harpy city of Asterion. They infiltrated from within."

Laina shrugged. "Well, I don't see any cities around here."

"Your grandmother knew an awful lot about the Harpies," Joan interrupted, giving the girl a skeptical look.

Laina blushed and turned her eyes away. "She knew all sorts of stories," she mumbled, perhaps embarrassed. Sora wondered at her response; Laina seemed troubled by the mention of her grandmother. The woman had died when Laina was ten, leaving her orphaned and homeless.

"There's a chance," Burn continued, "that this could be an auxiliary mine, used to gain access to Aerobourne. Perhaps if we follow these caves, we will arrive on the mainland of the Lost Isles."

"That's a very big if," Jacques muttered.

They all stood in silence, absorbing the information. Sora turned back and looked at the cave's entrance. It was pitch black against the afternoon light, the sun hesitating at its mouth, as though frightened of its depths. For a moment, she imagined that this was the empty eye socket of a giant skull, staring blindly out at the world.

Then she breathed a slow sigh of amazement. The original source of the Cat's Eye. She touched the necklace under her shirt, deep in thought, and was surprised to feel a small stirring in response. Suddenly, inexplicably, Sora was convinced that it was true. She felt certain of it. Her necklace had a way of communicating with her mind, sharing its soundless knowledge. *Yes*, she felt. And abruptly she became aware of the age of the stone, how long it must have been part of the world, wedged in some unseen cavern perhaps miles beneath the ocean. *This way.*

"He's right," she said suddenly. The group turned to her. She continued to gaze at the mine shaft, unmoved. "Burn is right. I know it."

"How can you be so certain?" Jacques asked.

"My necklace...." Sora's voice faded. No words could describe the feeling inside her. Suddenly she couldn't look away from the cave entrance, enraptured, spellbound. The great, gaping socket stared directly back at her, an unseen force in the darkness, beckoning silently. *This way.* The wind moaned, riffling through the trees in a sudden gust, as though trying to murmur the words. Her skin tingled. Magnetism.

She had to enter the cave.

"Jacques," Burn said suddenly, interrupting Sora's thoughts. "How are your wings?"

The Dracian frowned, surprised by the change of topic. "Fine," he said, tilting his head to one side.

"What do you think of flying back to the mainland?" Burn asked. "Could you do it?"

Jacques stared at the giant Wolfy. The rest of the crew turned to look at Burn with him, confused. For a moment, it seemed that Jacques would rebuke the idea, a troubled frown coming over his face. Then he brightened a bit and raised one eyebrow. "Actually," he said, "the thought has crossed my mind. I could probably make it. Using magic, of course."

Burn nodded, his eyes darting around the other Dracians. "Perhaps your people can set up a permanent camp in town," he said slowly. "Would you be able to fly back to the mainland and bring another ship to our aid?"

Jacques cocked his head to one side again, rubbing his chin. "I do know someone...." he said slowly.

"At the very least, bring back a ship to rescue your crew. You want to save their lives...right?"

Jacques nodded, though he didn't look convinced. "I will certainly try," he said grimly. "Even if I have to steal a damned boat."

Burn smiled at that. "Good," he said. "After you rescue your crew from this island, you can meet us to the north, where the main island sits. If all goes well, we will need a way to return home."

Sora's eyes widened, realizing Burn's plan. *Good thinking,* she thought in silent approval. It certainly solved one of their problems —getting home after this venture.

Jacques looked uncertain at this. He fidgeted for a moment. His pet crow landed on a nearby tree branch, squawking and fussing, as though echoing his thoughts. "'Tis an awfully long journey," he murmured. "And returning to these isles will be dangerous."

Burn took a step forward. Leaves crunched beneath his boots. His sheer size was intimidating, like a bear looming between the trees. "Aye," he said. "But not as dangerous as the plague that is spreading. We are all doomed if we can't lift this curse." He glared.

Sora shared a glance with Laina. She had never seen Burn look so threatening. Despite his size, he had always seemed a gentle, civilized giant.

Jacques paled for a moment. His eyes went from Burn to Crash, who was also staring with keen intensity. The three men were silent, the tension building amongst them. Then the Dracian put up his hands. A strained grin lit up his face. "Well played, Wolfy," he said. "I'll return for you. On my honor."

"On your life," Burn corrected.

Jacques swallowed, his smile tightening. Then the Dracian stuck out his hand and Burn clamped down on it, a fierce handshake. After a short struggle, Jacques wrenched his hand back.

"Ow," he groaned, flexing his fingers. "You don't have to break them!"

"My apologies," Burn replied, though his tone wasn't very sincere.

Jacques let out a long breath, then gazed up at the sky, as though appealing to a silent god. He turned to his crew. "Hear that, lads? You'll have to set up camp here for a while until I return with a boat."

The Dracians nodded and began to speak quietly amongst themselves. Sora listened to their banter with half an ear. They were deciding how to set up camp amidst the old buildings. There would be fresh water and enough game to live off of. As they spoke, they slowly filed away back down the mining tracks, seeming relieved to be departing from the caves.

"Dracians don't do well underground," Crash said, watching them go. "They are creatures of Wind and Fire. They don't like enclosed spaces."

Sora looked at him, a teasing smile on her lips. "I'm sure you will be perfectly comfortable, then," she said, nudging him with her shoulder. "You seem to like the dark."

Crash didn't respond to her humor. His eyes lingered on the mouth of the cave. "But not Harpies," he murmured.

Sora frowned. She had noticed Crash's dislike for them before. Every time the Harpy race was mentioned, he either grimaced or turned away. She had to wonder at that. A bad experience? Or just prejudice? Then her skin prickled and a wave of excitement passed through her. Harpies. By the end of this journey, she would finally meet the race of Wind and Light. *And to think, only two years ago I thought they were all extinct!*

Finally the Dracians were gone. Jacques went into the bushes to remove his clothes. The crow followed him, hopping from branch to branch, watching with keen interest. There was a shimmer of light between the trees, more forceful than daylight, causing Sora to squint. She could hear the crow cawing and flapping before it took off through the branches, flying swiftly away.

Jacques emerged in his reptilian form, his skin covered in brilliant gold scales, like a thousand small pebbles all knit perfectly together. Sora stared; he looked much different from Joan, when she had transformed underwater. He was taller, more muscular, though he still stood like a man. His wings were a vibrant, rich honey-yellow color, opaque in the sunlight and webbed like a giant bat. His face resembled a human, soft and smooth, the facial skin stretched tightly across his nose, which widened toward the base in a slight muzzle. His ears receded back into a perfectly round skull.

"'Til next we meet," he said, nodding to Burn and Sora. He turned away, his scales shimmering in the sunlight. A powerful gust of wind blew in from the south, and he opened his wings, stretching them to a grand length of almost fifteen feet. With a few quick moves, he leapt off the ground and into the air. The wind seemed to billow beneath him, carrying him upward at an impossible rate. Sora heard a slight jingling in her ears, the subtle ring of sleigh bells. Her Cat's Eye's warning. Magic. Jacques had the particular ability to control the wind, and he was carried above the trees, past the jungle toward the coast. Within minutes, he was gone.

The four travelers stood in front of the cave mouth and looked into its depths. Laina shifted nervously, glancing around with cautious eyes. Sora knew that the young girl was afraid; it was only natural. She wished she could be afraid too. But the Cat's Eye surged as she stared at the tunnel, filling her with strange excitement.

She observed her other two companions. Burn shifted the bag of supplies on his shoulder; he seemed full of trepidation, while Crash was as stoic as ever.

She took a step forward, impatient. *Yes. This way.*

They all started down the tunnel, tense with nerves. No one said a word.

* * *

The caves were dark, and the path steep. The four travelers followed the main mining shaft, ignoring the smaller tunnels that cut into the rock. They were careful not to trip over the tracks. Crash had brought several large branches with him, and he struck stone to flint, lighting a torch. The flame glittered off the side of the walls, catching tiny fragments of quartz and granite. Every now and then, they passed large iron wall sconces, where miners had once burned lanterns or oilcloth.

It was cold underground, and Sora found herself rubbing her arms, staving off the chill. The mouth of the cave became quickly invisible, lost in the earth. She tried not to glance over her shoulder at the darkness behind them. Distant sounds reached her ears: the vague drip of water, the disconcerting scratch of rocks. Pebbles falling. Rodents scurrying away from their torchlight.

After a while, Laina took her hand. The young girl was trembling. Sora wondered if they should have left her with the Dracians; perhaps it would have been a good idea. It hadn't occurred to her at the time; she had been too entranced with the caves. *Too late to send her back now,* she reasoned. They had come this far—she didn't want to turn back.

No one spoke. It was impossible to gauge how much time had passed. After a long while, the slope of the caves evened out, flattening and widening into small chamber-like caverns. The tracks came to an end, giving way to smooth rock. They passed another pile of mining carts in astonishingly good condition, protected from the elements. All were empty.

Crash lit a second torch. The flames revealed high domed ceilings, stretching up into the earth. Lava rock framed the walls, a smooth tan color. Stalagmites clung to the shadows, still dripping with water. The light danced off the irregular surfaces, casting oblong shadows, as though the rock itself was moving.

They passed through countless earthen chambers, strung together like beads on a necklace. Crash took the lead with the torch, following the path that the miners had made. There were still hooks embedded in the rock, places where they had once tied ropes or chains. She wondered how many men had worked these tunnels —how many Harpies had watched over them, overseeing the slaves, carrying whips and clubs, punishing them. How many had died under these conditions? A chill moved through her at the thought. The Harpies were said to be the First Race, the most advanced at the time of the War. And, in her mind, perhaps the most ruthless.

Then, suddenly, Crash came to a stop. Sora almost stumbled into his back.

"What? What is it?" Laina asked nervously.

Crash cursed under his breath. Burn left his place in the rear and edged around them, looking over the assassin's head. He pointed at the far wall. "Is that a door?" he finally asked.

"It looks like one," Crash replied, then continued forward, raising the torch high. Sora craned her neck to see around the two men.

The final cavern was smooth and carved, chiseled out by hand. At its far side was, indeed, a door. A tall, granite double-door with odd carvings and runes etched into its face. Sora and Crash approached it slowly, holding the torch high, examining its surface. She couldn't read the language—perhaps it was the Old Tongue like the template outside. Some of the runes resembled trees or stars, curling upward in a clumsy mosaic. There was an especially large drawing toward the bottom that looked like an animal. She recognized four legs and a long, curved back.

Crash passed the torch to Burn, then turned back to the door. He ran a hand over its surface. It was in perfect condition, untouched by time, as smooth as the day it had been created.

"It's written in the Old Tongue," he murmured.

"What does it say?" Sora asked. At Crash's silence, she turned to look at Burn. "Can you read it?"

The large Wolfy was gazing at the scripture. "Some of it is the Harpy language," he said. "I can't read all of it." He walked to the base of the door and brushed some of the dust from its surface. "*The War is won, and we have sealed this door,*" he murmured. "*Only a bearer can lift the ward.*" He continued to frown, his eyes searching the letters. "Beware the *garrolithe.*"

"*Garrolithe?*" Sora echoed. She turned to look at Burn. "What's that?"

Burn shrugged uncomfortably. "I don't know."

Sora blinked. They stood in silence, staring at the door. No one moved.

"Now what?" Laina finally asked. Her voice echoed around the chamber, small and thin.

"We have to open the door somehow," Sora said. She gnawed her lip in thought, stepping back, gazing up at the giant portal. The doors were almost three times her height. She couldn't imagine opening them by force.

"They must have sealed the Cat's Eye away," Crash spoke. The volume of his voice was unexpected. Sora realized that they had all been whispering, as though they didn't want to be overheard.

She glanced at him. The assassin stared at the letters that Burn had read, a frown on his face. "After the War was won, the stones were too dangerous to keep using, so the humans threw them back into the ocean and sealed off this cave."

"And only a bearer can open the door," Sora murmured. A thought crept through her mind, and the inscription started to make sense. "The ward is magic," she said. "Only a Cat's Eye can dispel it."

The three turned to look at her. Burn stepped away from the door and Laina moved too, staying close to his side. "It could work," the Wolfy said. He nodded to her. "Try it."

Sora grimaced. Anxiety twisted in her stomach, a strange foreboding. She wondered what they would meet on the other side —if the caves had been sealed off for more reasons than just the War. *What is a garrolithe?* She couldn't answer that question. It didn't stop her imagination, though. Was it a spell, a land formation, or a creature...? When she looked at the doors, she suddenly felt as though something stared right back, waiting for her on the other side.

She put her hand against the stone, this time full of purpose. The rock was cool to the touch, grainy, strong. She closed her eyes, reaching inward, summoning her Cat's Eye with her thoughts.

She wasn't sure what to expect, but the reaction happened immediately.

There was a flash.

For a moment her body tensed, her head tilted back—then she was gone, flying through the veins of the earth, seeping into the rock as though part of it. Her senses reached out, probing, hunting, searching for something. Her Cat's Eye seemed to know immediately where they were, what they were doing. It spread outward like a net, feverishly moving through the stone.

Then, suddenly, they made contact. Sora couldn't explain it in any other way. There was the sense of running up against something. She felt jolted, shocked by energy. It moved over her skin, cool and powerful.

Welcome. The voice was not her Cat's Eye, though it spoke in the same way. She felt as though it came from the earth, from something far deeper and older than she could fathom. Her body vibrated with it.

Her hands flew from the doors as though they'd been burned. She felt herself slam back into her body, ripped away from the earth. Sora stumbled backward, shaking, completely unnerved. The voice seemed to linger, warming her like a fire.

Crash caught her arm, keeping her from falling to the ground. Her head swam. She looked around, remembering where she was.

"What happened?" the assassin asked.

"I'm not sure," she muttered dazedly.

"The doors aren't opening!" Laina wailed. "It didn't work!"

Sora stared at the rock without truly seeing it, her body still humming from the strange voice. She waited breathlessly.

Suddenly, a low rumble shook the cavern. It started deep in the ground, working up through their feet, then to the walls. Bits of dust showered them, and Sora hunched forward, expecting the ceiling to collapse at any second. The stone creaked and moaned. The four travelers tensed, each staring upward, bracing themselves for the worst.

Then the doors slowly started to inch open. Finally, after several long moments, they stood ajar. There was just enough room for Burn to fit through comfortably. Sora had a feeling that this was not a coincidence.

White light poured through the opening, momentarily blinding them. Sora squinted against it, raising a hand to shield her face. *What? Light?*

Burn let out a long sigh of relief. "Looks like you did it," he said, his hand touching her arm. "Let's go."

CHAPTER 11

Silas escorted both of them to the basement—or bilge—of the building; a dark, airless underbelly with no windows and hardly any ventilation. Here the sick men were laid out on cots. There was evidence of food trays and water basins. They had been somewhat cared for, but Lori doubted the quality of care in a pirate city.

"We need to move them to a better ventilated area," she said immediately. She sniffed the air, noting the faint, musty scent of mold.

Silas looked doubtful. "The illness will spread to the rest of the ship."

She shook her head. "Not if we're careful. We'll work on them one at a time in an isolated room."

Silas still hesitated. Lori gave him a firm glare. "You asked me to save your men. Are you going to help me or not?"

At that, the captain conceded, spreading his arms in a slight bow. A wry grin quirked his lips. "Of course, madam. Anything to assist a Healer. Do you have any other requests?"

Lori didn't miss his subtle sarcasm. She ignored it. "Have three of your sailors cover their mouths with towels or cloth. They need to lift the first patient upstairs to a room with a large window and sunlight, preferably facing the ocean. And I'll need plenty of herbs —you might want to write this down."

Silas raised an eyebrow. "I have a keen memory," he replied dryly, and waited.

"Alright," Lori continued, walking along a row of cots, noting her patients' symptoms. "I will need elderberry, yarrow, rosemary, licorice root and chamomile, a full ounce each. This will increase their sweating and expel the toxins from the body. And for their fever blisters, I will require lavender, peppermint and lemon, enough to make about four-quarts of paste. Also, a jar of honey and several gallons of fresh drinking water." Her eyes lingered on the men's cracked, blistered lips; the harsh rasp of their breathing. They were terribly dehydrated. "Aloe," she said as an afterthought. "For their flaking skin."

Silas frowned at her. "Rosemary, chamomile, honey and water...." he paused. "I'll be back with a piece of paper."

Lori smiled. "Quick as you can."

Silas grimaced at her, then turned and left, shutting the door firmly behind him.

Ferran laughed softly from his position at the side of the room. "Very bold of you. It looks like Captain Silas doesn't like taking orders," he mentioned. He leaned up against a wall, a toothpick in his mouth, idly gazing at the sick men.

"He's a stubborn one," Lori agreed, preoccupied.

"That was pretty impressive, you know," Ferran said suddenly. He gazed away from her, at the cot immediately to his left.

She glanced up at him, surprised by the compliment. She usually received praise from farmers and merchants, but coming from Ferran, it felt different.

"This disease looks terrible," he continued. "If you weren't here, I would write them off for dead." He met her gaze.

Lori was struck by the irony. "Ferran," she began slowly, "if you weren't here, I'd be useless. All I'm doing is treating their symptoms. To fully recover, they need your Cat's Eye."

He cocked his head to one side, considering her words. "Eh," he finally shrugged. "I suppose you're right. But I stand by what I said."

Lori grinned.

Silas and his men arrived a minute later with cloths tied around their lower faces. Silas brought a sheaf of parchment, a quill and ink. He jotted down her list of ingredients and then quickly left for the kitchens. Meanwhile, the sailors lifted her first patient and carried him out into the hallway. Lori followed after them down the corridor, then up a short flight of stairs to the first floor. They entered a small room at the rear corner of the ship. A large window faced the ocean. She opened it, allowing in the brisk, fresh air.

The sailors laid the man on the bed. Lori had them wash their hands in a basin of warm water, then sent them into the hallway. "We'll need you when we are finished. Don't stray too far," she said. The sailors nodded.

She shut the door firmly, then turned back to their patient, already thinking ahead. "When Sora used her necklace against the illness, she had to place her hand over—"

"I know," Ferran said, gently cutting her off. He was standing next to the bed, looking down at the sick man intently. The only sound in the room was the man's raspy breath. Even at this distance, Lori could hear the fluid in his lungs. He was the worst of the lot, perhaps the first to become ill. Large welts covered his arms and legs. His lips were chapped and blistered, sallow skin and hollow cheeks.

Lori watched Ferran closely. When Sora used her Cat's Eye, she usually closed her eyes, at times placing a hand on the necklace.

Ferran did no such thing. He used the stone much more naturally, passing his cuffed hand over the body. The stone flared up brightly and a red glow spread around his fingers. After a moment, he placed his palm over the man's heart.

Immediately, the sailor jolted upward, going rigid, but Ferran pushed him firmly back down. Lori took a step back despite herself. Tendrils of darkness began seeping from the man's mouth and nose. With a burst of harsh crimson light, the Cat's Eye pulled the ropes of darkness into itself, drawing them from the man's body. It was far less violent than when Sora had done it. In her case, the tendrils had spewed from the farmer's mouth, landing across the room like a pile of rotted worms.

After several minutes, the darkness waned and the sailor's body went limp. Lori heard an audible change in his breathing—it sounded deeper, less constricted.

Ferran stumbled backwards, catching himself on the wall. He winced, holding his wrist as though sprained, his face pale.

Lori rushed to his side, instinctively grabbing his upper arm. "Are you alright?" she asked.

Ferran grimaced and spit out his toothpick. "Bitter," he grunted, and then, "This is not clean magic. It's tainted. I don't know how much the Cat's Eye can take."

Lori kept her hold on his arm, checking his skin, wondering if the plague could infect him while wearing the Cat's Eye. The stone had its limitations, just like the human body. Would the Dark God's power be too strong? She was struck by a terrifying thought—if Ferran became sick, there would be no one to cure him. She gripped his arm a little tighter.

Unexpectedly, Ferran placed a hand over hers. When she met

his eyes, she saw a reassuring smile on his face. "Don't worry about me," he said. "Worry about him." He nodded over his shoulder to the prone figure on the bed.

At that moment, Silas entered. He carried a small crate of supplies and two sailors followed him with a keg of fresh water. They set the keg down in the corner of the room.

Lori stepped away from Ferran quickly, and Silas gave her a curious look, his eyes passing between them. "Am I interrupting something?" he asked wryly. Then he looked at the patient on the bed. A slow smile touched his face. "He already looks much better. Is there anything else that you need?"

Lori nodded. "Just be ready when we call for the next one," she said. "It might be a little while."

"My men will be at your door," he promised. Then Silas deposited his crate on a desk in the corner. He turned and signaled for his men to leave. They walked out the door and shut it behind them.

Lori spent the next hour mixing a powerful herbal tonic that would clear the body of toxins. She treated the sailor on the bed, then she and Ferran administered a sponge bath, applying aloe to his dry, flaky skin. After a half-hour or so, the man opened his glassy eyes and gazed at Lori. She knew the look. He was coming out of his fever.

She finished the man's treatment with a blessing from the Goddess, passing her hand over his forehead, speaking words of power. It was not magic...but she hoped it would protect him, allow him to heal faster.

Finally, they were able to call in the sailors to carry the man away. He would be placed in an isolated room where he could recover in peace.

Lori watched them turn down the hallway out of sight. Then she wiped a tired hand across her brow. Her back was sore from leaning over the bed for so long, and she stretched it out, looking up toward the ceiling. "How many more?" she sighed. It wasn't truly a question.

"Six," Ferran replied, then approached her from across the room. He had a way of strolling rather than walking; shoulders relaxed, hands in his pockets. He paused by her side. "But first, I need to see to you."

Lori looked up at him, curious. "What?" she asked.

"Give me your hand," he explained. "I want to make sure you're not infected."

"Infected?" Lori gave him a searching look, trying to read his eyes. "I don't think you'd say that unless you already knew. Am I?" She glanced down at her hands, inspecting her skin, her exposed arms and elbows. But there was nothing unusual.

Ferran reached out and took her left hand. He smiled at her again, a lazy quirk of his lips. "The Cat's Eye sees it," he said, indicating the wrist cuff.

"Oh." Lori glanced at the stone. It was dormant for the time being; it appeared like nothing more than a deep ruby. A strange thought occurred to her. "Can you...*see* magic? That which is normally hidden to the eye?"

Ferran nodded. "I can smell it, too. In fact, that was the first way I communicated with the stone." His grip tightened on her hand. "Be still, this will only take a moment."

As she watched, the Cat's Eye began to glow gently at his wrist, spreading to his hand. Then Lori felt a strange sensation, like all of the air was being sucked from her lungs. She tried to pull in a breath, but it felt hollow, empty.

Suddenly, her knees buckled. Her muscles lost strength. She collapsed slowly, struggling to draw breath, raising her free hand to her neck. The skin puckered on her arms, a cold chill sweeping through her body. Her instincts told her to struggle, but she forced herself to remain calm, her eyes locked on Ferran's.

Then she saw dark mist slip from her mouth, thin tendrils winding through the air. The Cat's Eye pulled the cloud from her throat and into itself. The stone flared brightly—then released her.

Lori sagged forward. Ferran caught her by the shoulders, holding her up. She struggled to control her legs, but she felt weak and off-balance. Slowly, Ferran lowered her to the floor and sat next to her, supporting her with his shoulder, his hand locked in hers.

"Well?" he asked.

Lori struggled to catch her breath. "Not very pleasant," she replied. She glanced at him, noticing his pale skin and the slight sheen of sweat on his brow. "What about you?"

Ferran winced. "Like drinking cheap rum. Can't get the taste out of my mouth."

Lori nodded, still watching him. She wondered how many men they could heal before Ferran reached his limit. She would keep a careful eye on him. Otherwise he would probably push himself until he collapsed.

"You're worrying about me again," Ferran said, that lazy smile sliding across his face. "Don't worry so much. It's bad for your heart, Healer."

Lori raised an eyebrow. "This, from a shameless drunk?"

Ferran snorted. "I'm not a drunk. Shameless, maybe." Then he stood up, pulling her alongside him. "We should call in the next man. The longer we wait, the more chance of the plague spreading."

Lori nodded. They had wasted enough time. With a slight smile at Ferran, she turned and headed into the hallway.

* * *

Sora had never seen anything like this before in her life. It was magnificent—beautiful—awe-inspiring: The Shining Caverns.

The four of them stepped through the door filled with apprehension. Now they stood in shock. Sora's mouth was slightly open.

"By the gods," she heard Laina murmur next to her.

"I'll second that," came Burn's hoarse whisper.

The cavern around them was nothing like the dark, rocky tunnels from before. It glowed as brightly as daylight. *Sunstone,* Sora thought, remembering the word. She had never seen it before.

The first cave they entered was massive, more than one hundred feet wide. The ground was smooth and shiny. The walls were uneven and lumpy in contrast, but they were pure white, as though made of pristine quartz. Sora saw no evidence of mining carts or tracks. The caves appeared completely untouched.

A slight vibration moved across the walls. The air itself was thick with magic; it made her Cat's Eye shiver with excitement.

"Sunstone," Crash said, affirming her thoughts. His face was pale, drawn, as though he was in pain. Sora raised an eyebrow, watching him curiously. He didn't seem excited about the caves—he looked as if he was sitting too close to a fire. She wasn't sure what to make of that.

"It's beautiful," Laina said softly. Her voice echoed around the cave walls, carrying farther than natural. The stone had a way of stretching noise, tuning it, creating a perfect pitch. A simple word became like music. Sora's ears hummed with the sound.

Home, something whispered inside of her, and she took a deep breath, tasting the air on her tongue.

"Can you feel it?" Burn asked. His blunt voice broke the spell. "I've never seen so much sunstone in my life."

"Amazing," Sora whispered. She felt her Cat's Eye tug at her, encouraging her to walk forward. After a few moments, she realized that her body felt refreshed and rejuvenated. The magic of the caves was overwhelming, a direct source of energy. Indeed, each breath seemed to fill her stomach, stimulate her limbs. She flexed her injured arm, surprised to feel no pain. After a moment, she took off her sling, stretching out her limb. It seemed to be fully healed. *By the North Wind,* she thought. *Incredible!*

She turned to look at her friends, showing them her healed arm. She smiled at their expressions. "We need to go this way," she said. "Trust me." Then she turned back to the tunnel and started boldly forward.

Crash was the first to start following her, and the rest fell in step behind him. They walked in silence for a long way, each lost in wonder. Sora felt as if she was being led somewhere on an invisible chain. She couldn't fight it, and after a while, she didn't really want to. Her Cat's Eye moved inside her eagerly. Anticipation shot through her with each step.

As they passed, the walls captured their reflections like warped mirrors. The roof of the cave, which at first had been almost invisible, slowly lowered until they were walking down a narrow tunnel, like a hall of glass. The ground below them gradually became covered in white sand.

They came to a point where the path split into two tunnels, each veering off in a different direction. Sora turned to the left without even slowing her stride. The rest followed without question. They knew that the necklace was leading her.

Time didn't seem to pass—the light of the caves was unchanging. The travelers continued on, not knowing whether it was night or day, whether one hour had passed, or three. They were fueled by endless energy, bewitched by the white, shining labyrinth.

* * *

Volcrian's head snapped around as a cry echoed from the crow's nest.

"Look there! Up above!"

He squinted against the rain, searching the gray backdrop of the clouds. Finally, his eyes landed on a humanoid shape flying unsteadily through the windy skies. It glinted gold against the overcast sky.

Slowly and thoughtfully, a smile tugged at his lips.

"Cap'n, Cap'n!" one of his lackeys called. "'Tis some sort of demon!"

But not the demon I'm chasing, the mage grinned. Then he glanced at the small, wiry sailor who stood on deck; the man motioned wildly upwards. His shipmates paused, also staring.

"'Tis unnatural," one murmured.

"A sign from the Goddess," another said shrewdly. "These are bad waters."

"Aye," a third agreed.

"Magnificent, isn't it?" Volcrian said loudly, striding before his crew. The last thing he needed was a mutiny fueled by superstition. "A rare sight, indeed. 'Tis only a golden eagle flying overhead."

The first sailor looked at him suspiciously. He was a short, skinny man, perhaps underfed since a very young age.

"Doesn't look like a golden eagle," the man muttered.

Volcrian waved an idle had. "'Tis the sun playing tricks on your eyes," he said. "Why don't you break out a new flask of rum? Share it with the men? It's been a long voyage and you all deserve a break."

The men grinned at this, lopsided looks that would frighten their own mothers. They lumbered off across the deck, shouting to the rest of the crew, heading below to the bunks. Only a scattered few remained on-deck to tend the sails.

Volcrian turned back to the sea. His eyes narrowed, following the Dracian's form across the sky. He hadn't seen a fully transformed Dracian in quite some time. He wondered where the fellow was going to, and whether it had anything to do with his prey.

There was no chance of pursuing the lone traveler. It would take far too long to turn the boat around. Even as he watched, the winds picked up and the Dracian was carried into the clouds, lost from sight.

He leaned against the railing of the ship, looking down at the fierce water. The scent of magic was strong over the waves. It crawled across his skin: the vague tint of iron and a rare sweetness, like rust. His Wolfy senses were keen enough to pick it up.

The spells were old, tied to the waves below and the clouds above. Immense power saturated the skies, turning them dark and turbulent. These were war spells, cast during a time when nature had been irrelevant, when the Races had viciously tried to stamp each other out.

"We are halfway to the Isles," a voice reached him.

He turned slightly. The priestess stood about two yards away, smothered in her large cloak. She approached the railing and leaned against it in an identical fashion. "Our compasses are beginning to fail."

"You must guide the ship," Volcrian said. He wasn't worried. She wasn't a normal human anymore—not even a spirit, but something of his own creation. And as a vessel of magic, she had many uses.

"The dead can only do so much," the priestess said tiredly.

"More than you think," Volcrian murmured, momentarily lost in thought. Humans lived in a shell, ignorant to the ways of the afterlife. But the dead were far from asleep. No, they were sensitive to the balance in the world; they became part of it, ingrained in its threads, connected to a great energy that held all things together.

"Why do you follow them so?" the priestess asked.

Volcrian turned his icy gaze upon her. "What?"

"The assassin, the girl with the Cat's Eye—why do you care? Wouldn't you rather have peace?"

Volcrian glared at her, his anger bubbling to the surface. "My brother does not have peace," he growled. "And so I will not rest."

The priestess studied him with glazed eyes. The wind swept past her, blowing back her hood, carrying away strands of fine white hair. Her skin was the same lavender-gray as the clouds. In that moment, it seemed like a light glowed within her, something unseen by the physical eye. She quickly pulled her hood back over her head.

Volcrian eyed her in distaste. "You challenge me because you want me to release you," he said angrily. "You think you will be free after your body has perished. But the underworld has its own laws, my love. Your spirit will still be bound to me."

"The Goddess will come for me," the priestess said, raising her head a notch, a stubborn tilt to her chin.

Volcrian grinned viciously. "And what of *my* Goddess? The Lady of the Oceans?" he replied. "You think She won't claim you as Her own? You are tied to me, darling. Physically and spiritually."

The priestess shook her head stiffly. "Your blood stains me, but blood can be washed out."

"By what? Your purity?" Volcrian sneered. He turned back to the waves—they reflected the turmoil inside of him, the rage that yearned for release. "Stupid," he muttered. "Still clinging to your life, even as your hands decay in front of you. Your story is over, child. Accept it. You are my slave."

The corpse-woman was silent. She gazed out over the waves. He didn't care to watch her face. Her expressions were cold and numb, spread across stiff muscles.

"Your anger has cursed the world," the priestess said bitterly, quietly. "Your rage is killing everything. Can you not see that? It no longer glorifies your brother. Darker powers are at work."

"I don't care," Volcrian said bluntly. He felt an odd buzzing at the back of his mind, some residue of truth, but he shook it away. Perhaps his magic had changed him, created him into something new. But he welcomed it. He never wanted to feel powerless again.

He would kill the assassin, and then...then he didn't care what happened. Perhaps he would die as well, perhaps he would live on. But it didn't matter. He couldn't have peace until the killer was laid to rest.

"You are evil," the priestess said quietly.

"And you are a nuisance!" Volcrian snapped. "Go and consult with the other ghosts. I know you can see them. Find one to lead our ship through this storm."

The priestess stared at him blankly.

"Now!" Volcrian growled.

Her body shuddered and obeyed, turning toward the captain's cabin. Volcrian watched her wander away, her steps bent and uneven, as though one leg were shorter than the other. He glared at her back. She had no choice but to obey his orders, whether she willed to or not. He didn't like the fact that she remembered so much of her past life. Something had to have gone wrong with the spell. *Or the Goddess is protecting her,* his thoughts whispered, but he dismissed the idea. The Wind Goddess didn't care about Her creations. She was as distant as the wind and just as weak. If She had any power over the natural world, then She would have averted Etienne's death—saved him. But She hadn't. And now Volcrian knew that She couldn't.

He turned back to the ocean, closing his eyes, inhaling deeply. The saltwater almost smelled like blood. *Soon.* Soon he would have his prey trapped on a minuscule island...then there would be no escape.

CHAPTER 12

Lori left the sickroom with Ferran in tow. It was late morning aboard the *Aurora*. Five days had passed and they had barely slept during that time. Ferran had rested most of the previous night, recovering from his use of the Cat's Eye, while Lori watched over her patients. Thanks to her persistent care, the sailors appeared to be making a full recovery. Their appetites were returning and one had even climbed to his feet last night, demanding a trip to the gambling hall.

A few more days of food and rest and they should be fine, she thought.

Two sailors waited for them out in the hallway, each holding a rag over their mouths, reluctant to catch the disease. Lori smiled at them wearily. "No need for that now," she said. "They're all cured."

The men nodded and lowered their rags. "For how long?" one asked.

Lori paused; she hadn't given that possibility much thought. She frowned. "Until they contract it again, I suppose," she said. It dampened her spirits considerably. No matter how many Cat's-Eye stones they had, the plague would remain in the land, lingering in the soil, rotting the fields. They couldn't stop it like this—only delay it for a while.

"Where is Silas?" she asked. She was tired to the bone, but thoughts of *The Book of the Named* and the Sixth Race were circling her mind. "I want to speak with him."

The sailor nodded. "This way."

He split away from his companion and led her down a narrow hallway. Lori tried to keep up, forcing herself to find the energy. Ferran followed slowly behind, quieter than usual, one hand held to his stomach. Despite his night's rest, he still had dark circles under his eyes.

The sailor led them toward the stern of the ship. They walked for several minutes, turning down hallways and up small flights of stairs. Despite the thick wooden walls, she could still hear sounds from the great kitchens below, the smell of food wafting up through the floorboards, the occasional clash of plates, the shout of an angry cook, a furious quarrel of voices, and then laughter.

The sailor took them up to the very top of the ship. They opened a latch in the roof and climbed on top of the *Aurora*. Lori was struck by fresh air, brisk and salty, carrying the scent of the ocean. She paused at the top of the ladder and pulled in several deep breaths, feeling rejuvenated. The sunlight warmed her skin. She climbed the last few rungs and looked around. From this view, she felt like she was truly on a pirate ship. The top deck still carried mariner paraphernalia—lifebuoys, metal cleats, giant capstans used for reeling ropes, three masts, and even a crow's nest. From this perspective, the boat looked like it was ready to launch, leave port and take to the ocean. But of course, that was impossible.

At the very rear of the ship, a few steps led down to an ornately carved door with a large brass handle. She guessed these quarters belonged to Silas.

The sailor opened the door and gestured for them to enter the hallway. Lori's foot landed on a thick, hand-woven rug of dark green wool. A yellow and red pattern crisscrossed the weave, forward and back on itself like tangled vines.

Down the short hallway, they entered a large cabin that spanned the entire width of the *Aurora*. The rug ended, giving way to shining wooden floors of deep mahogany. The spacious room was bedecked with oil paintings and tapestries, gleaming hardwood furniture and stuffed armchairs. The artwork looked expensive and rare. *Probably stolen,* she thought wryly.

A giant desk stood in front of her, complete with quill and parchment, large wax candles and various compasses and protractors. Behind the desk was a series of long windows looking out over the city of Sonora. She gazed through them now, drawn to the sunlight. She could see the misshapen roofs stretching out before her, converted ships and wooden buildings, winding streets and a myriad of chimneys and flagstaffs. Bright blue water stretched into the distance, covered by a thin sheen of mist, slowly evaporating in the mid-morning light.

The city was curved into a horseshoe shape to match the natural formation of Rascal Bay, perfectly scooped from the cliffs. Lori's eyes followed the coastline, dipping inward and then out again. The *Aurora* was positioned at the very north end, built lengthwise, its bow facing the ocean while the aft faced the city. From this point, the buildings at the opposite end of the bay appeared like gray smudges, barely discernible from each other.

The sailor joined her at the window and undid the latch, opening it onto a balcony that bordered the entire rear of the ship, perhaps sixty feet across. A series of potted plants lined the railing, overgrown with vines of small purple flowers. The sea breeze was cool and refreshing, counteracting the heat from the sun.

A table and chairs stood at the corner of the balcony, the side closest to the ocean. She turned, noting the breakfast dishes: two covered plates and a steaming pot of tea.

Captain Silas sat in a large, comfortable-looking chair, his legs kicked up on the railing of the ship. On this morning, he wore a sleek shirt of canary yellow silk. Large brass buttons lined the front of the shirt, open halfway down his chest. He wore bright blue trousers buttoned at the calves, tall white stockings and buckled shoes. His red hair hung loosely around his shoulders, bright copper in the sunlight. Lori thought he looked more like a dandy than a pirate.

"Join me for breakfast?" he said, motioning to the two chairs opposite him. It wasn't truly a request, but Lori was not of a mind to refuse. She sat down immediately and uncovered a plate of bacon, eggs and beans. Ferran sat down a second later. They dug in with gusto.

Silas waited for them to finish eating while he sipped his tea. He commented on the weather, making small talk, though Lori's mouth was too full to really respond. Finally she sat back with a sigh, pushing the plate away.

"I assume you enjoyed the fare?" Silas asked, glancing back and forth between her and Ferran. Ferran took the remaining bacon from her plate and wolfed it down.

"It was very good," Lori conceded.

Ferran spoke around his mouthful of bacon. "New cook I take it?" he asked. "The last time we sailed, I found rat pellets in my oatmeal."

"Raisins," Silas corrected, his eyes narrowed. "Except for that one time on the Glass Coast, when we were low on rations."

Ferran winced, pushing away his empty plate. "It left an

impression," he replied.

Silas grinned at this, though it didn't quite reach his eyes.

Lori frowned. She hadn't realized the two had traveled together. *But of course they would,* she admonished. A collector and a treasure hunter would make fast friends. *Fast and fleeting,* she guessed. They certainly weren't very chummy now.

It suddenly made sense how he knew Ferran's last name. She winced at that. *Ebonaire.* She had meant to ask Ferran about that already—but there had been men to heal, and now was not the right time either.

"So to business," Lori said, decidedly changing the topic. "How do we retrieve the book?"

Silas gave her a broad smile. "Why, we go to the City of Crowns, of course."

"Of course," she echoed, her thoughts already moving ahead. She was filled with a keen frustration—she *had* to get the book for Sora, no matter what. But the City of Crowns was a vast metropolis, home to over a hundred thousand people. Where to begin?

She glanced at Ferran, who was watching Silas with a slight scowl. "It won't be easy," the treasure hunter said. "There are hundreds of nobility who could have hired those assassins to retrieve the book."

"Assuming it was the nobility," Lori pointed out. The men gave her a curious look, and she continued. "Perhaps the assassins were working on their own. And there's no guarantee that the book is still in the city. That's where the portal led to, but they could have moved on."

"We'll have to go there anyway to track it down," Silas said.

There was a beat of silence. "You're traveling with us?" Lori asked.

"Aye," Silas said. "To retrieve my book. I only intended to let you borrow it. And now that I know someone else is interested...I want it back."

"You want it...." Lori's voice trailed off. Her thoughts moved quickly, dissecting the situation. They had to travel to the City of Crowns—a journey she did not relish. And now they would have a third party in tow. Silas must not realize that they needed the book to reseal the Dark God. Their journey wouldn't end in Crowns, whether or not he was with them.

She considered mentioning it, but decided not to. They would deal with Silas when the time came.

"We need to consult our captive, find out where the book was taken," Ferran said. He glanced at Silas. "He has returned to consciousness, I'm assuming?"

Silas waved a hand through the air, as though swatting away a fly. "We've already looked into it," he said. "My men and I did the job. I didn't think a Healer would approve of our methods." He gave Lori a pointed look.

She raised an eyebrow. "You mean torture?" she asked bluntly.

Silas nodded.

Lori felt a surge of discomfort. No, as a Healer she could not condone torture. Not only was it cruel and barbaric, but prisoners often said all manner of things that weren't true—anything to make the torture stop.

"What did he say?" she asked stiffly.

Silas shrugged and took another sip of tea. "Nothing, really. You know how the Sixth Race are. They're trained to endure pain. He was hiding something, but wouldn't let the words pass his lips.

Just kept moaning on and on about the Dark God's wrath. He said that he didn't care if we killed him, because 'it's all going to end soon anyway.'" Silas glanced at Ferran, a mischievous glint in his eye. "Sounds like every fanatic I've ever known."

Ferran nodded but didn't return the smile. He appeared thoughtful. "Did he mean the Kingdom was coming to an end? Or the King's reign? Much of the nobility would like to see a regime change."

Silas nodded. "A political coup, perhaps."

Lori frowned. "Did he mention the plague? What did he say exactly?"

"Specifically, he said that the Dark God is rising and that humanity will be put in their place." The Dracian shrugged uncomfortably. "Then he just repeated it over and over."

"Nothing else? He didn't use any other words?" Lori prompted. She let out a short breath. "It doesn't sound like the nobility are behind this. The weapons of the Dark God wouldn't be any help to political radicals. Even if they summon the god, His power won't be easily controlled." She paused in thought. "The plague will continue to infect the Kingdom. What if the Sixth Race wants it to?"

"But who's to say that they won't become infected as well?" Silas asked skeptically. "Seems a bit risky, don't you think?"

Lori shook her head. "Maybe not," she said. A terrible sense of foreboding settled in her gut. Maybe the Sixth Race were immune to the plague. She had more questions—ones that Silas couldn't answer. "Can I speak to the prisoner?"

The pirate captain looked away, out over the city. "No," he said.

"What? Why not?"

"Because he's dead." Silas muttered.

Lori sat forward. "You killed him? But why?"

"He took his own life," Silas said sharply. He shook his head, his eyes wandering back to the coast. "Bit off his tongue and choked on it."

They sat in silence for a moment.

"Well," Ferran finally grunted. "That's one less assassin to worry about."

Lori glared at Silas. "You should have let me see him first! I can brew a tonic to loosen the tongue. He didn't have to die." She felt sick. The boy couldn't have been older than sixteen. The Sixth Race were peculiar, secretive and complicated, but that didn't make them evil. Well, not completely. It was disturbing to think that the boy would kill himself in such a brutal—and desperate—manner. He had been less afraid of death than of telling his secrets. *And now none of our questions will be answered!*

Silas shrugged uselessly. "What's done is done," he said. "Though had I known...."

"Well, now you do," she cut him off. "I should have left him in more capable hands." If she had known Silas would torture the boy, she would have intervened. Her vow as a Healer was to serve all races. *To aid all of the Wind's creations, to mourn their dead, to grieve with their families, to heal the sick, nurture the spirit and strengthen the mind. By the light of the East Wind, we are renewed.* She had failed to protect the boy. She should have known better.

Silas cleared his throat, then looked away.

"We need to make haste to the City of Crowns," Ferran interjected. "It's the only thing we can do now."

Lori grimaced at his words. She had lived in that city once. She had left in quite a hurry. The thought of going back was less than appealing.

"Shall we take your ship?" Ferran asked. "The *Starhound*, isn't it?"

"'Tis the *Dawn Seeker* now," Silas replied. "*Starhound* ran aground two years ago. Got me a new schooner, light in the water, fast in the shallows." He grinned. "I've already ordered my crew to make preparations. It will be a month's journey, maybe shorter if we take advantage of the rainy season. We'll take the Little Rain River, a tributary that joins the Crown's Rush at the base of the mountains. After that, we should make good time going with the current."

"The Little Rain?" Lori said curiously. "Will it be deep enough for a seafaring vessel?"

She waited for Silas' response, but the man wasn't looking at her. His eyes were suddenly transfixed over her shoulder. The ghost of a frown settled on his face.

Lori glanced behind her, unnerved. She blinked. A large black crow sat on the railing of the balcony, staring at them with a dark, round eye. It flapped its wings, squawked, then hopped back and forth in one leg. In its claw, it held a shiny brass button.

Lori considered the large button. It could have been from a jacket or boot. Numerous crows, seagulls and other birds occupied the city, flitting through the trees or soaring over the bay. But usually only tame crows collected shiny objects. She turned back to Silas questioningly.

Abruptly the pirate captain stood up from the table. He was still staring at the crow. "Excuse me," he said, then turned and dodged around his chair, walking hurriedly to the window, unlatching it and entering his quarters. As soon as he entered his room, Lori saw him bolt for the door.

Lori and Ferran exchanged a bewildered glance. They stood up and dashed after him, piling through the window and sprinting through the captain's quarters.

Silas ran across the deck and dove through the hatch in the ceiling, not bothering with the ladder. Lori and Ferran stumbled after him, trying to enter the hatch at the same time. Once they reached the hallway, Silas had already opened a second door to a long staircase and was jumping down it, taking three steps at a time.

They flew down the stairs after him. "Silas!" Lori called. "Where are you going?" But the captain didn't answer, only doubled his pace, reaching the ground floor. He opened a small utility door that spilled into a narrow, shaded alley. The street was paved with sandstone, surprisingly clean. Several clotheslines were strung between the buildings.

The crow soared by overhead. Silas continued to run down the alley to the main street. Ferran and Lori hurled after him, dodging around trash bins and into the crowded thoroughfare. The pirate captain turned toward the docks, following the crow to the waterfront. They passed by dozens of people.

As they neared the docks, Lori noticed the crowd growing larger and larger. Sailors, vendors, and residents alike were shouting animatedly amongst each other, pointing toward the sky, then to the bay. Some looked angry or frightened.

Finally, they reached the source of the excitement. Silas shoved through the clustered people and entered an empty space on the docks. The citizens of Sonora hung back, staring and pointing. Lori paused to catch her breath. She glanced around in confusion.

A red-haired man sat on the docks, leaning against a tall wooden post. He had a blanket wrapped around him and Lori suspected that he was naked beneath it. He appeared pale and shaken, drenched with sweat, his eyes closed in weariness. The crowd gave him a wide berth, mingling a few yards away.

"He fell from the sky!" one said, speaking to his companion. "Straight from the clouds!"

"He had wings," another said. "Did you see him? He was flying!"

"Gold wings!"

"Aye, I saw them too!"

"Toss him to the ocean!" a woman yelled. "He's bad luck!"

"Aye," another agreed. "He'll scare the fish out of the cove!"

Silas paused by the man's side. He reached out his hand slowly, hovering above the man's head, hesitating. Then he turned back to the crowd and waved his arms. "Get back, the drunken lot of you!" he yelled. Lori saw instant recognition pass through the gathering. A few had already detached and were walking up the street, away from the scene.

"Captain Silas," a short, scrawny pirate said. "Cap'n, the man fell from the sky...."

"And your breath stinks of ale," Silas growled. "Get back to whatever grimy tavern you crawled from, and tell the rest of these superstitious fools to do the same. That's an order!"

Lori noted the tattoo on the man's neck—one of Silas' crew. The sailor shifted, then turned to his mates. They grumbled amongst themselves but did as they were told, raising their voices to move people along. Eventually the crowd dispersed, the last stragglers casting suspicious glances over their shoulders.

"Help me carry him," Silas said to Ferran, his voice harsh and commanding. Ferran jumped to his side without question, lifting the naked man to his feet, pinching the blanket closed at his waist. One on each side, the two carried the half-conscious man back toward the *Aurora*. Lori followed behind them, frowning. He appeared to be a Dracian, like Silas. Beyond that, she couldn't tell if they were related by blood or were just friends. Curiosity burned inside of her. What was going on?

They entered through the front of the building. It was quiet at this time of day. Silas turned down a long hallway, signaling to one of his crew members. "Draw a bath in the master suite on the bottom floor," he said. "Bring a change of clothes from my cabin...and throw a few scraps to that crow on the balcony...."

By the time they reached the master suite, the two men were red-faced from exertion. The blanket-clad man had passed out; Lori could tell by his lulling head. They laid him down on a wide, soft bed. She worried her lower lip, taking stock of his symptoms. He didn't appear injured—only exhausted.

The large suite was decorated in canary-yellow wallpaper. A master bed covered in thick furs and large pillows was located in the center of the room. Several windows looked out onto the bay. There was a liquor cabinet, a dresser, a wardrobe, and a large bathtub with pipes attached. Lori was impressed. She had only heard of running water in a few major port cities—and the King's city, of course.

"Well?" Silas said, turning to look at her. "Is he injured? Sick?"

"Exhausted and malnourished would be my guess," she said, noting the dark circles under his eyes. Besides the pale skin, he appeared to be a healthy man in his prime. His muscles were strong and defined, well-shaped. There were a few bruises on his arms and legs, but they looked old, having turned slightly green in color. She lifted the man's wrist, checking his pulse, which was steady from sleep. "Get some water into him, and make sure he eats when he wakes up." She checked his lungs and his forehead, but he didn't have a fever. "Other than that, he should be alright. Let him sleep it off."

Silas still looked worried and hovered next to the bed. "I will stay with him until he wakes up," he said. "Can you check back in the morning? Then we will finish our conversation."

Lori wanted to refuse at first—it was urgent that they leave to the City of Crowns as soon as possible. But Silas appeared distraught, and she finally nodded. She wondered again who this man was. It was terribly risky for a Dracian to show his true form in front of humans; most didn't think the races existed anymore. Sailors were especially superstitious—it was a wonder that they hadn't stoned him from the docks.

The pirate captain stood at the foot of the bed, watching the man's face.

"Come on, Lori," Ferran said. He offered her his arm, giving her a slight smile.

She placed her arm in Ferran's and they walked out of the room, his pace casual and unhurried. As the excitement waned, she felt exhaustion slip over her; it had been too long since her last full night's rest. It would be wise to find a bed and lie down. She wouldn't be much use to anyone if she couldn't stand on her own two feet.

She glanced up at Ferran, watching his own tired face. She leaned into him slightly. "A soft bed sounds good about now," she murmured.

"I agree," he said.

"Any idea who that was?"

"No," he said thoughtfully. "But we'll find out soon enough."

CHAPTER 13

Deep in the Crystal Caves, a change occurred in the path. It narrowed and lowered until Burn had to hunch his shoulders, ducking his head around jutting rocks. He brought up the rear, behind Sora and Laina, with Crash in the lead.

Finally, the tunnel narrowed so much that they would have to crawl to continue forward. The walls glowed with steady white light, fully illuminating the path ahead. Sora wasn't particularly worried; she could see clearly in front of her and the caves were silent, absent of life. She hadn't seen a single living thing since entering—not even moss or fungus.

Then Crash held up a hand. "This could lead to a dead end," he said. "We shouldn't all enter at once." He turned to look at Sora. "You're certain that this is the correct path?"

She nodded. For a long while she had felt dazed, overwhelmed by magic and light. She looked at the thin tunnel before them: a long white hole. Burn would be hard-pressed to squeeze through on his hands and knees. She couldn't see where it ended; the path curved to the right, continuing out of sight.

She frowned and touched her Cat's Eye, uncertain. If they turned back now, who knew how many hours they would spend backtracking through the caves, seeking another route. *This way?* she asked silently. The Cat's Eye's presence was easily accessible in her mind, far more than before, amplified by the sunstone's energy. Immediately, she heard it answer: *Yes.* It rang through her thoughts like the chime of a bell.

"Yes," she echoed, answering Crash's question. "We have to follow the tunnel."

He gazed at her for another long moment, then nodded, turning back to the hole. "All right," he said. "I'll go first. Wait until I call for you from the other side." Then he knelt down on his hands and knees and started forward. He moved cautiously and avoided touching the sunstone as much as he could. He seemed especially sensitive to its light.

Sora glanced at Laina. The girl stood next to the cave wall, her hand slightly raised, hovering over its gleaming surface. The brightness of the rock illuminated her skin, causing her pale cheeks to glow, as though a hidden light had ignited inside of her. Sora frowned, staring at the young thief. Her eyes had turned from soft gray to lavender, an unusually vibrant color.

"Amazing, isn't it?" Sora asked, stepping up behind her.

Laina started and turned, as though shaken from a trance. She gave Sora a large, wan smile. "I can hear it humming," she whispered.

"Humming?" Sora asked.

"Yes...." Laina looked distant again, distracted. "In my bones. Like music."

Sora frowned, looking over Laina again. She wasn't sure what to make of that. She felt the power of the caves as well, but through her Cat's Eye, her mind. Not her body. And music? She listened, but there was only the very slight vibration of the rocks. Certainly nothing melodious.

"Sora!" Crash's voice reached her, echoing down the narrow tunnel. "It opens up. Come through!"

She turned back toward the hole, eyeing its width and height. She still worried that Burn might not be able to fit, but they had no other choice. This was the only way.

Getting down on her hands and knees, Sora started through the strip of rock, carefully edging her way forward. More than once her clothes snagged on the ceiling, and at one point she had to slither on her belly. The tunnel made a slight turn to the right, then continued a short ways before opening up at the other end. Crash's hand appeared at the mouth of the tunnel, assisting her to her feet.

She stood up and dusted herself off, the white sand clinging to her clothes in a fine powder. When she looked up, her eyes widened.

A sheer cliff dropped off at her feet. The ledge she stood on was only about two yards wide; she edged toward the side, glancing down. The cliff seemed to stretch into oblivion, an endless drop of pure white stone. The light was too intense, obscuring the bottom. She couldn't imagine how deep it was. She felt infinitesimally small in comparison—minuscule, irrelevant.

Then she gazed upward and her mouth dropped open. The crevice reached far above her, jagged white walls of towering stone, far higher than the tallest of buildings. In the vague distance, she saw the glint of massive stalactites. They appeared like shining white fangs, the great teeth of the earth.

Directly in front of her, a narrow bridge of rock spanned the chasm. The tunnel continued on its opposite side, turning out of sight. She stared. If they were to continue forward, they would have to cross over it.

Suddenly, a harsh wind blew past them, so powerful that Sora had to brace her feet against it. She put one hand to the wall, waiting for the fierce gale to pass, wondering at its source. *We're underground, aren't we?* She squinted up the ravine. It didn't feel like a natural draft, but like a large vibration passing through the rocks, building and building as it rolled through the caves. Finally, after a long minute, the wind died down and the air became calm again.

She let out a small sound of discomfort. The vibration had a way of lingering in her body, making her skin tingle. Her eyes returned to the narrow rock bridge and she could imagine centuries of wind wearing through the stone, until only this small strip remained.

Laina exited the hole behind her, then Burn, who had a few more snags in his clothes. Two scrapes showed on his back where he had forced himself through the rocks. The four travelers stared at the ravine, speechless, each assessing the path forward.

"Is it too late to turn back?" Laina asked in a small voice.

Sora grimaced. She had been thinking much the same.

"We're not actually going to cross that?" Laina continued. "It's impossible. We'll fly right off!"

"If we stay close to the ground and grip the rock, we should be able to make it," Burn's voice rumbled. "We don't have much of a choice, do we?" He turned to look at Sora, raising an eyebrow, and she realized that he intended the question for her. "Do we?" he asked again.

She touched her Cat's Eye and shook her head. "No," she said quietly. "This is the way."

They fell into an uneasy silence again. Sora took a deep breath to steady her nerves. The drop was far enough to make her head spin. Burn leaned over the edge of the cliff and her heart gave a thud of alarm, certain that he would fall. But the giant Wolfy remained unmoving as he gauged the distance. Then he glanced across the rock bridge to the tunnel on the other side.

Finally he turned around with a wide grin. "So, who's first?"

"This is madness," Laina muttered.

"No volunteers?" the Wolfy continued, unperturbed. "Great. Then I'll go."

Sora stared at him, surprised. "No!" she burst out.

Burn looked at her solemnly. He seemed resolved. "If the bridge can hold my weight, then it will hold all of us."

"No," Sora repeated. She shook her head. "I can't let you do that. If the bridge collapses, then we're all stranded on this side and you'll be dead." Her eyes focused past him on the windy ravine. "I'll go first."

"No," Crash interrupted her. "We need your Cat's Eye. I'll go."

Sora opened her mouth, wanting to argue, but his tone carried a certain finality; there was a heaviness to his words. He was staring at the bridge, his eyes narrow and calculating. Then he turned to face them. His confidence was palpable. "I can make it across."

"You're sure?" Sora asked.

He nodded wordlessly. Then, before anyone else could speak up, he approached the bridge. He knelt before crossing it, pressing his body against the rock, as sheltered from the wind as possible. He gripped the bridge with his hands, digging his fingers into small nooks and crannies.

The wind had carved the rock into a smooth surface, like rounded marble. It would be a challenge to find any handholds. After a moment, Crash slipped a knife from his boot and wedged it into the rock, giving his fingers a place to hold. He drew another knife with his right hand and did the same thing.

He made his way forward in this fashion, foot by foot, gripping with his knees and digging his knives into each side of the rock, slowly chiseling out handholds. A smart tactic, Sora realized. They would all be able to use them. Still, watching the wind whip over his back, blowing his hair wildly—she grew worried. Her heart lodged in her throat. One wrong move and he would plummet to his death.

Sora clenched her fists to stop them from shaking. *Stop worrying,* she told herself firmly. If anyone could cross, it was Crash. Still, she couldn't tame her imagination—the vision of him being torn from the surface of the bridge, the wind sweeping him into the ravine.

Finally, he reached the opposite side. Crash stood up, sheltered by the stone ridge of the second tunnel.

"Sora!" he called. "You're next!"

She gulped visibly. The last time she had crossed a rickety bridge, it had collapsed beneath her. That had been two years ago while crossing the Crown's Rush before entering Fennbog swamp. It seemed like a lifetime ago, yet the memory was still fresh and intimate. It was not an experience she wanted to relive—and this crossing was far more treacherous.

"Okay," she said, more to herself than her companions. She glanced at Laina. The girl stared at her with large lavender eyes, glistening with unshed tears. Sora had to look away. The girl's expression only made her more frightened.

Burn rested a hand on her shoulder. "I can go," he offered.

"No," Sora repeated, shaking her head firmly. "No...I can do this." She checked her staff and daggers, ensuring that the weapons were strapped firmly to her body and wouldn't fall. Then she crouched by the edge of the bridge, determined to cross before she could have any second thoughts. She inched her way forward, gripping with her knees as she had seen Crash do. Her fingers found the small creases in the rock, indents from his knives. The wind was fierce over the ravine, pressing her flat to the stone. She gritted her teeth in concentration. *Don't look down,* she told herself, and kept her eyes trained on the rock beneath her. *Don't look down!*

Once she was in the middle of the bridge, Sora felt the Cat's Eye stir in the back of her mind. She paused, unsure of what it meant, waiting breathlessly for the feeling to pass.

Then, as though rising from the very rock itself, a long, moaning howl carried through the ravine. It was purely animal— something between a wolf and a mountain lion—fierce and primal, impossibly loud.

Sora's entire body jolted. All of the hairs on her arms and neck stood on end. Without intending to, she looked down.

Her head spun at the drop. Sickening fear lurched through her, making her arms weak and her body quake. Then, at that moment, another gale-force wind blasted down the ravine. The rock vibrated beneath her hands, shaking her grip loose. She felt her body slide sideways.

Sora screamed. Someone shouted her name, but she was too panicked to know who. The gale plucked her easily from the rock bridge, like a hawk grabbing a mouse. She scrabbled for a hold, but her hands were useless against the smooth stone. With a shriek of pure terror, she was swept into the air—into empty space.

Her heart stopped.

She plummeted downward. The scream was ripped from her mouth, stolen by the wind. She clamped her eyes shut as the bridge flew away from her, her body as heavy and solid as stone. Her stomach went up to her throat, past that, to her head. She was diving, consumed by vertigo, spinning, her arms flailing, reaching instinctively for a handhold—there was only emptiness.

Her mind raced in panic, consumed by pure instinct, overriding all coherent thought.

Then something grabbed her from behind.

* * *

Krait lingered in the sitting room of a large stone house. Outside, rain lashed down on the flagstone streets. It was mid-afternoon, but felt more like late evening. Everything was cold, wet and subdued.

A week had passed since her narrow escape with *The Book of the Named*. She had expected Cerastes to meet her on the other side of the portal, but had arrived at an old tavern on Tourmaline Street. The heavy smell of the Crown's Rush was easily recognizable through the windows. In the City of Crowns, everything found its way into the Rush: heirlooms, old furniture, human waste and—at times—dead bodies.

A letter had been delivered to her room upon her arrival, telling her that Cerastes would summon her. That summons had arrived just two hours ago, while she sat in the tavern proper, listening to an old minstrel play. One minute, she had looked out the window. The next, a note had been slipped under her drink. One of the Named, she suspected, though she hadn't seen any of her brethren in the tavern.

She followed the letter's instructions, traveling down Tourmaline Street to a series of alleys that eventually led into the sewers. Small tunnels wove through the City of Crowns, ancient dungeons long since flooded by the Rush. She traveled to the center of the city, bypassing slums and heavily populated streets. Then she found her way under the great barrier wall into the Regency, a private sector of the city, exclusively home to the First and Second Tier.

When she climbed to the surface again, she found herself on a manicured street of large, gated houses, immaculate lawns and decadent statues.

Cerastes had given her an address. When she approached the large stone house, an old man opened the door. Without a word, he escorted her into a small sitting room and left her there, locking the door behind him.

The chamber was small and circular, with no windows and a single oak door. A large flagstone fireplace stood in front of her, an ornate golden clock upon its mantle. Two easy-chairs sat in front of the fireplace and a thick red rug spread across the floor. A small feast had been set on a large, polished table; she ate a roll of bread and cheese while she waited.

She wasn't sure if this was Cerastes' house; she could only assume that the Grandmaster would come for her here. In the meantime, she wondered why they weren't in the Hive. Why the City of Crowns? She watched the minute hand on the clock move in a slow circle. Its quiet ticking was the only sound to reach her ears. Eventually, she sat in one of the chairs, trying to relax. Her hand traveled to the book shoved in her belt.

Her mind strayed back to the *Aurora*. She dwelled on the memory of the pirate's stash—an entire room full of history. She had recognized only two relics from her own kind—an old, rusty sword that may have once been a Named weapon, though now eroded beyond repair, perhaps found beneath the ocean. Another was a piece of jewelry, to be worn during a joining festival, marking a woman's desire to mate. She had touched nothing in the room, but looked upon it all with eager eyes. She had never seen such a collection before. It was all that races had left: souvenirs, trinkets, the remnants of great civilizations that would never be restored.

She had searched for *The Book of the Named*, but among so many tomes it had proven difficult to locate. She had never seen it before and there were well over a thousand books packed onto the shelves.

Then the Dracian Captain had entered with his guests and pointed her right to it. She couldn't let the book be taken by someone else. She had acted fast...and she had left the savant behind.

He had been a young lad, new to the order, eager for an assignment. She had explained his duty clearly. If they were engaged in battle, he would do what was necessary to protect the book, even if that meant giving his life. He understood the sacrifice —had chosen it. And yet a glimmer of regret colored her thoughts. He had been very young and full of potential. Another few years of training and he might have taken a Name.

Yet this is the way of the Dark God, she reminded herself. *We might lose a few fingers, but his Hand remains.*

At that moment, the shadows of the room grew darker. Krait stiffened in her chair. It seemed that even the fire receded, rolling back on itself, shrinking against the growing darkness. She waited, her head tilted. The temperature dropped by several degrees, causing cold prickles to shiver across her skin.

She heard a key turn in the door's lock.

Cerastes entered the room, as majestic as a summer storm. He wore long, satin robes of midnight hues, with fine gold filigree embroidered on the sleeves. Around his neck dangled several pendants of different lengths and shapes, all made of expensive material: silver, gold, crystals and gemstones. A large medallion the size of a fist dangled toward his navel. The head of a boar was carved into its surface. The King's emblem.

Krait stared at the amulet, curious, wondering why he would wear such a thing. She had never seen him dressed so richly. In the Hive, he wore simple black linen, like every other assassin. Today he looked like an emperor.

He shut the door and locked it behind him. Then he turned to her. "You have the book?" he asked.

"Yes, Master," she said. She leapt to her feet, uncertain if she should bow first. She pulled the book from her belt and handed it to him, then got down on her knees, lowering her head to the ground.

"Good," Cerastes remarked. He ran his long fingers reverently over the frayed cover, then opened the book gently and turned a few pages, delicately holding each sheaf of paper between his thumb and index finger.

"There were others searching for it," Krait felt compelled to say. "Humans."

Cerastes raised a narrow, sloped eyebrow. "No matter," he murmured. "It is protected by spells. Only the Named can read it."

He thumbed through a few more pages and nodded. "Excellent."

Krait waited, wondering if she should speak. Then she said, "What now, Master? We have the book, but not the weapons."

"Yes, and our enemies will need this book to end the plague," Cerastes said. "And when they come here to the City of Crowns, we shall be waiting for them."

Krait nodded. *Waiting for them.* A vision of the Viper rose before her eyes, and she felt a tremor of anticipation. She would see him again and this time, she wouldn't be taken off-guard.

"For now, stay at the tavern on Tourmaline Street," Cerastes said briefly. "It is near the West Gate of the city. Watch for the Viper and his companions; I expect they will travel from the coast. Keep an ear to the ground. Alert me when they arrive. You can find me here, at this address." The Grandmaster paused, glancing over a passage in the book, then he closed it abruptly and tucked it into his robes. "I have matters to attend to in the city. You shall not see me for a while."

Krait nodded. "Yes, sir."

Cerastes pointed toward the far wall. The hair prickled on the back of her neck. Then the shadows began to melt and shift, circle inward on themselves, swirling lazily until they became thick, black mist. "Another portal, to take you back to the riverfront. Go."

Krait stood up and turned toward the far wall, quick to obey. Without a backward glance, she walked across the floor and launched herself through the mist.

* * *

Sora was far too shocked to scream. Something wrapped itself around her—strong arms, biceps almost as wide as her chest. Black skin, cracked and hardened like scales. *Scales!* Her head spun and only one thought made sense. *The garrolithe!* This had to be it—some sort of demonic monster that lived in the Crystal Caves. She had heard it howling before she fell. She remembered the vague drawings on the doors to the cavern. There was no other explanation.

The bulging muscles flexed around her small form. Sora shrieked and twisted away on instinct. The creature tightened its grip, turning her in its arms until she found herself pressed up against a broad, powerful chest, oddly human. She became confused—was it a monster or a man?

Two wings spread from the creature's back, snapping open against the wind. Their ascent slowed, drifting downward like a parachute. Sora panted with fear. Her vision swam. She was certain that she would black out before they reached the bottom of the ravine. *A good thing,* she told herself. At least she wouldn't have to witness her own death.

Then the creature slightly loosened its hold so she could breathe. She looked up despite herself. Gasped.

The beast's head was manlike. A straight nose, firm lips, strong chin. But the eyes chilled her—they were wide and almond-shaped, pitch black, no evidence of an iris or pupil. They absorbed all light, reflecting nothing back.

The skin of the face was smooth and ashen. Where a natural hairline would have been, the skin became hard, scaled, and dark black. Countless small horns, perhaps the width of her fingernail, jutted from the creature's skull. When the horns reached its shoulders, they became large blades of blackened bone, protruding through the skin, continuing down the arms, growing in length and width.

"No," she whispered, horrified. She was struck by instinctual terror, like a child waking up in the night, staring into darkness. She began to whimper—a desperate sound of primal fear.

Then the creature spoke. "Brace yourself." Its voice sounded like a low, crackling fire.

Her eyes caught on a silver line that ran along the beast's skin. Her mouth gaped. A long, jagged scar ran from the demon's jaw down to its chest.

WHAM!

They hit the ground at a fast glide, sending a shower of powdery white sand in every direction. All the air left her at once. They tumbled together, rolling wildly across the bottom of the ravine. The creature kept her pinned tightly to its chest, its wings wrapped around her protectively. Sora felt suffocated, terrified almost to the point of fainting.

Finally, after what seemed like an eternity of rolling, they came to a sprawled stop. The beast's heavy body was on top of her. It pressed her into the sandy ground, heat rolling off it in waves.

Sora lay with her eyes tightly shut, not daring to breathe. She didn't want to face the monster above her—didn't want to open her eyes to the reality.

Then its heavy weight seemed to lessen, to shift and grow smaller. Her chest eased, less constricted. Slowly the panic receded too, leaving her breathless and shaky.

"Sora?" a voice murmured from above her. She flinched in surprise. Hesitantly, she opened an eye.

No, it can't possibly be...."Crash?"

His shoulder was before her, crushing her into the ground. Then he shifted, moving so his voice was right in her ear. "Caught you."

She shoved him back, staring up at his face, the familiar green eyes and dark hair pressed to his forehead, soaked with sweat. He looked pale and wan, as though he had just run ten miles straight.

"No," she murmured. Had she gone mad? It was too much. She tried to shove him away, to scream, but he wouldn't budge.

"Get off of me!" she finally yelled. She struggled harder, pushing him with all her strength, trying to slip from his grasp. "You're not Crash! Who are you?" Terror struck again. The monster had to be using an illusion, trying to break down her guard. But she wouldn't be tricked.

"Sora," Crash repeated, grabbing her wrists, trapping her with his legs. "Sora, calm down."

"Calm down?" she shrieked, half-hysterical. A strange sound ripped from her mouth, somewhere between a laugh and a sob. "Don't tell me to calm down!"

"Sora, it's me," he said, looking into her eyes. Suddenly he released her wrist and cupped her face with one hand. He shook her slightly by the jaw. "Look. See? It's me. I caught you."

Sora tried to punch him with her free hand but was blocked by his shoulder. He maneuvered deftly and caught both of her hands in his, pulling them above her head. "Sora," he said. "Look at me. I'm right in front of you."

"No," she struggled, still trying to break his hold. "No!"

"Ask me anything," he said. "I'll prove it."

She trembled in his grasp, overcome by fighting instincts. She tried to shake her head, dislodge his hand, but he held her firmly, not allowing her to pull away. "Where did we meet?" she finally asked, certain that he wouldn't know the answer. She was waiting for the demon to resurface, to show some sign of itself.

"At your father's manor. You were running away."

She glared at him. "How long ago?"

He hesitated. "Two years?"

She paused. His response seemed genuine, his voice soft and unexpectedly patient. She watched him warily. Then she reached into her mind, beckoning the Cat's Eye. *Magic?* she asked silently. *Anything?*

But the Cat's Eye remained disturbingly dormant. She sucked in a slow, hollow breath. *No, no magic.* She looked at Crash again, finding the scar on the side of his jaw, the familiar angles of his face, sharp and masculine. His smooth forehead, the black bangs that swept across it so naturally, the sloped brows and straight nose. Hard, unforgiving lips. They had never been this close before; his nose was inches above her, his eyes focused, intense. She could read his expression. He was imploring her to believe him.

After a long moment, her chattering, panicked mind stilled. A small tremor ran through her body. She could feel every inch of him, every ridge of muscle imprinted on her flesh.

He didn't move. Didn't even twitch.

Sora frowned. "Crash?" she whispered uncertainly.

A sigh escaped his lips, a long breath that spoke more than words. "I believe..." he said slowly, his voice deep and hoarse. "I believe I should explain."

Sora nodded, unsure of what to expect. Something had just happened—something that defied the very laws of nature. She still wasn't sure if she was in danger, if she should be panicking, fighting away from him. She was owed an explanation.

She tried to turn, to roll away, but he surprisingly kept his hold. She paused, her breath quickening. He stretched her hands farther above her head so she was completely defenseless, exposed beneath his expressionless face. His eyes flickered over her, observing her prone position, and she felt the urge to squirm, to struggle. But she couldn't. No, his lower body held her down. She had the intense feeling that he didn't want to let her go—he didn't want her to run.

Somehow she managed to whisper, "What are you doing, Crash?"

Silence. It was so quiet that she thought she could feel the walls breathe. Then the assassin slowly released her. She noted that he was sweating.

"Nothing," he said.

"Right," she whispered in response. Then she slipped out from beneath him, scooting a short distance away. She needed space, distance, a chance to recover her thoughts. She glanced over him suspiciously, remembering the great beast, the bladed arms, the giant wings and midnight eyes. How was it possible?

Crash slowly raised himself into a sitting position. He looked weary, worn, exhausted. Sora realized that he was, indeed, shaking with the effort. She frowned.

"Are you all right?" she asked a little awkwardly. She couldn't help it. She was mad at him...but still concerned.

He settled next to her. His chest was bare and glistening with sweat. She saw his scar, a thin silver line starting at his jaw and gliding down his chest, all the way to the ridge of his pants. The same scar she had seen on the demonic beast.

She quickly looked away. She couldn't keep her thoughts to herself anymore. She needed answers. "What...what just happened?" she asked quietly.

Crash's face was blank. He didn't seem to know how to answer.

"What are you?" she asked again. He still hesitated, so she asked the question that she had been dreading, the one that had been on the tip of her tongue for a long time now. "Are you...human?"

He let out another short breath. "No."

The answer rang through her mind, sending a tremor through her body. Her heart sank. She had always suspected that there was something different about him—his inhuman endurance, his stealthy skill, his remarkable knowledge about the races. And there had been a name, something she had heard from only a few people, first from Dorian and then from the Dracians—*Dark One.*

Sora remembered the very first time she had seen him, the way his eyes had glowed. How he could see through the darkness like a nocturnal beast.

"What are you?" she whispered.

He replied quietly. "I am what humans, and the rest of the races, have come to think of as evil."

Sora just stared at him. Her mouth opened for a moment, trying to find the words. "You were the monster that saved me, then? That truly was you?" It seemed redundant to ask, but she still couldn't wrap her mind around it. How could someone change so completely? It was even more drastic than the Dracians, than any magic she had seen before, and...frightening. The beast had struck terror in her bones, deep and fierce, completely instinctual. It had risen from her belly up to her throat, turning her limbs to ice, chills puckering her skin.

"Yes, I caught you," Crash answered.

"How?"

He responded slowly, like he had to search a long time for the answer. "You know that the Elements each made a creature?" he said. "They each combined with the Wind, and so the races were born?"

"Yes."

"Well, the story is incomplete. It says that Wind and Darkness did not create a creature, which is true. But Darkness *did* create a race. One of Shadow and Fire. It was a bastard creature made of an elemental raping. Because it was done in secret, we were called the Unnamed."

"A Sixth Race?" Sora asked quietly.

He nodded. He seemed intent on looking anywhere but at her face. "Yes."

Sora sat back, closing her eyes for a moment, trying to clear her mind. All of Laina's stories had been true. There was a Sixth Race of Darkness—born in secret, living in the shadows. Centuries of existence, yet the humans had no record of their civilization, no knowledge of their people.

Crash pushed on, as though he wanted her to understand fully. "I grew up in a small, secluded colony called the Hive. Our existence was kept secret. It's the only way we could survive. The Harpies see it as their duty to destroy our race. They wish to extinguish us from the world. They think it will put an end to evil." He shook his head slowly. "Perhaps they are right."

Sora watched him carefully. She still felt cold, disturbed by this new knowledge. She swallowed. "You turned into a...a...."

"A demon?" Crash said; she saw his lips move in thought. "You may call it that. It wasn't a wise thing to do, but I lost control."

"Control?"

He nodded. "When our emotions grow too intense, our demons escape. We become them. Sometimes...sometimes we lose ourselves to them."

Sora heard the dark implication of his words. She didn't know what it meant to become a demon, but the monster's aura had been dangerous, instinctively terrifying. She wondered what sort of destruction it could cause. She remained quiet, absorbing everything. It changed her entire view of the world. When she had first met Crash, she hadn't believed in the races. She had thought they were extinct. And all of this time—all of these years—there had been a Sixth Race, one of Darkness and Fire, keeping to the night, hiding from the world. It was a lot to accept.

But he saved my life, she thought, glancing up the length of the ravine, which disappeared into the distance, obscured by the light of the sunstone. She couldn't imagine how long they had fallen —what could have happened....

"And you risked this change for me?" she finally murmured.

"It was not a question of choice."

Sora nodded. She wished that he would look at her. She felt that would make everything easier. She reached over and touched his arm, making him jump. "You look tired," she observed.

"The change drains my energy," he said softly. Surprisingly Sora glimpsed what might have been uncertainty in his eyes. Fear? *No, it can't be....*

But the sight melted the chill inside of her—it made her

suddenly warm. He was afraid—perhaps because he had exposed so much. Suddenly, she felt pity. It came out of nowhere, bubbling up through her chest. An outcast race, shunned and feared for his entire life, taught to live in shadow and secrecy. *He must feel so alone.*

A cold wind gusted through the ravine, sending clouds of white sand into the air. Sora shivered. She wondered if Crash could feel the cold. As a creature of Darkness and Fire, she doubted it. She had never seen him shiver, except for the few times he had been wet. She shook her head again, mulling over their conversation.

Perhaps two years ago, she would have abhorred him, terrified of his demonic form. Back when she had been a rich noble, sheltered from the world, living with her nose in a book.

But everything had changed since then. She had seen another kind of evil: Volcrian's thirst for vengeance and the wraiths he had created. The way he had slaughtered Dorian without a second thought. She and Crash had traveled so far...and he had saved her life so many times...she couldn't allow herself to feel threatened by him now.

She was surprised by this epiphany. No, she didn't fear him. The demon, perhaps, but that seemed natural, something rooted in her body. He was her friend. It shouldn't matter if he was a monster, a human, or even a figment of her imagination. They had been through too much.

Sora moved closer, pressing their shoulders together. He stiffened at her touch. She glanced at him, a slight smile on her lips. Tentatively, she grabbed his calloused hand. "You're still Crash to me," she said softly.

He looked at her. She saw something strange and unknowable pass through his gaze. Then a soft smile parted his lips. She felt her chest constrict. His smile took her breath away.

"Thank you," he murmured.

Sora looked him over again, taking in his smooth, tanned skin, and her eyes found his scar. It was long and painful-looking in this light. Impulse seized her—they were sitting so close together, his face mere inches away. She reached out a hand, touching the top of the scar, running a finger along his jawline. She felt a trickle of warmth move through her at the touch, some unknowable energy. Her hand trailed from his jaw to his chest, tracing the line of silver.

Crash made a sound low in his throat and grabbed her hand, firmly yet gently pushing her away.

She sat back, awkward, avoiding his eyes. *I went too far,* she thought, angry at herself. *Goddess, what was I thinking?* She couldn't even explain it to herself. He had seemed so lonely in that moment—and she had felt so close to him.

"Does that scar ever hurt you?" she asked, trying to forget what she had just done.

"No," he answered, his voice deep and rich.

She found herself blushing stupidly. She stared resolutely at her hands, desperate to focus on anything else. Another cold wind blasted through the ravine and a shiver passed through her body.

"Maybe we should—uh—keep moving," she mumbled.

"I need to rest," Crash answered. "We can move to the cliff wall. The rock should shelter us from the wind."

"Can you feel it, then?" she asked, suddenly curious. "How cold it is?"

"No."

She frowned. "Then how...?"

Crash took her hand again unexpectedly. He held it up, placing it lightly on his chest, over his scar. She swallowed, jolted by his touch. She could feel the pulse of his heart beneath her palm.

"Your fingers are cold," he told her softly. "Come."

He stood up stiffly. Sora could tell that his legs were weak, though he was trying to hide it. She pulled one of his arms around her shoulder, offering support. She thought she might have seen a look of amusement pass over his face, but he didn't make any comment.

They staggered toward the wall of the ravine. The assassin's weariness was so great that it affected her, too. She assisted him to the ground and leaned against the side of the wall, exhausted. She went to move away but Crash gripped her hand, pulling her back down next to him. He settled her in the crook of his arm.

"What...?" she started to ask.

"You'll get cold," he whispered, his eyes already closing, "and I need you here."

Why do you need me? Sora wanted to ask, but the assassin was already asleep. She watched him for a moment, his quiet breathing, the relaxed slump of his shoulders.

Then a smile came to her face, perhaps a little smug. She liked his words, no matter what they meant. She watched him for a minute longer, lingering on their conversation, on all the mysteries to this man.

Only then did she have the courage to lean close and place her lips against his scar. She wasn't sure why, only that it felt right. When she drew back, she thought she saw a slight curve to his mouth, but decided it was her imagination.

Sora dozed off next to him, completely at peace.

CHAPTER 14

Lori sighed. It was mid-morning, the next day. She and Ferran sat in the hallway, waiting for Silas' arrival. They were outside of the master suite where the sleeping Dracian still lay unconscious behind the door. A pair of burly sailors had escorted them to the room, but the captain himself was still absent.

Lori glanced at Ferran. He sat next to her in an identical fashion, his knees pulled up, his lengthy arms slung easily across them. In one hand, he twirled a half-chewed cinnamon stick. She watched it dance between his fingers, moving up and down his long digits.

She had thought about Ferran a lot since arriving in Sonora. He always slept shirtless, the phoenix tattoo clearly visible on his chest. She could remember him getting it shortly after Dane's death. She had thought perhaps the tattoo was to memorialize Dane. It had not occurred to her that it was the same emblem as the Ebonaire family's, a golden phoenix rising from a field of red.

"You never told me you were an Ebonaire," she finally said to him. It seemed as good a time as any to bring it up. The question had been dancing on her tongue for days now, but the opportunity to ask had not yet arrived.

He gave her a sideways glance. "You don't seem pleased by that."

Lori raised an eyebrow. She could hear the humor in his tone— dry, cocky, yet somehow guarded. She wasn't sure how to take that.

"It's been eighteen years," she finally said. "We were friends once. That's quite a big detail to leave out."

Ferran shrugged. His cinnamon stick picked up speed. He glanced across the hallway, his eyes traveling over the faded, floral wallpaper. "All right," he said. "So I'm an Ebonaire. I made the mistake of telling Silas. We were drunk at the time."

Lori leaned slightly toward him. "So...what happened?"

"He tried to hold me for ransom."

Lori almost choked at this. The thought was somehow comical. A pirate captain holding Ferran for ransom? It sounded just like something he would get mixed up with. "I take it that's when you parted ways?" she asked.

Ferran shook his head. "No," he grimaced. "He sent a letter to my father asking for ten thousand gold coins. My father wrote him back."

"And?"

"He paid Silas one hundred gold to throw me to the ocean."

Lori was quiet. She thought at first that he might be joking, but Ferran's face was solemn, his lips pressed firmly together. "Did Silas...?" she asked.

"Yes...but close to shore. That was the last I saw of the good ol' Captain...until now."

She hesitated, then reached out and touched his arm. Ferran jerked away, then flashed her a quick smile. "I told Silas it was a bad idea, that my family wouldn't pay," he said. His smile felt empty, somehow. "The Ebonaires see me as a disgrace. We haven't spoken since I was eighteen."

"That's...a long time," Lori agreed. Twenty years.

"Aye."

She fell into thoughtful silence. The Ebonaires were one of the richest families in the realm. First Tier nobility, highly respected and influential. Their bloodline went back to the War of the Races, when Calvin Ebonaire had led the human armies into war. They had been contenders for the throne and were said to be mixed with the royal bloodline—she knew of at least two queens who came from their family.

It was difficult to reconcile the two images. Ferran, raised by the First Tier, surrounded by wealth. Lori tried to imagine him dressed in expensive garb, decorated with all the pins and insignia of city nobility. He would have studied fencing, tutored privately under the most learned scholars, attended the King at court.

But she could only see the man next to her now, lounging against the wall, penniless and wandering, wasting his time in taverns and gambling halls. She couldn't imagine how he must feel, cut off from his roots for so long, with no anchor, no future.

"Why did you leave?" she finally asked.

Ferran shrugged. "A scandal, of course. I didn't have a lick of sense, especially at eighteen."

Lori had to smile at this. She remembered the young Ferran well: hot-headed, overly confident, ready for a fight. There had been a lot of anger in him...*and there still is,* she sensed. He was just a bit better at hiding it.

"I was a cocky little bastard," he continued. "Prince Peric and I were close friends. We grew up together at court and studied with the same tutors. We were the same age and considered cousins. Second cousins, perhaps, but close as brothers...." Ferran paused, frowning. "When we grew older, the prince became obsessed with the War of the Races. He wanted to find a Cat's Eye and use it. He was bored, over-educated and with too much money. We both were." Ferran shook his head, turning his eyes heavenward. "There was one noble family in the city who claimed to own a Cat's Eye. The prince offered to buy it, but the man wouldn't sell. Peric was upset and plotted to steal it, but it's hard to slip a thief into a noble's house. So I volunteered."

Lori winced. She could see where this was going.

"Anyway, I broke into the family's treasury during a party and took the Cat's Eye. I grabbed it without thinking and it bonded to me. Once I realized what had happened, I told Peric, who was furious. I fled the city, figuring that the noble family would press charges and the full blame would land on me. As I said...foolish." Ferran shrugged. "Word spread, rumors abounded. Next thing I knew, I was being hired by collectors to hunt down rare artifacts." He stared harder at the wall. "My family refused to talk to me. They said I had blackened the Ebonaire name."

"And that was the last time you saw them?" she asked softly.

"Yes," Ferran murmured. Then, after a moment, "I received a letter a few years back that my father had died. My brother is now Lord of the estate."

Lori's heart twisted. His father had died, and Ferran hadn't seen him in his final days. Twenty years since the scandal and she still noted the rigid set of his shoulders, the way he lingered on the memory. She tried to put a hand on his arm again, and this time he allowed it.

He turned and gave her a half-smile, the corner of his lips turning up, entirely roguish. "I made myself a new reputation as a treasure hunter," he said. "Guess I lost that too."

Lori shook her head. "There's more to life than a reputation."

"Aye," Ferran said skeptically. "Peasants say that. But to the First Tier, it's everything." Then he looked away again.

His remark might have stung, but Lori didn't take it personally. She bit her lip, casting around for some kind of encouragement, a reassuring word, but nothing came to mind. Ferran wasn't young anymore. The seeds of his childhood had taken root and firmly grown into a tree, complete with knotted branches and curling leaves. She couldn't comfort him as she would a young man. He knew better. Perhaps a reputation wasn't everything...but in his case, it had changed who he was, taken away his father, his House, his name. It was like telling a poor man that he didn't need gold.

"What about Dane?" Lori asked suddenly, dredging up a thought from the past. "Dane said he had worked at a noble's house...."

"He was my footman," Ferran replied. "And a close friend. When I left, he came with me."

Lori nodded. It made sense now. Dane had told her that he and Ferran grew up together. He had never elaborated on the details and she had never thought to push. In the whole scheme of things, she realized now that she had barely known Sora's father. He had been a boy, really. Both of them, so young, never even married. She had never tried to seek out his family. He had claimed that his mother was dead and his father...his father had left him as a child. *Goddess, I can barely remember now.* So many details were missing. She shook her head. After the fiasco she had caused with Lord Fallcrest, she had only wanted to disappear, to become a ghost herself.

She remembered her own parents, already deceased. They had

died of old age on a farm close to where Lori now made her home. She never told them of their granddaughter—she had tried to forget that Sora even existed. Her daughter would grow up to be a wealthy noble, and would play no role in her life. The guilt still stuck in her throat, squeezing it shut.

She wondered, suddenly, who she had been to get caught up with two adventurous young boys. Nothing good had come of it. Nothing except Sora, perhaps. Who had that young girl been, so many years ago, when Ferran and Dane had wandered through her town? She felt as though she had changed over the years, grown from an insecure girl into a confident woman, sure of herself, capable of reading people, of healing them, embracing them or turning them away. And yet deep in her core, at the butter-soft center of her heart, that young girl still lived. The one who held onto the future, who created silent hopes and dreams, kept hidden from her matured self.

That girl wanted to tell Ferran that everything would be all right. That his life wasn't for nothing. That his mistakes were all part of some great journey, an extravagant tapestry that couldn't be fully glimpsed. She wanted to promise that someday, it would all make sense. That all of the strands would come together and that there would be a great release, some cathartic closure to this open-ended world.

But she knew better than that. He didn't need to hear those words—he needed her silence.

The sound of footsteps disrupted her thoughts. Lori looked up to see Silas striding toward them. Today, the pirate captain wore a stark white shirt with broad cuffs. Ruffled lace decorated the neckline of the shirt, which was open at the chest, exposing his defined muscles and a small patch of red fuzz. His pants were of fine black leather and his boots were tall, encasing his knees, buckled at the heel.

"Oh, good, you're here," he said. It was an offhanded comment; he expected them to be there anyway. He took a large brass key from his belt and inserted it into the door. Lori and Ferran both got to their feet and watched the door swing open.

The room beyond was filled with sunlight. After they entered, a maid swept in with a tray of food, leaving it on the bedside table before rushing out of the room. Lori paused, staring at the massive bed. Their visitor was tangled in a mess of quilts. Silas pulled up a chair to sit next to him, and the man stirred in his sleep, throwing his arm over his eyes.

"Oh," he groaned. "The sunlight is foul!"

Silas reached out and tapped the man's arm. The gesture spoke of familiarity. "Jacques," he said. "Jacques!"

The Dracian moaned pathetically, then finally put his arm down, staring up at the pirate captain. Lori studied the man's face. He looked slightly older than Silas, perhaps because of the thick facial hair around his chin and jaw. They had identical blue eyes and similar noses, sharp and straight, aristocratic. Jacques' hair was a slightly deeper auburn, coarser, while Silas' was pure copper, smoothed back against his head. But Lori could see the resemblance now; they had to be related.

"Silas! You scurvy dog," Jacques muttered. His voice was hoarse. He reached for the tall glass of milk on the bedside table and took a deep swig. "Where am I?"

"Sonora, the pirate city," Silas said. "In the *Aurora*. You don't remember?"

Jacques shook his head slowly, as though his skull was tender. Lori could imagine that he had quite a headache. He was probably dehydrated. "I flew for a week straight across the ocean. The winds lifted me...." He closed his eyes. "Damned if I ever fly again. There were storms. 'Twas terrible."

Silas nodded and helped the man into a sitting position. "What are you doing here, brother?" he asked.

Ah. That explained one thing. Lori waited anxiously for Jacques' reply, her interest piqued.

Jacques' eyes widened, as though the memory had just come to him. "Our ship sank," he said. He grabbed Silas' arm in a strong grip, looking up into his brother's face. "You must come at once. Tristan and the others are stranded...."

Silas pried his brother's hand off. "Slow down!" he exclaimed. "What about Tristan?"

"'Tis a long story," Jacques said. "A girl came to us in Delbar. Sora was her name, and she wore a Cat's-Eye stone. There were others with her, a small band of four. They needed passage overseas to the Lost Isles."

"Wait," Lori said, interjecting.

Jacques looked up at her, startled. He probably hadn't noticed her presence until now. The Dracian's eyes widened with a spark of recognition. She had never met the man before, but if he knew Sora, he must notice the resemblance. Many had commented on it.

"What news of my daughter?" she demanded. "Where is Sora? What happened?"

"Your daughter....?" Jacques asked. Then he sat back, the headboard thudding solidly against the wall. "Now this is strange indeed...."

"Out with it!" Lori snapped. "What happened to your ship?"

Jacques looked at Silas. "Then you know of the plague?" he asked swiftly. "Of the Dark God's weapons?"

Silas waved a hand in Lori and Ferran's direction. "Aye," he said. "These two have filled in the details. What happened to Tristan? And...to Sora?" He glanced at Lori, unsure of the name. She nodded.

"Our ship sank," Jacques repeated, addressing all of them. "We were stranded on a small island. It's connected to the Lost Isles, but not part of the mainland. There was no way to get back to Delbar, so I flew for help. We have need of a ship. They're still trapped there on the island. I doubt the Harpies will help them...."

"Harpies?" Silas and Lori both said at the same time.

"Aye," Jacques nodded. "Sora and the others decided to travel through a cave, hoping to make their way to the main island, where the Harpies live. The others remained where I left them. The whole lot."

Silas sat back in his chair, quiet for a moment. His expression was one of intense thought. Lori had the sudden urge to punch something. Here she was, dallying around in a pirate city, while Sora risked her life on an isolated, dangerous island. She clenched her hands into fists to hide the fact that they were quivering.

Ferran stepped next to her and laid his large hand on her shoulder. "We have to go," he said. "We can't just leave them stranded."

"And my son is with them?" Silas asked. "Tristan?"

Jacques nodded.

Silas stared at him for a moment...then lunged out of the chair and grabbed Jacques by the throat, wrestling the man down to the mattress. "You bastard!" he roared. "You dirty scumbag of a brother! If anything's happened to my boy, I swear I will slit your throat!"

Jacques choked and wheezed, trying to wrestle the pirate off him. He searched the bed and grabbed a heavy satin pillow, the only object at hand, then swung it at Silas, hitting him viciously on the head, the shoulders, wherever he could. Silas sat back, trying to protect his face. The two men yelled and screamed at each other.

There was a short, loud tearing sound, and then the pillow ripped open. Hundreds of feathers exploded out of it, permeating the air, drifting across the room.

Lori and Ferran watched the fight in bewildered amusement. Then she turned to look at her tall companion. "The book will have to wait," she said quietly. "We need to rescue Sora."

"My thoughts exactly," Ferran replied.

Lori was surprised by his firm tone. She blinked, wondering where this new Ferran had come from. He was hardly the man she had met a month ago, drunken and useless, lying on the floor of a filthy tavern. Now his jaw was set with determination, his voice full of purpose. She searched his eyes for a long moment. His words almost gave her hope.

It was essential that they retrieve the book, but she couldn't leave her daughter on the Lost Isles. That was out of the question.

The fight on the bed had died down. Jacques rolled Silas off onto the floor. Then he stretched out, splayed across the mattress, gasping for breath.

Silas got to his feet. His hair had come untied and fell wildly around his shoulders, a silken mess. "It's decided, then," he said firmly. "We leave in the morning. I have already prepared a ship to the City of Crowns, but it appears we are taking a detour." He eyed Jacques with a modicum of distaste. "A long detour."

CHAPTER 15

Sora opened her eyes, groggy from sleep. Crash sat next to her, alert and awake, staring down the length of the ravine. When she stirred, he moved to stand up.

"Shall we continue?" he said.

Sora sat up, wincing, and looked around. He stood a few yards away, ankle-deep in the white sand. She paused, memories rushing back to her—the ice bridge, the plummet, the demon....

She tried to smile but failed. Their fall from the rock bridge seemed like a dream, a horrible nightmare conjured in her sleep. She stared up the side of the ravine, trying to put her thoughts in order. At this distance, she couldn't even see the thin bridge of stone that connected the two sides of the chasm. They had fallen a long, long way.

"Burn and Laina," she said suddenly. "What are we going to do about them?"

"Nothing for the moment," Crash replied. "We have no way of reaching them now."

Sora looked back at the ground. He was right, but it didn't sit well with her. Without the Cat's Eye, her two friends might become lost in the caves, wandering for an eternity. She had no idea how far these underground caverns stretched. *But there's nothing we can do,* she admitted to herself. There was no way back up the side of the cliff. They would have to continue forward.

She stood up and brushed the white sand from her clothes. It sparkled against her hands like stardust, sticking to her skin, impossible to wipe off. Then she turned to Crash. Despite her acceptance of him, it was still strange to think that he wasn't human. It left her slightly unnerved—uncertain. The past two years seemed oddly false. *Everything I thought I knew about him....*The trust they had built, the nights they had shared by the fire, blanketed by stars, heavy with the smell of road dust and wind....Was any of it real?

She looked away awkwardly, unsure of what to say.

"We should see where this wind is blowing from," he said after a moment of silence. "Perhaps we can find a place to climb up."

Then he turned and started walking.

Sora fell into step a few paces behind. After a short while, Crash stooped down and picked something off the ground.

"Your staff," he said, turning and offering her the weapon. Sora took it from his hands, surprised. True to its name, the witch wood remained undamaged, not even a scratch.

"Lucky it fell this close," she murmured. She felt much better with a weapon in her hands.

They continued down the narrow canyon. Crash strode in front of her, blocking her from the majority of the wind. Sora found herself gazing after him. She thoughtfully considered the past few hours.

"Crash?" she called, and he looked back at her, raising one eyebrow.

With a deep breath, she said, "I need to know something."

"What?" he asked.

"If we're going to travel together, I need to know that you're not keeping anything from me." There, she said it. It was hard enough to trust him—he was a trained killer, after all, and now some sort of demon. She still didn't understand all of the details. But she had to learn more, to rediscover him. She couldn't let this get in the way of their journey.

Crash looked at her calmly, giving thought to her words, then slowly nodded. "Alright," he said. "No more secrets."

Sora was surprised that he had agreed so easily. Her lips parted, letting out a silent breath of relief. She had been braced for an argument, some sort of denial or justification. But none was forthcoming.

"Is that all?" he asked.

"Uh...yes."

"Alright."

They continued walking. Sora squinted as the sand blew up in her eyes. Wind and time had turned the stone to a fine chalk. It clung stubbornly to her clothes and hands, glittering mischievously, caking under her nails and coating her boots.

She felt slightly disappointed. Despite her words, nothing had changed at all. He was still quiet, in fact, probably more so now than he had been for the past few days. *What did you expect?* her inner voice chided. *If you have questions, just ask!* The thought was still intimidating. For so long, she had respected his closed manner. His silence was like a fortress, an impenetrable wall that needed to be climbed. *Silly,* she told herself. *Just say something.*

Sora blurted out the first thing that came to mind. "Laina didn't see anything, did she?"

"See what?" he responded.

"Your...uh...?"

"Transformation," he interjected. "No, I believe she fainted."

She heard the distaste in his voice.

"That's fortunate," she said helpfully.

Crash shook his head. "I should have given it more thought...but there wasn't time."

Sora frowned, thinking back on the horrible experience. There had been a sound...a strange howling noise. She shuddered. Had it been an echo of the ravine, or something more? Something alive?

She glanced upward at the massive cliffs. She hated to think of what might have happened if Crash hadn't dived after her. She would be a bloodied, flattened mess on the ravine floor.

She remembered his wings. His strange, hardened skin, black as night. Claws....

"What if you hadn't come out of it?" she asked suddenly. "Your transformation? That...creature? What if you'd remained in your other form?"

Crash paused. "Then you would have been in danger."

His blunt answer took her off-guard. Sora stared at his bare back, the firm muscles and broad shoulders. She was speechless for a moment. "You mean...you would have attacked me?" she asked softly. A bit of fear bloomed in her. She could remember the intensity of the monster, its dark aura, the way her body had shuddered and convulsed.

He shook his head. "I knew who you were, I knew what I was doing, but...." his words hung in the air.

"You can't always control it, can you?" she asked.

"No, I can't."

"Are all of your people like that? Barely containing this...this *thing*....?"

He shook his head again. "Most, maybe. But there are those

who embrace the demon and learn to summon it, to use it. It's a long and difficult process. For some, it takes a lifetime."

Sora frowned at this. "Why don't you?" she asked. It seemed like a worthy cause, if it would make him safer, more in control.

He shrugged. "There are other dangers in using one's demon."

There it was—the half-answer she had expected. She waited for him to elaborate, but he didn't. She pushed on. "What kind of dangers?"

He was definitely growing uncomfortable. She could tell by his quickening pace, the set of his shoulders. She hurried until she was directly behind him, almost at his side. She reached out and touched his arm. "Crash?"

He flinched slightly. When he looked at her, his expression was hard, guarded. "We are not like the Dracians," he said. "Our other form is not ourselves. It is a separate creature."

"I don't understand," she said cautiously.

He sighed, irritated, rubbing his hand across his face. "So many questions!" he suddenly growled.

Sora paused, but she didn't retreat as she once had. Instead, she glared at him. "We agreed—no more secrets."

"I know," he said harshly, giving her a cold look. Then he went back to walking, focused on the trail in front of them. "You're not going to like what you hear."

"I'm prepared," she said immediately. *Am I?* She pushed the thought away.

When Crash spoke next, he sounded angry, impatient. She had seen him like this before—but not for a long time. "Inside each of the Unnamed, there is a shard of the Dark God," he said. "Some of us suppress it, others of us embrace it. Those who embrace the

Dark God, who learn to summon and use its power...the demon takes over their minds. They become...twisted." He looked at her as though he truly wanted her to understand—as though his words carried a terrible weight. "They become the demon, and the man is lost."

Sora felt the hair prickle on the back of her arms. "Forever?" she finally asked.

He nodded.

She frowned. "And this can happen to you?"

Crash turned back to the path ahead. "Yes."

It felt as though something had just slid into place. She understood, suddenly, why he had left behind his home, his traditions. And she understood the darkness she saw in him, the moments when he turned away, when he seemed like an untouchable force.

An awkward silence enveloped them. She ran her hand down her staff anxiously, in search of something to say that would bring him back.

"And what of your life in the Hive?" she asked. She remembered the word he had used from the day before. A colony, he had explained. "Did you have a family? Brothers or sisters?"

"We are all brothers and sisters in the Hive," Crash replied. "We are raised communally."

Sora's brow furrowed. "That must make marriage difficult," she said, trying for humor.

"We don't marry."

"Ah...."

"We have seasonal festivals where men and women can join," he explained.

Sora felt the conversation take a different turn. She hesitated, wondering if this was truly worth knowing about—but curiosity got the best of her. "Join...? You mean...make love?"

An odd expression passed over Crash's face. "You could call it that."

A blush crept up from her neckline. She had very little experience in that arena. Lily, her handmaid, had given her all sorts of bawdy details about young men and haystacks. But as a member of the nobility, she had been expected to wait for marriage. Which, of course, had never happened.

Occasionally she thought about it, but since living with her mother, the subject hadn't come up. Which was probably a blessing. She couldn't imagine how that conversation would go.

"And the women of your race...prefer this?" she asked with a sideways glance. "Not to be married?" It was a foreign concept. She had been raised with only one model for a family, one way of rearing children. Everything he was telling her seemed wrong, somehow cruel.

"They do."

She fidgeted with her staff. "And have you participated in these...festivals....?"

He cast a glance at her. A wry grin curved along the corners of his mouth. He looked at her a little too long, and it made her stomach squirm, her cheeks flush self-consciously. "Several times," he said. "Would you like more details?"

"Uh, no, I'm fine," she said briefly. *Yes!* her mind admonished. *Yes, ask him!* No, it would be far too awkward, she could already feel the blush spreading from her cheeks up to her forehead. She wondered what he must think of her. She felt terribly clumsy and naïve at that moment.

His smile widened and he laughed softly, turning away. "Innocent," he murmured.

Sora frowned, trying to regain her speech. "Well...uhm," she licked her lips. "Some people value innocence." Her blush deepened, and she wondered why she felt the need to defend herself.

"A valid point," he said, and met her eyes again. He held her gaze intently.

Sora almost tripped over her own feet. She slowed down a bit, allowing him to move in front of her. She needed a moment to regain her composure. So Crash had been with women in his colony —fine, she hadn't expected him to be a virgin. He had a good handful of years on her, anyway—seven or eight; she had never asked directly. Still, for some reason, the thought of him being with a woman of the Sixth Race...some tall, beautiful woman who had no qualms about joining...who was experienced in the ways of making love....

Her thoughts made her choke. More disturbing was how her body reacted—she felt warm, slightly weak....She forced her mind away from that territory. *Dangerous,* she told herself, *to be thinking of him like that.*

Suddenly the assassin stopped in his tracks. Walking up to him, she noticed that he was staring hard into the distance. Concerned, she said quietly, "What is it?"

"Listen," he said.

Sora paused, turning her head. It took a long moment. Then, from the hollow distance, she heard a reverberating howl. It began with the low-pitched ferocity of a wolf, then grew in volume, amplified by the sunstone walls. It ended in the high shriek of a wildcat.

A shudder went down her spine. She almost dropped her staff.

"What was that?" she asked, her mouth dry.

"I don't know," Crash said, then he turned to look back the way they'd come. "But it's getting closer."

"What should we do?"

"Run."

Crash bolted down the crevice, grabbing her hand and hauling her behind him. It took a moment for Sora's legs to catch up. She was still stunned by the eerie howl. Now that she was listening for it, she heard another one begin. It rumbled low to the ground, then ended high in the air, a shrill and furious pitch. Her breath caught. It was the same howl that had shaken her from the rock bridge. Fear raced down her spine, through her legs and into her boots.

"Faster," Crash breathed.

Within a minute, she heard another sound—the thunder of feet against the ground. Or paws. A creature of some kind. She chanced a look over her shoulder, but all she saw was a rising cloud of white dust, kicked up from whatever was following them.

"We're trapped," she panted. "We should save our energy and fight."

"Look ahead," Crash said, and pointed.

Sora narrowed her eyes, squinting into the white distance. "What?" she asked.

"It looks like a wall...or perhaps a door. I think we can climb it." He didn't sound very certain.

Sora gripped her staff, her mind whirling, trying to come up with a solution. "How far?" she panted.

"Under a mile."

So they would reach a dead-end. The thought unnerved her. But given the circumstances, they could only keep running. She mentally reached out to her Cat's Eye, hoping for some sign, some indication of what to do. *Yes,* the necklace breathed. *This way.*

Suddenly, the ground dropped out from under them. The sand hid a steep slope from their eyes. They skidded downward, holding each other for balance, then staggered back to their feet at the bottom. They leapt back into a full run, sprinting onward, moving as one. The creature's howls increased in volume.

Finally, the end of the ravine came into view. Sora would have gasped if she weren't running for her life. True to Crash's words, there appeared to be a wall in the distance, but as they neared, she noted strange irregularities along its surface. No, not a wall—a door. A giant door, perhaps hundreds of feet high, stretching far up the edge of the ravine. No human could have opened it—or built it, she suspected. Perhaps an ancient relic from the Harpies. She had difficulty thinking it was real, it was so large.

As they grew closer, bold designs carved by ancient hands stood out on the door's surface: suns and moons, stars, swirls and lettering. The doors were carved from sunstone, as smooth as glass.

"Climb!" Crash yelled, and he threw himself on the doors, starting upward at a formidable pace.

Sora stared after him, shocked. Climb? The doors looked shiny and slick, though the carved shapes would offer handholds and footholds. But the howling was now so intense that it made her head hurt. It ricocheted off the walls, echoing through the cavern. The creature was almost upon them.

She shouldered her staff. When she reached the wall, she used her momentum to run up its side, then grabbed onto a large star-shaped carving that was several yards above the ground. She pulled her weight up the side of the door, but she couldn't move half as fast as the assassin.

"Higher!" Crash called down. "Hurry!"

Sora fought for balance on the slick stone, hand after hand, fingers crammed into the crevices, digging for purchase. All she could do was focus on the space in front of her.

Wham! Something slammed into the door beneath her. She almost lost her hold. Sora quickly regained her footing and climbed a few more feet. *Wham!* It struck the doors again. She chanced a look over her shoulder and stiffened in terror.

A massive jaw gaped open beneath her. It was lined with fine-edged teeth. White saliva foamed at its lips. And above that gray muzzle were bright, burning eyes, the color of blue fire.

The beast was massive. It appeared to be a great cat, its body long and sinewy, covered by a thick coat of white fur and a long, lashing tail. Sprouting from its neck was a mane of iron-gray quills, short and bristling, as sharp as needles. Its paws were like giant clubs pounding against the door, thick and heavy, leaving jagged tears in the rock. Spiraling horns protruded from its skull and smaller spikes jutted from the ridge of its neck. Its muzzle was blunt, thick, wide. Its ears were small, pressed against its head in fury.

This was the *garrolithe*.

Sora forced herself to keep climbing, trying to stay calm. She was at least twenty-five feet above the ground now. The great beast kept leaping at her, but couldn't quite reach.

"Sora!" Crash yelled. "Here! Take my hand!"

She looked up. He was crouched on a ridge of stone next to the great door, higher up on the wall of the ravine. She maneuvered toward him, wedging her feet into the stone ridges, gripping the rock with her fingers. Her muscles strained, filled with adrenaline. She tried to focus on the door without losing her grip.

Finally, finally, she was close enough to reach out. Crash grabbed her wrist firmly and dragged her upward, pulling her onto the small ridge next to him. She fell back against him, shuddering, her knees suddenly weak. He held her firmly back from the ledge as they stared down at the beast. The creature had given up on the door and was looking up at them with startling intelligence. Its eyes glowed with blue light, no pupil or iris, unnervingly flat.

Then the beast turned and walked toward the side of the ravine. Its coat shimmered with light. A moment later, it dissolved into the sunstone, melting into the wall of the cavern.

Sora stared at the place where the beast had disappeared. For a moment, she thought she saw the outline of its body embedded in the rock, shifting with the light, and then it was gone.

"Goddess take me," she murmured. "What was that?"

"The guardian of the caves," Crash replied, his voice equally soft.

Sora touched her Cat's Eye, her hand shaking. "It wasn't natural," she said.

"No, it wasn't."

They sat for a moment longer. Sora still felt like she wanted to scream. The Crystal Caves had turned from a mystical labyrinth into a gilded death trap. The *garrolithe* was by far the worst of it. The beast didn't seem like something that could be killed. She wondered who had created it, where it had come from, how it was possible.

"Look," Crash murmured. He nodded to their left, where the ledge met with the side of the door. A large crack worked its way up the wall, creating a break between the door and the rest of the ravine. It was deep and wide, large enough for a human to pass through.

Sora nodded. "Let's go," she said immediately. She didn't want to sit on this ledge too long. The beast had dissolved into the sunstone walls—who knew where it would appear next. Perhaps directly next to them, ready to rip out their throats.

"I'll go first," Crash said.

Sora blanched. "No, I'll go first!"

He gave her a small smile. "Lost your nerve, have you?"

She scowled at him. Yes, she was terrified, and she wasn't afraid to admit it. "I'd be a fool not to fear that beast," she snapped. "You're not leaving me behind."

Crash turned back to the crevice. "We don't know where this hole leads. I'll go first. If it's safe on the other side, I'll call to you." He glanced at her. "I'm not leaving you."

Sora gritted her teeth. Of course she knew that, but it didn't calm her nerves. She forced herself to nod.

"Be quick," she said. "If you're gone for more than a minute, then I'm coming through after you."

He nodded firmly. Then the assassin started forward, twisting and shifting his lean figure through the narrow crevice. Sora watched nervously, checking over her shoulder, scanning the ground below. The beast's paw prints were filling in with sand. In another minute or two, they would disappear altogether.

"Crash?" she called after a little time had passed. She listened for his response but didn't hear any. "Hello?" she called again. Her voice echoed dully off the rock, but there was no reply.

She let out a short, irritated breath. She couldn't wait any longer—she felt as though the beast still lingered, hidden somewhere behind the walls. "I'm coming through!" she called, then turned sideways, easing herself into the crack. It was an impossibly tight fit; Crash had made it look easy. She inched forward, one foot at a time, guiding herself along the wall.

In the enclosed space, the light of the caves was as good as darkness. The wall in front of her was so white she couldn't see the details in the stone, its shape or shadow. She kept pausing to blink, trying to clear her vision. She felt like she was staring straight into the sun.

Her ankle caught on a rock and she had to twist for a moment, struggling to free it. Then her clothes snagged. At one point she had to stoop down, trying to fit under a jutting overhang. She bumped her head against the sharp stone, letting out a curse of pain. "Damn!" she muttered fiercely at the cave wall. "The winds take you!"

Then Crash's voice drifted to her, faint and muffled. "Sora? Are you all right?"

"Yes!" she called back. "Everything is just *fine!* I don't need help!" She continued to curse as she squeezed her way through the narrow spot, sucking in her breath, scraping her ribs. She paused twice to dislodge her staff from the rocky ceiling. Finally she spilled out of the crevice, losing her balance, tumbling to her knees. She barely stopped herself from landing flat on her face.

Crash's boots were directly in front of her. "Easy now," he said and offered her a hand up. He looked amused, perhaps laughing at her—at least inwardly. She glared at him but took his hand anyway.

Once on her feet, she brushed off her clothes and tried to recover a bit of her lost dignity. Then she turned to survey the new cavern.

Her eyes lit up. At first, she didn't know what she was looking at. Mounds of sunstone faced her, cut through with long veins of color, as vibrant and varied as a rainbow. It was very different from the ravine they had just left. This chamber was huge, a vast cavern stretching at least a square mile. The roof was high above, made of jutting stalactites of bright green, red, blue, silver...the colors were endless.

In the middle of the chamber stood a giant pillar of sunstone. It spanned from the floor to the ceiling, supporting the massive cave. The pillar must have been thousands of feet in diameter, large enough to encase a small town. Veins of brightly colored rock ran up and down it, several yards wide in some places.

Their ledge stood about fifty feet above the floor of the cavern. The walls were covered with the same bright sheets of rock. This close, Sora could see thousands upon thousands of tiny round stones bunched inside the veins, forming up through the sunstone.

The colorful jewels were amassed much thicker on the floor of the cavern, where they piled up from the ground, resembling coral reefs. Only a few sunstone paths remained, cutting natural passages through the colored rock, perhaps where water had once flowed. The paths twisted around each other, creating a giant maze as far as her eye could see.

Awestruck, Sora stepped toward a nearby wall, squinting more closely at the veins. *Cat's Eye.* An entire cavern of Cat's Eye.

An odd tingle moved through her necklace, into her skull and down her spine. Then the stone moved on her chest—actually moved! It spun in a lazy circle, dancing with excitement. She could feel its euphoria bubbling up inside of her and had the urge to laugh, an intense happiness that she couldn't explain. *Home,* she heard. *Heart.* It warmed her, forcing a smile to her lips. It was as though she could feel the cave's heartbeat, a vibration that echoed through the expansive cavern. She understood now where the winds came from. *Here we are,* she thought. *Where humanity discovered the Cat's Eye—where the War changed.*

"By the North Wind," she whispered. "Crash...look at them all."

The assassin nodded, also gazing at the cavern. "They're growing through the rocks," he said.

Sora glanced at him. "Growing?"

He nodded.

"But stones don't grow."

"Cat's Eyes do. Here, anyway." His eyes scanned the cavern. "The ocean amplifies magic. All of that energy has to be stored somewhere, or else it would tear apart the earth. They say that's how the Cat's Eye formed."

Sora felt a rush of understanding. "Like a coal becoming a diamond," she murmured. "The magical pressure builds until the sunstone turns into a Cat's Eye."

"Exactly."

She considered that for a moment. "This is a dangerous place," she finally said. "We should be careful not to touch any of them."

"Naturally," he agreed. "I think this is where your Cat's Eye has been leading you. Can it find us a way to the other side?"

She nodded. She could tell by the reaction of the necklace. The

Cat's Eye still spun at the end of its chain, circling in her thoughts as well.

"Do you think Burn and Laina will find their way here?" she asked, reminded of her friends and suddenly worried. This new cavern was radiant—but would they know its danger? Burn, perhaps. But not Laina.

"If they stayed on the same path," Crash said. "We should search for other tunnels."

She nodded and turned to the side of the ledge. Footholds had been carved out of the rock; it wasn't a true staircase, but a vague remnant of times long past. Crash followed her down the steep slope of the wall, digging their feet into the indents. Both were careful not to touch the ribbons of Cat's Eye, their colors vast and varied, bright as gemstones, glinting in the light.

Once on the floor of the cavern, the Cat's-Eye stones turned into large mounds, some taller than her head. They passed through pillars of rock, navigating the maze, searching for a sign of their lost companions.

CHAPTER 16

Sora and Crash made countless turns. Through her necklace, she could sense an exit toward the opposite end of the cavern. But it wasn't the direction where she thought Burn and Laina might arrive. The Cat's Eye had originally led them through a tunnel that would have connected to the far right of the cavern, close to the giant doors.

After an hour of fruitless searching, Sora paused, raising her head. A faint murmur reached her ears. She turned, trying to see above the giant mounds of rock. Crash stopped walking, too, and turned toward the sound.

"Sora!" she heard again. The voice was dim, but grew louder with each echo. "Sora!" it repeated.

"This way," Crash said, and turned down another path.

Hope bloomed in Sora's chest. "I'm here!" she called, jumping up, trying to wave her hand around the rocks. "Hello?"

"Sora!" the voice cried again. This time she recognized it. *Goddess...Laina!*

They made a few more turns and then found themselves at the entrance of another tunnel. It curved up and sideways, turning out of sight back toward the ravine. Burn and Laina stood at its mouth, relief on their faces.

Burn approached Crash and they shook hands, clasping at the wrists.

"Well met, Wolfy," the assassin said.

"Same to you," Burn replied. He nodded back to the tunnel. "We crossed the stone bridge and followed the path. It led us directly here. I had a feeling we were on track. There was no other way forward."

Laina launched herself at Sora, gripping her in a tight hug. "The Goddess must be protecting you!" she gasped. "I thought you were dead, but Burn gave me hope! How did you survive that fall?"

Sora's mouth opened. How indeed? She didn't want to uncover Crash's secret; she didn't think Laina would understand. The two already didn't like each other. But there was no other plausible excuse.

"I don't know," she finally said. "I passed out. Crash is very skilled. He managed to do something miraculous...again." She tried to smile.

Laina's eyes narrowed, looking at her shrewdly, her lips pursed. "I passed out, so I didn't see it myself," she said, lowering her voice. "But it must have been some kind of magic." She took Sora's hand. "I'm glad you're alive, but I don't trust Crash. I think he's keeping something from us. Please watch out for yourself!"

Sora released Laina's hand. "Of course I will," she said, inwardly relieved. Laina's own explanation was ironically close to the truth. She tousled the girl's short hair. "Let's find a way out of these caves, shall we? I'm starting to miss fresh air."

Burn nodded. "Agreed. Do we know the way out?"

She caught his look and touched her necklace, asking for a direction. She waited. The stone seemed preoccupied, buzzing about in excitement, chattering against her thoughts. She forced herself to concentrate. Finally, she pointed to their left, across the cavern to its opposite side. "There," she said.

They started in that direction. Sora walked in front, Laina beside her, with Crash and Burn bringing up the rear.

As they walked, she noticed Laina's eyes lingering on the Cat's-Eye stones. The girl finally let out a low whistle. "I bet these gems are worth a fortune," she muttered. "I wonder if we can pry a few out."

"Don't," Sora replied, and caught Laina's hand as she went to touch the stones. "They'll bond to you."

Laina looked at her quizzically, then brightened. "Cat's Eye!" she exclaimed. She looked back at the veins of rock. "I didn't recognize them at first. Why not take one for myself? Then I'd have a necklace like yours. We'd both have protection." She reached out her hand again.

Sora kept a firm grip on the girl's wrist. Honestly, she didn't know what to say. "The stones are dangerous," she tried to explain. "They'll bond to your mind. If you touch one, you can't reverse it...Trust me. Keep your hands down."

Laina had a stubborn look on her face that meant trouble. Sora hoped the girl would listen. She released her wrist, but kept a close eye on her.

They continued to walk and Sora's thoughts traveled forward to what might happen once they left the caves. They would arrive at the Lost Isles—and Harpy territory. With any luck, Volcrian would arrive within a few weeks' time, having followed them across the ocean. She was certain he would come. He had already devastated the mainland with his hunt for vengeance; he wouldn't let an overseas voyage get in his way. Then there was the matter of the Harpy's sacred stone circle. How would they pin him down to the rocks? How powerful had his magic become? And what if, somehow, her Cat's Eye was destroyed in the fight?

Her eyes roved around the cave again. What if...what if she took one of the stones with her? There was no rule saying she had to use her own. Up to this point it had been her only option, but what if she could remove one of the stones without touching it? Wrap it in a cloth, tuck it into her pocket until the time was right. It would be a risky affair...but worth it, if it kept her from having to sacrifice her own necklace...and possibly her life.

They continued to walk for a while longer until Laina finally groaned. "My feet ache," she said. "Can we rest for a bit?"

"Just five minutes," Sora said, glancing around the cavern. They were next to an unusually large mound of Cat's Eye; an ideal opportunity. She stopped the group and made a show of stretching her arms and neck. Burn set down his bag and Crash knelt on his heels, resting.

The pillar of Cat's Eye jutted above their heads. Bright orange stones protruded from it at odd angles, like overripe berries waiting to burst. Sora wandered to its opposite side until she was almost out of sight. Then she bent close to the ground.

She quietly took out one of her daggers. She carefully wedged the blade underneath a small stone, putting force against the hilt, prying it outward. She held her breath. It was a risky thing to do—she already bore a Cat's Eye, and didn't want to mix energies. She had to avoid direct contact.

Yet no matter how hard she tried, she couldn't quite dislodge it. She needed more leverage—more strength.

"What are you doing?" Crash asked from above her.

She looked up, not having heard his approach. Then she glanced around for Laina. The girl was standing several paces away, her back turned. "Quickly," she said. "Help me pry this off!"

Crash studied her for a moment, then the stone. She saw his thoughts pass behind his eyes. It didn't take long for him to understand her reasoning. He simply nodded, then knelt down and took the dagger from her hand. With a short, firm thrust, he dug the knife under the stone and pulled outward, forcing it from the rock.

After a long moment, the stone came loose with an audible *pop!* It fell to the floor, a speck of bright orange against the white sand. Crash quickly tore a strip of cloth from the bottom of his pant leg and picked up the stone, folding it into a square. He handed her the small bundle. "Be careful," he said, and searched her eyes briefly.

She smiled. "That's the idea. This little stone might just save our lives." Then she tucked it into her pocket and climbed back to her feet.

At that moment, Burn poked his head around the corner. "Are you two quite finished?" he asked, glancing back and forth between them. A strange grin lingered on his face. "We should continue."

Sora quickly stepped away from Crash, wondering at Burn's look. She scowled at the Wolfy and sheathed her daggers. "Of course," she said.

Burn continued to grin, but she walked away from him up the path. She would wait to tell him about the Cat's Eye—at least until they were out of the caves. She didn't want Laina overhearing, then trying to take one of her own.

They traveled for a while longer. After about twenty minutes, Burn came to a halt. He turned, staring behind them, his ears flicking distractedly. Sora stopped as well and tried to see what he was looking at, but the shelves of stone were too high.

Finally he said, "The wall of the cave is moving."

Sora's hands grew clammy. "What do you mean?" she asked.

"Strange," he murmured. "It looks like a reflection of some kind...." Then his voice dropped a notch. "Something's coming through the wall of the cave."

"Something?" Sora asked. A chill ran across her skin. She knew immediately what it was, but she didn't want to believe it. "What does it look like?"

"Like...like a big white beast," Burn replied.

"A beast?" Laina asked skeptically.

Then Sora heard it—a long, wailing howl that started low in the chest, like a rumbling avalanche, and ended in a shriek. Her muscles locked. She was terror-struck.

Suddenly Crash was behind her, shoving her forward, drawing his sword. "Go!" he said, and pointed toward the far end of the cavern. They were halfway across—still a long way to run. "Find another tunnel. Get out of here!"

Sora tripped forward. She pulled out her daggers, whirling to face him, digging in her feet. "No!" she exclaimed. "If you're going to fight, then I'm standing with you!"

"Take Laina," Burn ordered. "Make sure she's safe."

That changed things. With a resigned breath, Sora sheathed her daggers and grabbed Laina's hand. "Come on!" she yelled, and they took off running. Crash and Burn followed them at a slower pace, their weapons held at ready.

Sora tried to listen through the howls, wondering how close the beast was, but the noise echoed forcefully from the walls, turning one voice into a hundred. It was deafening. She put on a renewed burst of speed, Laina sprinting beside her.

After a minute, she could make out a tunnel in the wall ahead of them. Its darkness caught her eye, carved from solid rock, not the bright sunstone of the caverns; possibly an exit. She had a feeling that the monster wouldn't be able to follow them through it. The beast seemed tied to the sunstone—imprisoned by it, perhaps, to keep trespassers out.

She dragged Laina down a side path, through a narrow strip of Cat's-Eye shelves. They were inches away from brushing up against the stones, and had to turn sideways to pass, raising their arms. Crash and Burn paused behind them, looking through the gap.

"We can't fit," Burn said. "Come on, this way." The Wolfy turned in a quick circle, peering over the rocks for an alternative route. Then he nodded. The men ran in another direction, taking the path forward.

Sora and Laina cleared the narrow stretch, just as a long howl issued from behind them, shockingly close. The sound sucked away her breath. Sora glanced over her shoulder, horrified, to see a white glow hurling through the cavern. The beast wasn't chasing after the men. No, it was coming after her and Laina. *Goddess!*

Only one possibility presented itself. She shoved Laina forward, pointing at the mouth of the darkened cave. "Go!" she yelled. "Keep running!"

"What are you going to do?" Laina demanded, stumbling in front of her.

"I'm going to lead it away. Just stay inside that tunnel!" And Sora ducked down an opposite path, running away from the exit. *What are you doing?* her thoughts screamed at her. *This is a very bad idea!* It went against every bone in her body, but she had to draw the beast away from Laina. She had to protect her. The creature was made of magic—she didn't think it could be killed, which meant her Cat's Eye would be their only defense. Again. She cursed the necklace silently, wishing that she had never worn it—that it didn't have to be such a terrible burden.

She darted down another corridor of stone, weaving among the mounds of Cat's Eye. The howls picked up; she could hear the thrum of giant paws, its massive weight hitting the ground. The beast kept to the narrow path between the Cat's-Eye stones, which slowed it down. That gave Sora a sense of hope. Perhaps it wasn't immune to the stone's power. Perhaps she had a chance.

Then the monster leapt over a ridge of stone and landed directly in front of her, blocking her way forward. Sora screamed and fell, sliding across the slick floor, sand flying up in her wake. A massive paw swiped just inches above her head. She narrowly missed the bristling quills of the beast's mane.

Then suddenly she was on the opposite side of it, stumbling to her feet, still running. She found a path that seemed to circle back to the granite tunnel. She couldn't be certain, but she dodged down it anyway, the *garrolithe* only a few meters behind. The narrow rock shelves kept the creature at bay. It couldn't leap over them and couldn't push through them, so kept to the rear.

Then, suddenly, a dead end.

Sora's jaw dropped. She came to a skidding halt. A ledge of sunstone stood before her, the wall of the cavern, tall and impenetrable. There wasn't enough time to climb it. She drew her staff and whirled around, bracing herself. A second later, the *garrolithe* appeared. Its breath rose in clouds of mist. It barreled toward her, charging between the Cat's-Eye shelves. There was nothing she could do. The beast lunged, flying at her, its mouth wide enough to swallow her whole.

Sora screamed, falling back, the sound ripping from her throat. "No!" she yelled in panic and grabbed her Cat's-Eye necklace, forgetting her staff.

Flash!

Instantly, a brilliant green light blasted outward, different from what she had expected. Usually the necklace encased her in a dome of protection, but this time it was on the assault. The energy spread out in a wave. The beast roared, a sound that shook the caverns, billowing up sand from the floor. Sora was stunned by the sound, as though she had been struck by a battering ram. She fell back against the sunstone wall, paralyzed.

A rope of green energy wrapped around the beast like a noose, dragging it forward, into the necklace. The *garrolithe* screamed again, enough to make her bones ache. In seconds it would slam into her, knocking her into the wall, perhaps killing her from the force. She braced herself, panic-stricken, waiting to be crushed.

The green light flashed again. The *garrolithe's* jaws were inches away....

And then, suddenly...it was gone.

A gale-force wind struck Sora's body. She slammed back against the wall. Something heavy and solid impacted her chest, a phantom of the beast's energy. Then a great weight bore down on her Cat's Eye, making her neck ache. She remained pinned against the wall, unable to move, but the *garrolithe* had disappeared. All that remained was gusting sand and the echo of its horrible howl.

Had the Cat's Eye...taken it? Absorbed it? *What happened?*

After a long moment, the caves were reclaimed by silence. Sora slid to the ground, panting, still unable to move. She closed her eyes and held her necklace tightly, her heart thudding in her chest, the air wheezing in her lungs. She forced herself to breathe.

Suddenly, she heard the pounding of feet. Crash and Burn rounded the stone corridor, dashing toward her, their weapons drawn. They looked ready for battle, their lips firm and eyes hard.

Shock registered on their faces when they saw her. Burn skidded to a stop, quickly assessing their position, then whirled around. "Where is it?" he demanded. He swung his greatsword in an easy arc, whirling it through the air. "Where is the beast?"

Crash ran to her side, kneeling down, touching her wrist. "Are you injured?"

Sora wasn't sure how to respond to that. Physically? No, she was fine. And yet her Cat's Eye kept spinning through her mind, monopolizing her thoughts, bucking and rolling, as though somewhere deep inside it was still battling the monster. She felt sick and dizzy, overwhelmed. She could only shake her head, the words stuck in her throat.

Crash frowned. Then he grabbed her arms and pulled her to her feet. Sora staggered forward and almost vomited; her stomach churned, her throat retched, but there was nothing to throw up. She coughed instead, struggling to control her lungs.

"What happened?" Crash asked. He kept a firm hold on her arm, her balance unstable, as though she stood aboard a ship at sea.

"My necklace," she finally gasped. "I think...the beast is gone."

"Let's not take any chances," Burn said immediately, still searching the caverns with a keen eye. He turned and grabbed Sora with one arm, lifting her off her feet and slinging her easily over his shoulder. Then he started back down the path they had followed, setting a fast pace. His greatsword remained in his left hand, ready for a fight.

Sora didn't blame them for being cautious. Although the monster had been taken by the Cat's Eye, she didn't feel that it was truly gone. The beast's power still clung to the caves, resonating from the stones. She felt sickened.

A minute later, they reached the granite tunnel where Laina awaited, curled up on the ground, her knees tucked to her chest. She was visibly shaking. When she saw Sora, she stood up, wide-eyed and wordless. Crash passed by her brusquely, barely sparing her a glance. Burn paused next to her and lowered Sora to her feet. He searched the caverns one last time, then slowly sheathed his sword.

"This looks like an exit," Crash said, drawing their attention. "Let's get out of here."

Sora couldn't agree more.

Shaken and hesitant, the four started up the long, rocky tunnel. It was pitch black, carved through hard granite. The path turned to the left, then sloped upward, cutting through the rocks. As they walked, the glow of the sunstone was soon lost behind them.

"Sora," Crash said suddenly. "Give me your staff."

She slung the weapon from her shoulder and held it out to him, unsure of what he intended. Then she heard the end of the staff knocking against the ground; Crash was testing the floor of the shaft for weaknesses. They continued forward, Crash checking the path, searching for crevices or holes. Sora took Laina's hand, then Burn's, not wanting to lose them in the darkness.

In this fashion, they continued steadily upward, moving as swiftly as possible. The caves grew cold and moist; the chill of the deep earth. The energy of the sunstones drained out of her, reminding her that she hadn't eaten in days, hadn't drunk any water, hadn't slept. She began to stumble over unseen rocks, unexpected dips in the ground. Her body grew heavier and heavier as they walked. It became difficult to keep up with the men; Laina was dragging her down, similarly affected.

No one spoke. As time stretched on, Sora found herself growing nervous. She couldn't guess at the path ahead—what if it narrowed down to a small tunnel and they had to crawl their way through? What if animals lived here, hidden in the blackness? Bats or underground snakes? It seemed that all of her senses were heightened. She heard every shift of stone, each crunch of a footstep, every tap, tap, tap of her staff against the ground.

Then, suddenly, Sora heard water. She stopped in her tracks, causing Laina and Burn to stop too. The sound was still distant, but it wasn't like a mere trickle or stream. No, it was like the rushing currents of a mighty river.

"Crash?" she asked hesitantly.

"This way," his voice answered from the darkness. "We're not far now." She realized, suddenly, that he could probably see quite well, and the staff was really for their own benefit. Some of the tension loosened from her shoulders.

The thought of seeing true daylight again lent fuel to her steps. Her skin prickled in anticipation. The water increased in volume until it echoed from the walls of the cave, encasing them in a rush of sound.

Finally, she saw a dot of light on the horizon. She blinked

against its brightness, hardly able to believe her eyes. Light. Real, natural daylight. She resisted the urge to run forward, to chase after the sun until she caught it.

Moss grew on the rocks around them, clinging to the damp walls. Moisture made the air heavy, sweet and refreshingly cool. As they neared the mouth of the cave, Sora realized that she was staring at the back of a waterfall.

They paused before it. The rocky floor became smooth and slippery. Their clothes were dampened by a fine mist cast off by the water. The current fell hard and fast over the cave's mouth, occasionally splitting to one side like a parted curtain. She caught a glimpse of thick green foliage and a blue sky. They appeared to be high up on the wall of a cliff, looking over a long river basin of thick wilderness.

Crash walked forward to investigate. He moved agilely on the wet stone, crossing under the waterfall, exploring the cliff on the other side. When he returned, he was completely drenched, his hair plastered to his head, droplets running down his face. He handed Sora back her staff.

"There's a ledge and a path to the left," he told them. "The rocks are slick. Watch your step."

Burn nodded and took Laina's hand, leading the girl to the side of the cave's mouth. He picked her up and passed through the falling water, climbing along the stone cliff. Sora watched until they disappeared, then she approached the thundering water. She couldn't wait to clean herself off.

Crash followed her. She could feel his eyes on her back, studying each step, each subtle movement. She wanted to sigh. He acted as if she might slip at any moment—as if she couldn't handle herself on a rocky ledge.

"Just because I fell once doesn't mean I'll do it again," she snapped over her shoulder.

"I know," was his only reply.

It canceled out all argument. She cast him an exasperated look. She knew this tactic—he might agree with her, but it wouldn't stop him from watching her every move.

"Well...you're making me nervous," she remarked.

She saw a slight smile on his lips. "Don't be—if you think you can manage." A subtle challenge laced his tone. She raised an eyebrow. *Challenge accepted.* Then she turned to one side and slipped through the waterfall. It cascaded over her body; mountain water, cold as ice. She sucked in a quick breath, not quite prepared.

She moved swiftly, wanting to show Crash that she didn't need any help. Her mother had taught her how to balance on slick surfaces. They had trained throughout the entire winter, battling on ice and snow, jumping and kicking. A few slick rocks should be no challenge at all.

Sora navigated through the waterfall and found herself at the edge of a steep cliff. The stone was the color of lead, darkened by moisture and covered in moss, but jagged and easy to climb. She maneuvered sideways, gripping with her hands and feet, swiftly climbing across. She jumped the rest of the way to solid land, where Burn and Laina waited.

Crash followed close behind her. Finally the four travelers stood in full daylight, having left the Shining Caverns behind.

Sora turned and surveyed the world around her; she felt like she had just hatched from an egg, like everything was new and wondrous.

They stood upon a tall ridge at the very front of a canyon. The cliff walls were covered in thick foliage and shrubbery, all vibrant green, sloping down into a long river basin. She couldn't count the species of trees—they were tropical, like the island she had just left, crammed close together and impossibly dense. The waterfall spilled over the edge of the canyon and continued at its base, wandering through the forest, out to the distant silver rim of the ocean.

And far off in the distance, just before the curve of the sea, was a gleaming white city. Sora felt her breath catch, surprised by the sight. She squinted, making out the vague silhouette of buildings, perhaps ten or more miles away. The city sprawled for several miles, interrupted by patches of towering trees. Occasionally a domed structure or tiered roof would disrupt the canopy, indicating that the city was still present on the forest floor. The buildings were overtaken by foliage, on the verge of being swallowed up by the wilderness.

"The Harpy city of Asterion," Burn murmured. The four continued to gaze at the shining white structures, so far in the distance.

"It's beautiful," Laina murmured. She perched at the very edge of the cliff and leaned out over the waterfall, one hand raised to shield her eyes from the sun. "If only my grandmother could have seen this....I guess we're at the right place, then?" she asked.

"Seems like it," Sora replied.

Crash turned toward the trees abruptly. "We should take cover," he said.

Sora snorted at this. "Really? The city is a day's walk away, if not more! I doubt we'll be noticed."

Crash gave her a hard look. "Harpies fly," he said sharply.

She rolled her eyes. "Right," she said, "But I doubt they'll attack us. Once they hear of our quest, they'll want to help, just like the Dracians." It made sense. The Harpies had once been the most advanced of the races. Surely they weren't as barbaric or warlike as the Catlins. *Not all the races are bad,* she thought. The Dracians, after all, had quickly come to their aid.

"Into the trees," Crash ordered, pointing over her head. "Away from the path."

"Why?" Laina asked loudly. She glared at the assassin and crossed her arms stubbornly. "I'm tired! I don't want to trek through the woods."

"I agree," Sora said slowly. "We're all tired...."

Crash's gaze turned cold. She recognized that look—the mask of an assassin, the one who had kidnapped her so long ago, who wouldn't be argued with. A shudder of trepidation passed through her.

Why is he so vehement about this? She knew the truth of his race, his dark heritage, their division with the Harpies, but she doubted that such lines were still drawn. The War of the Races had been more than four centuries ago. Surely the animosity had subsided.

"We don't want to be taken by surprise," Burn said gently, breaking the tension. "I doubt the Harpies are eager for visitors. It would be better to meet them on our own terms."

Sora nodded. She could see the sense in that. But she still eyed the assassin, wondering if he was being paranoid or if the Harpies truly presented a threat.

Burn withdrew a long knife from his belt and started hacking into the thick foliage. He cut back a series of vines so they could pass. Laina followed him, still grumbling, casting Crash a petulant look. Sora fell into step next, leaving the assassin in the rear. He walked silently behind her.

Her thoughts quickly turned to food and rest. The forest appeared to be full of game, the air rich with bird calls and scampering feet in the underbrush, lizards or small rodents. Perhaps they could hunt down a deer or a boar. Even a wild hen would be welcome. She was hungry enough to eat tree bark.

"I can't wait for a good meal," Laina muttered, echoing her thoughts. Sora silently agreed.

CHAPTER 17

A droplet of water struck Sora's cheek. Her eyes snapped open, taking in their makeshift campsite. Crash was already awake, sitting in the shade of a tree, eating a large red fruit. Several more fruits had been left in a pile next to the ashes of last night's fire. From the angle of the sun, she judged that it was midday. They had slept for a long, long time.

She sat up, pulling in a deep breath of air. Gray clouds mingled above her, broken up by gaps of blue sky. Not truly a storm, but capable of rain. Another droplet landed on the back of her hand and she smiled. It felt good to be outside the caves, back in the natural world. She took in a deep breath, tasting moisture on her tongue. She could hear the rush of the waterfall in the distance. They had only hiked about a mile into the forest before exhaustion had forced them to stop.

The Cat's Eye still throbbed dully at her chest, though not as terrible as before. She touched it briefly, remembering the *garrolithe*, wondering if that was somehow still inside the necklace. *How could such a thing exist?* She couldn't imagine the beast being contained by the stone. In her dreams, the monster had haunted her footsteps, following her through the labyrinthine depths of the Crystal Caves. She had glimpsed its reflection in the sunstone walls.

The rest of her companions began to stir around her. Burn sat up to her left, his hair tangled with leaves and twigs. Laina yawned next, pulling herself up into a sitting position. Sora grabbed a fruit for herself and bit down eagerly. Warm, sweet juice burst into her mouth.

"What now?" Laina asked, after they had eaten.

"We need to find a circle of sacred stones," Sora replied. She had been dwelling on her vision, the one spurred by her Cat's Eye at the start of this journey. *I hope we can find them in time. Volcrian can't be far behind us after that detour.* "They're somewhere on this island."

"That doesn't give us a lot of direction," Burn said slowly.

"The stones were next to the ocean," Sora recalled. The vision had been burned into her mind crisp and sharp by the Cat's Eye, as though she had just awakened from it. She was fairly sure she could draw the stone circle, given a quill and parchment. She touched her Cat's Eye, asking for a direction. She waited.

Disturbingly, the necklace remained quiet.

She tried again, sinking into her mind, searching for the stone's presence. She found it...but her connection felt clogged, blocked by something. The stone tried to communicate, but it was a dim murmur that she couldn't understand. She wondered if the *garrolithe* had anything to do with it. She frowned, uncertain.

"Well?" Laina asked impatiently. Sora was brought back to the present. Her friends were waiting. She swallowed, trying to hide her confusion.

"I remember the ocean," she repeated, then got to her feet, shouldering her staff. "We can follow the river. Let's hurry. There's no time to waste." She sounded tense, even to her own ears.

Burn frowned at her, but stood anyway, pulling up Laina beside him. "I'll lead for now," he said, a tactful way of taking charge. If he wondered about her hesitation, he didn't voice it aloud. He turned toward the river and started cutting back the underbrush. As he made headway, Laina followed at a safe distance.

Sora waited while the path was cleared. Crash caught her eye from across their campsite. She returned his look with a half-smile. *Everything's fine,* she thought. *Really....*Then she touched the necklace self-consciously. Had she broken it, somehow? Was that possible? Her thoughts raced, filling her with anxiety.

The assassin turned away and scattered the ashes from the fire, obscuring their camp with leaves and brush. Then he lifted up Burn's large satchel, swinging it over his shoulder. They followed the new trail through the trees.

The day was surprisingly cool, the forest lush and alive. Eventually, Burn found a deer trail and they followed it parallel to the river. All Sora cared about was getting to the coast. Once on the beach, they could start looking for the sacrificial stones. She tried to keep her thoughts focused on that, and not the failure of her necklace, or the possibility that Volcrian had already arrived. He would surely follow them—but how quickly?

They passed through tangled brush, odd roots and large ferns. The deer trail turned along the banks of the river, where it broadened into a walking path. It appeared ancient and abandoned, the stone cracked and worn. They came across large stone pillars, broken and toppled across the trail, as though long ago this had been a magnificent garden, full of statues and gazebos. Flagstones jutted from the ground at odd angles, puncturing the earth, the remains of a disheveled garden path. The trees changed as well, showing a greater mix of deciduous leaves: sycamore, ash and chestnut. They weren't native to the island; that she could tell.

Looking at the dense wilderness, Sora could almost imagine what it must have been like some four hundred years ago. Grand, perhaps. Manicured. Ornate.

"The gardens of Asterion were one of the great wonders of the Races," Burn said as they climbed over another fallen pillar. It was made of white limestone, carved with intricate shapes, some of which resembled feathers or flower petals. He sounded somewhat wistful. "Now it is a wilderness."

"A shame," Laina observed. "I wish the island had never fallen. My grandmother said that when Aerobourne fell, the days of true civilization ended."

"I think humans have done pretty well so far," Sora said, remembering the docks of Delbar and the bell-covered walls of Barcella. Humans might not have magic, but their world was vast and sprawled, their buildings large and majestic, full of history and tradition.

Laina gave her a narrow look. "Not when you're a street rat," she sniffed. "All ghettos look the same. My grandmother said that no Harpy ever went hungry in Asterion, and none were poor."

Sora sighed. Of course the girl would say that. "I doubt that's true," she commented.

Laina glared at her, but didn't reply.

After walking for another hour, Sora heard a dull chiming at the edge of her hearing. She paused between a large fern and a ruptured flagstone. Instinctively, her eyes traveled up to the sky.

"What is it?" Burn asked.

"The necklace...." Sora said, touching the stone. It still felt stifled and distant; she couldn't hear it as she once had. The jingling of bells was very dim, and yet....

Suddenly, she saw a speck on the horizon, a small white dot. After a moment, it was joined by two more white flecks. Sora stared at the quickly approaching figures. They moved much faster than birds, almost three times the speed, like arrows. She squinted, trying to make out more details.

"What...what are those?" she asked, pointing.

She heard Burn inhale sharply. He reached for his sword, an automatic gesture. "Crash," he growled. "They've seen us."

The assassin watched the sky, hesitating only for a moment, then grabbed Sora's arm. Hard. "Into the forest!" he snapped. "Take cover!"

Sora ran with him into the woods. His urgency was contagious. She wasn't sure if she feared the Harpies, but she found herself reaching for her knives. The points of light were approaching at a formidable pace. They would be above them any minute now.

Burn and Laina fell back, struggling through the deep underbrush. Sora looked back, spotting them a few yards behind. This area of the forest was dense with short scrub-oak and tall, broad maples. Perhaps at one time the grove had been crisply pruned and maintained, but now, thick, thorny bushes spread between the trunks, mingling with hemlock sprigs and poison ivy.

"Wait!" she heard Laina call. "We can't catch up."

"Watch out!" Burn yelled.

Suddenly, a burst of light filtered down through the trees, as though the sun had fallen toward them, brightening the earth. The light fell directly over Laina and Burn. Sora turned away, shielding her eyes. The back of her neck turned pink from the heat. She stumbled through a thick patch of bushes, hardly able to see.

Crash grabbed her upper arm again, leading her forward.

"Damn," she heard him mutter. "They're fast."

Sora could barely jog. The light felt like a barrier—she couldn't raise her head, couldn't straighten her back, her eyes were narrowed to slits. She could hear Burn and Laina fumbling and cursing, falling farther and farther behind.

Suddenly, a powerful voice rang out through the forest. It fell on her ears like a whiplash. "Stop."

Laina and Burn froze in place, unable to move. Sora's legs locked; her body vibrated with sound, as though she were a musical instrument struck by some unseen hand. Yet the Cat's Eye jingled fiercely in retaliation, breaking the spell, setting her legs free. She continued to run into the forest, leaving Burn and Laina behind. *There's no time! They're right on top of us!* Crash was by her side. He, too, was able to shake off the command, though he moved more sluggishly now.

Another flash of light. Something flew past her, as quick as a crossbow bolt. Sora cried out, shocked, wondering if she had been hit. Then something wrapped around Crash's legs, dragging him to the ground. The assassin let out a short cry as he went down.

Sora came to a skidding halt, her heart in her throat. She had never heard him make such a sound before. "Crash!" she screamed, dropping back to his side.

The assassin writhed on the ground. He reached for the weapon that bound his legs, but flinched back, hissing in pain.

Sora recognized it; she had used a smaller version of the weapon back at her mother's house when hunting. It was a bolas, a pair of weights attached to a chain, meant to trip an opponent—or entangle fleeing prey. Except instead of a regular chain, this one glowed white-hot, enchanted by some unknown magic. The weights on either end were not iron or rock, but sunstone.

The bolas bound his legs together tightly. The assassin's eyes were clamped shut, his face averted from the light. She could see welts and burns rising on his skin. The chain smoked where it touched his clothing.

"Goddess," Sora pleaded. She rolled him over, trying to free him from the web of light, but when she touched the bolas, it was like fire in her hands. She dropped the chain with a short hiss, her fingers already blistered.

"Run, Sora," Crash gasped. "Run!"

It was too late. The wind suddenly picked up, blasting through the trees, shaking leaves to the ground in a small hurricane. Sora squinted as a cloud of dust blew toward her. She got up on her feet, standing protectively over Crash's figure. A fierce determination filled her. She would not run from these beings. She had nothing to hide. She was here for the good of the Kingdom, the entire mainland.

The light brightened, then faded, though it did not fully disappear. Two men and a woman descended through the branches. They landed softly in the dirt, elegant, perfectly controlled. Sora raised her chin and tried not to feel intimidated.

At first glance, the Harpies appeared no different from humans, though perhaps slightly taller, long-limbed and willowy. They wore strange armor that looked like plates of glass instead of iron. It glinted in the sunlight, opalescent. Each suit of armor was studded with sunstones.

But their wings entranced her: possibly twelve feet or more in length, shining like starlight, pure white against the yellow afternoon sun. After landing, the glow slowly faded from their wings and they appeared like ordinary flesh and bone, similar to the doves she had kept at her manor.

They all had identical white-blond hair and large, luminescent eyes of various pastel colors, light green, light blue and...lavender.

Sora glanced to where Laina stood a few yards away. She and Burn were still rooted to the ground, frozen in place. Her hair was a tad darker than the Harpies', and yet her fine-boned features were the same, the paleness of her skin, the shade of her eyes.

Sora swallowed hard, choking on realization.

"I am Talarin." The first of the Harpies spoke, a tall female with long legs and giant wings, the largest of the lot. Her hair was thick and fell to her waist. It was pulled back by a large helmet that covered the crown of her head, then spiraled backwards and up, like a seashell. "You are trespassing on our land. We have come to escort you to our city. You may come peaceably...or not."

Sora's eyes shifted to the two men behind Talarin. One held a strange kind of crossbow made of white wood. It didn't appear to be loaded, and yet he held it trained on her, prepared to shoot. *I'd be a fool to run now,* she thought. The weapon had to be magic. Nothing else made sense. Her Cat's Eye might protect her...but she couldn't abandon her friends.

Sora nodded. "We've traveled to your island from the mainland. We are here on important business. We must speak to...er...." Did Harpies have Kings? Queens? She had no idea. "Whoever is in charge."

Talarin stared at her with sharp lavender eyes, as bright as amethysts. Then her gaze slid to the assassin on the ground. A look of disgust passed over her face. "Our Matriarch will decide who she wishes to speak to."

Sora opened her mouth. "Release him," she demanded, pointing to the assassin. "Then we'll come willingly with you."

Talarin sneered at her. "I'd much rather kill him." She raised her hand, signaling the man with the crossbow.

"Wait!" Sora said, and moved in front of Crash. She was at a huge disadvantage, and if she put up a fight, she would lose even more credibility. "All right," she agreed. "We'll come peaceably."

Talarin nodded in acceptance, then quickly motioned to the man on her right. "Feros, carry her."

Sora didn't have time to react. The male Harpy lunged forward, carried by his wings. Then, he was behind her. He grabbed her hands and tied them behind her back, all within a matter of seconds. She was stiff with shock.

"Mythas, take the Dark One," Talarin ordered.

The other Harpy shouldered his crossbow and glided swiftly to Crash's side. Sora was forced to stand back. She looked down at her fallen companion. He lay motionless in the dirt, his eyes averted, slightly glazed with pain, focused on the trees. Yet she could see a hardness in his gaze. Anger? Hatred?

A cold chill swept through her. She suddenly wondered what the Harpies would do. They seemed far more focused on capturing him. Perhaps Crash hadn't been exaggerating—perhaps he truly was in danger. She tried to quell the fear that accompanied that thought.

"No!" she burst out. "He'll cooperate! He won't fight you!"

"He'll fight," Talarin snapped. "Mythas, hurry up. Put a collar on him. Tell Caprion we've caught one—and he's *Named*."

Sora didn't like the woman's tone—full of cruel anticipation. She opened her mouth again, but didn't know what to say. She instinctively reached out to her Cat's Eye, trying to summon its power, perhaps use it as she had in the Crystal Caves. But the stone barely stirred.

Mythas knelt next to Crash's side and took a sunstone from the pouch on his belt. He held the sunstone out and Sora saw it flare up like a vibrant torch. The Harpy channeled his energy into it, making the stone glow brighter. Crash gritted his teeth, shut his eyes, and his body went rigid. She couldn't imagine what the stone was doing to him, but it looked...searingly painful.

Then Mythas knelt down and placed the stone at the base of Crash's throat. She almost cried out as his skin smoked and singed. Red welts began to form. She half-expected Crash to retaliate, lash out, fight back...perhaps scream...but he only lay there, unmoving. *Bound,* she suddenly realized. Bound by the sunstones.

Talarin walked back to Burn and Laina. The Harpy warrior grabbed one of them in each hand. When she touched them, a white light surrounded their bodies. The forest became saturated with unknown energy—it permeated the air, thick as sunlight.

The Harpy spread her wings and then leapt from the ground, carrying both of her companions upward, compelled by an invisible power. Sora couldn't believe her eyes. Laina would have been easy to carry, but Burn was almost seven feet tall, a towering mountain of dense muscle and bone. Yet the Harpy made it look effortless.

The other two followed Talarin's lead. Within minutes, Sora found herself carried far above the forest, toward the distant City of Asterion.

* * *

From above, the City of Asterion was covered by wilderness, the ancient buildings obscured by trees, barely discernible from the forest itself. Yet the buildings stretched on and on, from the center of the island up to the coast. Sora looked, but caught no sight of the sacred stones.

They landed in an empty courtyard of white stone, somewhere just outside the city proper. It was surrounded by a high, white wall. The Harpies flew swiftly, yet touched down with the gentleness of a blown leaf.

The giant marble slabs of the courtyard were cracked and displaced. Weeds poked up through the gaps. The walls were tall and arched, covered in moss and hanging ivy. Wildflowers had taken root in the deep shade, some finding purchase amongst the split rocks. A great stone threshold led into a large temple. The courtyard was completely enclosed. Sora had the feeling that one could only fly in or out.

Talarin released both Laina and Burn, then turned to Sora's captor, Feros. "Go check on Mythas," she commanded. "Make sure the Dark One is still bound."

"Where did you take him?" Sora asked. She couldn't stop herself. She needed to know that they wouldn't kill Crash.

"Do you wish to speak to the Matriarch or not?" Talarin snapped. Her voice lingered in the air, echoing around the old stones.

Sora caught a wary glance from Burn, and she hesitated. If she seemed too sympathetic to Crash, perhaps the Harpies would become suspicious—and much less inviting.

"Yes, of course," she answered Talarin's question. "As soon as possible." Talarin nodded to Feros, and the Harpy took to the air again, lifting easily from the courtyard. Within seconds, he was gone from sight. Her gut twisted sickeningly.

"I will escort you to the Matriarch's chambers," Talarin spoke again. Her voice was firm and curt, like a soldier. "Come."

They walked through the courtyard into a garden of sorts. Wild jasmine clung to every surface. A large fountain spilled clear water into a limestone pool. The garden felt serene and yet somehow forbidden, as though rarely looked upon. They passed through it quickly and entered the temple.

The hall before them was much different from the walls outside. So different, in fact, that Sora felt that she had come to the wrong place. Every surface was pristine, dusted and shined, made of brilliant white marble. The hall was brightly lit by sunstone pillars on either side. Long midnight-blue curtains fell from the ceiling, clasped to the walls in a decorative fashion. The floor tile was black-and-white, paved in a dizzying pattern. Other than that, it was empty; there were no chairs, tables or windows.

"I will leave you here," Talarin said. "When the Matriarch calls for you, simply enter through those doors, and you will find yourself in her chamber." Talarin paused, glancing over Sora, Burn and Laina with a cold look. "If you run, we will kill you."

Sora nodded, her mouth going dry. Then the lady Harpy turned and walked swiftly from the room. Every couple of steps, she seemed to hover in the air, gliding forward on her powerful wings.

As soon as she was gone, Sora turned to Burn, fear clogging her throat. "What are we going to do?" she hissed. "Where did they take Crash?"

"Keep your voice down," Burn murmured. "These hallways

echo. Let me do the talking."

Sora blinked. "But...."

"I doubt the Matriarch will be very sympathetic to a girl with a Cat's Eye," Burn said, his voice soft and rushed. "Don't forget the history of your two peoples; the Harpies certainly have not."

Sora was speechless. She hadn't considered that before. *Stupid!* she thought. Once again, caught by her own naiveté. Of course the Harpies would look upon her less than favorably. She was the reason why their island had crashed into the ocean—the cause of their civilization's collapse. Perhaps she was in more danger here than she realized. Maybe even more danger than Crash.

She quickly checked her necklace, making sure it was hidden under her shirt. Good. Perhaps the Harpies hadn't noticed it yet.

"Their voices," Laina said softly, drawing her attention. The girl was staring up the long hallway toward the doors on the opposite side, her eyes soft and large. "Their voices are so beautiful. How did they stop us from running?"

"It is their magic," Burn said tightly. "Harpies carry the magic of song and star, of Wind and Light. Their voices hold influence over nature. They can sing powerful spells that bind your limbs and control your mind."

Sora's eyes widened. "But what of that light in the forest?" she asked, and gingerly touched the back of her neck. It stung like a severe sunburn.

"Their wings emit the light of the stars," Burn explained briefly. "The larger a Harpy's wings, the more powerful they are. But their light is used mainly to destroy the children of the Dark God, the Sixth Race." He looked at her sternly, acknowledging that she knew the truth about Crash. "They see it as their sacred duty to rid the world of darkness. Usually they kill the Unnamed on sight."

"I knew it," Laina sniffed, her nose turning upward. "See? I told you that my grandmother wasn't a liar. The Harpies protect us from evil. Don't worry, Sora," she added, suddenly full of certainty. "They won't hurt us. They want to protect the world!"

Sora nodded, but she didn't believe what Laina said. The girl's ideas were just as naïve as her own. She was simply spouting off words, saying whatever might be reassuring.

And Laina clearly hadn't yet realized Crash's true identity.

Sora had the sudden, vicious urge to strangle her. *Don't you understand?* She wanted to scream. *They're going to kill him! They're going to torture him with sunstones and then burn him into oblivion!* It made her sick, desperate with panic.

Burn touched her shoulder lightly, as though hearing her thoughts. She looked up into his broad, calm face, his deep gold eyes. "Don't worry," he said. "I will speak for us."

Sora nodded again, this time gratefully. Burn might be their only chance to save Crash's life.

At that moment, a low rumble moved through the hallway, a deep vibration that reached Sora's bones. Suddenly the doors opened in front of them, leading to the next chamber. A low, melodic voice drifted through the air, seeming to emanate from the sunstones on the walls.

"You may enter," intoned the voice.

Sora looked at Burn one last time, then clasped Laina's hand. The three travelers walked down the marble hallway, toward the brilliant white doors.

CHAPTER 18

In the next chamber, the ceiling arched above them in a perfect dome, stretching perhaps thirty feet tall. At its apex was the inlaid design of a giant star, apparently made out of pure gold, that had to be at least ten feet wide. The craftsmanship was extravagant, detailed, perfect. Chiseled filigree decorated its surface. Sora's eyes lingered on the star, wondering how long it had taken to create, and how they had managed to fasten it so high above the ground. *Of course, they can fly,* she admonished herself. But it didn't make the sight any less impressive.

Polished glass floors reflected the light of six large sunstones, embedded around the top of the walls, evenly distanced from each other. In the center of the room stood a large, raised dais and a massive throne carved of white marble. The back of the throne matched the starry ceiling, spiking upward in five great points tipped with gold, as though echoing the sunrise. Every surface contained inlaid patterns, rich with swirls, circles and symbols. It reminded Sora of an ancient and sacred temple, a place of worship and power.

A woman sat atop the throne. Her white gown was long and flowing, made of sheer fabric, layered over her body like fine sheets of ice. A halo of light surrounded her, a soft glow that teased the eyes; her presence seemed to fill the chamber, as palpable as a song. Her white-blond hair fell to her waist in glorious waves. She was strikingly beautiful, more than an ordinary mortal, her features perfect and ageless. She seemed young and old all at once, her skin flawlessly smooth, yet her eyes were ancient, heavy and bold.

Burn knelt to the ground and Sora followed suit, making Laina kneel as well. They bowed, their heads lowered, waiting. Beads of perspiration sprang up on Sora's brow.

"Rise," the Matriarch said. Her voice rang around the chamber, amplified by the stone walls and domed ceiling. It was middle-pitched, low for a woman, rich and soothing.

Sora stood up. Recalling her life at the manor, when she had been a noblewoman trained in the art of propriety, she kept her hands clasped before her and her head slightly lowered out of respect. She hoped the Harpy would interpret her stance as subservient, rather than think she was hiding something.

"A Wolfy," the Matriarch said, her eyes landing on Burn. A long, slow smile curled on her lips. "I didn't think your race survived the War."

"Most of us did not," Burn said briefly. His voice was harsh and grating next to the Matriarch's, like hearing a cymbal crash after the most beautiful serenade. Sora winced, surprised by the difference.

"What brings you to my island?" the Matriarch asked. She didn't sound terribly interested, and yet her eyes were keen with intelligence, observing all three travelers. Sora felt as if the Harpy could see right through her, and resisted the urge to touch her Cat's Eye.

"It has been a long journey," Burn said. "We have come as friends to ask for your help in a very serious matter."

The Matriarch nodded. "Does this concern the Wolfy bloodmage that is sailing to us?" she asked bluntly.

Sora sucked in a short breath. So they knew. Of course. They probably had knowledge of every ship that entered their waters.

Burn seemed equally surprised, and paused for a moment before answering. "Yes," he said. "That is exactly why we are here."

"Then state your purpose," she said, her voice dropping a notch, somehow threatening.

"The mage follows us on a misplaced hunt for revenge," Burn said quickly. "He has used several spells against us that are condoned as black-blooded magic."

"Raising the dead?" the Matriarch asked.

"Yes..." Burn replied. Once again, he didn't seem to expect the Matriarch's knowledge. Sora was relieved. The Harpies knew of blood magic and its uses, apparently to a great extent. That would make their quest much easier to explain.

Burn continued. "The bloodmage is not as skilled in his craft as he would like to believe. There have been consequences. The Dark God's power is beginning to leak back into the world. It has tainted this mage with a dark magic that he doesn't understand, far beyond the abilities of a simple Wolfy. We think it is possessing him. We have lured him to this island in hopes of destroying him before more damage can be done."

The Matriarch abruptly stood up. A glimmer of light passed through the room, and the Matriarch's wings shimmered into existence. They were...*massive,* spanning almost twenty-five feet across, half the width of the chamber. And yet they were not as solid and bright as Talarin's. They flickered, ghostly shapes that emanated from her shoulders, there and yet...not there.

Sora wondered at this. Perhaps the Harpies' wings were made of pure magic. Pure light. And maybe their manifestation could be controlled.

The Matriarch stepped down from her dais and stood immediately in front of Sora, who looked up, filled with a sense of dread.

"It's been many years since a human has been to this island," she spoke, her voice rich with magic. "Why are you here?"

Sora opened her mouth, yet didn't know what to say. Her eyes darted to Burn.

The Matriarch smiled cunningly. "Talarin says our voices do not affect you," she said smoothly. "I can see that this is true. Allow me to guess." The Matriach's hand shot out, and grabbed Sora's Cat's Eye through her shirt. Sora stood in shock, staring down at the Matriarch's long arm. The fabric shielded the stone, but it glowed bright green at the Harpy's presence. Sora heard the dim chime of bells.

The Matriarch released her after a moment. "We have known of your presence since your ship sank," she said, turning back to Burn. "And I daresay, we know your plan to use our sacred stones. This is why you have led the bloodmage here, is it not?"

Burn nodded silently.

The Matriarch strode around her chamber, deep in thought. "We, perhaps even more so than those on the mainland, know of this rising darkness." She turned and gave Sora a strange look, one that made her feel small and insignificant. "Humans do not know the dangers of the Dark God. They do not know the history of what happened before. And even if they did, they would not know how to stop it from happening again." Her lip curled. "A Wolfy bloodmage, I could care less about. But it is the sacred duty of our race to contain the Dark God. To ensure that He does not rise again. And for that, I will help you."

Sora hesitated, struck by the Matriarch's words. "You mean, this has happened before?"

The Matriarch looked insulted by her question. "Of course, child," she said. "It is the way of the world. The sun has risen and set for thousands of years, and yet the hours of the day are the same. History repeats itself. Do you know how old I am?"

The question caught her off-guard. Sora's lips parted. "N-no," she stuttered, unable to turn away from the woman's luminescent eyes.

"I became the Matriarch of this island more than four hundred years ago," she said, her voice ringing with authority. "I watched it crash into the sea. And over those years, I have watched darkness come and go from the mainland, lingering on the horizon, yet never spreading. It is a human darkness. A weak, petty thing, like rats fighting in the streets for bread. Something easily crushed, that time itself will resolve." She continued walking forward until she stood inches away from Sora. Her presence was so powerful that Sora's knees shook.

"But this shadow that rises now, that of the Dark God...." the Matriarch continued. "It covers the mainland in a thick blanket, and is the consistency of tar. It is not something easily dispelled. We are creatures of Light, yet there is a darkness greater than the night shadows—greater than we can penetrate. It absorbs all that it touches. It is evil, young one, of a like that you cannot fathom, because humans are momentary creatures, your lives short and fleeting. You only know the evil of a few decades, that which hardens you, that might throw you out onto the streets."

The Matriarch shook her head. "No, the power of the Dark God runs much deeper than that. It is chaos. Pure, natural chaos that was birthed with the world, that tore apart the mountains and boiled the seas. It consumes life and destroys it, not because it is hateful—but because that is its nature." The Matriarch stared at Sora unwaveringly. "Do you understand?"

Sora nodded, barely able to move.

The Matriarch smirked softly. "Then you know why you sound so pathetic. Even if you kill the mage, the Dark God's power will continue to seep into the land. You cannot seal it away with a little Cat's-Eye stone." Her smirk grew into a cold sneer. "You and the necklace will be destroyed in this endeavor, and the First Race will clean up your mess."

The Matriarch turned away. Sora pulled in a long breath, released from the vise-like grip of the Harpy's eyes. What was the woman saying? That the Harpies would help—but only after she and Burn failed? Her brow darkened. *Old hag,* she thought.

The Matriarch continued to speak as she returned to her throne, stepping slowly and gracefully up to the dais. It was only then that Sora realized that the Harpy wasn't truly walking on the ground, but a few inches above it; her feet were not touching the floor.

"The nature of the Sixth Race is one of chaotic destruction," she continued. "It is deeply embedded in every one of them. They mimic people of flesh and bone, but do not be deceived. Inside each of the Unnamed lives a shard of the Dark God. A demon waiting to be released, barely controlled by years of discipline. Their race is vile, their power drawn from death, from the fire and darkness of the underworld. You have brought one to our island." She sat down fluidly, relaxing back into her chair as though she were discussing the weather. "Why?"

Crash. She was speaking of Crash. Sora's hands grew clammy and hot. Fear constricted her lungs.

"He is our captive," Burn cut in abruptly.

The Matriarch turned her bright eyes upon him. "Captive?" she asked.

"Yes. We have brought him here to lure the mage to this island. The mage is on a quest for revenge and hunts him tirelessly. It was the only way to make him follow us."

Sora felt her chest loosen slightly. *Brilliant,* she thought, turning to look at Burn, mentally congratulating the Wolfy. *Just brilliant.*

"I see," the Matriarch said slowly, her eyes looking from one to the other. Sora could tell that she wasn't convinced, and tried not to look away from her.

"For this reason," Burn said, "I'd ask that you not kill him until the mage is dead. In case something goes wrong, it is the only way to lure him out."

The Matriarch looked at Burn, then at Sora, then at Laina for a long moment. "I will allow you to carry out this plan on our island," she finally said. "But we will restrain demon in our prison. He cannot walk free." Then she nodded to Laina, as though noticing her for the first time. "And what of this halfling?"

Halfling? Sora had never heard such a term before. She glanced at Laina, who had been riveted by the Matriarch the entire time.

The Harpy motioned Laina to approach her. "Come closer, child. I see our blood in you."

Laina's eyes widened even more, if that was possible. Sora felt her heart plummet. No, the girl couldn't be mixed with such an arrogant race. It didn't bode well for anyone. What if she started speaking and revealed their alliance with Crash? It would undermine the Matriarch's trust, fragile as it was. They might all end up in prison.

"Your Majesty," Laina said, bowing awkwardly. Sora winced. She was fairly certain that wasn't the appropriate title for a Harpy Matriarch.

But the Harpy smiled anyway and held out her hand. "You were born on the mainland?" she asked, glancing over Laina's disheveled appearance. Sora wanted to wince at that too. All three of them probably looked ratty and tired, like dogs dragged out of a swamp.

"Yes ma'am," Laina nodded. At least the girl was on her best behavior.

"How very interesting. I have yet to meet a halfling from the mainland. Welcome to the City of Asterion." The Matriarch lowered her hand and glanced over Laina with a wry expression. "Would you care for a tour?"

Laina's mouth dropped open. "Would I!" she exclaimed. Then, recovering herself, she cleared her throat. "Yes, ma'am. I mean, I'd be honored."

"Wonderful. Then I will arrange it for you. Caprion!"

The Matriarch cried out the name like a bugle call. It rang through the air, echoing, echoing....

Abruptly Sora felt a presence at her back. Prickles ran over her skin. She turned, surprised, as a second figure entered the room. He must have been waiting in the hallway. How long had he been standing there?

The man was slightly taller than Crash. He had the build of a warrior: wide shoulders, trim waist, muscled chest. He was dressed in a soft white tunic, very plain, with brown leggings and tall black boots. Just like the Matriarch, his wings were hidden from view, a slight halo around his back.

But his face...his face was unlike anything Sora had seen before. It was perfectly symmetrical and beautiful, beyond anything human. His nose was straight and sharp, his jaw square and pronounced, his lips full and firm. His eyes were a sharp violet, a shade richer than Laina's and Talarin's, smoky and vibrant all at once. His hair swept across his brow in platinum waves, falling just below his ears, as though he had forgotten to trim it recently.

He, too, had a presence like the Matriarch, except it was more masculine, louder, as though a raging star of fire had entered the room. Sora's eyes dropped to his belt, and she saw a familiar dagger hanging there, dark against his light clothing. It belonged to Crash. Her breath caught.

"My Lady of the One Star," he said, addressing the Matriarch with a slight bow. His voice was as pure as river water. Then he turned to the rest of them, regarding the three visitors with a cool facade.

"This is Caprion. He is the Guardian of our city and the General of our army," the Matriarch said, a hint of pride entering her voice. "He is the first seraphim to be born since the War."

"A seraphim?" Burn murmured.

Sora glanced at the Wolfy, wondering what a seraphim was. Some kind of special Harpy? A rare breed, perhaps?

"Caprion, these are my new guests," The Matriarch said, though to Sora, it sounded less than inviting. "Do keep an eye on them while they are in the city. They are not to travel unescorted." She gave the orders flippantly, as though bored.

"My Lady," Caprion nodded.

So there will be guards at our door? Sora thought. She couldn't help but feel insulted. The Matriarch had done nothing but mock them since arriving in her chamber. Despite warning them about the Dark God, she obviously didn't plan on doing much. No, the Matriarch would sit back on her throne and watch the show from afar, just as the Harpies watched the mainland.

I should have listened to Crash, Sora lamented. *We should have avoided the Harpies from the beginning.*

"See that the halfling has a tour of the city. I will dine privately with her tonight." The Matriarch stood up from her chair. "If you have any needs while you are under our care, please address them to Caprion. He will see that you are supplied with all that is reasonable."

Wonderful, Sora thought. She eyed the dagger at Caprion's belt again. *He must know where Crash is.* This, at least, gave her some hope.

The Harpy General turned on his heel and walked back into the long hallway, obviously expecting them to follow. Sora paused for a half-second, wondering if she should bow or say something in farewell, but there was no time to linger. She hurried to catch up to the General, her shoulders stiff with tension. She shared a look with Burn and knew that he felt the same.

* * *

Caprion escorted them back into the courtyard. The setting

sun cast an orange glow across the white walls. He paused outside, then created a strange series of symbols with his fingers, like intricate sign-language.

A cloud of pale light surrounded them. Sora sucked in a sharp breath, hoping her Cat's Eye didn't respond to the magic and deflect the spell. Yet the necklace remained quiet—which was equally disturbing.

Caprion watched her reaction closely, making her nervous.

With a final motion of his hand, he easily raised them all off the ground. Sora's heart hammered against her ribs. She felt as though she were standing on solid air. It was unnerving, watching the courtyard drop away from her, yet still having the sense of standing upright.

The three travelers glided quickly over the wall, landing outside of the building on a stone pathway. Caprion landed gracefully behind them.

"That was amazing!" Laina burst out, turning to look at the Harpy General. She seemed oblivious to the danger they were in— or perhaps, after the Matriarch's invitation, she felt more like a guest of honor. Sora watched her in annoyance.

Caprion smiled faintly. "Your quarters are this way," he said, and turned, leading them down the path.

Sora fell into step behind him, scowling at his back. So far, every Harpy she had met had the arrogance of the First Tier. They acted as though they were each kings in their own right. It reminded her vaguely of her life back at the manor, always aware of her inferiority, always trying to live up to some unattainable ideal. That grated on her nerves.

They passed through a quarter-mile of dense trees, leaving the city proper. After about twenty minutes, Caprion showed them to a large oval-shaped building made of white limestone. Sora thought it resembled an upside-down bowl, perhaps two stories high, chiseled with emblems of the sun and moon. A balcony encircled the second tier. She could see windows spaced evenly apart, made of heavy marbled glass that captured the light. The sun was beginning to set, so the glass was turned bright orange. She could imagine at midday, the windows would become like vibrant prisms, reflecting all sorts of colors. She had never seen anything like it on the mainland.

There was no sign of a door. With another casual sweep of his hand, Caprion lifted them up and set them to the second-story balcony, where a large archway led into the building. They landed on the smooth limestone and Caprion motioned for them to enter. Sora passed beneath the archway into the large dome.

An inner-balcony made of wood circled the upper floor, and Sora could see rooms branching off, connected by simple beaded doors. A winding staircase led to the bottom floor; the ground was paved with wide, smooth bricks of rusty red. A large fountain sat low to the ground, empty of water and collecting leaves. It looked like a ghostly memory, something left over from another time.

"I will post two of my soldiers on the floor below," Caprion said, leading them in a semi-circle around the second-story walkway. "The only way to leave this building is by flight. If you have need of anything, tell my men and they will assist you. You are not to travel unescorted. If you do, we will find you very easily." He didn't bother to look at them as he spoke.

Sora considered that; she had a Cat's Eye and could evade their spells, if she could get it to work correctly. She wondered if she would be able to slip out quietly during the night to find Crash's location. She was desperate to see him—but would it be worth it? If she tried to escape, she would lose the Matriarch's trust, as fragile as it was.

Her eyes lingered on the blade at Caprion's belt. Crash wouldn't give up his dagger without a fight, which meant he was still bound by the sunstone...*or dead,* she admitted. But she didn't want to dwell on that possibility. *It's Crash. He'll find a way to survive.*

Still, the sunstone had completely debilitated him....

Caprion paused, indicating a series of beaded doors. "These are your rooms," he said. "Pick whichever you'd like." He turned to face them, speaking in his melodic voice. "There are many buildings in Asterion that you can only reach by flight. There is no use going off to explore on your own. You will find yourselves...quite limited." As he glanced over them, his expression was similar to the Matriarch's—as though they lacked some essential appendage.

"What about my tour?" Laina asked.

"I will return in an hour for you," he said. He arched an eyebrow. "Make yourself presentable." He glanced over their tattered appearance but refrained from further comment.

Sora watched him turn and walk away. As with the Matriarch, it took her a moment to realize that he wasn't truly walking, but hovering over the ground.

She looked down at two other Harpies in the building, standing next to the silent fountain. They were large men in shining armor with swords strapped to their sides. Their wings were clearly visible, with spans of around twelve feet. She looked at their boots carefully, but if their shadows were any indication, they were standing evenly on the ground.

What of Caprion's wings? she wondered, her gaze returning to the General's back. Only he and the Matriarch hovered as they walked, as though touching the floor took more effort than flying. Would his wings be as wide as the Matriarch's, and just as grand? How powerful? *A seraphim Harpy....*From his air of confidence, she had the feeling he was a formidable warrior.

"This is wonderful!" Laina said, turning to grin at them. "I'm going to have a tour of the city! Can you believe it? Me! The Matriarch spoke to me...." Her eyes were alight with excitement. Laina whirled toward the closest room, a definite bounce in her step. "I have to get ready," she gushed. "See you in an hour!"

Sora stared after her as though the girl had gone mad. But of course, Laina's imagination had been fueled by her grandmother's stories, and now she had the full attention of the Harpy Matriarch. Sora shook her head slowly. *A halfling.*

"I don't like it," Sora said softly, after Laina had disappeared. "She's too trusting."

"I agree," Burn replied. He hesitated, and then added, "I'll have a quick word with her. Make sure she understands the gravity of the situation."

Sora nodded. "Do you think the Matriarch is trying to use her? Get more information out of her?"

Burn let out a long, slow breath. "The Harpies are very intelligent," he said, "and long-lived. I wouldn't doubt it. I just hope the poor girl doesn't get used and thrown away. I don't think Harpies are especially fond of halflings. They are a proud race."

Sora had to agree. It made sense—why would someone as

domineering as the Matriarch take interest in a half-human girl, unless it was to pry information out of her? Laina had played directly into her hands.

It made her somewhat sad. She couldn't imagine what the girl must be feeling. To be an orphan for so long...and then to discover that she was part of an ancient race, even if it was only by half. What would Laina do to find a sense of belonging?

She sighed, reining in her thoughts, forcing herself not to worry. Laina was young, but her heart was in the right place. She wouldn't betray them so quickly.

Sora walked through the open archway into her room, in search of a bucket and washcloth.

CHAPTER 19

The wide room beyond had a huge window that opened out onto the balcony. A bed with white, gauzy curtains sat against the wall farthest from the tub. The mattress was lumpy but not completely uncomfortable, and free of bed bugs.

After bathing in a large white tub, Sora dressed in an outfit of white silk that had been left out. Her clothing was both intricate and simple: a white undershirt made of sheer mesh that conformed tightly to her skin, a pair of white breeches and tall white boots, made of butter-soft leather, clasped at the knees, and a long white robe, similar to the silken nightrobe her mother had worn on summer nights. The robe tied at the waist with a thick, silvery sash. Once the ensemble was put together, Sora felt quite comfortable in the light, airy fabric. She found a hairbrush laid out next to the bed, carved of bone, and brushed her hair. Then she pulled her hair back in a fishtail braid.

Sora stood in front of the mirror for a moment, looking at herself. She barely recognized her own face. Her hair was lighter than before, bleached by the sun. There were fading bruises along her cheekbone, and her jaw stood out far more than it used to. She looked tan, hard and lean. More than that, her expression troubled her. She tried to smile, but it didn't quite reach her eyes. The smile looked forced, somehow. Insincere.

Goddess....Since when had she become so hardened? She looked far more like a warrior than she felt.

Just then she heard the sound of voices in the hallway.

Sora shouldered her staff and stood just beyond the beaded curtain, listening. Caprion's unmistakable voice rang through the domed building. "Klaren will escort you around the city tonight. Please remain in her line of sight at all times. Afterwards, the Matriarch has invited you to dinner."

"Thank you!" Laina replied. "I feel honored!"

Sora could sense Caprion's smile, the vague crook of his lips, without even seeing his face.

The seraphim continued to speak. "Burn, the Matriarch would like you to accompany Laina on her tour of the city, but you will retire before dinner. We will have a separate meal served to your room."

"I thought the Matriarch only wanted Laina to see the city," Burn rumbled, a deep croak compared to Caprion's rising tenor.

"She often changes her mind," the seraphim murmured. There it was, that smile again. Sora grimaced, imagining the Harpy's expression.

Burn's silence was his only response.

A series of footsteps passed by Sora's door. She could see the faint outline of silhouettes through the beaded curtain, including one with large white wings. She closed her eyes briefly. Good, they would be leaving her behind. Maybe she would have the opportunity to sneak out after all. She had to locate Crash....

"Ahem."

Sora took a surprised step backwards. Caprion's face suddenly appeared through the beaded curtain. She was shocked by his sudden appearance, the way he looked at her with his vibrant amethyst eyes.

"You're coming with me," he said directly.

Sora felt her skin tingle. The power of that voice....She found herself stepping forward, not even questioning. But then she shrugged that compulsion off, relying on a small tendril of her Cat's Eye.

"Where?" she asked instead.

Caprion frowned. He looked like he wasn't used to being questioned. "I'm going to show you the city," he said.

Sora's eyes narrowed. She didn't trust this man, not in the least. He wanted to keep an eye on her, make sure she didn't cause any mischief. But why not just station extra guards at her door? What game was he playing at?

"Fine," Sora said resignedly. She briefly checked herself, making sure she had all her belongings. Her staff, daggers, and the extra Cat's Eye folded in cloth, shoved in her pocket....

Then she followed Caprion into the hallway. He glided in front of her, covering far more ground than his steps should allow. Sora had to walk swiftly to keep up with him. Two guards stood in the foyer below and saluted him as he passed, lowering their eyes in respect. He ignored them.

Once they were outside, Sora watched as he raised his right hand, creating the same signs as he had before. She saw the soft glow surround her body. "Where are we going?" she asked. This time when he lifted her into the air, it was far less shocking. He hovered next to her, flying effortlessly through the night, his wings still invisible.

"To Asterion's eastern district," he explained. "There is something I would like you to see."

Sora didn't know what to say to that.

The two landed a few kilometers away. The trees slowly fell back beneath them, becoming more widely spaced, until she could see the buildings of the city easily. Towering structures, stretching up and up, crossed by white limestone bridges and buttresses. Their windows were the same as the small domed building where she was staying: large and oval-shaped, capturing the very last rays of the sinking sun and turning the light into rainbow hues.

The pair set down in an empty market square. Sora looked up at the massive buildings that were far larger than anything on the mainland, stretching five or six stories or more. They resembled tall spears jutting from the ground, with spiraling towers and domed peaks, balconies upon balconies on each floor. The walls were inlaid with stone murals, patterns and filigree. None of the buildings had doors, she noticed. All of entryways were tall stone arches that opened onto the ground floors. Some were obscured by hanging beads or mats.

Limestone blocks paved the ground beneath her. Just like the riverside garden, almost half the blocks were broken and splintered. Weeds and grass grew up through narrow crevices. Wild ivy had taken root, climbing over porch steps and tall pillars, scaling the architecture. The great walls looked chipped and worn, slowly crumbling before the elements.

Everything had a sense of age and silence, as though she stood amidst a lost and abandoned city.

"Where is everyone?" she couldn't help but ask.

"This is the business quarter," Caprion explained. He stood in the center of the market square, watching her closely. "Everyone has gone home for the day. Before the Great Fall, this city was one of the largest in existence. Shop owners would live above their businesses, crammed on top of each other." He nodded to the darkened windows of the upper stories. They looked dirty and unused. "Our population has dwindled over the years. Now there are more than enough dwellings to choose from."

Sora nodded. *Why is he telling me this?* She gazed at the hollow courtyard, the haunted windows of the empty buildings. The shadows were slowly lengthening on the walls, the sun crawling ever- lower in the sky. It was eerily quiet.

"Come," he said, and strode away toward a narrow alley that led between the buildings. Sora hesitated, glancing around once again. She had no choice. She had to follow him.

They traveled up the alley, through closely packed storefronts, half of them abandoned. Some looked like they hadn't been used in years, their doors smothered in cobwebs and ivy. She followed Caprion over piles of rubble and clumps of ferns that sprouted up from the ruined sidewalk. It felt like the forest was slowly invading the city, spreading into every corner. Within another hundred years, she could imagine the entire city being overtaken by dandelions and scrub brush.

Eventually they left the compact business quarter and entered a stretch of forest, following the paved pathway that curved slightly upward. Sora saw evidence of benches and tables, half-buried under moss. Perhaps long ago this had been another courtyard, a beautiful outdoor cafe or a public park, where citizens would sit and enjoy the midday sun.

The pathway connected with a wide thoroughfare at the base of a giant hill. The forest fell back behind them and the hillside curled at their feet, rolling into the air, stretching up and up, covered by tall dry grass. Sora leaned back, impressed by its height.

The hillside dwarfed the surrounding countryside like a giant's grave, higher than even the buildings of Asterion and almost a mile across.

This new road could fit several wagons side-by-side. Lining the street was a series of tall statues, each larger than life. Caprion led her around the base of the hill, following the road. They passed the statues slowly, giving her time to observe each one. All were Harpies with grand wings, either carrying swords, scrolls or books. Some of the Harpies had two or three sets of wings lining their backs. These statues were always dressed in elaborate armor and carried fierce weapons, swords of fire or massive war hammers—albeit of stone.

They reached the end of the series of statues. The road continued, winding up the hill out of sight. The stars had come out, glinting in the darkness, the only source of light other than the strange glow that emanated from Caprion's skin. Toward the top of the hill, she saw what looked like a temple, now just a vague mound in the darkness.

"Where are we?" she finally asked, turning to her escort.

He was watching her again. "This is the Road of Remnants," he said quietly. "And beyond this is the Singing Chamber."

"The Singing Chamber?"

"Yes." Caprion turned away, looking toward the top of the hill. "It is a deep bowl in the earth, carved from a bed of sunstone. Young Harpies go there to find their wings."

"Find their...?" Sora frowned, unsure if she understood.

Caprion continued. "We are born of Wind and Light. All Harpies have powerful voices from the moment we are born. But to truly unlock our magic, we must find our stars." His eyes looked to the sky, the star-strewn blanket above them. "We cast our voices far out into the heavens...and hope that one day, our star sings back. When we find it, then our wings emerge and we are able to harness the full power of Light."

Sora frowned even more. "So not all Harpies have wings?" she asked, eyeing his back.

He shook his head. "No, not all. It is a terrible thing for a Harpy to have no wings."

Sora nodded, absorbing this fact. Then she asked the question that had been on the tip of her tongue. "Do *you* have wings?" she asked.

Caprion turned to look at her, a glimmer of surprise on his face. "Of course," he said. Then his look slowly melted into a mischievous smile. Sora felt her heart begin to pound. *Beautiful.* It seemed unfair that one of the races should be so damned pretty.

"Would you like to see my wings?" he asked quietly.

Sora paused, glancing around nervously, wondering if this was some sort of trap. Just what were they doing out here, all alone? Why had he brought her to this place? Had the Matriarch ordered it? Was it some elaborate ploy so she would reveal her Cat's Eye?

Yet she had the feeling that this was a rare opportunity. That he didn't offer the sight of his wings to just anyone....

"Yes," she finally replied.

"I can't show you their full intensity," he explained. "The light would blind you."

Sora nodded.

Caprion closed his eyes, raising one hand before his chest in a half-prayer. Immediately, the air shimmered behind him.

A mantle of light appeared across his shoulders. She saw the shape of giant wings unfurl from his back. She clenched her fists, amazed at their size. The wings took up the entire width of the road, similar to the Matriarch's.

Then another set of wings began to unfurl, and Sora took a step back, pressing a hand to her mouth. They were shorter, smaller and translucent, more like the impression of wings. After a minute, she counted as many as six protruding from his back. Then she had to turn her face slightly away, raising her hand to shield her eyes. It was too bright. She felt heat against her skin, similar to a sunburn.

By the North Wind! How many were there? Six? Eight?

Her Cat's Eye finally responded. It jingled fiercely, tightening in her chest, prepared to defend against a magical attack. Sora put her hand on the gem unconsciously, pressing the stone through her shirt, trying to calm herself. Caprion's wings were beautiful, yes, like staring into the depths of a star, yet they also terrified her.

"A...seraphim...." she murmured.

"We are born purely for war," Caprion explained.

Sora continued to avert her eyes. *This* was a seraphim? She suddenly imagined the floating island of Aerobourne from so many centuries ago, the intense magic that had lifted the island from the ground, and the flying warriors, like shards of starlight come to life, that had guarded this city. How had anyone ever fought against this race? How had the humans ever won? It seemed absurd. An entire army...with *this* power....

Slowly the light faded and the wings became a vague shimmer on his back, then silhouettes, then they were gone. His voice returned to normal as well, no longer striking her like a bell. "Do not be afraid," he said quietly. "I did not bring you here to harm you."

"Then...then why?" Sora asked. "Why did you bring me here?"

"I wanted you to see the ruins of our city," Caprion replied. "I wanted you to understand what has happened to our race."

Sora stared at him suspiciously. "Why?" she asked again.

"Believe it or not," he said, "you are the first human I have ever met. You also strike me as someone who might understand what I have shown you."

Sora was surprised by his words. She had been so caught in the foreign majesty of this place, that she hadn't realized how out-of-place she must seem. Humans were so common...how could she possibly be the first he had met?

She considered his words and glanced over her shoulder, back to the ruined spires of the city. "And what have you shown me? An abandoned marketplace?" she asked.

"A ruined people," he corrected.

"You don't seem all that ruined to me," she said skeptically, thinking back on the Matriarch.

"The Harpy race is proud...but we are dying," Caprion said. "Every generation is smaller than the last. Our numbers are dwindling on this island. That is why we do not rebuild our city. There is already too much space for us."

Sora nodded at this. It made sense, but she still didn't understand what he wanted from her. Perhaps the reaction showed on her face, because he glanced away, as though self-conscious. A cloud suddenly shifted across the moon, casting his face in half-shadow. "I want to leave this island," he said simply.

She stared.

He clasped his hands behind his back. "I am either the last of the seraphims...or the first of a new generation. Either way, I have a duty to my people, and I can't fulfill it here."

She frowned. "But why leave...?"

"There are many Harpies scattered across the mainland. I want to find them. Unite them. Bring them home...." he paused. "And I want to know what else lies beyond the ocean. We have watched the mainland for centuries, and yet we do not truly know what has changed, what the humans have done." He nodded to her. "I don't think the races are meant to perish...but I don't think they will survive, either. Not without help."

"But why wait? Why not go there yourself?" she asked, still uncertain.

He looked her over from head to toe. "I need a guide."

Her eyes narrowed. "Why me?"

A wan smile came over his face. "You don't trust me," he said.

"No."

Her abrupt answer took him off-guard, she could tell. He hesitated, glancing at the ground; he wasn't used to being refused. His voice probably held the same power over other Harpies as it did over Burn and Laina. A small, grim smile was on her lips. He would not be able to manipulate her that way.

"What if...I could guarantee the life of the assassin?" he finally asked.

Sora's eyes dropped to the dagger at his belt. He read her reaction immediately, resting a hand on it, giving her a knowing look. "The Matriarch speaks fiercely of the evil of the Unnamed," he said. "She is good at that. Yet the age of the First Race is long gone, and our Matriarch is full of bravado. She won't admit that times have changed. She remembers those days of glory, and she is proud." He seemed wistful about it, almost sad. "But she speaks in fear. It has been centuries since we went toe-to-toe with the Unnamed. She is afraid of them, of what is happening on the mainland. We are too out of touch; we know nothing of the human world anymore. My people would rather live in isolation than face what they don't know." He shook his head slowly.

"Oh?" Sora asked. "And you are so very different?" He acted better off than his own race—but it felt like more arrogance. "You're not afraid of the Unnamed?" she pressed.

His smile broadened. "No," he said. "I do not fear them. My light outshines their darkness."

Sora couldn't help but bristle. It was a bold claim to make. She thought of Crash's dexterity, his unmatched skill. She had seen him in countless battles, the best and the worst. To an assassin, killing was easier than fighting. Perhaps she hadn't met any others of the Sixth Race, yet she knew that they were formidable opponents. *You haven't seen them yet,* she wanted to say to him. *You don't know what they're truly like.*

Oh, and you do? her inner voice spoke up, interrupting her thoughts. She bit her lip. Only a few days ago, Crash had been a simple man—not a demon, not some unknown offspring of the Dark God. The truth of his identity suddenly bothered her, sticking in her throat, the gravity of it. He was not human, but something else. Something she didn't understand.

"Come," Caprion said, and held out his hand. "There is one last thing I wish you to see."

Sora eyed his hand warily, uncertain of what to do—yet she couldn't back down. There was nowhere for her to go.

The white glow surrounded her. They immediately lifted up

into the air, rising above the trees, gliding smoothly across the forest. They sped through the night, passing over countless acres of woodland. Most of the ground below was obscured in deep shadows.

Finally, an open space in the trees revealed a small building cradled in the foliage. The structure must have been important, for there were guards stationed all around. They looked up as she and Caprion approached. A half-minute later, she found herself standing lightly in the grass, in front of an open archway that led into a dark building. The soldiers glanced at her, then turned away when Caprion approached, lowering their eyes respectfully.

The building was domed, similar to the one she was staying in. Yet it was far plainer, with no fancy mosaics or molding. It appeared to be built of thick gray granite sunk into the ground, impenetrable.

"Where are we?" Sora asked as Caprion passed her, heading toward the open archway. He motioned for her to follow, and she fell into step behind him.

As he approached the entrance, a large Harpy moved to stand in his way. This Harpy was Caprion's height but far wider, packed with muscle, his armor making him appear twice the size. He had a thick jaw and a broad neck that sloped into powerful shoulders. His eyes were similar to Caprion's, perhaps a slightly darker shade of purple.

"Sumas," Caprion said shortly.

The large guard nodded to them. "I can't let the human enter," he said.

Caprion raised an eyebrow. "She is my guest," he said. "Stand aside."

Sumas stared stoically at the Harpy General. Sora frowned up at him, but the guard intentionally ignored her, his expression like stone. He was the first soldier she had seen who stared Caprion in the face. "The Matriarch forbid anyone to enter," he growled.

"And you suggest that I am disobeying the Matriarch?" Caprion said pointedly.

They stared at each other intently for a moment, then Sumas' gaze wavered. His eyes shifted downward and he grimaced.

"Stand aside," Caprion repeated, his tone ringing in the dead air. The Cat's Eye shivered. Sora felt the voice's power tingle across her skin.

Sumas stepped to one side, allowing them to pass. She could feel his eyes upon her, hard and unwelcoming. It made the hair stand up on the back of her neck.

Inside, the building was less than accommodating. Everything was dark, thick stone. There were no chairs, no windows, no items of comfort. Only a solid, round floor and at its center, a stairwell leading downward.

"Where are we?" Sora asked again, slightly alarmed. She didn't like the idea of going underground alone with this man. She didn't trust him. Not yet.

"The holding cells," Caprion said. "We have a larger prison, but we have no use for it anymore."

The holding cells. *Crash!* Sora felt her heart leap, thudding erratically in her chest. She wiped her sweaty palms and stared at the darkened staircase. It was swallowed by deep shadows, as though leading into an infinite abyss.

Caprion paused halfway down the stairs and nodded toward the bottom. "I assume you want some privacy. Go ahead."

Sora stared at him, suspicion rising again. It seemed like far too grand a gesture. Here she was, fully armed, not bound. She could easily walk down there and break Crash out of the holding cell.

Then she glanced behind her at the series of guards. There were at least eight of them, and maybe more out of sight. Too many for her to fight alone.

"Right," she murmured to him in passing, then climbed down the stairwell. The air grew colder as she descended, chilled by the earth.

He nodded, but, true to his word, he didn't follow her.

Sora reached the bottom floor. She found herself in a pitch-black underground chamber. She stood there for a moment, waiting for her eyes to adjust, but there was no source of light.

On instinct, she touched her Cat's Eye. *I need light,* she thought, directing her intentions toward the necklace. She hoped it would obey her this time.

The necklace stuttered. Then there was a dull hum in her ears. The stone began to glow through her shirt. After a slight hesitation, she pulled it into the open, and a soft green light fell upon the dark room.

Immediately her eyes found the far wall. Directly in front of her, perhaps twenty paces away, was a granite wall. Thick metal shackles were clamped on it, rusted by moisture.

Sitting on the floor, his hands bound behind him by shackles, was a familiar figure.

Sora's heart leapt to her throat. She quickly stepped toward him.

Smack!

She bumped head-first into an invisible wall and almost yelped in surprise. Wincing, she rubbed her nose, her eyes tearing up. *What was that?* She raised her hands and extended them outward, feeling along the hidden barrier. Her hands tingled with magic. The guards must have resurrected some sort of shield to keep him imprisoned. Otherwise, he could easily break through the rusty shackles and make an escape.

Except...he wasn't moving.

Her brow furrowed with worry. She quickly touched her necklace, sending a silent command. With a soft chime, the Cat's Eye stirred and she felt a familiar sense of inhalation. The magic was slowly absorbed by the stone. It took much longer than usual.

The barrier dissolved and she rushed to Crash's side. But as she neared, she felt a strange density in the air, as though the shadows were growing gradually darker. The room became increasingly colder. She could actually see small puffs of frost rising from her breath. She paused a few feet away from him, staring down at his body.

The assassin's shoulders were slumped forward and his head was bent down. She couldn't tell if he was unconscious or not. Sora forced herself to cross the remaining distance. She felt like she had to climb through the air, swim through it like a dense fluid. The shadows grew deeper, and to her keen eye, she noticed that they were moving...which was strange, as there was no light to displace them. *What is this?* It didn't feel like Harpy magic...or magic of any kind, really. She tried to suppress the fear that rose in her throat. *It's just Crash,* she reassured herself. *He won't hurt you.*

"Crash?" she murmured quietly. She knelt down next to him. With a trembling hand, she reached out to touch his shoulder.

His head jolted up. He shifted away from her, twisting his body as though he would attack. She fell back with a cry, raising her arm to defend herself, even though the man was chained to the wall. The shadows shifted again, rising from the floor, covering him like armor.

Then his eyes met hers. They narrowed. Then widened.

"Sora," he rasped. It was a horrible sound, his throat as rough as shredded wood. "What are you doing here?"

Her eyes went to his neck. He wore a thick metal collar, which was also chained to the wall. It was studded with a large sunstone at the front, tight against the base of his throat. Angry red blisters surrounded the collar. Red burns covered his skin, seeping blood.

"Crash...." She couldn't keep the horror from her voice. She sat back on her heels, closely observing him. Bruises covered his face. His lip was split, his eyebrow, his cheekbone. "What have they done to you?"

He shook his head slightly, then winced. His breath sounded painful. It came in short, uneven gasps. "I've had worse," he croaked.

She put her hand against his shoulder, pushing through the shadows that surrounded him. They were thick in the air, tangible, like a gauzy curtain.

"I'm going to get you out of here," she said, reaching for the shackles. They were made of thick iron, but perhaps she could pry them from the wall. She wondered if her daggers would have any effect.

"No."

She paused. "What?"

He was breathing heavily with the effort of speaking. He

coughed a little, spitting out flecks of blood. Her face paled at the sight.

"We can't escape," he gasped. "I can't fight them like this."

Sora let out a short breath. She knew it was true. And she was far too weak to carry him—he was a good eighty pounds heavier than she. They wouldn't get far...and in the process of escaping, the Harpies would turn on them. They couldn't afford to be imprisoned right now. Volcrian was on his way.

She felt tears of frustration rising, and she squeezed her eyes shut, trying to control herself. "Then what do we do?" she asked through gritted teeth.

There was a scraping noise as the shackles moved. Then, abruptly, his hand touched her face. He stroked the back of his fingers along her cheek...*so* incredibly gently.

She flinched in surprise and looked at him. He was staring at her, his expression hard and solemn. She knew that look: fierce and calculating, like a caged wolf. It was the face of a warrior—someone much stronger than she could ever be.

"You must convince the Harpies to set me free," he said hoarsely. Then he lightly pressed a finger to her forehead. "Use your head," he murmured. "You're good at that."

Sora felt a small smile on her lips. He ran his finger down the side of her cheek again, then pinched her chin, giving it a light squeeze. "Yes, smile," he murmured. "You must look...like you don't care."

But I do care, she thought. The truth of it resonated throughout her body, her eyes widening fractionally. *I care a lot.*

His touch lingered on her face, a silent connection that slowly warmed her blood. She had never felt so close to anyone in her entire life. She didn't want to leave. No, she wanted to stay in the darkness, gazing at him, listening to his ruined voice.

"What?" she asked softly, trying to understand his expression. It was fiery and soft all at once, as though she had spoken her thoughts aloud—as though he had heard every word.

"You're beautiful, Sora," he said.

Her breath caught. Her lips parted. She stared at him, unsure of what to say, and she suddenly had the intense urge to hide her face. *Truly?* she thought, wallowing in inexplicable shyness. *At a time like this?* But she couldn't deny it. She cast her eyes away, trying to hide her reaction. Why would he say something like that?

She clasped his hand, forcing out a strangled laugh. "Growing sentimental on me, Crash?" she whispered, trying to make light of it.

"Maybe," he replied roughly. "I won't make a habit of it." But when she met his gaze, she saw a vague glint of humor. A slow smile pulled at his cracked lips, and his expression became hooded, almost lazy, gazing at her. She felt her stomach clench. She wanted to melt into a pool and disappear.

There was a sudden noise above them, the sound of voices and footsteps. Sora broke eye contact, pulling back. "I should go," she said quickly, though it was hard to turn away from him.

His gaze shifted over her shoulder to the staircase. "Be careful," he murmured.

She nodded. "You, too." Her words seemed completely inane.

He grinned again, and blood seeped from his torn lip. "I'll see you soon, Sora," he said softly.

She lingered for a moment more, looking down at him....Then she turned back toward the staircase, tucking her Cat's Eye away.

The stone's light slowly faded, returning to a simple rock. She felt sick and empty leaving him like that, uncertain if she would really see him again. Part of her wanted to break through the shackles, help him to his feet and run into the night...but she already knew it would be futile. It took all of her strength to walk away. She didn't let herself look back.

I must look like I don't care, she reminded herself, thinking of his words.

She took the stairs slowly, feeling winded, exhausted. Caprion stood at the top, his figure outlined by moonlight. She steeled herself as he came into view, hardening her expression, allowing a hint of disgust to touch her lips. Gazing at the Harpy, it was easy to feel. *How can they do this?* she thought, unable to stifle her bitterness. *Such a powerful race. Where is their mercy?*

He nodded to her and motioned for her to follow him. "Come," he said quietly. "There is one more place I wish to show you."

Sora followed him silently. They didn't speak, but walked away from the holding cells, past Sumas and into the night. The large soldier stared after them, but this time, his angry gaze didn't affect her. Sora was lost in thought, her mind still trapped in that dark cell, sitting next to the assassin.

They walked for a distance into the trees, up a woodland path that curved to the left, cutting through acres of wilderness, back to the city. As soon as they were out of sight, Caprion paused, creating a few symbols with his hand. The white glow surrounded her body, and again they lifted easily into the air, flying through the night.

Within twenty minutes, they reached the ocean. Sora gazed down, consumed by a strange familiarity. She recognized this view from her vision, as though she had somehow gone back in time, stepping into an old dream. A series of cliffs towered above the waves; on top of them, separate from the forest, was a wide meadow of clear green grass. There stood a circular stone monument, like a giant crown embedded in the earth. The rocks were huge, perhaps thirty feet tall and almost ten feet wide at the base. Their surface glinted black in the moonlight, smooth and glassy, like polished obsidian.

Toward one end of the ruins was a slight hill that led up to the peak of a cliff overlooking the ocean. A small stone pedestal stood there, an ancient mound of rock, eroded by centuries of rain and wind. The waves sounded loud and fierce, crashing against the cliff face in massive swells, as though trying to climb the rock.

They landed amidst the circle of sacred stones. The grass was thick and dewy from moisture, strewn with shards of broken rock. At its center was a stone bed, like an embalming table, large enough to lay a body on top.

Standing on the grass, Sora felt dwarfed by the large pillars of stone. They glinted in the moonlight, blacker than the night. The air was tense with suppressed power, as though at any moment the grass might burst into flames. She waited for her Cat's Eye to respond, certain of the presence of magic, but it seemed to have fallen dormant again.

Caprion turned to look at her. "We call this place *Terren Morte*," he said. "In the Old Tongue, it meant the Garden of the Dead. We would sacrifice our enemies to the One Star, the God of Light. It was a...very old ritual," he finished, glancing around the stones as though at a loss for words.

But Sora wasn't thinking of the large stones. Her eyes were still on the dagger that Caprion wore. "Why did you take me to see the assassin?" she asked quietly.

"To gain your trust," the Harpy General replied.

Sora let out a slow breath. "And you can guarantee his life and freedom?" she asked. "If I take you back to the mainland?" It seemed like a simple enough request. She didn't even have to do anything. Just allow him to travel with them.

"Yes," Caprion replied.

Crash wouldn't like it. He barely tolerated Laina—a full-fledged Harpy seraphim would not be welcomed. But what choice did she have? She couldn't allow his torture to continue. She could still see the burns along his skin, the blistering wounds, the seeping blood. How long until infection set in? She listened to the rush of the ocean for a moment, allowing its rhythm to wash over her, calming her, giving her strength.

"All right," she said finally. "You can come with us...in exchange for his release."

Caprion nodded solemnly. "I will hold you to your word."

"Of course."

"In that case, we are allies now." Caprion's expression became grim. "I think you should know that the Matriarch does not plan to help you."

Sora winced. "I know," she replied.

"She hates the Cat's-Eye stones as much as the Unnamed. She saw the island fall," Caprion said, his eyes lingering at the base of her throat. "She hopes that the bloodmage will kill you and destroy the necklace. Then we will finish the fight."

Sora frowned, unnerved. "And if I survive?"

Caprion paused. "Then she will kill you herself."

Sora remained silent, absorbing his words. Caprion glanced

upward at the stars, his eyes searching them, as though reading some hidden message. "The Wolfy mage approaches," he finally said. "He will arrive in two days' time. The Matriarch is meeting with Laina tonight to find out the truth of your partnership with the assassin." He shook his head slowly. "Once she knows, she will kill you both before the mage ever reaches the island."

Sora's eyes widened. She stared at Caprion, stunned. "W-what?" she stuttered. "But why?"

"It is our sacred duty to destroy the Sixth," he said. "And if you are aiding him, you are a traitor in our eyes. At least, the eyes of my people." Caprion looked back to the stars. "Personally, I think it is quite brave of you."

Sora felt numb. "What should we do?" she asked quietly.

"Leave," Caprion said. "As soon as possible."

"But...." She glanced around at the stones, her mouth dry. "We're on an island. We can't hide from the Matriarch for long."

"You can with my help," Caprion said. A smile alighted on his perfect face. He looked confident and sincere. "The Matriarch trusts me with all of her whims. She will ask me to hunt you down, and I will lead the search party astray. This should give you enough time to deal with the mage. She won't interfere with your battle."

Sora nodded slowly, hardly able to believe it. She put her hand on her face, closing her eyes, wishing for a moment of peace. "Just one good night's rest," she muttered.

Caprion laughed unexpectedly. It was a bright sound, more than charming. "You might still have that," he said, "but it wouldn't be safe for you to stay in the city. I have brought you here for a reason. This is how you plan on killing the mage, is it not? You will use a Cat's Eye to steal the life from him."

"Yes," Sora agreed, "that was our plan." At least the Harpies seemed familiar with what she hoped to do.

He pointed to the far-off pedestal at the top of the cliff. "Your Cat's Eye should be placed there," he said. Then he pointed to the bed of stone in the center of the circle. "And the mage must lie here. The stones will do the rest. It won't be easy to pin him down. Have you thought of that?"

Sora frowned at him. No, she hadn't...but with Burn's strength and Crash's skill, she thought they might be able to do it. A little trickery would help. She had been so focused on getting to the stone circle, she hadn't thought yet of fight.

"Why are you helping us?" she asked, staring at him, her suspicion returning to the surface.

"Because I am a seraphim," he replied simply. "And I, too, would like to lay the Dark God to rest."

Sora wondered if he knew what that would take.

Caprion continued urgently. "Tonight, when I return you to your room, gather your companions and travel here to the ruins. You can hide in the forest, while I will see to the assassin." He paused in thought. "Stay hidden among the trees. The Matriarch will organize a search party, and I will ensure that they don't find you. When the mage arrives, you will have to fight him on your own."

Sora nodded. "What about afterward?" she asked; she almost didn't want to. A cold dread filled her when she thought of the aftermath of the battle. If they weren't dead, they would have the Harpies to contend with.

Caprion glanced at the stars again. He listened for a long moment, turning slightly away from her, his eyes searching the sky.

Sora listened as well, but she heard nothing. She wondered what he was doing. Could he actually communicate with the heavens? It seemed impossible, and yet....

Finally, the Harpy said, "There is a second ship approaching through the storms. This one is captained by a Dracian."

Sora's heart quickened.

Caprion read her response easily. "I take it you know them?" he asked.

"Yes," she replied. *Jacques!* Could the scoundrel actually be coming to rescue them? She remembered his promise from before they had entered the Crystal Caves. It seemed like months had passed, though it had only been a week or two at most. "They are friends," she explained. "They're coming to take us home. You'll accompany us," she added.

Caprion nodded. "Then I will make sure that they can approach the island safely." He glanced at the stars again, distracted. "Have we covered all of the details?"

Sora frowned. She hadn't realized they were planning everything out—it had happened without her intention. Honestly, she felt much more confident than she had thirty minutes ago. "I think that's all," she said, feeling the tension loosen in her chest.

"Good." Caprion reached out a hand to her. "Come, we must go back now. Laina will have returned to your quarters. I don't want the Matriarch suspecting anything."

Sora stepped toward him and took his hand, surprised by how easy it was. The glow traveled down his wrist and through their fingers, transferring up her arm until her entire body was surrounded with light. Then they lifted up again, floating into the sky, carried by a brisk wind from the ocean.

CHAPTER 20

Caprion deposited her on the balcony outside her room. He nodded to her briefly. "Remember," he said. "Leave tonight as soon as you can. Come dawn, the Matriarch's soldiers will arrest you. Be gone long before then."

Sora nodded wordlessly, and watched the majestic Harpy step off the balcony into the open air. He walked a few steps, then flew upward, sailing back toward the Matriarch's temple.

Then she turned around and entered her room. She crossed through it quickly and headed for Burn's chambers. In the hallway, she glanced down at the bottom floor and noticed that the two guards were missing from around the fountain. Caprion's doing? She couldn't be sure. He hadn't spoken to anyone on their return, but perhaps he'd already planned for her agreement, for their escape.

She brushed through the beaded curtain into Burn's room. His chamber was the mirror image of her own, everything exactly the same, from the position of the bed to the color of the curtains. The Wolfy was lying down, his arms folded behind his head, staring at the bed's canopy.

He looked at her when she entered, sitting up, his gold eyes quizzical. "There you are," he said, raising a light-brown eyebrow. "Where....?"

"We need to leave," Sora said. "Now."

Burn frowned. "What happened?"

She paused, not knowing how to explain. It had taken half the night for Caprion to outline his intentions, and even then, she wasn't completely convinced that he was trustworthy. "Caprion took me on a tour of the city," she said briefly. "He told me that the Matriarch plans on imprisoning us. We need to leave tonight."

Burn's expression grew darker. Sora knew that this brief explanation would not satisfy him. With a deep breath, she quickly rattled off the details of the evening, describing her visit with Crash and the location of the stone circle. Burn listened intently, gazing at the canopy in thought.

"I made a deal with him," she said. "Hel'l travel with us in return for Crash's release."

Burn gave her an alarmed glance. "Sora...."

"I know, it's risky," she agreed. She put up a hand to stop him from speaking. "But you should have seen Crash. He was injured...." her voice died in her throat. She pushed herself to continue, "I need you to promise me that, if I die in battle, you'll see that Caprion gets passage overseas."

Burn looked at her gravely. "Of course," he said, still considering her words. He looked troubled. "I am so very sorry, Sora, for dragging you into this. It really is my fault. I should have forced you to get away from Volcrian when you had the chance. You're too young...."

She reached out and took his hand, giving him a quick smile. "But I'm here, right? We have to make the best of this." She squeezed his big hand tightly. "I know what I'm risking."

"As do I," Burn sighed. It was a heavy sound. For a moment he looked terribly sad, full of regret. "And you've already risked too much."

Sora frowned at him. She didn't know what to say. The silence stretched.

"Can we trust him?" Burn finally asked, changing the subject, referring back to Caprion.

Sora hesitated. "I don't know for sure. I know it sounds unlikely...."

"What do *you* think?" he pressed. "You spoke to him. I trust your judgment."

She thought back over the events of the night, Caprion's words and his actions. "I think we can," she finally said.

"Then we will. Gather your things quickly."

"I already have them," she replied, indicating her daggers and staff. She grinned slightly, and Burn gave her a look of approval.

"Always prepared," he said. "But I'll need a minute to pack my bag."

"Then I'll speak to Laina," Sora said. She sighed inwardly. She wondered if everything had gone well with the Matriarch—if the girl was over her infatuation, or much the opposite.

She left Burn's room quickly and rushed down the hallway. Now she would have to confront the young girl. She anticipated resistance.

When she entered the room, Laina was standing in front of a mirror, staring at her own reflection. Sora paused. The young girl was dressed in a similar white shirt and breeches, with an airy robe covering her small frame. But her hair had been intricately braided on top of her head, woven through with flowers and gold pins. Had the Matriarch done it? One of her handmaids?

"Sora!" the girl said, turning to look at her. "Can you believe it? I have Harpy blood!"

Sora gave her a wary smile. "Yes, it's wonderful," she said sincerely. "I'm happy for you."

Laina beamed at her, then pranced away from the mirror, opening the wardrobe on the opposite wall. "Just look at all of these clothes that the Matriarch gave me! Have you ever seen such beautiful fabrics? I could buy a month's worth of bread with one dress alone!"

Sora gazed into the wardrobe, looking at the various colored garments. They were beautifully crafted, though a bit out of fashion. She doubted the Harpies kept up with mainland trends. Laina didn't know that Sora had once been part of the nobility, and had worn fancier dresses in her younger days. She thought of the dress she had worn for her own Blooming, a frilly pink thing of various layers, jewels sewn into the neckline. She had ripped it to pieces after the dance, tossing it into a closet

"Laina," she said quietly, clearing her throat. "We need to leave tonight."

Laina's smile melted into a look of confusion. "But you can't! The Matriarch has a feast planned for us tomorrow. Besides, aren't you and Burn being held captive?"

Sora put her hands on her hips. "We're all captives here," she ground out.

Laina raised an eyebrow. "Not me," she said. "The Matriarch has given me my own house. Can you believe that? A real house!"

Sora wanted to roll her eyes. The girl was completely clueless. The Matriarch was bribing her in order to get information. After speaking with Caprion, she highly doubted that the Harpies cared about a half-breed girl.

"What did you tell her?" Sora asked bluntly, taking a step

toward Laina.

The girl's eyes widened. "What do you mean?"

"I mean, what did you speak about over dinner? Did you talk about Crash?"

Laina grinned. "Oh, don't be so worried! She knew that we were all traveling together. I told her that I didn't like him much, and she said that it was in my blood." Laina raised an eyebrow. "She also told me something *terrible* about him. Do you know *what he is?*"

"You told her we were all companions?" Sora stuttered, still hung up on the first part of Laina's disclosure.

Laina had the decency to look ashamed. "I'm sorry," she said briefly. "But she already knew!"

Sora thought of Caprion's warning and wondered if his soldiers would turn up soon. She took a deep, steadying breath. "Never mind that," she said stiffly. "We're in danger here and we need to leave. Now."

"Why?" Laina asked, her voice turning stubborn. "I like it here!"

"We're not safe," Sora repeated with urgency. She took a few steps toward the girl, reaching out to grab her arm. Laina backed away angrily. Sora continued, "Tomorrow the Matriarch is going to have us arrested, maybe killed, and Volcrian...."

"Ugh!" Laina burst out, throwing her arms up in the air. "You're so concerned about Volcrian! The Matriarch is going to protect us. Besides, I feel good here, like I belong." She paused, glancing at the mirror again. "My entire life, I've felt unwanted and alone, and now I know why. The Harpies understand me, Sora." She stopped and looked at her. "They think I still have a great-aunt alive. Someone who knew my grandmother...or my grandmother's mother, something like that. They're very long-lived. The Matriarch says she will take me to meet her...."

Sora felt her frown deepen. She didn't like the direction of this conversation. Had the Matriarch influenced her so completely? "But you also have a human family, don't you?" she said softly.

Laina pointed a finger at herself, her face twisting into a scowl. "If I do, then they don't want me," she said. "And I am better than that! I feel like I have a place here. Some day, I might even have wings!" Then she laughed, a sound that was far too cynical for a thirteen-year-old girl. "I know what this is about," she said knowingly. "You're jealous!"

Sora balked at that. "What? No!"

The girl's expression turned snide. "Then it's about your dear, precious assassin, isn't it? Poor Crash finally got put in a prison, where he belongs!"

Sora straightened up, her shoulders going tense. "You don't know what you're talking about."

"Oh?" Laina taunted. "Don't I? I knew he was evil since I first laid eyes on him, but you just wouldn't listen to me." She looked inordinately pleased with herself.

Sora didn't know what to say to that. Laina and Crash didn't like each other, but that wasn't so unusual. Sora hadn't liked Crash either when she had first met him.

"He's from a bastard race," Laina continued, "an abomination, a creature of the Dark God! And I, a lowly street child, am one of the First Order chosen to destroy his kind!" The girl made a dramatic flourish, and Sora looked on in shock, unable to believe her ears. "What worries me the most is how badly you've been tricked. You are so far under his thrall that you can't even see the truth."

"His thrall?" Sora repeated. She didn't know whether to laugh at the girl's outburst or reach for her daggers.

"Yes! You might not realize it," Laina said, leaning closer to her, as though sharing an important secret, "but the Matriarch told me everything. Crash has you under a spell."

"What?" Sora choked.

Laina nodded, her soft gray eyes now sharp and fevered, imbued with passion. "Yes, a spell. I've known it since I first saw you together! It's very, very obvious."

Sora almost laughed at the girl's expression. She looked far too convinced for her own good. "Laina, you don't understand," she said, trying not to grin. "Crash can't put me under a spell, it's impossible."

"No, Sora, you're not listening!" Laina yelled.

Sora flinched backwards, surprised by the outburst. A tremor moved through her Cat's Eye, warning her to be cautious. The Harpies were playing with Laina's mind. She wasn't thinking straight.

"I need to make you understand!" Laina insisted. "Crash has you under his influence. He's using you, manipulating you to get what he wants. Can't you see that? Dear Goddess, he's not even human! He's less than human, less than an animal! How can you let him touch you?"

"What are you talking about?" Sora snapped, her voice hardening a notch.

At that, Laina exploded. She started ranting at the top of her lungs. "You're his lover, Sora!" she screamed. "It makes me sick to think of it! How many times?" she demanded. "How many times have you let him use you? I admired you for so long—I thought you were such a good person, with such a strong sense of honor...." Her voice wavered. For a moment, her expression changed and Sora caught a glimpse of that young girl again, the one she had rescued from the jailhouse, uncertain, vulnerable. Then Laina's gaze clouded with anger. She took a deep breath and began advancing on Sora purposefully, as though she meant to attack her. "I'm here to stop it," she spat. "I won't let him use you anymore. I won't let you become his whore!"

Smack!

The sound cracked the air. Sora's hand stung from the slap, her breath heaving in her lungs.

Laina collapsed to the ground, shocked into silence, her arm thrown protectively over her face. A strangled sob ripped from the girl's throat.

"Don't you ever," Sora hissed, "*ever* speak like that again! Crash is not my lover and he would *never* treat me like a whore!"

Laina stayed on the ground, still trembling from the blow. Sora's fist ached from the force of it. She might have broken the girl's nose, she didn't know for sure. She had lashed out viciously, unable to control herself.

But as she stared at the girl, she felt the guilt and pity drain out of her. Suddenly, Sora was filled with a cold hardness. She had endangered all of their lives. They were lucky that the Matriarch herself wasn't in that room, waiting to imprison them. Volcrian was all that mattered now.

Sora leaned over Laina's body, speaking fiercely into her ear. "If you want to live with the Harpies, so be it. You have my blessing.

But once we leave, we can't come back for you." She paused. She wanted to say more, but she couldn't waste any more time. "Take care of yourself." Then she stood up, turned away, and strode swiftly from the room.

Burn was waiting for her out in the hallway. Considering his long ears, Sora was certain that he had heard everything. He gave her a sad look, but didn't question the situation. Instead, he fell into step behind her.

"I didn't want it to be this way," Sora said as they dashed for the outside balcony.

"I know," he said hollowly. "But she made her choice."

His words struck her more than Laina's actions had. Burn had always been fond of the girl, catering to her like a daughter. And yet he still followed Sora down the stairs without hesitation. He understood the gravity of the situation—exactly what was at stake.

Yet Sora couldn't shake the feeling that they were abandoning her...and for him to say that....

It's because of Volcrian, she thought, reining in her emotions. *We don't have time for this now.*

Sometimes being a warrior meant that she had to be logical. Crash had taught her that, and Burn knew it, too.

They ran into the night, making for the nearby woodland. Sora could remember where the circle of stones sat, several miles to the east of Asterion. They started in that direction, using the stars as their guide.

* * *

A flicker of light entered his vision. Crash gritted his teeth.

Pain coursed through him with each heartbeat, focusing him, fueling him.

The light approached through the dark cell, taking on the figure of a man. He walked a half-inch above the ground, no footsteps. When Crash used his demon's eyes, he could see a halo of six wings surrounding the man's back. They glimmered translucently.

He recognized the bastard—the one who had taken his dagger, who had chained him to the wall. *General,* the soldiers had called him, not that his title made a difference. He would bleed the same as any man.

The Harpy knelt before him. A sickening vibration passed over Crash's skin. The sunstone flared at his neck in response; pain shot up his throat, down his limbs.

He coughed up blood and spat at the man's boots. The General didn't flinch. Wordlessly, he took out a key and began unlocking Crash's chains. They fell to the ground with a loud clank. Next, the man released the iron collar with its sunstone. As the collar was pried away from his flesh, Crash felt a great surge of agony, his muscles cramping, his skin tearing. Then the pain passed. All of the strength left him, as though a great wind had swept through his body. He caved forward, struggling to breathe.

The man fully removed the collar and tossed it to one side. Crash could only sit, holding himself up with his arms, gathering enough strength to attack.

"Before you kill me," the General said in a low, taunting voice, "you should know that I've come to release you."

Crash spat more blood at his feet. "Why?"

"Because I promised the girl with the Cat's Eye that I would."

Crash bristled, immediately suspicious. "Why are you helping us?"

"Let's say we have a common enemy," he murmured. He settled his right hand on his belt, directly upon Crash's Named weapon—the Viper. "The Matriarch told me to kill Sora tonight."

"Touch her, and I'll rip off your hands."

The General paused, glancing at his slumped, bruised body. A look of distaste touched his lips. "Fortunately for you," he murmured, "I didn't."

At the General's mocking words, Crash felt a cold fire light within him. His muscles tightened. His head throbbed. With the sunstone removed, nothing restrained his demon's power—only his own will. "Why are you telling me this?" he asked quietly. *I'm going to tear out your throat.*

"Because I want you to trust me."

Crash could have laughed. Hatred surged. He grinned up at the Harpy, full of malice.

The General spread his hands in appeasement, like comforting a sick man. "We are on the same side, you and I. We both want to see the bloodmage killed, and your party return safely to the mainland."

"And why would you want that?"

"For the sake of good deeds, of course," he replied, and flashed a condescending smile, sharp as a knife. "I don't need a reason to do what is right...unlike an assassin."

Enough. Crash's hatred fueled his strength. He launched to his feet. His shadow lengthened, enveloping the Harpy in a rush of black smoke, twisting around his white body and dousing his glow.

The Harpy stumbled back, taken off-guard. He flailed

uselessly. The shadow wrapped around his arms and legs in a thick web. It tightened around his throat and smothered his wings, extinguishing their light like a snuffed candle. The room fell to blackness.

Instantly, Crash stood behind him. He slipped his dagger from the man's belt and held it to his navel. At the touch of the blade, the General went still.

"Harpies," Crash spat. "Pathetic, always preying on the weak. You've never fought one of the Named, have you?" He dug the blade a little deeper. "Never let your guard down."

The man struggled against the grip of Crash's shadow, choking on it, suffocating. It damped his voice, stifling his magic. "I released you for Sora," he wheezed.

"A mistake on your part," Crash growled.

"I spared her life!"

Crash paused. He was sorely tempted to shove his blade clear through the man's intestines, but a small, nagging doubt entered his thoughts....

"If you come near her again, I'll kill you," he said.

He turned, his shadow wrapping around him, and vanished into the early-morning darkness.

* * *

By the time they could hear the ocean, the sun was already breaking the horizon, casting gold light across the water. Burn paused at the edge of the stone circle.

They found a large tree with a gap between its roots, and set up camp inside the hollow trunk, hidden from sight. They took turns sleeping as the other kept watch. Several times, Sora heard distant horn-calls or shouting voices. But Caprion kept his word, and no figures descended from the sky.

Toward late evening, there was an ominous rustle in the foliage above them. It was Sora's turn to keep watch. She sat at the very edge of the tree roots, hidden amongst a thick bushel of ferns. She peeked up at the sky. No sign of Harpies....

A shadow dropped from the tree next to them. She bit her lip, barely containing a cry. At first she thought it was a large jungle cat, but the figure uncoiled from the ground and stood there, leaning against the tree trunk, one hand held out to support himself.

Crash.

She rose silently to her feet, wanting to run to him, but he crossed to her first. "Hush," he murmured, glancing toward the sky. "They're still searching for us."

His voice shocked her. It was raspy and sore, huskier than she remembered. Painful to listen to.

Sora couldn't contain herself. She embraced him in a swift, fierce hug. His arms wrapped around her and he pushed her back into the shade of the tree roots, until they were hidden once again. They both knelt down in the shelter of the ferns. She sat back to look at him, drinking in the sight.

He must have swum through a stream, because his hair dripped with water, and was pressed against his head in a bristling black mess. His eyes gleamed in the fading sunlight. Bruises and burn marks covered his skin, though she was surprised to see that many of his wounds were already healing. Another trait of the Unnamed? She didn't want to ask. She only cared that he was safe. She had spent the majority of the day agonizing over the thought of him being tortured, wondering if she should go back to the holding cells and break him out. But she trusted Caprion, not wanting to jeopardize their plan. Once again, the Harpy's word had proven true.

The worst of the burns were around Crash's neck, where the sunstone had been. The skin was cracked and peeling, caked with blood. That explained the rough timbre of his voice. She was certain the sunstone would leave a scar.

"You look terrible," she said, worried.

"And you look tired," he replied.

She bowed her head in agreement. It had been difficult for her to sleep during the day. "How did you get out?" she asked wearily.

Crash frowned slowly. He indicated the dagger at his belt. "A Harpy released me," he said. "He told me that you asked him to."

Sora blinked, taken aback. "Oh," she muttered. "Good." She held his eyes, hoping he wouldn't ask any questions. He wouldn't respond well to her deal with Caprion, and she was too tired to argue with him. How much had the Harpy told him?

He frowned, watching her closely.

"You tracked us through the woods?" she asked, trying to change the subject. "We should move camp, then. If it was that easy for you to find us...."

"I wasn't followed, and I knew what to look for." A bit of amusement entered his eyes. "I taught you how to cover your tracks. Remember?"

Don't smile! Sora told herself firmly. But she couldn't control her expression. How could she forget? All of those grueling months traveling through Fennbog swamp, learning his techniques, how to fight and defend herself. It was a long time ago, but this was the first time he had acknowledged it. She grinned at the dirt, still not looking at him. She liked it that he remembered those days.

"Does that make me your student?" she couldn't help but ask. She wondered if he would recognize the question, because she had asked it once before, back in the swamp, two years ago, when she had been terrified of him.

He paused, looking away. He seemed surprised by the question, though he hid it well. She could read him much better now than she used to. "You were my first student," he said briefly, echoing his words from the swamp. Then he glanced at her. "I suppose you still are."

She grimaced. "I thought I'd surpassed you by now," she said, attempting humor.

He smiled quietly in response, but his eyes remained dark, his expression fading with the sun. She sensed him pull away, and immediately regretted her words.

He looked around their camp, quickly noting Burn's sleeping figure inside the tree. If he wondered about Laina's absence, he didn't mention it. Something told her that he was relieved to see her gone...and that he already suspected the reason why.

"Volcrian will arrive on the island tomorrow," Sora said, remembering Caprion's warning. "The sacred stones are a quarter-mile to the east. I figure we can lure him there...."

Crash nodded, accepting her plan without question. "Have you learned what you must do with your Cat's Eye?" he asked warily.

"Yes." She thought of Caprion's words, their meeting at the sacred stones. Then another thought occurred to her. She reached into her pocket, took out a folded piece of cloth, and held it out to Crash.

He paused before touching it. Briefly, he said, "I can't open this."

"It's a second Cat's Eye," Sora explained quickly. "I thought I might use it instead." But would it require a bond to work? Would it activate once they put it on the pedestal? She couldn't control it without touching it, and she wasn't sure what that would do to her.

Crash seemed to read her mind. "It could work," he said. "And it's better than the alternative."

She pocketed the small stone again and smiled at him, though it didn't quite feel genuine. "Tomorrow..." she started to say, then paused, unable to finish the thought. *Tomorrow, we might fail.* "How will you fight Volcrian? Do you know what to expect?"

Crash shook his head slowly. "His magic has changed since our last meeting," he murmured. "But he's still flesh and bone. We can restrain him if we get close enough. Easier said than done."

Sora raised an eyebrow. "I take it you've tried that before?"

He nodded. "Don't allow him to get hold of your blood. You saw what he did to Dorian."

"I won't," she promised.

They paused, lingering on the thought of Dorian, on the battle to come. "I'll take watch," Crash said abruptly, and motioned for her to lie down next to Burn. "You should rest. You need it."

She raised an eyebrow. "You're the one who just escaped," she replied. "Are you sure you're not tired?" He looked tough, but she could see the drag of his shoulders, the way he knelt without moving, conserving his energy.

"I just spent the last day sitting in a cell," he observed. "I'm more than rested."

She wanted to argue with him. He might have been

imprisoned, but he had also been tortured and brutalized. A serious injury could be far more tiring than physical exertion. Yet his expression was determined, and she didn't think she had the strength to convince him otherwise. She could feel her own exhaustion overcoming her.

She finally crawled into the shadows beneath the tree roots, settling down in the cool dirt. Her white clothes were already stained by mud and grass. It might not be as comfortable as a bed, but at least it was familiar.

Under Crash's watchful eye, she was finally able to slip into a deep, restful slumber.

CHAPTER 21

Crash sat at the base of the tree and waited for her to fall asleep. He watched the gentle rise and fall of her breath. *She's safe.* It loosened the tension inside of him, if only a little.

Satisfied that Sora was completely unconscious, he turned back to the forest and knelt on the ground. With his index finger, he quickly drew a series of symbols in the dirt: a circle for protection and three ancient letters, S for sky, E for earth, V for vision.

Shadows began to gather and congeal inside of the circle. With a nudge of willpower, he sent the shadows climbing up the side of the tree, easily hiding the campsite. To a passing traveler, it would appear simply that the shade was a little darker than usual, yet no eyes could penetrate it. The Harpies would easily miss the campsite from above, especially once the sun was down. They didn't see well at night.

He usually avoided working magic in front of observers. It was a lesson long ingrained in him. The Sixth Race did not share their secrets—their true power lay in obscurity. And every time he used his magic, his demon came that much closer to the surface. He felt a burning power rise within him, a crimson wave of anger and frustration.

He had kept the creature subdued for years, locked securely inside his body. In fact, he hadn't allowed the demon to surface since leaving the Hive. Yet for the last month, the demon had been eager for release, testing his discipline, pushing his boundaries. He was finding it more and more difficult to keep it under control.

But why now? Because of Sora? His eyes slid to her sleeping form, and he felt that conflict again, a natural instinct to shelter and protect her. He thought back to the Crystal Caves, when she had fallen from the rock bridge. The demon had risen in her defense. He had thrown himself off the ledge without thinking, his body acting on his own accord, the demon launching from his skin like a rabid predator. And yet it hadn't harmed her. That was unheard of.

When the beast came to the surface, he couldn't always control its will. Often, Crash existed only as an observer through the demon's eyes. He didn't want to scare Sora, so he hadn't told her the full truth. The demon could have easily chosen to kill her, and yet it hadn't. Why?

My control never should have slipped. He wasn't usually this undisciplined. Perhaps he was growing weaker....Or perhaps the demon could sense the rising power in the land, and was bucking to welcome it.

He comes, that dark voice inside of him murmured, writhing. The demon sought the attention of Crash's thoughts, reminding him that he wasn't alone in his own body.

Silence, Crash commanded.

The demon just grinned in its cage.

He sighed and sat back, wincing as he shifted his sore muscles. He didn't want to show his weakness in front of Sora. She, of all people, needed him to be strong. But the Harpies had dealt him quite a bit of damage. His back ached like fire, his muscles burned and his body was desperate for food. But there was no time to go hunting now. He would have to wait until nightfall to see if he could catch an unwary rabbit or fowl. He needed to eat meat.

His wounds were healing rapidly, but it would be a long time before his voice recovered, perhaps a month or longer. The worst pain came from his neck; it was as though his throat had been clawed out by a wildcat, thrashed and bloodied. It burned when he breathed, and ached when he talked. The sunstone had left a nasty welt beneath his jaw. It was uncomfortable for him just moving his head.

His thoughts traveled to the day to come. Volcrian would be on the island before long. There was little time to prepare. Crash's sword and knives were lost to the Harpies, but he still had his Named dagger.

His lip wrinkled in disgust, and he touched the blade, remembering the Harpy who had released him; the man sent to kill Sora. Cold fire rushed through him. He should have killed the man when he had the chance; gutted him through like a fish. He didn't like leaving loose ends—and Harpies were dangerous.

But the thought of Sora had stopped him; the thought of admitting to her what he had done. *Foolish*—to let her influence him so much. Despite sparing the Harpy, he still couldn't summon her steadfast conscience. He only felt the black pit of his body, the dark force just beneath his skin, eager to consume. He didn't know if he could ever see life the same as she did. In this way, the teachings of his Grandmaster still lived on, rooted into his mind, inextricable. *The wave rushes in, then rushes out,* he heard, echoing across the years. *It cannot just come in and in and in— then the whole world would be an ocean.*

Life needed to be tamed. It needed to be cut back. Otherwise, it would consume itself.

We are the outgoing wave. The harvesters.

He had known this when he had taken a Name. He had been eager for it. Ruthless.

And yet a conscience must have developed over time. It must have, because eventually the coldness had become too much.

He shook his head, looking at Sora as though her sleeping form held some answer for him. Tomorrow, she would use her Cat's-Eye necklace to kill the mage. She might have to create two bonds with separate stones. He didn't know if that was possible. There was still a chance that she could die. It left a deep hollowness in his gut, a sensation that he was not familiar with—and not comfortable with.

He could imagine the disappointment of his Grandmaster, knowing that he cared for the girl. *She is weak*, the voice whispered in his head, taunting him. Yes, she was weak, and part of him reveled in that. A foolish thing to do, but there it was.

He still meant his words, the ones he had spoken to her in the forest, when she had confessed her fear. He would die to protect her. He welcomed the thought. It would be a fitting end to his life—perhaps a kind of redemption. Not that the Dark God would recognize such a gesture. But perhaps...perhaps there were other forces that would take pity on him, that would save him from a fierce and fiery afterlife.

Are you growing sentimental on me, Crash? her voice asked, drifting through his memories.

The thought was accompanied by the ghost of a smile. Was he?

He pulled out his dagger, running his hand over the sharp blade, gazing at the worn snake that wrapped around its hilt.

* * *

It was Sora's watch. She was somewhat relieved. She fingered her Cat's Eye, thinking of the day to come.

She had slept soundly for a few hours, but had awakened to the sound of Crash and Burn's voices, discussing the battle ahead. Their words lingered in her mind.

"What of Sora?" Burn had asked. *"She's our only weakness. If Volcrian goes after her first...."*

"We won't let him catch us off-guard," Crash answered darkly. *"Keep her as far from the fight as possible."*

"But we can't protect her from the Cat's Eye," Burn replied. *"She will sacrifice her life for us. I'd rather she kept away from the fight altogether."*

"We need her necklace," Crash murmured. *"And there's a chance that she'll survive."*

"Yes, and there's a bigger chance that she will die. And then what? We've already wasted Dorian's life. Shall we throw her to the fire, too?"

Crash hadn't responded. His silence worried her more than his words. Would they be able to defeat Volcrian, or was the Dark God's power too immense? She wasn't anyone special, after all. Not as skilled as her companions. Just a girl with a bit of jewelry. As Burn had said, she was their greatest weakness.

Now she sat with her back against a thick tree root. The sound of crickets permeated the air. The silver glow of the full moon illuminated the forest, revealing small insects and animals that skittered about the ground. A wave of bats passed overhead, diving for moths, shrieking through the night.

She felt for the second Cat's Eye in her pocket. It was smaller than the one at her neck, barely the size of a pearl. She planned to use it...but she didn't know if it would work. Perhaps she could place the new stone upon the pedestal instead of her own, but without a bond, she had no way of controlling it. What if it didn't react properly? She couldn't command it with her will. Too many things could go wrong—and too many people depended on her.

You can't worry about this, she told herself. *You'll make yourself sick.* She tried to distract herself, but her mind was set on torturing her. Laina's face arose in her thoughts. She felt that familiar pit of guilt open up in her stomach. The girl's betrayal still frustrated her, and she wondered if she had done the right thing by leaving her behind.

What else could you do? her inner voice said. *Bring her to fight Volcrian?* A valid point, but she wasn't reassured. Laina was only thirteen. She had played straight into the Matriarch's hands, simply used as a tool for information. She couldn't condemn a child for that.

I can't abandon her, she thought.

She chose it, her inner voice argued.

She's too young to know better.

And she's too stubborn to be saved. Let her make her mistakes.

Sora sighed. She glanced over her shoulder, her gaze lingering on the sleeping figure of Crash. He lay next to Burn, almost invisible beneath the tree roots. She sighed. How many nights had they spent like this over the past two years? Far too many to count. She found it difficult to imagine her old life of riches and prestige.

At least I have a home to return to, she thought. She wondered what her mother was doing, if Lori was still at the farm, healing the sick and watching the horizon for her lost daughter. Neither Burn nor Crash had a place to go when this was all over. What if they succeeded in killing Volcrian? What then? *But our quest isn't over yet,* she reminded herself. No, this would only solve half of the problem. They needed to destroy the sacred weapons somehow...and they only had two of the three.

Sora scratched a bug bite on her arm. She couldn't keep dwelling on these thoughts. Her mind wasn't providing any answers—only more worries. She was too restless. *I need to walk,* she thought; burn off a little extra energy. Just a short walk, not far from camp. Her eyes quickly scanned the night sky, but she didn't see any evidence of the Harpies, not since Crash had arrived. She was fairly certain that Caprion's plan had worked, and that they were safe for now.

She stood up and glanced back at her companions. *I'm sure they'll be safe for a few minutes,* she decided, and quietly strolled into the woods. She decided to head for the sacred stones, and take one last look before it became a battleground.

The calm forest engulfed her. Sora took careful note of which direction she headed. The wind brushed through her hair, cooling her forehead, tickling through the trees. Various birds and frogs could be heard chirping, hidden in the canopy. After a few minutes, the knot in her stomach began to loosen.

An owl hooted deeply and a small rodent scurried at her feet, ducking into a large fern. Sora paid them no heed. They were animals, untroubled by her concerns. No matter what happened tomorrow, this forest and all of its creatures would live on. *For a while,* she thought—until the Dark God's power overcame the earth, and then who knew what would happen. She couldn't draw comfort from that.

Sora stepped through a patch of tall bushes and found herself at the edge of the ruins. *Terren Morte,* the Garden of the Dead. She looked up, gazing at the shiny black pillars with their perfectly smooth surface. How had the stones become so dark? They looked to be the very opposite of sunstones—rocks made of pure night.

She hovered in indecision. It would be too risky to enter the open field, yet she wasn't quite ready to head back to camp. Something about the mystic ruins held her attention. She loved the ancient beauty of the terrain, the giant stones beneath the stars, silent and firm in their vigilance. If only she could contain such strength. She leaned back into the shadows of a tree, pressing her hands against the bark, feeling its cool, rough surface through her shirt.

Perhaps a minute later, she slowly became aware that she wasn't alone. She glanced to her right, where a large pine grew a few strides away. As she gazed into the shadows beneath its branches, she saw a familiar silhouette take form, like a phantom materializing from the air.

She managed a smile. "Checking up on me?" she asked wryly.

Crash turned to face her. She could make out his eyes, glimmering like a nocturnal beast. For a moment, the sight made her uncertain, reminding her of what he was.

If he noticed her pause, he didn't mention it. "Couldn't sit still?" he asked softly.

She shook her head, suddenly at a loss for words. What could she say to him? Nothing came to mind. She turned back to the ruins and they stood in silence for a few moments, studying the large black stones.

"I can't stop thinking about tomorrow," she finally said. She couldn't tell him the full truth—that she was afraid of what it might bring. This might be her last night in this world.

"Me too," he admitted.

Sora didn't expect that. She blinked. He stood closer to her, though she hadn't noticed him move. He was almost shoulder to shoulder with her now.

"Are you...having second thoughts?" she asked, remembering his private conversation with Burn.

"No," he replied.

This was the Crash that she had come to know: one-word answers, a mask of quiet indifference. Yet she knew him better now. His silence was a shield—and at times, a door. His words were like small keyholes, allowing her moments of insight.

"I thought taking a walk would clear my head," she said brusquely. "But I suppose that's impossible. Are warriors always filled with this much doubt?"

He paused thoughtfully. "It gets better with time," he murmured.

"How do you deal with it?"

He turned to look at her, observing her quietly. She stared resolutely out at the stone circle, focusing on the stars, the rush of the ocean, the moist air. Pretending she didn't need to hear his answer.

"Doubt is a product of fear," he finally said. "And fear is a response of the body." He followed her eyes out to the ruins, also studying the large black stones. "I haven't felt it in a long time."

She curled one of her hands into a fist. Her mind returned to the note he had left her more than a year ago, folded into the hilt of the Dark God's weapon. *For the first time I felt fear.* Perhaps he had truly meant it—more than she could know. She still kept the note in her room at her mother's house, hidden in a desk drawer. She hadn't showed it to anyone. It had been private. A part of him that he had shared in confidence.

Either way, his advice wasn't very helpful. He might be able to rise above his emotions, conquer the impulses of his body, but she wasn't like him. This was her first true battle. She thought back to her fight with the wraiths, the Catlins, even the *garrolithe* in the Caves. She had been afraid, but not like this. Not with the long, drawn-out expectation of her own demise. She felt as though she stood on the deck of a ship barreling through the ocean, unable to stop it from crashing against the rocks.

She turned to face him. They were inches apart, their chests almost touching. She looked up at him with her neck stretched a bit, since he was so much taller than she. "Why are you here, Crash?" she asked directly.

He almost stepped back, shifting in place. He stared down at her, his face fully visible—wolfish and cunning, his hair longer than before, sweeping down to his jaw, black as pitch. She had the sudden urge to touch his hair, to brush it away from his face. *Why not?* she thought suddenly. *If this is our last night together, then why not?*

She felt a little wild in doing so, but she forced herself to reach up and move his hair to one side. It was soft against her fingers, slightly tangled from sleep.

He gripped her hand suddenly. She didn't see him move.

"Sora," he said quietly. She couldn't tell if it was a warning, or if he was simply surprised.

"I might not be here tomorrow, Crash," she said, her voice breaking. Fear constricted her chest. She wasn't...she wasn't ready to face death. And she especially wasn't ready to watch any of her friends die. That was an even worse outcome. The vision of Dorian's body, cold and lifeless in the fields, flickered before her eyes. She hadn't been able to save him. Volcrian's wraith had struck him down easily. A terrible guilt seized her about Dorian, and her throat closed with grief.

Crash watched her face. He frowned. "I'm not going to let anything happen to you," he said quietly.

She shook her head. "You can't promise that." *And I don't want you to.* She didn't want to survive while the rest of them perished. She didn't want to live through that kind of pain.

"Why are you here?" she repeated. He hadn't answered her question before.

"To check on you."

"Is that all?"

He hesitated. Then he let out a long, frustrated sigh. His hand still clasped hers, his fingers playing along her small knuckles. "I suppose I should say something meaningful, hmm?" She could sense a slight smile on his face, a shade ironic. "I'm not good at comforting people, Sora."

She winced at that. It was true. She tried to tug her hand away, but he didn't let her go.

"Do you think I might die tomorrow?" she asked, searching his face.

He finally dropped her hand. "I don't know," he said briefly.

Finally, an honest answer. "Then what?" she pressed. She knew that she was pushing him, perhaps asking too much, but she had to. She couldn't let this rest. "What do you want to say to me? This might be your last chance."

He turned away, distancing himself from her. She expected that, and took a step after him, close to his back. "You've saved my life far too many times to count," she said. "You vowed to die next to me. You...you...." Her voice hitched, a terrible reaction, one that irritated her greatly. Her words came out soft and strained. "You told me that I was beautiful." It meant something, didn't it? What was he hiding from her?

A brooding silence fell between them. For a moment, he seemed angry. She almost relished the thought. Maybe she could provoke him to answer; force him to explain himself.

Then he turned, advancing swiftly, closing the space between them. He took her by the shoulders, propelling her backward until she was pressed against the tree.

When he looked down at her, his eyes were deep emerald, lit with black fire. Her breath caught. He was brilliantly handsome in the darkness, secretive and scarred, smothered in shadows. She felt terrified and excited all at once, filled with a strange anticipation.

"You're very frustrating," he said, his voice hoarse from his wounds.

She grimaced. "I know."

"You shouldn't doubt me."

She stared at him, surprised. "What?"

"You need to trust my words."

She opened her mouth to reply, but suddenly his lips were upon her.

Sora froze in shock. He pressed his mouth against hers, hard and then soft. His hands gripped her shoulders, holding her still, giving her no chance to escape. After a long moment, her body relaxed, her head tilted back. She sank against him, unable to resist, responding naturally.

The kiss deepened. He teased her lips, tempting her to open them. Her breath shuddered and she tried to meet him, clumsily mimicking his technique. His hands squeezed her shoulders. Caution? Encouragement? She couldn't tell. He tasted warm and coppery, slightly metallic, like a clean blade. Heat flooded her, blossoming in her chest, pooling lower in her belly. Her heart pounded. She didn't know what to do—she had never been kissed before, and she certainly hadn't imagined it would be like this.

A low, unexpected sound escaped from her throat. Her cheeks flushed, embarrassed, unsure if it was a natural response.

Then he stopped, pulling back without warning. She fell against him, her legs weak. She felt loose, pliant, absolutely speechless.

He gazed down at her, his eyes hooded and unreadable. She could barely look at him, suddenly intimidated.

"I'm sorry," he said.

She looked up at him searchingly, her lips still humming from the kiss. "Why did you stop?" she asked softly.

He paused. "You're vulnerable," he finally replied. "You don't want this, Sora."

She frowned at him, uncertain. *I don't?* By the way her body was responding, she was pretty sure that she did. The sensations were startlingly intense, difficult to suppress. Her mind began speeding up, imagining all sorts of scenarios.

"I...I've never done anything, uh, like this...before..." she started to say, then stopped. *Oh, dear Goddess.* If he felt as awkward as she did now, at least he was better at hiding it. He waited for her patiently, his hands warm on her shoulders, his body brushing hers.

She couldn't believe what she was trying to say, but she pushed through it, determined not to leave anything undone. "Don't let my innocence stop you," she finally finished. She focused hard on the grass beneath them, the small pine cones that littered the forest floor.

"Some people value innocence," he murmured, repeating her own words from the Crystal Caves.

She gave a small, nervous laugh. "Right," she agreed. "But tomorrow...."

"You're not going to die, Sora."

She glanced up at him. "How can you be so sure?"

He didn't answer, but pulled her tight against his chest, wrapping her in his strong arms. She was enveloped by the warm scent of him: trail dust and woodsmoke. "You have to trust me," he whispered.

She buried her face in his shirt. He made it sound so simple, so easy. "Then take away my fear," she said, her voice small, muffled by fabric. She didn't want to be afraid. She had tried not to be. But when he was this close, she felt completely undone.

He reached between them, tipping her head up. For a brief moment he searched her eyes, looking for something, she didn't know what. But he must have found it, because he set his lips against hers again, softly this time, gently. He kissed her with a sense of controlled power, as though holding back something monstrously strong. She could sense the shadows shift around them, moving on their own accord, clasping her in a dark embrace, an extension of his own body. She felt completely consumed.

He broke away again, muttering against her lips. "I will do this," he said, "until you can't think anymore." He trailed his lips across her mouth, tendrils of fire slipping through her body. "Then we will go back," he murmured, "and you will sleep."

She began to tremble, barely able to stand. His arms clamped her to his chest, strong and secure, sliding across her back. One traveled up to her neck, cradling the back of her head, adjusting her position. He opened her mouth easily, capturing her tongue, controlling her.

After a long moment, he finished his thought. "Tomorrow we will fight, and you will be safe, and this will have never happened."

Why? she wanted to ask. *Why can't this happen?*

Because he's an assassin, her inner voice answered through the foggy cloud of her mind.

I don't care, she thought.

You do, the voice murmured. *And he knows it.*

She couldn't argue anymore. Crash's hand wove into her hair, and then she was truly lost.

CHAPTER 22

Dawn broke across the ocean, spilling over the brink of the world. Gray water trapped the light, carrying it to a pale beach, curling over the white sand and washing away a series of footsteps.

Volcrian took a deep breath of the fresh sea air. His eyes searched the sky. The Lost Isles, the sacred home of the Harpies. He didn't see any now. The storms had been fierce on the ocean and he was certain that the Harpies knew of his arrival, but they weren't here to greet him. A grim smile crossed his face. Perhaps they were hiding?

He didn't really care about the Harpies. He wanted the assassin. And the moment he set foot upon the island, he felt a firm warmth seep up through the soles of his boots. It sang in his blood, provoking his anger. The Viper was near. *Fool*, he thought. *What is he playing at?* If the Viper thought to evade him on this island, he was sorely mistaken. Volcrian would find him eventually. There was no place left to run.

He glanced over his shoulder, back toward his ship. It dipped and wove on its anchor, a little less than a league offshore. Several small boats sailed between the beach and the larger vessel—his crew. He grinned. One by one, he had slaughtered the men and bled them dry, turning their corpses into loyal servants, just as he had the priestess. Yet unlike the priestess, these men were far easier to control. They gazed at him with empty, glassy eyes, doing whatever he said without question. Their spirits were weak, easily manipulated.

He would meet the Viper with a small battalion at his back. No matter what the assassin's tricks, he and his companions would not survive.

Volcrian didn't know why, but it seemed like in the past few months, his powers had grown immensely. Sometimes he lay awake at night, feeling the energy burn through his limbs. At times he had trouble focusing, he was so full of thirst, the need to crush the assassin's throat—and anyone who got in his way. *Is that an effect of the blood magic?* He felt like something else was growing within him, something far larger than he could explain. He hardly glanced at his grandfather's book anymore. He felt as though the spells were born into him now, a new knowledge that arose with his growing power.

As the day brightened, he could feel the familiar itch of a headache behind his eyes. He grimaced, rubbing his temples. He had suffered from migraines almost as soon as they left Delbar. He could only assume that it was the spirit of his dead brother hovering over him, pressuring him to complete his task. *Soon,* he promised. *Soon, Etienne. Soon we will rest.* He could tell it was almost time. Somewhere deep inside, he felt everything drawing to a close.

Before him lay the thick jungle of the Lost Isles, a solid wall of wilderness. As he looked at the trees, he felt a strange vibration in the air. He twitched his long ears and could almost hear music. Yet the sound went deeper than that, settling just below his diaphragm.

Sacred ground. A place where his magic could be amplified. The power emitting from it was palpable, like a beacon of light teasing his eyes. He would begin his search there.

"You're in a rather good mood," a wry voice said from behind him. It was barely intelligible. The priestess's vocal chords had begun to rot.

He glanced at the woman over his shoulder. She stood on the beach as the rest of the dead soldiers dragged their boat to shore. Her tattered brown cloak swirled in the wind, obscuring her figure. He could see large, gaping holes in her cheeks, a glimpse of white bone through the rotting flesh of her face. A swarm of flies had come to investigate, hovering around her head, crawling over her shoulders. She didn't notice.

"Four years," he said. "Four years I've been waiting for this."

Her eyes were almost pure white, but he could sense her looking him over, glancing from his face to his hands. "Only four years?" she asked slowly, a hint of challenge in her voice.

It bothered him, and he passed his hand over his face. His headache was growing worse. No, not four years. Longer than that, much longer....A sudden darkness leapt within him, growling in his stomach, clawing at his chest. *Eons,* it seemed to say. *A star's lifetime, trapped in the earth. The heat, the miserable, suffocating pressure, the crumbling depths of a grave....*

He needed blood. He craved it. He wanted to tear this island apart with his hands.

When he looked back at the priestess, he saw a grim set to her face, as though she knew his thoughts. He glared at her. "Four years since Etienne's death," he growled, pushing through his rage. "Don't worry, my dear. Soon you will join him in that afterlife."

She watched him impassively. He finally turned away in disgust.

The rest of his crew had reached the shore. They wandered up behind him, stiff and slow. It was the one downfall of his spell; a corpse didn't retain the natural elasticity of a body.

But Volcrian had one more minion at his command. Two of his wraiths had been destroyed by the Cat's Eye, but that only leant strength to the third one. As each wraith perished, its power was channeled into the next. So the last wraith would harbor the ferocity of all three combined.

He drew a knife from his belt and ran the blade down the center of his crippled hand. He barely felt the deep gash. Blood welled up from his skin. He clenched his fist, allowing the blood to drip through his fingers. *Where are you?* he asked the wind silently. *I need you now. Come to me.*

He waited. The minutes stretched on and he twitched his ears, listening for the faintest sound in reply. He called again, sending his will out over the ocean, speaking through the currents and the waves, magnified by the salt water. The ocean was the blood of the earth, a potent vessel for magic. He knew that if he waited long enough, his call would circle the entire world, echoing from sandy beaches to stone wells, up rivers and down streams. Yet he couldn't wait that long. The wraith shouldn't be that far away.

He felt a bit of perspiration on his brow. He knew that his minion was still in existence, yet when he reached for that inner bond, that strand that tied them together—he couldn't find it.

Volcrian frowned. Fifteen minutes passed. Twenty. Thirty. Still nothing.

"Are we going to stand here all day?" the priestess groaned at his back. "I can feel my muscles locking."

Volcrian gritted his teeth in frustration. The wind was cold and brisk next to the ocean, not good for an army of rotting corpses. Yet if he moved much closer to the ruins, the sacred ground would disrupt his call, making it impossible to be heard by the wraith. *Where has it gone?* A sense of doubt entered his thoughts, a strange foreboding. Either the wraith had been destroyed somehow...or it had found a new master. *But how is that possible?*

Volcrian shook his head. He didn't know, but he couldn't waste any more time. With the dead sailors at his command, he doubted he would need the wraith anyway. They would easily be able to overpower the assassin and his companions. Perhaps the corpses were slow and unwieldy, but they had monstrous strength, fueled by blood magic—and they couldn't be killed.

"Come," he finally said, and whirled toward the jungle, heading swiftly for the trees. The corpses plodded along behind him, the priestess in the lead. They likely wouldn't reach the ruins until midday, but as he entered the trees, he felt a rush of certainty return to him. Yes, the Viper was here. He could feel it in his bones. And by nightfall, the assassin would be dead.

* * *

Sora climbed over a fallen log, dappled with dense sunlight. It was a few hours past dawn. She had taken a brief detour in the woods to relieve herself, and was now headed to her appointed place—the far side of the ruins, close to the pedestal that stood on top of the cliff. Once there, she was to stay safe and out of the way, separate from the fight.

Burn and Crash would wait in the circle of stones, luring Volcrian into the open. There was still no sign of the mage, yet the forest felt different today. Subdued and quiet, it seemed that an ominous hush had fallen over the island. She hadn't seen any Harpies in the sky and she doubted that she would.

As she walked, her mind inevitably returned to the night before. She lightly pressed a finger to her lips. *Crash....*

Last night, he had kissed her. More than just kissed— devoured. She had felt completely overtaken, swept up in his presence, his hands, his mouth, the heaviness of his breath....How could a simple touch be so powerful? She still felt consumed, anxious, humming with the memory.

She didn't know how long they had spent under that tree. Her mind had become lost in the darkness, in the sensation of his body, in the way his calloused hands had moved over her skin, in the heat of him, his scent....She could barely remember being lifted from her feet, clasped in his arms and carried back to their camp.

As promised, he had made her forget her fear, her worries, her trepidation. And yet they had only kissed. Perhaps it was for the better. He had refrained from taking her innocence, and in the light of day, she felt a sense of relief. She hadn't truly been ready to part with it, and she didn't know how it would have changed things.

Sora climbed over a fallen long, still lost in thought. When she woke up that morning, the assassin was absent from their camp. Burn assured her that he had gone to scout for Volcrian, to see if the mage had arrived. As far as she knew, he still hadn't returned.

And as the morning crept by, the thought of confronting Crash became more and more terrifying. It was almost as frightening as their fight with Volcrian. *This will have never happened,* his voice repeated to her, over and over again. Perhaps he meant it. If she tried to address what he had done—what *they* had done—would he deny it? Brush it off like some sordid dream? Declare it was a mistake? *Was it a mistake?* Her stomach fluttered at the thought, squeezing uncomfortably.

Wrapped up in such troubling doubt, Sora didn't notice the brightening light that fell through the trees, strengthening in vibrancy and power. Suddenly, a figure landed directly in front of her. She yelped and fell back, raising her staff, prepared for an attack. She lashed out without thinking. *Thwak!*

A reassuring smack met her ears, but when she finally saw her opponent, all she could do was stare.

"C-Caprion?" she stuttered in surprise.

The Harpy General had a slight grin on his lips. It faded as he looked at her, and a frown touched his face, thoughtful. His hair looked tousled and messy and his clothes were streaked with dirt, much different from the last time she had seen him. His eyes had faint circles underneath, evidence of a sleepless night. His gaze shifted, focusing on the air around her body, as though he could see something that she couldn't. Then his frown deepened. Sora bit her lips, suddenly nervous.

"You look...." he paused, still gazing at her. "Did the assassin...." Finally, he shook his head. "I suppose it doesn't matter."

She yanked back her weapon, realizing that Caprion had grabbed it from midair. He released it willingly.

"What?" she demanded, on-guard.

Caprion shook his head again. "His aura has mingled with your own, that's all."

Sora frowned, unsure of what he meant. Her mind briefly returned to last night, the shadows that had risen around her body, cradling her, tightening their grasp....Either way, it was none of

Caprion's concern.

"What are you doing here?" she asked bluntly.

"I came to tell you that Volcrian has landed on the island," he said.

Sora's heart skipped a beat. "Oh."

"He's not alone," he added. "He is accompanied by twenty men and a woman. He is controlling them with his blood magic."

She nodded, alarmed. So many?

"Also," he said, "you should know that the Matriarch and her soldiers are laying low for the moment, watching to see what he does. I led them away from you. I think she suspects my involvement, but she hasn't said anything directly."

Sora let out a sigh of relief. At least they didn't have to worry about the Harpies for now. "Thank you," she murmured. "And what about the Dracians? Are they nearby?"

Caprion nodded. "They should arrive by nightfall. Perhaps tomorrow morning if the winds change."

She shifted on her feet; their arrival was sooner than expected, but still worrisome. If she succeeded in killing Volcrian, she would have the Harpies to contend with. Caprion might be able to distract them for a while, but they would catch on to his game soon. There were very few places to hide on an island.

He seemed to know how she felt. Perhaps it was obvious on her face. "Don't worry," he said. She could hear the ring of command in his tone. Too bad she was immune to it; she could have used the extra confidence. "The dawn star was clearly visible this morning. It is a sign of luck. I think you will succeed."

Sora raised an eyebrow. A sign of luck? "That's encouraging," she said. It came out more sardonic than she intended, but Caprion didn't seem to take offense. He nodded over her shoulder, toward the ruins.

"I will return for you tonight," he said. "I, too, wish to leave this island as soon as possible. Together we will find a way."

Sora gave him a slight smile. He was trying to reassure her. She appreciated the attempt, though it didn't work. "It's good to know that we have help," she affirmed. "You've done more than enough...."

"Not enough," he interrupted her. "Not until Volcrian is dead and we are safely away from the Matriarch. I won't be able to join you in the fight—it would be too suspicious—but know that I am counting on your survival. We *will* leave this island together." He smiled in return. "Until nightfall." Then he bowed his head slightly in farewell.

She watched him turn back to the trees. A halo of light glowed around him, illuminating the forest in a bright glow, outshining the sun—then he leapt into the air. Sora squinted, her hand shielding her eyes. Then he was gone.

She sighed, turning back toward the ruins and continuing on her way. Crash still didn't know about her alliance with Caprion; he distrusted the First Race and would suspect the worst. But Caprion was the only reason why they all weren't in prison right now, awaiting Volcrian's arrival behind bars.

She clutched her staff in sweaty hands and continued walking.

A minute later, she exited the forest and stepped onto the dewy grass of the ruins. The black stones were just as she had left them—tall and ominous in the daylight. A hollow wind swept through the clearing, carrying the distant crash of the ocean's waves.

Her eyes found the treeline across from her, where Burn supposedly stood watch. She had to tell him about Caprion's warning: Volcrian was on the island and he had a band of warriors at his back.

She took two steps, then winced. Something sharp stung her hand. She looked, puzzled, and saw a small bead of blood slide down her index finger toward the ground. She lifted her finger in front of her eyes. A bee sting?

Quite suddenly, she couldn't move.

At first Sora didn't know what was happening. She twisted around, but her feet were firmly planted in the dirt, as solid as stone. She caught herself on her staff, struggling to stay balanced.

"I'd suggest you stop moving before you fall over," a soft, silky voice drifted to her.

All of the hair on Sora's body stood on end. The voice's breathy quality caused a shiver to run down her spine. She had never heard it before, but she knew who it was. Who it had to be.

She turned, looking over her shoulder, slightly to her left. About ten feet away stood a man, one she dimly recognized from a vision long ago. In person, however, he wasn't quite as tall as she'd thought. His shoulders were broad, though not as muscular as Crash. He was covered by a midnight-blue cloak. He wore a midnight-blue cloak. His steel-silver hair and blue eyes reminded her of an arctic sky, sharp and bright. His lips were pale, twisted into a smile that didn't reach his eyes. It left her feeling chilled.

One long, sloping ear twitched, and that sick grin widened. "It seems that you are quite firmly trapped," the mage murmured, and began to walk forward. Sora's stomach lurched with each step. The closer he came, the more she could smell something heavy and sour in the air. The stench of rotten meat.

"Volcrian." She hadn't meant to say his name, but it fell from her lips like poison. The Wolfy's fangs glinted at the sound of it.

"So you've heard of me," he murmured. "Sora Fallcrest, isn't it? My, but you are a pretty young thing."

Sora blanched. She hated how he said her name—mockingly, like an insult. She hadn't used her surname Fallcrest in more than a year. It was a taunting reminder of her past, of the life she had left behind, of the family she didn't belong to.

He approached her from behind. Sora felt a surge of anger that shocked her into action. She sent a silent command to the Cat's Eye, and the necklace twisted against the force of his magic, trying to break free. Blood magic was more complicated than that of the other races—it wasn't purely energy, but made of physical matter, difficult for the stone to absorb. She focused her mind, commanding the necklace—and with an audible snap, her legs returned to her.

She stumbled forward, not expecting the shift of balance. Volcrian lunged at her at the same time. She ran a few steps, then felt his hand snag her hair, wrapping it around his wrist, dragging her backward. A shriek escaped her lips. He pulled her against his body, holding her with bruising force.

The taint of his magic made her skin crawl. He was icy-cold, clammy, like a dead corpse. Sora struggled, trying to slip from his grasp, but he was far stronger than he appeared. Unnaturally strong. He held her effortlessly, dragging her into the air by her neck, her legs kicking futilely. She tried to bring her staff around to hit him, but it was at a bad angle. He was using her body as a shield.

"Bastard!" she choked in outrage. "Let me go!"

"Keep struggling and I'll snap your neck," the mage hissed. His hand tightened viciously, cutting off her air. Sora went limp, knowing a threat when she heard one. *This is all wrong!* she thought, screaming in her head. *This wasn't the plan!*

Volcrian held her up like a caught fish, facing the treeline across the clearing. He breathed deeply, sniffing the air. Finally he paused, facing a particularly thick patch of shrubbery; she felt his hand clamp a little harder on her neck. She was forced to breathe in small, short spurts through her nose.

"I know you're there, Viper!" he called out, almost friendly. "I can smell you!"

A pause. Nothing stirred but the wind.

If anything, the breeze only seemed to make the mage more certain. "Oh, come now, my friend," the Wolfy barked out jovially. "Do I need to persuade you? I have a pretty girl here who I believe you know. I could kill her, if you'd like."

Sora grasped the mage's hand, trying to pry his fingers from her neck, but his grip was like iron. His strength was inhuman, fueled by magic. He dug his nails into her throat and she felt a burning sensation. Blood leaked through their entwined hands, staining her shirt. She closed her eyes briefly, trying to gather herself. *I must remain conscious,* she repeated over and over again. Her head began to swim.

A shadow emerged from the treeline. Sora's eyes fastened onto it desperately. It had to be Crash, though her vision was growing blurry, interrupted by white dots. He stood against the dark shade of the forest, his clothes ripped and stained, his features grim.

"Kill her then," he called.

Sora would have gasped if she could breathe. The assassin's voice was cold and strong, rough from his brutalized neck. This was not Crash speaking—it was Viper, the trained killer. A knot of fear formed in her belly. *He's bluffing,* she thought desperately. *He has to be!*

Volcrian shifted. He seemed disappointed by the turn of events. "How dull," he murmured quietly, as though personally confiding in her. Then he shook her viciously, like a small kitten. Sora stiffened, trying not to break her neck.

"Maybe I'll have some fun with her first," he said loudly, his voice carrying easily across the clearing. They stood perhaps a hundred feet apart, not quite yelling distance. "She's a firm young thing. And if her blood is any indication, she hasn't been touched yet."

Crash watched him silently.

Sora's skin crawled. She writhed against Volcrian, kicking futilely with her legs. It was a position that her mother had warned her about. There was no easy trick to make him let go. His nails dug deeper into her skin, and she heard his voice in her ear. "Tsk tsk," he muttered. "Oh no, you aren't going anywhere."

Suddenly, someone lunged out of the trees. Burn charged at Volcrian's back, his longsword already swinging through the air. A guttural cry ripped from his throat.

Volcrian staggered in surprise and loosened his hold. It was all that Sora needed. She sank her weight downward and then up, cracking her head back against his chin. The Wolfy stumbled and released her.

"Run, Sora!" Burn roared. His blade whirled past Volcrian,

barely missing the mage's head. She scrambled to her feet and grabbed her staff, then took off across the clearing, running toward the nearby cliff.

"Priestess!" Volcrian yelled from behind her. "Stop her!"

What? Sora didn't know who he was talking to. She looked around, prepared for an attack, then noticed several bulky shapes emerge from the jungle ahead of her. They limped awkwardly into her path, moving so strangely that at first she didn't know what they were: human or animal? The wind changed, blowing against her face, and she almost gagged from the bitter, bloated smell of dead flesh.

A figure in a brown cloak ran to cut her off. It moved faster than the rest, though still clumsy in the long grass. The wind shoved the cloak's hood back and she saw the face of a dead woman staring at her. Sora stumbled out of pure shock. The woman's flesh dripped from her bones, flaking away with each gust of wind. She could see patches of teeth through the rotted holes in her face. In her hand was a long, naked dagger.

Sora felt her gut sink. So these were the men that Caprion had mentioned. Only they weren't men at all. They were corpses.

The priestess paused, blocking her path. The other corpses reached her side, fanning out in front of her. They stood between Sora and the tall cliff that led to the Cat's Eye's pedestal. She had no choice. She would have to force her way through.

Sora ran forward, brought her staff up, and jammed it into the chest of the first corpse. The body imploded, crumpling inward, oozing with blood and putrid gas. She held her breath as she slammed her weapon into the man's head, his skull shattering beneath her blow.

Yet the body did not fall. It continued to lurch toward her, hands grasping at her weapon, trying to pull it from her grasp.

Sora fell back and touched her Cat's Eye, desperate for help. The necklace was slow to respond; it jingled distantly. A shield of green light fell around her, moving inward until it sunk into her skin. She felt strengthened and protected—for the moment.

A cry of fury ripped from her throat, and she launched herself again at her foe. Two more corpses converged on her only a few yards away. They were slow, but strong. *I can handle this,* she thought, and she ducked down, sweeping her staff under the first corpse's legs. It fell onto its back, flailing helplessly on the ground like a toppled turtle. *That's one,* she thought. *Twenty more to go.*

CHAPTER 23

Out of the corner of his eye, Crash watched Sora sprint across the wet grass toward the hill. Numerous shapes were emerging from the trees and wandering into her path. He didn't know what they were, but he could see that she was sorely outnumbered. "Burn!" he called. The giant mercenary stood facing Volcrian, his sword held at the ready. The two Wolfies appeared to be at a standoff. "Burn, help her!"

The hulking warrior must have heard him, because he turned and dashed back to the treeline, following it to Sora's position. Volcrian watched him go, his blue cloak brushing in the wind. Then the mage turned to look at Crash. He could see the man's smile at this distance. He gritted his teeth, a black rage boiling inside.

Crash drew his dagger and started across the grass, closing the distance between them.

"You seem very eager to die," Volcrian called. He drew a saber from his cloak, a thin blade used for fencing. Crash barely glanced at it.

"Thought you could escape me?" Volcrian continued. "You certainly had a good run."

Crash didn't reply. There was no point in speaking to a man who would soon be dead. He felt a grim satisfaction move through him at the thought. This was a kill he would enjoy.

Volcrian waited until he was only a yard away. Then he whipped the saber up and lunged. Crash parried the blow with his dagger, sparks flying between the blades. The mage whirled and attacked again, unfastening his cloak and allowing it to fall to the ground. He lunged forward once, twice, thrice—Crash was able to block, but he was surprised by Volcrian's strength. The mage's blows were unnaturally hard, close to breaking the saber's blade. Such a sword was built for speed, not force.

Crash saw an opening. He ducked under Volcrian's swing and lunged forward, ready to stab the mage under the ribs.

Surprisingly, the Wolfy grabbed his arm and pulled him forward, as though assisting Crash with his attack. Then he dropped his saber and slipped a small knife out of his sleeve. He brought the knife down on Crash's arm just as the dagger entered his body.

The mage stumbled backwards. Warm blood sprayed across the grass, dampening his shirt. Volcrian clamped a hand over the wound, then looked up, a smile still plastered on his face. They stood a few yards apart. The Wolfy was breathing hard, his skin shiny and pale.

Crash stared at him. An average man would have collapsed to the ground, entering his death throes. But not this mage. *Blood magic*, he realized.

"First blood is spilled," Volcrian hissed, then let out a breathy laugh. "Go on, stab me again. It will only make me stronger!"

Crash paused. There were spells that could strengthen a mage's body, he knew that much. The blood lost to the mage would work as a sacrifice, and fuel his strength until he was killed. Dorian had described it to him once, long ago, when they had first met. It was simply called *bloodletting*.

Then Crash felt a burning sensation. He looked down and saw

a bloody gash on his forearm. The pain sharpened his senses, heightening his adrenaline. The demon slammed against its inner cage, knocking on his chest, eager for release. Crash took a steadying breath, trying to contain it. *Not now,* he thought desperately. *Gods, not now!*

When he looked up again, the mage had raised his hand to his mouth and was sucking on his fingers. Blood graced his lips. "The Unnamed tastes like burnt ashes," he said. "How very appropriate."

Crash's eyes widened marginally. It had been a ploy. The mage had attacked him in an attempt to get his blood—and it had worked. *Clumsy,* he thought. *I'm too distracted.* He needed to stop worrying about Sora and focus on the fight.

Suddenly, his head swam. He felt a strange sense of vertigo. Crash dug his feet into the ground, unwilling to fall.

Then something snagged his boot.

He paused, glancing down. The very tail end of a tree root protruded through the grass, tightly wrapped around his ankle. He frowned, uncertain for a moment; several other roots had ripped out of the ground, tearing up the earth. Crash slashed at them, cutting down two on his left, but more rose to take their place. Another root grabbed his second foot.

When he looked up once again, the entire clearing seemed to have changed. The large obsidian stones were taller, more menacing, spaced closer than before. The trees had grown darker, leaning forward with malicious intent. Clouds were gathering in the sky, pressing down above his head. He had the intense impression that everything was staring at him. It seemed like a thousand eyes lay hidden in the grass, in the black branches of the trees, in the rocks that littered the ground.

"Did you think it would be that easy?" Volcrian crowed. His voice sounded different now, larger, echoing. "I've been preparing for this moment a long time. My magic is more than strong enough!"

Crash swept his hand over his eyes, trying to regain his composure. He had been foolish to attack first. The mage had obviously planned it this way. Crash's anger had gotten the best of him. *I need to step back.* He was an assassin—he knew better than to rush headlong into the unknown.

A sick grin spread across the Wolfy's features. "Any last requests?" he called.

Crash looked at him coldly. "Just that your brother might be here," he said, "so you can die in front of him."

Volcrian's facade slipped and his eyes filled with manic fury. He threw back his head and howled. Then the mage drew his knife across his own arm. Black blood spilled from his veins, falling to the earth and singeing the grass. Smoke rose from the mage's feet. The air thickened with an unknown magic, becoming dense and warm.

The tree creaked at Volcrian's back. Suddenly its branches began to move, knocking together and bending forward like grasping arms. Crash ducked down, slicing through the thin tree roots that held his feet. Then he launched to one side and rolled away just as a massive tree limb smashed the ground exactly where he had been standing.

The trunk righted itself and appeared to turn, watching the assassin run across the grass. *What kind of magic is this?* he thought, his eyes narrowing.

Volcrian stood at the base of the tree, protected by its strong limbs. Crash gritted his teeth. The only way to reach him was to go through the tree.

He sprinted forward, dodging the thick pine needles. Twice he almost lost his head to a whizzing branch. He ducked and wove, jumping, turning. The sky was blocked out by dense foliage and surrounded him in an inescapable net. He pushed on. He could avoid the larger limbs, but the smaller ones whipped at his body, drawing blood from old injuries. He shook them off, bearing the pain, racing toward his foe.

And all the while, Volcrian's laugh rang maddeningly through the air.

* * *

Sora stumbled back, her brow dripping with sweat. She didn't know what to do. She could have killed twice as many men by now, but the corpses kept rising and coming back to life. They were tireless. Half of them didn't even have heads anymore, and still they came on.

"Sora, behind you!" The voice reached her a moment before Burn appeared, charging from the treeline, arriving not a moment too soon. He passed by her so closely, they almost collided. With his giant sword, he struck down three corpses at her back, cleaving easily through their bodies. They burst open under his blade, spewing out rotten pus and bile. Sora wanted to vomit. She could barely breathe through the stench.

Yet even cleaved in half, the bodies still writhed on the ground, turning toward them, crawling forward on blind hands.

"What are we going to do?" she panted, finding herself back-to-back with the giant Wolfy. They turned as one, looking around the clearing. They were surrounded by corpses.

"I'll give you an opening," Burn said. "Then you run up the cliff."

She didn't like that idea. "You can't take on this many," she panted.

Burn smiled grimly. "Watch me."

With a ferocious roar, the Wolfy lunged again, sweeping his blade through the air. Everywhere he swung, he sliced through flesh. Sora watched him, in shock. He moved swiftly, skillfully, wielding the massive sword with ease. Within a minute, the corpses had either fallen back or were chopped down to the ground, squirming on the grass like dying worms.

"Go!" he yelled to her.

Sora shook herself into action. She launched into a run, dashing between the bodies, yelping as a severed hand grabbed her foot. It clung to her ankle, but had no way of pulling her down. She smacked it off with the butt of her staff, then kept moving toward the hillside. She was close now. Almost there....

Wham! Someone tackled her—the dead woman in the brown cloak. Her body was light and empty, the weight of a child. Sora twisted and threw her off, but the woman kept coming, scrabbling at her feet. She grabbed at her legs. Sora regained her balance and kicked the woman down to one side.

Finally, she was at the base of the hill. She started scrambling up. The cliff was steep and tall, and toward the top it became almost vertical. She could already feel her muscles straining.

The dead woman followed behind her, propelled by her bony arms and legs, scuttling like a vicious spider.

Crash had almost reached the trunk of the tree. With a burst of strength, he leapt over a swinging limb and raised his dagger in both hands. Volcrian turned toward him, his face contorting into a scowl.

It all seemed to happen very slowly. The assassin flew through the air, aiming for the Wolfy's chest, straight for his heart. In his mind, he was already playing out his next attack, a thousand different parries and blows, depending on how the mage planned to defend himself.

Yet Volcrian did nothing. He just stood and watched.

Crash surged through the last of the branches and struck him fully in the chest.

The mage's body crumpled beneath him, then vanished in a misty cloud of vapor and blood.

Crash hit the ground hard and stumbled, regaining his feet in an instant. He hadn't anticipated the hard impact—the mage's body should have been beneath him. He whirled, staring at the ground, at the blackened tree trunk, at the deep shadows between the pines. It felt as though everything was moving, swaying back and forth, including the ground.

"Nicely done!" Volcrian's voice called to him. "Beautiful form, perfect control! Only you missed."

Crash whirled toward the voice. Through the thick pine needles, he could catch a glimpse of the mage's silver hair. The man stood several yards behind him, toward the center of the sacred stones, beyond the reach of the tree.

His heart thudded—doubt entered his thoughts. How was it possible? Volcrian had been directly in front of him, solid flesh....*An illusion?* he thought, his mind racing. *A double of some kind?* He didn't know enough about Wolfy magic to understand how it worked. Mages tended to be tactical masters. Back in the War, they had kept to the fortress walls, far removed from direct combat. Their spells had served to strengthen and protect the mercenaries on the ground.

Crash felt the tree creak above him. It was still groaning and twisting. He noticed that the limbs had begun to draw inward to the trunk, slowly shutting out the daylight. He cursed under his breath —he had hesitated too long. Another few seconds and the branches would enclose him completely, locking him into a suffocating prison. His body would be completely crushed.

He leapt at a thin patch of branches and struck them with his dagger, trying to cut his way through, but the blade was too short. He couldn't cut fast enough. He fell back against the trunk, panting, his feet cushioned by dry pine needles. He was now surrounded by dense shadows. He could feel the weight of the tree pushing down upon him; a slow, shuddering moan as its wooden limbs contorted, closing the last of the space.

He shut his eyes, his grip tightening on the dagger, trying to think of a solution.

And in that darkness, a voice spoke to him. *You need me.* It slithered up from his gullet, writhing in the back of his throat. *Let me out.*

No, he thought. He couldn't trust the demon. It had its own agenda, its own desires and needs. There was no way to know for sure that it would go after Volcrian. He could try to direct it...but he couldn't control it. What if it turned its sights upon Sora and Burn?

You're going to get us both killed, the demon whispered. *Then what will happen to her?*

Her. The word jolted him. Its only concern was Sora, and it disturbed him that the demon knew his deeper motives, that he kept hidden even from himself.

But of course it would. It resided in that same place at the bottom of his skull, where the darkness pooled like thick, black water.

You're not going to have your way, Crash said. *Not like last time.*

The demon hissed. The sound was like fire running down his spine. He was losing his grip; heat coursed through his arms and legs, his muscles cramping, his heartbeat tripling in speed. He gripped the dagger harder, bowing his head, grinding his teeth. A vein throbbed in his neck. He could feel his shadow lift from the ground, coiling in the air, taunting him.

You need me, the demon growled. *You're nothing without me.*

No, Crash swore.

Yes, the demon grinned. *It's so easy. Just let go....*

Crash couldn't stay in control. With a strangled yell, he fell to his knees, panting and heaving. He felt the skin split along his back, bones and tendons thrusting up from his shoulder blades, creating his wings. Horns jutted from his neck and arms, tearing through flesh. The pain was intense, consuming his entire body. Blood spattered the tree trunk, dripping to the ground, burning all that it touched with toxic acidity.

And then—rage. It poured from his mouth, his skin, his lungs. Igniting. Consuming.

Dark energy rolled off his skin. With furious strength, the Viper rose to his feet. He reached out and scored the tree with his claws, rending the bark.

The wood burst into flames.

* * *

The earth shook and Sora was almost thrown off her feet. She was just beneath the summit of the hill. She stumbled to her knees, her hands gripping the dirt for purchase, trying not to slide backwards.

She glanced over her shoulder at the sacred stones below. Past Burn's figure and the struggling corpses she saw a dark cloud roll across the ground. Was it smoke? It looked like part of the forest was on fire. She squinted, her heart in her throat, looking for a sign of Crash and Volcrian, but they were obscured by mist. *This isn't good,* she thought. *How will I know when to use the Cat's Eye?*

Something clawed at Sora's ankle and she jumped. The dead woman's corpse was just beneath her, struggling over a rocky overhang, her fingers scrabbling at her boots. Sora turned back to the cliff and started upward, pulling herself over the final ledge, huffing and heaving as she reached the top.

The stone pedestal stood before her. It was old, worn down by wind and rain, barely standing. She stared at it, trying to catch her breath. Her muscles were exhausted from the long climb and it took a moment for her to recover. The Cat's Eye shifted on her chest, responding to the pedestal, humming with latent energy. Yes, this was the right place.

She stood up just as the dead woman arrived behind her.

Sora turned as the woman lunged. Her long, bony arms grasped for Sora's neck, the dagger swinging wildly. She easily caught the woman's arm and pulled, intending to trip her, but there was a terrible ripping sound as the flesh tore from her body. Sora stumbled back as the arm came off. *Ugh!*

The skeletal hand stabbed down clumsily, gouging her shoulder with the knife. She gasped in surprise and pain. Then she dislodged the knife and held the arm away from her—it twisted in the air like a caught snake. She threw it away on impulse, sending it plummeting over the side of the cliff. It fell toward the ocean.

Sora stood for a moment, her stomach rising into her throat, thoroughly disgusted.

The woman attacked again, throwing her body on top of Sora, clinging with one hand while she attempted to bite her neck. No, not her neck—the Cat's Eye! The corpse was trying to yank the necklace free.

Sora screamed, grappling with the lightweight body. The corpse was full of tireless energy and came at her like a frenzied beast, kicking and clawing. She dropped her staff and grabbed the woman by the shoulders, locking her in a vise-like grip, prying her off.

At that moment, the Cat's Eye stone let out a fierce chime and a burst of green light exploded from the necklace. It pushed the corpse back, toppling her over. She would have gone over the cliff, but she grabbed the stone pedestal at the last second, clawing her way again to safety.

The necklace died down, returning to the back of Sora's mind. Then she heard a voice—guttural, rasping, barely intelligible.

"Kill me," the corpse gasped.

Sora took a step back, surprised. "What?"

"Too long...too long I have been trapped in this body," the corpse groaned. "I cannot let him control me anymore. You must kill me!"

"But...." *But you are dead,* she wanted to say. How did one kill a corpse? "I don't know how...." The woman was still clinging to the pedestal, but this time, it was as though she were holding herself back. Resisting some inner force.

"The necklace!" the woman gasped. "Quickly, I can't hold back much longer! Use the necklace to rid me of this curse! I beg...I beg you...." The corpse's eyes rolled wildly in her head, and then she let out a fierce scream, like the cry of a banshee, lunging over the pedestal, gnashing her teeth, leaping at Sora with murderous intent.

Sora ran to meet her. She grabbed the woman's outstretched arm and sent a quick command to her necklace. She didn't know if the stone would work very well against Volcrian's magic. The corpse was solid, after all. But she had to try. "Free her!" she screamed, forcing the command through her entire body.

There was a brilliant flash of light—the sound of countless bells clanging. The Cat's Eye let out a ferocious burst of white energy, unlike anything Sora had seen before. She felt the energy burn her skin, scorching her chest.

The light intensified, capturing the woman's corpse, lifting it from the ground, obliterating it in a matter of seconds. The flesh crumbled beneath her hands, burned away, turned to ash. The woman's skull melted before her eyes, disintegrating into the air.

In its place was a white, misty substance. For a moment, Sora saw another person standing before her, hovering at the edge of the cliff. By her blue robes, she knew it was a priestess of the Goddess.

The woman rose into the air, a small smile alighting on her lips, serene. For a moment, she looked at Sora—then turned and opened her arms. A great wind gusted over the top of the cliff, and she was carried away.

Sora fell to the ground. She felt as though her body had been squeezed dry. She gasped brokenly, struggling to breathe, unsure of what had just happened. Usually the necklace absorbed magic, but she had never felt it expel energy before, especially with such force. *What did I do?* she wondered. *What was that...thing?* A human spirit? Could it be?

Then she heard a loud, vicious roar from the field below. It echoed through the air, carrying far out over the ocean. She crawled to the edge of the hill, looking down at the battle. Burn was still fighting the corpses, though it wasn't much of a contest, since most of the bodies had been hacked to gory pieces.

Beyond him, though, was a terrifying sight.

Sora's body turned cold with fear—dark, instinctual fear that rose from her stomach, paralyzing her limbs. She stared, unable to look away, a scream lodged in her throat.

* * *

Viper charged from the forest into the center of the stone circle. He could hear the trees screaming behind him, consumed by black flames. Large branches crashed down around him, still reaching for his body, swinging at his head—but he broke through them easily. His strength was immense, and before him—his prey.

Volcrian stepped back as the demon came on, the fear naked

on his face. Viper relished the expression. He could smell the Wolfy's sweat, feel it on the back of his throat, taste it with his tongue. *Yes. Yes. Yes.*

Volcrian raised his hand, and a flurry of bats appeared in the sky, diving at Viper's body. He leapt up to greet them, catching one in his mouth and crunching it between powerful jaws. The mage kept waving his arms, summoning roots from the ground, ripping apart the earth, sending stones flying through the air. But still the demon came.

Crash observed, trapped in the heated depths of the demon's body. Through his new eyes, the mage did not appear like himself. No, he saw a dark energy surrounding the man, seeping into the air —a tainted aura. The Dark God. He recognized the way it smelled, how it pierced his nose like ice. Yes, the Dark God was possessing Volcrian, worming into his mind. Crash grimaced inwardly. No wonder his magic was so strong.

Suddenly, the temperature dropped. Cold air arose from the ground. Volcrian stumbled backwards, his body shuddering, and the tainted aura began to spread. It wrapped up the mage's neck and over his face, clasping the Wolfy in a dark shroud. He let out a muffled scream and fell to the ground, his body twitching and convulsing.

As soon as Volcrian fell, the earth seemed to tilt, and Viper stumbled to one side. A sense of nausea passed through his body, and he blinked. His vision swam briefly, then cleared. The day grew brighter, the mist lifted, the standing stones pulled back into their original positions. He turned and glanced at the trees, noting that they no longer loomed threateningly toward him. All the broken branches and torn limbs had disappeared.

An illusion, he realized. Volcrian had drunk his blood and manipulated his mind. The entire time, he had been fighting ghosts.

Crash turned back to his opponent. When Volcrian had collapsed, he had lost hold of the spell. *Now. Do it now.* The demon started forward, stalking across the grass, and paused over Volcrian's body. The mage's eyes stared sightlessly up at the sky—then slowly turned black, as though filling with ink.

The Dark God didn't want to lose this battle. Oh no, He wanted to use the mage as a vessel, and if Crash waited much longer, he would be dealing with much more than blood magic.

Kill him, Crash ordered, asserting his will.

No, the demon rebuked. Excitement surged. Its mouth watered in anticipation. *He comes.*

Crash's focus tightened. He thrust himself forward, pushing the demon back. *Remember your true master,* he commanded. He forced himself to take control of his body, pushing into his arms and legs, reclaiming his throne.

No! the demon bellowed. *No! No! No!* Crash could feel the creature digging in its claws, scrambling for a foothold, trying to reclaim its freedom.

But his will was stronger.

Crash broke through the demon's control and lunged forward. He needed to utilize the demon's body while it still lasted. Now that the beast's mind was in remission, his new form wouldn't remain for long. He had to work quickly. He could already feel his strength wane.

He grabbed Volcrian by the neck and dragged him across the ground. The mage's body shuddered and twisted, in the throes of a seizure. The stone table was only a few yards away, and he threw Volcrian's body on top of it, pressing him into the hard rock.

"Sora!" he yelled, hoping that his vocal cords would work. What came out was a strangled roar, but somewhere in that sound was a name. "Sora, now! Use the Cat's Eye!"

* * *

Sora stared at the demon in the field below. She couldn't seem to make her feet work. She knew it was Crash—reassured herself of that fact—and yet he looked like a monster, blackened skin and giant wings, spikes along his shoulders as long as swords.

The beast roared, its voice carrying for miles around. It sent another bolt of paralyzing fear through her. She had the intense urge to cower behind the pedestal. Inside that roar, she thought she heard words, but she couldn't be certain.

Then Burn's voice reached her from below. "The Cat's Eye!" he yelled. She had to strain her ears to hear him. "Use the Cat's Eye!"

Sora nodded and forced herself to turn toward the pedestal. She felt as though her body was fighting her, clumsy and stiff. She reached into her pocket, finding the small stone wrapped in a piece of a cloth. *I hope this works,* she thought desperately, and plunged the stone onto the pedestal.

It spun slightly on the flat surface, moved by the energy of the sacred ground. But after a few seconds, it slowed down and rolled to a stop. Silent.

I need to bond with it, Sora realized. She didn't have any other choice. They had to kill Volcrian. If she waited any longer, it might be too late.

She didn't give herself a chance to turn back. She grabbed the stone with her bare hand. A jolt of electricity shot through her body as the new bond was formed. Its presence burst into her mind, searching for a place to fit. She felt a terrible, jarring pain.

The new bond clashed with the one that was already in place. She heard a strangled tussle of sleigh bells, and the second Cat's Eye began to smoke in her hand, burning a hole in her skin, trying to embed itself into her flesh. The two necklaces were wrestling with each other, fighting for dominance in her body. She pressed the second stone onto the pedestal, forcing it down with her weight.

Then she screamed. She felt as though her mind was being split in two. She couldn't balance any longer, and she collapsed to her knees, gripping the pedestal for support.

I have to do this, she thought, her head throbbing. She struggled for control, forcing her limbs to work.

"Finish him!" she yelled, directing her command to the second stone. Another wave of fire crashed through her; hot energy ran down her arm, channeling into the Cat's Eye.

There was a fierce, terrible *crack!*

Sora was thrown back to the edge of the cliff, losing hold of the pedestal. She rolled to a stop, inches away from plunging to her death. When she opened her eyes, the world was spinning—colors, objects and light were all swirled together, like a spun painting. At its center was the Cat's Eye, creating a vortex of energy that would devour all that it touched, amplified by the power of the standing stones. Not even the wind could escape it.

* * *

Volcrian was panicking. Somehow, he had lost control. He had blacked out for a moment—he didn't know what had happened—but now the demon held him down by the throat. He didn't know what the assassin planned to do.

Suddenly, he felt tendrils of power snake across his skin, weaving over his hands and legs, tying him down to the table. Terror struck him. He recognized the fierce pull of the Cat's Eye, far stronger than he remembered.

The ropes of energy crushed him to the stone slab. He felt a terrible suction at his chest, paralyzing his lungs, his pulse beating erratically. He felt as though his heart would be torn from his body. Bones snapped. A rushing noise consumed his ears, like the torrents of a mighty river. He could feel his strength drain out of him, his skin becoming paper-thin.

Then, a burst of excruciating pain. A scream ripped from his throat. Volcrian felt himself being pulled forcefully upward, leaving his solid, warm flesh behind. The howling wind and his own yells vanished from his ears. He no longer felt the demon on top of him, his vision darkening.

Dear brother, I have failed.

* * *

A spiral of light emerged from the Cat's-Eye stone, swirling like a tornado. Instead of stretching upward, it bent down toward the sacred circle—to the stone slab where Volcrian's body lay.

Strange sensations shot through her. Sora felt his fear, his rage, his deep sorrow. She watched his soul lift out of his body. Volcrian's spirit flew through the air, sucked into the Cat's Eye like a wind-tunnel.

She felt Crash's spirit next, but it was gone before the Cat's Eye could catch hold of it. Then the stone's power began to overflow, seeping over the edge of the pedestal in a wave of white light.

Static snapped over her skin, leaving small burn marks. The Cat's Eye sought out her body, trying to recreate the broken bond. Sora grabbed her own necklace and begged it to protect her, to stop the light from touching her. She didn't know if it worked. She felt as though she would be burned to ash.

The smaller stone could withstand no more. With a sickening crack, it split in two. Abruptly, the wind-tunnel dispersed. The magic vanished, trapped forever inside the two broken halves.

A backlash of power clapped the air, shattering her senses into a thousand shining shards.

CHAPTER 24

Crash opened his eyes with a groan.

He lay on the grass next to the stone table, in the center of the sacred circle. He raised himself slowly into a sitting position. His head throbbed. His hands shook. Numerous cuts and bruises covered his body, and blood still seeped from the thick gash on his forearm. He winced and ripped off the sleeve of his shirt, wrapping it around the injured limb, binding it tightly.

How much time had passed? A day? An hour? He glanced at the sky. The sun was still high, a little past noon. He must have fallen unconscious for a matter of minutes.

He stood up, using the stone table to support himself. There was no sign of Volcrian's body—only a blackened stain on the granite and a few scraps of cloth, the leather from his boots. The table reeked of burned flesh. Crash gazed at it for a long moment, reflecting on the battle. So many years of running—it was finally over. So why didn't he feel relieved?

The rest of the clearing was torn up from the fight; there were long rents in the earth and shattered rocks, patches of scorched grass. The wind blew eerily across the field, carrying dead leaves with it. The black stones stood in their silent circle, looking on impassively.

Hells, he thought, his headache intensifying and pulsing down the center of his skull.

Then his eyes traveled beyond the clearing to the tall cliff that rose above the sea. He couldn't see anyone standing on top of that hill. His hands suddenly turned cold. *Sora.*

He pushed off the stone table and stumbled across the grass. It took him a minute to regain his coordination. He was exhausted from the demon's transformation; he felt empty, drained to the bone. He had to summon all his remaining strength just to walk to the base of the cliff.

Burn was sitting there in the shade of a tree. Countless dead bodies littered the grass. They already looked decomposed, their flesh gray and bloated, as though they had been dead far longer than a day. Crash only noticed in passing. He nodded to the large Wolfy, who raised a tired hand, his head bowed toward the grass. He didn't appear to be injured, yet he was too tired to rise to his feet.

Crash turned back toward the hill—it was tall and steep, an intimidating height, considering his exhaustion. Long grayish-green grass swept over the hill's surface, and a brown dirt path marred by footprints cut up its side. He started upward as fast as he could. *I promised her.* He repeated in his head that mantra of strength, over and over again. *I promised her.*

Panting and sweating when he finally reached the top of the slope, he paused for a moment, regaining his breath. Immediately his eyes landed on the cracked Cat's Eye on top of the pedestal. Part of the gem had melted into the rock. He didn't dare get too close, for it still hummed and smoked with energy, like a sputtering fire. From the size of the stone, he was certain it was the second Cat's Eye, the one that Sora had taken from the Caves. At least that meant her bond was still intact. Hopefully.

Then Crash saw a prone figure behind the pedestal. His heart slammed within his chest. Without thinking, he scrambled around the rock and knelt to the ground, bending down near the girl's head.

"Sora," he whispered. He rolled her body over, his hands shaking; she was pale and cold. He touched her face gently, his fingers playing over her soft skin. *Gods, don't let me be too late.* He knew she wasn't dead—she couldn't be dead—he had promised to keep her safe.

Foolish, the dark voice murmured from far back in his mind. The demon swam languidly about, grinning at him. *You knew you couldn't keep that promise.*

Leaning down, he placed one ear to her chest and listened, trying to hear above the hammering of his own heart.

For a long moment, there was nothing but silence. Crash's hands tightened on her shoulders. He felt a terrible pit open in his stomach—a hole that could swallow him effortlessly. He was too late; he had failed her. *No....*

A faint murmur. Was that her pulse? It was barely there, the whisper of butterfly wings, perhaps a trick of the mind. He waited, not daring to hope. After a long pause, he heard another dull beat. A murmur of life. She wasn't quite gone yet.

His chest tightened; he needed to act swiftly. Her breath stuttered, fading. He turned her face toward him, checking her mouth for obstructions, trying to understand the strange state of her body. Was she paralyzed? In a coma?

He didn't know how to fix a broken bond, but he wasn't even sure that was the problem. Her necklace was still intact, but her lungs weren't working. It didn't matter—he would give her his breath.

He carefully covered her mouth with his—and breathed.

* * *

Sora fell through a black hole, spinning and ricocheting off bits of memory. Visions of her distant past flickered before her eyes, disorienting. Voices shot past her ears: Lily's hum in the morning, beckoning her awake; her stepfather's low rumble, annoyed by her childish games; the sound of horses and chickens from her mother's farm rustling beneath her bedroom window.

As the darkness dipped and turned, Sora felt herself start to fade. Her hand came into view, and she saw its outline become fainter and fainter, disintegrating before her eyes. It was almost transparent.

*Burn...Crash...*she thought hazily, though she couldn't quite summon their faces. *I'm falling....*

Suddenly there was a light before her, a tiny white ball flying closer and closer. It chased after her through the surrounding darkness. Her eyes locked on it, unable to look away. She saw the silhouette of a hand reaching for her. A strong, glowing hand....

She stretched toward the light, suddenly desperate to be there. The glow came closer and closer, until it was just inches away. She turned her body toward it, grasping, straining with effort. So close....

Finally, their grips locked.

* * *

The ground was hard and cold beneath her. She could hear the distant roar of the ocean in her ears. A brisk wind touched her face. She was terribly, terribly cold.

A cough fought its way from her throat. Something moved against her mouth, then pulled away.

"Sora?" a voice asked.

She opened her eyes a crack, squinting against the harsh light. It took a long moment to focus. Finally, Crash's face came into view. *Crash.*

"You...you're alive," she gasped. She felt as though she were speaking at full volume, but the sound leaked from her lips, weak and raspy. The voice of an old woman.

"I suppose I am," Crash echoed, and a wry smile crossed his face. "And you are, too." He looked pleased with that. She tried to smile back at him, but her face felt stiff and numb.

She lifted her head, but the world swam around her. Then she slumped back down. "I can't move," she muttered. Her voice was even quieter than before. Why couldn't she move? *By the North Wind....*

"Shhh," Crash murmured, placing his hands on her shoulders, holding her down. "Don't get up. I think your body is in shock...the Cat's Eye...." his eyes shifted to the stone pedestal behind them.

Sora followed his gaze. *Yes, the Cat's Eye.* She remembered now. He probably didn't understand what happened very well, but it made sense to her. She had broken the second bond. It hadn't been strong—she had used the stone for only a matter of seconds. Yet her body was certainly affected. She wondered how close she had come to death. That thought left her chilled.

"Volcrian's gone?" she muttered, unsure if Crash could hear her.

He glanced down, meeting her eyes. "Yes."

"And...Burn?"

Crash's hand gently cupped the side of her face. "He's fine," he said softly.

She let out a slow, painful sigh. "Good." Her strength faded with the word. Holding a conversation was far too taxing. *But...but....*There was something terribly important that she had to tell him. *Something...*she tried to remember. Her senses were slipping away, soft and fleeting, like darting birds.

But Caprion, she finally realized. Caprion would be coming for them tonight, to take them to the Dracians. She had to tell him....

"Come on," Crash murmured, slipping his arms under her and lifting her from the ground. He paused for a moment, adjusting to her weight. He seemed almost as tired as she was. Worry entered her thoughts. They were vulnerable for the moment, unable to defend themselves if the Harpies were to attack.

He turned to the slope. "We'll find a place to set up camp."

Sora tried to keep her eyes open, tried to formulate a sentence. But the more she focused, the more she couldn't seem to grasp the words. They swirled about on her tongue, mixing and dissolving. She licked her lips. "The Harpies...."

"Don't worry, they won't find us." Crash's tone was firm. She stared up at his face as he carried her, trying to force her thoughts through her mouth, gripping his sleeve in frustration. But it was futile. Her vision slowly melted into darkness.

* * *

Lori stood at the bow of the ship, the sunset fanning out behind her. The water caught the light, reflecting the bright colors, turning the ocean to molten gold.

To the east was a wall of impenetrable clouds, heavy and tumultuous. With Jacques' wind magic and the help of Ferran's Cat's Eye, they had subdued the storms long enough to pass through. Lori shuddered, remembering several sleepless nights combating the waves. This was where Sora's ship had capsized, splitting and sinking into the ocean. She didn't want to imagine that. Deep, biological instinct paralyzed her at the thought.

Before them were the gray shapes of the Lost Isles, becoming dim and vague in the fading light. They were perhaps a few miles offshore. She could hear the Dracians shouting to each other in excitement, pointing over the railing, calling orders to bank the sails.

That morning Jacques had left to find his missing crew, flying over the ocean to one of the smaller isles. They had returned almost two hours later, coasting down from the sky, about fourteen of them.

One woman swam up alongside the ship, her scales bright blue in the water, in sharp contrast to her auburn hair. "Drop me a rope!" she called. The pirates had pulled her up willingly, gazing at her scaled form, taut and athletic. A few of Silas' crew were human, but they didn't seem fazed by the Dracians. Considering their Captain, they had probably seen a few odd sights over the years.

Now they neared the Harpies' island. It was the largest of the lot, arching over the waves like a giant green turtle. Lori leaned forward, sighing. She had a terrible sense of doubt in her stomach. She had only met a few Harpies in her life, but none of them had been very warm or helpful. They stayed aloof, uninterested in human affairs. She wondered if the Harpies of the Lost Isles would be any different. Was Sora even there? That thought worried her the most. What if her daughter hadn't made it...or worse, had perished along the way? Her throat closed at the thought.

"Almost there," a voice said from behind her. Ferran leaned over the railing at her side, a foot taller than she. He cast her an easy smile, his gray eyes glinting. "Don't worry so much." He stretched out a long finger and poked her in the center of her forehead, pressing against an unknown knot of tension.

Lori relaxed her brow, but she couldn't bring herself to smile back.

"They'll be there," he said quietly.

"Aye," she replied. "If they're not dead."

Ferran nudged her shoulder with his. "You always assume the worst. It's a wonder you can sleep at night."

She shrugged. "Bad things happen."

"Right," he replied. "But no sense anticipating them. If you don't know, you don't know."

Easy for him to say, she thought. It wasn't his daughter risking her life, venturing to a strange island, isolated from the human world. "So many things could have gone wrong," she murmured.

He gave her a stern look. "If Sora is anything like you, then she'll be just fine," he said. His confidence took her off-guard. "There are strong women in your family."

She wondered if that was a compliment. Perhaps. But he didn't know half of what she had gone through since she left Sora at the manor. No one did. And now wasn't the time to tell him.

Suddenly, a glint of light caught her attention. She turned back to the island, squinting against the fading sunset. At first she thought it was a star, but it was too low on the horizon. She pointed. "What's that?"

Ferran frowned. "Not sure...."

The light grew at a rapid pace until she saw the vague silhouette of a body. A minute later, a man appeared in the sky. His skin glowed with a strange light, noticeable against the sunset. He hovered over their ship for a moment.

Lori felt her heart quicken. A Harpy. Would he turn them away? It didn't matter—they would go to the island, no matter what.

A series of shouts arose from the Dracians. Jacques and Silas appeared on deck, roaring to the crew, keeping the men in order. The two Dracians stared at the man in the sky.

"Who are you?" Silas called, and pulled his sword from his

waist; it had a short blade that was curved near the tip. "What do you want?"

"Explain yourself, Harpy!" Jacques called.

Silas elbowed him in the shoulder. "I'm the Captain," he glared. "I'll do the talking."

The stranger landed on the ship and the sailors scurried away from him, giving him a large berth. Jacques and Silas took a step back. Lori could understand their reaction—the air hummed with a strange, completely foreign energy. She could feel the vibration on her skin, like music but with no sound.

The man turned to look at her. His eyes brushed over Lori, studying her. When he spoke, his voice had the purity of a bell, swift and striking. "Do you know Sora?"

Lori put a hand on her chest. It took her a moment to gather her breath. "Yes," she said. "My daughter."

The man nodded. "She is on the island. If you anchor your ship a ways from the eastern shore, I will bring her to you. And her companions."

Companions. So the assassin and the Wolfy were still alive. Lori was shocked by this news—it had quite literally come out of the blue. "What of Volcrian?" she asked.

"Dead," the man replied.

Lori's mouth gaped. Her memory of the mage was still sharp and disturbing. Sora had defeated him? But how? She couldn't imagine.

"I will bring them tonight," the man said shortly. "Anchor your ship and wait for me." His voice hummed with power, commanding that they obey. Then he gave the Dracians a narrow look. "No tricks."

Silas stared at him. It was the first time that Lori had seen him speechless.

Then the Harpy briefly turned, raising a hand in farewell, and launched off the boat back into the sky. She gazed after him. His figure quickly dissolved into a small light, heading back toward the island. His visit had been so brief, she could barely come to terms with it.

"Who was that?" Ferran asked.

Lori shook her head. "I don't know," she murmured.

From behind them, Silas let out a short, harsh sigh. "Harpies," he grunted. "Imperious lot, aren't they?"

"Not very friendly," Jacques agreed at his side.

"He said he would bring Sora to us," Lori said. "Should we trust him?" She turned to look at the two Dracians.

Jacques glanced at her, then at Ferran. He shrugged. "I don't see why not," he finally said, and sheathed his sword. "If that's Sora's plan, then we should follow it."

"Perhaps," Silas murmured, "but it could be a trap."

Ferran shook his head slowly. "When he said 'no trickery,' I don't think he meant us," he said quietly. "He must have been in a hurry."

"I wonder why," Silas mused.

It was a question left to be answered. Lori turned back to the horizon, gazing at the distant island, now more desperate than ever to see her daughter. Did they dare wait by the coast, anchored offshore by the will of some unknown stranger? She didn't know. Her hands tightened into fists, and she glared hard at the island. She wasn't used to this level of uncertainty, but they would have to wait it out.

* * *

Crash and Burn made camp in a small alcove on the beach.

They had reclaimed the Dark God's weapons from a stash in the forest, then walked almost two miles from the sacred stones. He would have liked to go farther, but their exhaustion was too much, and he needed to tend Sora's wounds.

She lay behind him now, breathing softly. He had cleaned her shoulder with salt water and bandaged it for the time being. Burn rested next to her, propped up against the far wall, his longsword in easy reach.

Crash remained focused on the ocean, for any sign that the Dracians had arrived. But darkness was falling, and a ship would be hard to recognize. He didn't truly know if they would come, or if he would have to contend with the Harpies for the following weeks, until he found some other way off the island.

He blinked his tired, dry eyes, trying to clear them of dust and sand. A few more hours and it would be Burn's watch. He was used to struggling through such long nights, but damn, it helped to have a flask of fresh water and a fire for company. His throat ached; his muscles throbbed. He hadn't felt this weary in a long time.

Suddenly, a vibration passed over his skin, raising the hair on his arms. Crash shuddered instinctively and drew his dagger. At the edge of his hearing, he heard a distinct, high-pitched keening sound.

Behind him, Burn sat up. He immediately turned to Crash, who held up his hand, signaling for him to remain silent. Harpies couldn't see well at night. If they were patrolling the area, they might pass by overhead and miss the small campsite.

A moment later, a gust of sand kicked up on the beach, propelled by a new wind. A soft light illuminated the deep shadows, slowly growing with intensity. Finally, a tall figure landed on the beach. His wings were hidden, but Crash blinked, summoning his demon's eyes. A halo surrounded the man; the impression of six wings.

His face turned grim. *Bastard.* He recognized the wide shoulders and long neck, the imperious tilt of the head.

"Caprion," Burn said quietly.

Crash glanced over his shoulder. "You know him?"

Burn nodded. "He had dealings with Sora."

Crash turned back to the beach. He scanned the sky, but didn't see any other Harpies. Had the man come alone? A vague smile touched his lips—*he'll be that much easier to kill.*

Caprion walked quickly toward them. Crash stood and blocked the entrance to the alcove, his dagger raised threateningly. Burn exited the alcove behind him, his large sword in hand, its tip hovering above the sand.

"What do you want?" the Wolfy called.

Caprion paused a few meters away. "I've come to take you to your ship," he said quietly. "Where is Sora?" he glanced around. Burn saw an expression of worry on his face. Caprion's lips turned down; his brows pinched together. "Is she dead?"

Crash glared. "What business is it of yours?"

"She didn't tell you?" Caprion raised a brow.

"She told me," Burn replied. Crash turned to look at him, and the Wolfy shrugged uncomfortably. "It slipped my mind," he murmured. "I was more focused on Volcrian."

"Told you what?" Crash asked softly, suspicious.

Caprion laughed—it was not a kind sound. "So the girl kept a secret from her assassin?" he grinned. "I'm not surprised."

Crash turned back to the Harpy. "State your purpose before I slit your throat," he snarled.

Caprion ignored him, focusing instead on Burn. "The Dracians are approaching on their ship. I will take you to them."

"We're not going anywhere with you," Crash said bluntly.

Caprion spoke again to Burn. "Come with me," he said.

Crash heard the compulsion in that voice. The Wolfy took an automatic step forward, but he raised his arm, blocking Burn from approaching the Harpy. Humans and Wolfies were the most susceptible to the voice's power, perhaps because they couldn't use magic themselves. He pushed Burn back with one hand and tightened his grip on his dagger.

"You don't trust me," Caprion said, watching him. Then again, he asked, "Where is Sora?"

"Leave, or I'll make you," Crash glared.

Caprion almost looked amused. His eyes swept over them, noting their exhaustion. "I highly doubt that. You won't catch me off-guard twice."

Crash shifted his stance, prepared for a fight. He didn't care how weary his body was—he would defend Sora to the death, if necessary. Killing the Harpy would be worth it.

"He's a seraphim," Burn said in warning, and gave the assassin a meaningful look.

Crash didn't flinch. "Stay out of my way," he said, his voice having dropped a notch. Lethal. He faced the Harpy, a deadly silence filling the air. He wasn't afraid of a seraphim. They might be bred for war, but the Named were trained to kill.

Suddenly a female voice called out from behind him. "Let him be!"

CHAPTER 25

Sora awakened to the sound of voices. She sat upright in the small cove, her muscles sore and stiff. Her eyes immediately traveled to the beach outside where Crash and Caprion faced off, staring at each other murderously. It took her a moment to register what she was seeing. She wasn't sure what was going on, but it didn't look very promising.

"Let him be!" she called out, hoping her voice was strong enough to be heard. Thankfully, it was. She didn't know if she meant to caution Crash or Caprion—only that she had to stop the fight.

Burn turned to look at her in surprise, his sword held tensely at his side. She saw Crash stiffen, not expecting her intervention.

"He's here to help us," she repeated.

Caprion immediately approached the alcove, unperturbed by the assassin. She pushed herself up, struggling to stand, but the ground tilted under her. Her head began to throb and she sat back quickly, taking in a deep breath. *Not quite recovered, I see.*

Crash backed into the shallow cave and stood in front of her, blocking the Harpy from coming any closer. He held his dagger at the ready, his expression grim. She sat at his feet, gazing at Caprion around the assassin's legs.

"Crash," she said softly. He glanced down at her. He looked as he did when she had first met him—strong, intimidating, filled with dark purpose. She shook her head slowly. "I didn't tell you before. I didn't know how," she said.

He frowned.

"Caprion and I made a deal," she continued. "He promised to set you free. He called the guards away from your prison. He made sure they wouldn't find us in the forest."

Crash looked back to the Harpy, his eyes narrowed.

"He wants to travel with us to the mainland," she said. "I promised him safe passage overseas if he guaranteed your life."

The assassin glared. "I don't need a Harpy's help," he said fiercely. "He's not coming with us."

"Yes, I am," Caprion interjected, "unless you want the Matriarch and all of her soldiers here in the morning. She still wants Sora dead. Now is the time to flee." He stood there calmly, his eyes traveling from Burn to Sora, then to Crash again.

"How do we know you won't take us straight to the Matriarch?" Burn called.

"I have an agreement with Sora." He gave Crash a narrow look. "Some of us stand by our word."

The assassin clenched his fist. "Keep talking like that, and I'll cut out your tongue."

"Wait. Don't fight." Sora tried to stand again, but fell back onto the sand. She let out a breath of frustration. Why wouldn't her body obey? The will was there, but not the strength. She suddenly wished that she wasn't a human—that she was a Dracian or a Wolfy mage, with magic at her command. She needed more stamina.

Her attempts to move drew Crash's attention. He abruptly turned away from the Harpy and knelt by her side, the dagger held out like a shield. He spoke without looking at her, keeping his eyes trained on the enemy. "Don't move," he said quietly.

She glared at him. A bit of anger arose in her thoughts. She wasn't a weak child. "I'll move if I want to," she said stubbornly. *Except that I can't.*

Crash glanced at her. His look was firm, pointed. *Don't argue.*

She turned her glare upon Caprion. "How far away are the Dracians?" she asked.

"They're anchored about a league offshore. I can fly you to their ship." Caprion nodded to Burn. "Perhaps I can take him first while you sort this out."

Sora nodded. "That might be best."

"No," Crash said. "I don't trust him."

Sora sighed. She gave him a weary look. "He released you from the holding cells," she said. "Isn't that enough?"

The assassin paused, his look darkening.

Then Burn drew their attention. "It'll be all right," he said, and gave them a savage smile. His fangs glinted. "I'll risk it."

She could almost hear Crash's thoughts. *But I won't let you.* She touched his arm out of reflex. "Don't worry," she said softly. "He's a warrior. He can handle himself. Let him go."

Finally the assassin looked down. It was the most agreement she was going to get. She motioned toward Caprion. "Go," she said to him. Then to Burn, "We'll join you soon."

The Harpy wasted no time. He turned and made a brief signal with his hand. A soft glow illuminated Burn's body, starting at his boots and traveling up to the top of his head. The Wolfy glanced down at himself and gripped his sword close to his body.

Caprion lifted off the ground, effortlessly gliding into the night. Burn rose up behind him, as though drawn by invisible strings, following in his wake. The Wolfy gave them one last glance over his shoulder as they flew out over the sea.

It was a strange thing to watch. Sora felt her Cat's Eye murmur uncomfortably, provoked by the surge of magic.

Once the two were gone from sight, she turned back to Crash. With Caprion gone, their small cave was consumed by shadow, hidden from the light of the moon. She waited for her eyes to adjust, then watched the assassin scatter the remains of their camp, covering their footsteps in the sand, destroying all traces of their campsite.

She opened her mouth to speak, but Crash cut her off. "Why didn't you tell me?" he asked. Then he paused, a strange expression passing over his face. "Why would you make a deal with a Harpy?"

Sora tried to understand what he was feeling. He, more than any of them, had been demonized by the First Race. They had put him in a cell, burned his throat, bloodied him, scarred his body. The memory made her sick: the dark hole of the jailhouse, the sunstone collar around his neck. They had treated him as less than an animal.

But Caprion had proved to be different. Right? Without his help, they would have been imprisoned too, perhaps already dead. The battle with Volcrian would have been impossible. And now he was fulfilling his final promise—to help them reach the Dracians.

"What else was I supposed to do?" she said defensively. "You asked me to get you out of that cell. There was no other way. The Matriarch was going to arrest us."

"There are always other ways," Crash grunted.

"Perhaps for you!" Sora tried to stand up again, ignited by anger, but fell back again to the sand. *Damn!* "We don't all have incredible combat skills and magical powers!" she exclaimed. "Caprion and I spoke for a long time. He wants to leave the island and see the mainland. He...."

"Then why not fly?" Crash snapped, his voice uncharacteristically hoarse from his wounds. It made his words sharper. "You're too trusting. You don't know what their race has done, what they are capable of."

Sora rolled her eyes. "He wanted a guide. The mainland is a

big place, Crash. He wants to unite his race and bring them home. That's all! Not all Harpies are evil."

He let out a short, irritated breath. "And not all humans are evil, not all Dracians, not all Wolfies—but the Harpies never admit to what they do." He flung his dagger on the ground, embedding it in the sand. "They started the War of the Races, they caused their own destruction, and yet they blame the Sixth Race for all of the darkness in the world. Caprion might fulfill his half of the deal, but you don't know what he'll do once we reach the mainland. You don't know his true intentions." Crash frowned bitterly and looked down at the knife. "A seraphim," he murmured, more to himself than to her, his voice dripping with irony.

Sora wasn't sure what to say to that. She hadn't realized that the Harpies had started the War, but she knew that they had once enslaved the humans, treating them like beasts of labor. The Matriarch was certainly arrogant.

Still, the war had been over four hundred years ago and they couldn't keep lingering on the past. "This is a different age," she said softly. "We don't know Caprion's intentions, and he doesn't know ours. Yet he's willing to trust us."

"Of course. He has the advantage," Crash said dryly.

Sora sighed. She was fast growing tired of arguing. She didn't have the strength for this. "He's done his part, and I will do mine. You can't make me break my word, Crash. Let's just get off this island. I'm ready to go home."

The assassin lifted his dagger out of the sand and sheathed it. Then he knelt by her side again, reaching out to touch her wounded shoulder, swiftly inspecting the bandage. As he unfastened the cloth, he said softly, "We're not going home yet. We need to find the third weapon."

Sora winced as he unwrapped the bandage, then put on a fresh strip of linen. His hands were warm and dry, steadying her as he worked. She felt a strange warmth move through her at his touch.

"I know," she said, trying not to grow distracted by his closeness. "That's what I meant." *No, I really want to go home.* Couldn't they rest for a while? She had the strong urge to lean against him, bury her face in his shoulder and sleep. She wanted to disappear, awaken in the wilderness somewhere far away from humans and Harpies and magic. Her mind felt like it was tied up in knots, ready to snap apart from the strain.

The assassin finished wrapping her fresh bandage and sat against the wall next to her, their legs almost touching. "How do you feel?" he asked softly.

She glanced at him. Changing the subject? She took that as a sign that he was relenting. She let out a slow breath and flexed her left hand. It was sore and stiff and felt burned, and there was a deep pain centered on her palm, but she couldn't see it very clearly in the darkness. "I'm fine," she said. "Just tired."

He nodded. A strange tension filled the air. She wanted to touch him somehow, to share his warmth—but it seemed like that familiarity was gone.

Because of the kiss. She bit her lip, thinking about it—the heat of his mouth, his firm arms. Why had he done such a thing if he wouldn't acknowledge it now? Why did he let it hang between them, tangible and heavy, like a third person nudging them apart?

"About last night," she started to say, then paused. Crash glanced at her, then away. Not very comforting. "I don't want anything to change between us."

He shifted slightly. "What's changed?"

She blinked. *Uh, everything.* "I don't know," she said lamely.

He hesitated, then reached over and clasped her hand, still not looking at her. Sora was surprised by his touch. She looked down at their interlocked hands, frowning, unsure of what it meant.

"Nothing's changed, Sora," he said quietly.

She wondered at his words. *Nothing's changed.* Meaning, they would go back to the way things were? Remaining distant, him pulling back whenever she got too close? Or did he think about the kiss as much as she did? *Nothing's changed*—their embrace under the tree meant something, and he still thought of it. They were headed in the same direction—but where, exactly?

She was trying to formulate a question out of all that, but was distracted by a vague sound from the Cat's Eye. A small chime. A slight vibration passed over her skin, and she heard the sand moving outside the cave, being kicked up into the air.

Caprion landed a moment later. His eyes searched the darkness. She wasn't sure if he could see the two of them or not; he seemed uncertain. "Are you ready?" he called.

Crash stood up and lifted Sora to her feet, supporting her with one shoulder. She wavered and he tightened his arm, correcting her balance. Together, they walked out of the cave toward the Harpy.

"We're ready," Sora said.

Caprion nodded. He made another series of hand signals. The white light emerged from the ground, slipping over their feet, up their legs, their chest, their shoulders. With a flick of his wrist, they shot into the air, flying faster than Sora had before. The night flowed around them like black velvet, soft and cool, deceptively peaceful. The ground sped by, and then the ocean waves. In the distance, she could see a vague flickering light—a ship. At first it was small on the horizon, like a toy boat, but it grew larger and larger as they neared. It was a schooner, three-masted, anchored off the eastern shore of the Isles, listing slightly in the tide.

Crash kept her hand in his the entire time, his grip tight. She wondered if he enjoyed the experience—or if he was waiting for the

Harpy to drop them into the ocean.

They continued toward the ship, leaving the Lost Isles behind.

* * *

As they approached the deck, Sora could see a large group of people standing toward the aft of the boat, watching the sky eagerly. Countless fingers were pointing at them, and then there was an uproar of shouts and excited cries, though the voices were shredded by the wind.

She kept a close eye on the approaching deck. At the speed they were going, she didn't want to slam face-first into the wood. Yet Caprion brought them up short, hovering just above the railing of the boat, then gently set them down toward the very rear of the deck. The Harpy staggered when his feet touched the deck, and he leaned up against the railing, sweat drenching his brow. Transporting so many people so far had taken a lot of strength.

The first person Sora saw was Burn. He had collapsed on a wooden bench, his shoulders sagging in exhaustion. She took a step toward him, but before she could go any further, a blond arrow shot across the deck.

"Sora!" she heard. "Oh, my daughter!"

In shock, Sora found herself gripped tightly in her mother's embrace. "W-what are you doing here?" she stammered.

Her mother didn't answer, only held her closer. Sora couldn't quite believe it. *What's going on?*

The crowd rushed up behind Lori, eagerly calling Sora's name. Finally, her mother released her from the tight hug, but kept one arm around her shoulders, unable to let go of her daughter.

Sora looked on in surprise. She recognized the Dracians that they had left on the island, and she summoned up a relieved smile.

Joan reached out and touched Sora's hand, then Tristan approached, taking both of their hands in his.

"Where is Laina?" Tristan asked, his eyes filling with doubt. "Is she...?"

"She's alive," Sora answered wearily. "She decided to stay with the Harpies."

Tristan frowned in disappointment, then he nodded. He didn't ask what Laina's reasoning was. Sora could only assume that the Dracian knew of the girl's heritage.

He ruffled Sora's hair and then turned away, joining Burn on the bench. Joan followed after him, heading quickly to the Wolfy.

Sora's eyes scanned the mingling crowd. There was a mix of humans and Dracians on-board, and many of the sailors were unfamiliar: tall, broad men with piercings and tattoos, corded with muscle, decidedly cutthroat. They hung at the back of the group, watching with wary interest. Jacques' crow circled above them, though she had yet to see the man. She noticed that Caprion had momentarily disappeared. Was he still on the boat? She glanced skyward, but didn't see any evidence of the Harpy.

Crash slipped from behind her and traveled around the fringe of the crowd to where Burn sat. She caught his eye, wishing she could follow, but he shook his head. Then he gave her an ironic half-smile. She returned it. For the moment, she was the center of attention. She couldn't fathom why.

Finally, her mother stepped away from her side, removing her arm. She glanced over her daughter's body. "You're wounded," she said briefly. It was almost an accusation.

"We fought Volcrian," Sora said. Her voice felt dry in her throat.

"And?"

"We won."

It felt empty. The memory of Volcrian's demise left her strangely uncomfortable. Her head throbbed: a sudden, short burst of pain. She grimaced. Was it a remnant of the broken bond? She couldn't be sure.

Her mother searched her face, then smiled—a genuine look that was full of strength. "Of course," she said. "I can see it on you. You look tired...but strong. I was a fool to worry."

"Oh?" a new voice spoke from behind her. "A fool to worry? Is that so?"

Sora looked up, surprised. In Tristan's place stood another man, one she had never met before. She stared. He was tall and lanky; his body held an easy, athletic grace, like that of a long-distance runner. He was dressed in a brown greatcoat with a stained tunic underneath, and tall leather boots. By his face, she could tell that he was older, perhaps in his late thirties, with chestnut brown hair and quick gray eyes. There was a roguish, weathered charm about him. She could see that he had been handsome in his youth, but age was slowly creeping into the lines on his brow, the scuffed tan of his skin.

"Sora," her mother said, stepping back and turning to the new man. "This is Ferran. He's an old friend of your father's."

Sora stared at the man, taken aback. Ferran. She had never heard that name before. "You knew my father?" she asked softly.

"I did," he said, with a slight nod. There was a definite warmth in his eyes. He looked at her for a long moment. "Though I must say, you take after your mother."

Sora grinned, at an unexpected loss for words. His presence was puzzling. She knew that her real father had died before she was born. Lori had told her as much. But her instincts still recognized another man—the cold noble who had kept her under his roof for seventeen years. It always left her feeling conflicted. She had known for over a year now that she wasn't related to the Fallcrest family, and yet it was the only family she had ever really known.

She glanced from Ferran to Lori, almost frowning. "But why are you two here?" she finally asked. *Not to sound ungrateful....*

"Your mother asked me to accompany her," Ferran started.

"He's a treasure hunter," Lorianne cut in. "Or at least, he was. We were looking for a certain book that tells us how to destroy the sacred weapons. We found it, but then it was stolen...." She paused, and Sora could see the words moving behind the woman's eyes. Her mother's face was always intelligent and expressive—when Lori was thinking, it felt like the entire room thought with her.

Ferran cut in. "It's a long story, and it can wait for now. You look exhausted. Have you eaten?"

Sora shook her head. Now that the excitement had waned, her body felt heavy and tired. All she wanted to do was sit on the bench next to Burn.

Her mother took her hand and pulled her toward a series of cabins at the center of the ship. "Let's get you a plate of hot stew, and I'll look at that wound on your shoulder."

"Crash tended to it," she mumbled, allowing her mother to drag her across the deck.

Lori pushed her way forcefully through the crowd of sailors and Dracians. "And I'll make sure he did it right," she replied.

Sora knew better than to argue. Her mother was just as stubborn as she was—perhaps more so. She glanced over her shoulder to where Crash and Burn still sat on the bench. Several more Dracians surrounded them, and she recognized Jacques' crow hovering above the crowd. She felt overwhelmed by so many people. For the past month, she had been isolated with her friends—and had grown far closer to Crash and Burn than she could explain. She felt a strange yearning. She didn't want to be separated from them, even if they were on the same ship.

But then her mother opened a door and led her into a long, narrow hallway. Ferran walked casually behind them, his hands thrust into the pockets of his brown coat.

A whistle sounded as they went below deck. She could hear the clunk and screech of the anchor being raised. The ship tossed and rocked, free upon the waves, and several more whistles sounded as various sails were released. Her stomach sank, and a familiar, swimmy sensation filled her gut. Seasickness. She wanted to groan.

Her mother led her into the sickroom and closed the door behind them.

* * *

Close to dawn, Sora stood at the fore of the ship, watching the waves break across the bow. A pale blue light the color of a robin's egg was flowing across the eastern sky. Soon a new day would begin.

Her mother had given her a special calming tonic to ease her stomach. Still, Sora found herself needing a taste of fresh air. She was trying to keep down the three plates of stew that she had eaten —and simultaneously organize her thoughts.

The night had been a long one, with no time to sleep. Jacques and their new captain, Silas, met with all of them in the main cabin. She had listened to her mother's story, forcing herself to focus, despite the cobwebs of sleep that clouded her thoughts.

She remembered Caprion's attendance. The Harpy sat quietly in the corner, his light permeating the room. He hadn't said much— just listened. The Dracian crew tried to engage him in banter, but the Harpy merely stared at them, hooded and aloof. Eventually, the Dracians gave up and moved away, allowing him a wide berth.

Meanwhile, Sora had grown dizzy from her mother's story, hardly able to believe it: *The Book of the Named*, the Shade, and now a voyage to the City of Crowns. She looked back and forth between Lori and Ferran, noticing how closely they sat together, the way their eyes often met. Just friends? Why hadn't her mother mentioned him before?

Sora picked at the wooden railing of the boat. She felt unexpectedly shy around Ferran, unsure of what to think of him. He didn't look like the kind of company her mother would keep. His appearance had a definite hard edge, just like Crash. He was used to rough places, the alleyways and backstreets, perhaps even a criminal himself.

And now they would all have to travel together to the City of Crowns.

She couldn't deny it. She didn't want to go there. On her last run-in with the King's guard, she was almost arrested. She wondered if she still had a price on her head—if they still thought she had been the one to kill Lord Fallcrest. And there was always the slim chance of running into someone who recognized her. The First Tier wouldn't know her and the Second Tier only visited the City of Crowns once a year. But, gazing at the night sky, she couldn't resist the sense of dread creeping over her.

In fact, none of the people in the meeting seemed very eager to go. Her mother looked troubled, and she had gazed intently at the wall, her thoughts circling tangibly. Ferran sat next to Lori, rolling a cinnamon stick in his mouth, similarly preoccupied. His eyes had drifted to Crash numerous times, especially while discussing the Shade. It seemed as if very few people trusted the assassin. No one spoke to him directly, and he hadn't interjected his opinion—he simply met their eyes, look for look.

She sighed, fingering her Cat's Eye, feeling the salty sea-mist on her face. A new day—a new destination. All she wanted to do was crawl under a rock.

Jacques' crow cawed overhead, swooping past her. Startled, she glanced over her shoulder, then paused again. Someone was standing behind her on the deck. She immediately recognized Crash's silhouette against the flickering lanterns of the ship. Her stomach tightened at the sight, and she clutched the railing nervously. How long had he been standing there? Had he followed her from the meeting? *What does he want?*

She nodded to him, unsure of what to say.

The assassin walked to her side wordlessly and leaned against the railing, gazing at the sea. The wind tousled his black hair, blowing it across his forehead in unkempt waves.

Sora swallowed. Her fingers itched to touch his hair, but she restrained herself. When he stood this close, she felt completely off-balance. Her mind summoned the memory of their night beneath the tree—her first kiss. They had yet to speak about it in depth. Now that they were barreling across the ocean toward the City of Crowns, she wondered if it even mattered. She should be worried about the Dark God and the journey ahead.

And yet....

"Your mother told you to rest," Crash murmured. He glanced sideways at her. "Your body is still recovering from the broken bond."

She shook her head, a wry smile on her face. "I'm an adult too, you know," she muttered. "I'm fine."

"You're tired," he replied, studying her face.

"I'll survive," she grumbled.

They stood in silence for another moment, looking out at the waves. He leaned toward her until their shoulders were touching, sheltering her from the wind. She looked up at him, searching his face. She felt nervous, like she was slowly melting into the deck of the ship. *What has he done to me?* she thought. *This is Crash. An assassin. He's untouchable.*

And yet, he was also her friend.

The thought made her bolder. After a slight hesitation, she leaned into him as well. She slid her fingers over the back of his hand and entwined them, dangling their hands over the railing. He glanced down at her small palm over his large one.

"Sora..." he began softly.

"What?" she said, resisting the urge to pull back. She felt somehow guilty. Had she done something wrong?

His eyes flickered over the waves. "We can't."

Her heart shuddered at those words. Here it was—the rejection she had been anticipating. She had braced herself for it, but she still felt as though she couldn't breathe. "What do you mean?"

A strange smile twisted his mouth: wry, self-deprecating. "You know what I mean. Your mother, Ferran and the others...they won't accept it." He still didn't look at her.

"Won't accept what?" she asked bluntly, and gave him a pointed look. "That our hands are touching?"

Crash snorted. "Don't act so naïve. It doesn't suit you."

"Naïve?" she replied, almost offended. "You give me half-answers. Why can't you just speak your mind?" *I thought we were supposed to be past this.* Hadn't he agreed to be more open with her?

"I am of the Sixth Race," Crash said harshly. "They understand that more than you do. They won't accept it. We can't be close like this."

Sora looked at him in surprise. *Of all reasons....*"Just because of their opinions?" she asked, stunned. "Since when do you care about that?"

"Since I started caring about you."

Her lips parted.

He seemed to realize his words after saying them, and shifted uncomfortably, clearing his throat. "I'm not good at this, Sora. In our world...we don't engage with others...we don't...." He paused.

"You don't fall in love?" she supplied, though love was such a strong word, and what they had was like a thimble in comparison, a small seed struggling to grow in the dirt.

"We're not supposed to," Crash relented. "And anyway...I don't know how."

Sora looked at him for another long moment, then back out to sea, licking her dry lips. She thought about his words, puzzling over them, trying to find something tactful to say. "I don't think anyone really knows how to love," she finally offered.

"Let's stop calling it that," he said quietly.

"All right...but you know what I mean."

He shook his head slowly. "You don't understand. I can't be that person for you."

"You shouldn't care what others think...."

"I would hurt you, Sora." He finally met her eyes, hard and solemn. "Whatever this is...it can't happen."

She didn't know what to say to that. How could he be so logical? So certain? All of his excuses seemed small in the face of what they had been through. Didn't he trust her by now?

She squeezed his hand, letting him know that she understood, though it was a lie. Truly, she didn't understand anything. Her throat closed. *This is much harder than I expected.*

Then her eyes landed on his lips. Memories surged. Perhaps she went mad for a moment—lost her wits. Suddenly she couldn't stop staring at his mouth. So close. *Why not?* He had already rejected her—what did she have to lose? *One last time.*

She went up on her toes and pressed her lips against the top of his scar, at the ridge of his jaw. Her heart pounded. She felt dizzy with courage.

Crash went still. His entire body turned rigid under her touch. Then he abruptly released her hand.

He grabbed her face and turned her head, crushing his mouth down on hers. She gasped against him, surprised. Butterflies flooded her stomach.

His kiss was full of pent-up yearning, unspoken need. He stroked her lips, easily tilting her head back. His tongue entered her open mouth, soft and teasing. She responded clumsily, attempting to follow his lead. He squeezed her jaw in response. Her knees weakened. Her cheeks flushed. She leaned into him more, pressing against his shoulder, gripping his arms, unwilling to let go.

He watched her the entire time, his eyes on her face, gauging her reaction. She shuddered from the intensity of it. They were so close; he held her in the palm of his hand. He could tighten his fist, and she would break in his hold. *Please tighten,* she thought, pressing close. *Please don't let go.*

Then, abruptly, he stopped.

Sora gasped, bereft. Her lips felt stung. He released her gently and stepped back, still watching her impassively, his eyes filled with a strange darkness, a brutal hunger that she didn't understand.

"I can't," he repeated hoarsely, his throat full of rocks. Then he turned and walked away.

She watched him go. A small part of her trailed after him, having abandoned her body. She held out her hand to call him back, but the words wouldn't come. How did one argue with an assassin? How could she fix this, when she didn't even know what she wanted?

She dropped her hand, leaning back on the railing, trying to regain herself. He had a point. She knew he was dangerous. There was a certain darkness in him that scared her—she had seen it plenty of times. He had kidnapped her, held her hostage, forced her through a treacherous swamp, dragged her into this entire situation. If she had a lick of sense, she would take his advice and forget about everything.

And yet...he had protected her, saved her life, proven to be far more gentle than he believed possible.

She turned back to the ocean, twisting her fingers together. In the light of a new day, there was a silent expectation, as though the sun's illumination would make all things known. And yet she was just as troubled as the night before. Nothing made sense.

Her gaze traveled to the distance. Somewhere far away, the City of Crowns awaited, and the mysterious, ominous Shade. How were they supposed to track down such an organization? And where was the third weapon of the Dark God? The assassins had *The Book of the Named*—perhaps they already had the third weapon, as well. This next leg of her journey felt even more intimidating than the last. She simply did not know what to expect.

Sora sighed. The sun pierced the horizon, mounting the distant waves, spilling across the ocean. She needed to rest and recover—not waste her energy worrying about Crash. There would be time for that later.

She turned her back to the sun and headed toward her cabin, burdened with doubt. The gray water slowly lightened with the sky.

...so what's next?

CAPRION'S WINGS
A novelette.
Release: January 31, 2014

By the age of nineteen, all Harpies know how to fly—except Caprion. He has yet pass the test of the Singing and gain his wings. His family has disowned him in shame and people are beginning to talk. Now an evil voice haunts his dreams, taunting him, drawing out his worst fears—that he will remain wingless forever.

Caprion decides to find the root of this insidious voice, no matter what it takes. He journeys to the secret prisons of the Harpy underground, where he meets a young slave named Moss. In those sunless, decrepit cells, a forbidden friendship is formed. Can Caprion and Moss find the source of the voice? And can Caprion save Moss from a terrible fate?

Join young Caprion as he journeys down, down into the earth, finding his wings and forging a friendship that will change him forever.

Get ready for....

Ferran's Map
(The Cat's Eye Chronicles, Book 4)
Release: Summer 2014

The next full-length installment of The Cat's Eye Chronicles! Sora and company must travel to The City of Crowns. They arrive just in time for the Winter festival, two weeks of extravagant parties, fine wines and legendary debauchery. Intrigue abounds as she and Crash infiltrate the First Tier and track down Grandmaster Cerastes. She will be forced to face her past, don the guise of a noblewoman and uncover the Shade's dark intentions. Add *Ferran's Map* on Goodreads today!

Want more?

Visit *The Cat's Eye Chronicles* website!
www.catseyechronicles.com

If you like Paranormal Romance, check out T. L. Shreffler's *The Wolves of Black River* series!

The Wolves of Black River

Mark of the Wolf
Blood of the Wolf

Want more of the world?

Visit *The Cat's Eye Chronicles* website!

WWW.CATSEYECHRONICLES.COM

LEARN ABOUT
THE RACES
THE WORLD
THE CHARACTERS
THE AUTHOR

VIEW
FAN ART
BOOK TRAILERS
TRIVIA GAMES
WRITING PROGRESS
PERSONALITY QUIZZES

AND BUY YOUR OWN CAT'S EYE NECKLACE!

About the Author

T. L. Shreffler is a noblewoman living in the sunny acres of San Fernando Valley, California, a mere block from Warner Bros. Studios. She enjoys frolicking through meadows, sipping iced tea, exploring the unknown reaches of her homeland and unearthing rare artifacts in thrift stores. She holds a Bachelors in Eloquence (English) and writes Epic Fantasy, Paranormal Romance and poetry. She has previously been published in *Eclipse: A Literary Anthology* and *The Northridge Review*.

Feel free to connect online! She loves hearing from readers, reviewers, orcs, elves, assassins, villains, figments of her imagination and extraterrestrials looking to make contact. Her online accounts are as follows:

Email: therunawaypen@gmail.com
Author Website: www.tlshreffler.com
Facebook: www.facebook.com/tlshreffler
Twitter: @poetsforpeanuts

Printed in Great Britain
by Amazon